THE RELUCTANT SAINT

(A NOVEL)

WUNDERFOOL

W/P

PRESS

Also by Brad Whittington

Novels

Welcome to Fred

Living with Fred

Postcards from Fred

Escape from Fred

Muffin Man

Strange Vacation

Open Season

Endless Vacation

Essays

Build Your Own Relgion
And other bad ideas from The Door

Non-fiction

What Would Jesus Drink?
What the Bible Really Says About Alcohol

BRAD WHITTINGTON

THE RELUCTANT SAINT

(A NOVEL)

PATRIOT PEST CONTROL

ISBN: 978-1-937274-29-0
Published by Wunderfool Press
Austin, Texas

Dewey Decimal Classification: F
Subject Heading: Fiction / Mystery & Detective / General

Contents

What they're saying about Whittington

Whittington spins an enjoyable literary story and is definitely a novelist to watch.
–Publisher's Weekly

Brad Whittington is an artist with a pen.
–Ethan C. McDonald, DancingWord.com

It is always a joy to find a new writer who knows what he's doing.
–Rick Lewis, Logos Bookstore

Whittington is a welcome new voice in the world of fiction.
–Cindy Crosby, author of By Willoway Brook

Who can resist a story of someone else's alienated youth if that someone else is as talented as Brad Whittington?
–JT Conroe, author of The Blue Hotel

The pacing, humor, honesty, and believable characters made me turn page after page in rapid succession until there were none.
–T Leigh

Brad Whittington paints some of the best word pictures I've seen.
–Cammi Ellis

What they're saying about Muffin Man

Brad Whittington is not only back, he's at his best. I haven't been this excited about a new fictional detective since Martin Walker's Bruno, Chief of Police. Have no doubt: Muffin Man delivers!
–J. Mark Bertrand, author of Back on Murder and Pattern of Wounds

I love the way Brad Whittington writes. Smooth and snappy as jazz. Whittington has baked up a winner in Muffin Man. With dry wit, poignant humanity, and a setting as rich as Texas earth, Whittington proves his flair for storytelling once again.

A great book.
–Tosca Lee, NY Times bestselling author of Demon: A Memoir, Havah: The Story of Eve, and The Books of Mortals series

For Brenda

For giving me Chrystal

Rendezvous
by Ted McMahon

Let's meet in Santa Fe
where we can stroll holding hands
along the *acequia madre*
then sip espresso
at the bookstore on Garcia Street.

Let's meet in Santa Fe
and bask like lizards
on the rocks at Bandelier
or explore the secrets
of remote creek beds.

Let's meet in Santa Fe
to share our stories and let
the whisper of cottonwood leaves
fill the silences between.

Let's meet in Santa Fe
and eat *posole* with our eggs
and laugh, and love, and turn
the calendar to the wall
for a few brief days.

DAY 1: THURSDAY

Chapter One: Quandary

There was something about narrowly escaping the deadly attentions of an international assassin that lent an air of luxury to the simplest of life's experiences. And so it was that when Hensley Fletcher set foot in Galveston fresh, off a cruise ship and into the waiting arms of the Secret Service, he did so with an unexpected sense of gratitude and bonhomie. Particularly since he had spent most of his life flying under the radar of the authorities, whether federal or local.

Even so, when Special Agent Harris breezed through customs and gestured to the open back door of the cliché black SUV, Hensley faltered, as perhaps even the most seasoned lion tamer might when placing his head between the massive jaws of a beast. It was the Secret Service, after all.

He glanced at Davison, who was making some remark to Harris, and then at Masie, who waited patiently, and the moment passed. He climbed in and made room for the others. Harris rode shotgun.

Despite it being the first week of June, the temperature was a balmy eighty. But after a few blocks, the SUV took on the dank atmosphere of a locker room just after the big game. Not surprising since the three of them hadn't had a chance to change clothes after they fled the resort five days ago.

Harris turned in his seat. "Relax and get plenty of rest. Tomorrow will be a full day." He targeted Davison with his next comment. "Since this whole Cancún fiasco went down after you officially retired from the service, it might get a little ticklish. And a lot of people want to talk to all three of you about the incident on the ship."

The SUV came to a stop in front of the Tremont House, a four-story Victorian hotel that took up an entire block. Given the state of federal budgets, Hensley had expected something more along the lines of the No Tell Motel. The warmth of human kindness swelled in his breast. This Harris fellow knew how to do them up proper.

As they piled out of the SUV, Hensley approached Harris, toying with the idea of thanking him with the two-cheek air-kiss he frequently employed in Europe. However, Davison shot a glare his way, and Hensley confined himself to the two-fisted handshake and a heartfelt, "Sir, I shall forever be in your debt. You have but to say the word . . ."

Harris extracted his hand from the grip. "Couldn't leave Davison's brother out in the cold." He smiled. "Company policy." He gestured to an agent standing under the entrance canopy and spoke to the group. "As a precaution, we've posted a protective detail."

Hensley inspected their protector. Since they were safely out of danger in the good old US of A, he suspected that this gatekeeper's primary goal was assuring that they made it to the debriefing tomorrow. And by *they* he meant *Hensley*.

If so, the joke was on them. Hensley intended to enjoy room service and whatever other amenities he could accrue at the largess of the state for as long as it lasted.

Approximately half an hour and exactly one shower later, Hensley wrapped himself in a towel, absorbed the life-affirming delight of a well-chosen beverage ordered via room service, and turned his thoughts to the puzzle that, despite all the chaos of the past few days, remained uppermost in his mind.

After a few minutes, Hensley recalled that speculation was the pastime of fools. He picked up the room phone and navigated the maze of button-pushing required to call Philadelphia.

"Ellis, my good man. Hensley Fletcher here, recently of Cancún, calling from Galveston, safe within the protective embrace of the Secret Service. Do you have time for a few questions regarding the matter of which we spoke last week?"

"Yes."

Hensley smiled. That was Ellis, ever the picture of efficiency. "How long have you been the Stone family legal adviser?"

"Fifty-seven years, three months, and eleven days."

"Since before Uncle Rex assumed control of the estate."

"Correct."

"Was he in the habit of making frequent alterations to his will?"

"I'm afraid that is privileged information."

Ellis was also ever the picture of rectitude. Hensley took a go at it from another angle. "In your office last week, you expressed surprise that Rex had changed his will to leave the entire estate to Masie Wright."

"You are correct."

"Was that due to the nature of the change or the timing?"

"Both."

Just as Hensley expected. Uncle Rex wasn't one of those eccentric millionaires who responded to every perceived slight with the threat of disenfranchisement. "The most recent intelligence is that Masie refused to accept the inheritance."

"Perhaps, but you should know that from a legal perspective her wishes are immaterial to the validity of the will, which I am bound to honor in my capacity as executor."

"But you also said there were grounds to contest."

"Yes, mental competence. But you may have some resistance in that regard."

"From whom? Masie doesn't want the money."

"A few minutes ago, Davison offered to submit a deposition affirming that Rex was of sound mind."

"Was Masie a party to this conversation?"

"Not that I am aware."

It appeared that devious forces might be at work. Clearly, Davison had done a one-eighty in the matter of one Masie Wright. Far from suspecting her of manipulating Uncle Rex into changing his will, he was now endorsing her as the rightful heir.

Not that Hensley suspected Davison of foul play. His brother had ever been the consummate Boy Scout, but they were both up against a dark horse, even if Davison didn't realize it.

Circumstantial evidence notwithstanding, Masie looked legit enough. That was the problem. More like too legit by half.

Hensley could think of only one reason why someone would turn down two hundred million dollars, and it wasn't to trade it for what was behind door number two. It was to dispel all suspicion before finally acquiescing to the will and walking away with the lot, free and clear.

Any woman worth her salt could fake sincere for a week. As far as Hensley could tell, most married women had learned to fake it for decades.

It came down to who was right, Hensley or Davison. Was she a sinner or a saint?

"This matter bears further investigation," Hensley said. "I shall be in touch with breaking news as required."

"In the event I need to contact you, may I reach you at this number?"

"At present I can't predict my future movements with any degree of certainty. I'll have to contact you."

Tomorrow they would be ferried to the Federal Building for a debriefing regarding their Endless Vacation experience. He would bask in this land of milk and honey as long as possible, but eventually he would have to find another landing spot from which to launch his next adventure.

He hung up the phone and turned a reluctant gaze upon the man-in-black outfit he had cast on the bed when he entered the room. It was long past its sell-by date, considering he'd donned it in Cancún five days ago.

Regretting the impossibility of ordering a fresh change of clothes via room service, he donned the now overfamiliar, aromatic ensemble and headed down to the in-house cafe for dinner, waving to the watchdog in the lobby on the way.

The menu offered a range of options, from sandwiches to entrées, each of which he examined carefully. While Hensley appreciated the singular focus that led John Montagu, the Earl of Sandwich, to instruct his servants to construct the eponymous collation so as not to be distracted from his work, in Hensley's world, a meal was not a distraction necessitated by the requirements of the body but an experience to be savored.

Whether ordering a full meal or simply a refreshing beverage, one did so only after careful consideration of a host of factors, the goal of which was to engineer optimum pleasure.

After perusing the menu at the counter, Hensley settled on jambalaya, paired it with a Turbo Dog Louisiana dark ale, and took a seat at the bar. He was about three bites in, and very good bites they were, when someone climbed onto the stool next to him.

"Didn't take you long to find the restaurant," Masie said.

Judging by the fresh outfit, Masie had spent her time shopping instead of discussing the terms of the will with the family retainer. "Greetings and felicitations, my dear lady. I can offer an unqualified recommendation in regard to the jambalaya."

"I ordered the tomato and mozzarella panini."

"Doubtless an equally excellent choice." Hensley scanned the room. "Will Davison be joining us?"

"Your brother is having dinner with Harris."

"Doing Secret Service stuff, no doubt."

"I think it's more of a reunion. Evidently they've known each other since prep school."

A server delivered Masie's sandwich, and conversation gave way to dining. Hensley took a reflective sip of the Turbo Dog and considered The Case of Masie and the Money.

It wasn't like he needed the whole nut, or even half. While he had, on many occasions, lived for weeks or months as the guest of the absurdly wealthy, in the course of his life he had learned to thrive on almost nothing.

In the nineties he had spent three years studying Wing Chun in the mountains of Guangxi, living off the equivalent of a thousand dollars a year. And just before this most recent interlude in Cancún, he had been living in a small Nepali village. A spartan existence by any measure.

At present he was relatively flush, thanks to the two thousand dollars Davison had thrown at him a few days ago, accompanied with the demand that Hensley make himself scarce in any location in which Davison found himself. Hensley had accepted the money but declined to vacate. Fortunately Davison hadn't demanded a refund.

It was a goodly sum, and Hensley knew how to make it last. It would serve to keep body and soul together for the nonce.

But as one approached the twilight of life—not that fifty-three was old, mind you—one began to give thought to the waning years, even a vagabond who lived by his wits. After all, it was a race to see which would fail first, the wits or the body, and Hensley didn't fancy dying in a gutter somewhere because he could no longer keep an audience spellbound with his charm.

Hensley finished off the jambalaya, downed the last of the ale, and dropped his napkin on the plate. He glanced at Masie. Considering how things had worked out, Hensley wasn't willing to take Davison's word on Masie's position about the estate. What sane person would turn their back on a fortune out of principle? Hensley would wager that he had as many principles as the next guy, but principles could take you only so far. At some point, one would always require a ready supply of solid currency.

He turned to Masie. "Could I interest you in a libation at the Rooftop Bar?"

Masie finished her sandwich at a leisurely pace and washed it down with the last of her ice water. Then she looked at him.

"I was looking forward to an early night. It's been four days since I slept in a proper bed."

"A nightcap then. It's still an hour until sunset."

She shrugged, and they took the elevator to the bar four floors above the street.

The temps were dropping into the seventies on the roof, but being on the gulf, the humidity was as close to one hundred percent as to make no difference. Hensley rolled up his sleeves as he smiled at the bartender.

"Remind me of your name," he said, although he'd never seen the man in his life.

"Julien." He swirled a cocktail napkin in front of Hensley and then another next to it as Masie stepped up. "What'll it be?" he asked without looking at either of them.

Hensley shook his head with a world-weary sigh. All business and no heart, this one, not realizing that as the man behind the bar, he was surfing the swirling maelstrom of mankind, the star-stuff of humanity, a million stories sitting on these stools every year, looking for a moment of connection, a moment of something real, something true.

The boy was a youngster, barely in his thirties, tanned and slender as a reed in his black short-sleeved shirt and black jeans, ponytail, tats. In five years, his metabolism would change. In ten he'd be a beefy bartender, as clueless as a boiled frog, wondering why the young girls no longer flirted with him. In twenty he'd be asking himself if this was all there was. And if he kept on this way, it would be.

"Yes," Hensley said. "Now I remember. Julien." He held out his hand and Julien automatically shook it. "Reginald Kite. I was in here a few months back on business, and I'll never forget what you said to me."

Julien froze and studied Hensley. "Really?"

Hensley caught his eyes and held them with an expression of intensity that had given princes pause and stopped knife-wielding thugs in their tracks. It didn't fail him now. Julien stood like a bird charmed by a snake.

"I went home and followed your advice, and I'm not exaggerating when I say it changed my life."

The sound of Masie's swift intake of breath echoed in Hensley's left ear, but he didn't break eye contact with Julien, who studied Hensley like he was a treasure map.

A waitress stepped up to the bar station and slapped an order on the counter, but Julien didn't even flinch.

"I could have missed out on the greatest love of my life," Hensley said. "I had to go to Paris to track her down, but because of you, we are now together and happier than we've ever been."

He swung out his arm and pulled Masie close. "Dovey, this is the man I told you about." He looked at her. She returned the gaze with a searching intensity that eclipsed Julien's confused stare.

"Selfless in his service, generous in his wisdom. If any man deserves the encouragement of seeing the fruits of his labors, it's my main man Julien."

Masie whispered between clenched teeth. "What are you talking about?"

"Just play along," Hensley breathed back.

Masie composed herself and turned to the bartender. "I don't know how to thank you."

"Uh . . . it was nothing, ma'am," Julien replied, still attempting to dial up a memory of the event.

"Let's celebrate," Hensley said, back to full volume. "What will you have, love?"

"Me?" Masie scanned the shelf behind the bar. "Do you have a pinot noir?"

"Absolutely," Julien said, springing into action.

Masie extracted herself from Hensley's embrace and whispered, "What are you—"

"Later, my love," Hensley replied softly. When Julien turned back to them with the glass of wine, Hensley said, "For me, a Hendrix martini, heavy on the vermouth with a slice of cucumber, and a bowl of olives. I'm sure you remember."

Julien looked him in the eye with a smile. "Of course, Mr. Kite."

"Please, call me Reggie," Hensley said. "It's not like we're strangers."

"Of course not," Julien said. "One classic martini coming up."

Hensley and Masie waited in silence as Julien did the needful and delivered it with a flourish. Hensley took a sip. "Excellent, as always." He charged it to the room with a generous tip that the Feds should be happy to pay, considering the circumstances, and led Masie to a set of armchairs bookending a coffee table in a corner away from the crowd.

"What was that?" Masie said as she sat down.

"The man was a drone. Didn't you see him?" Hensley settled into his chair and took a generous sip of the excellently prepared martini. He couldn't have done better himself.

"I'm not your long lost love."

"Of course you aren't." He munched serenely on an olive.

"Why?"

Hensley frowned. He didn't expect to have to connect the dots for someone clever enough to land a two hundred million dollar estate on the strength of two days of work.

"He's not at McDonald's. This is a high-end bar, and if he doesn't learn that he's not in the business of serving drinks but in the vocation of serving humanity, he's going to burn out a bitter old man." He took another sip of the martini. "Plus, it got me a level of service I could never have bought with something so crass as the promise of a good tip." He set the glass down. "And I bet every customer he serves tonight will benefit as well."

Masie slouched in the chair with her elbows on the armrests and her wine glass held in front of her face with both hands, regarding him as if he were a specimen under glass in a natural history museum.

Her confusion was not surprising. She had not yet experienced the full spectrum of the Hensley persona. Where she was concerned, to this point he had, of necessity, played the role of the antagonist. This was her first glimpse of Hensley, the philanthropist.

"What exactly are you up to?" Masie said.

"I'm just a man who worked the other side of a bar before Julien was born. Who learned that lesson in his teens from an old woman in Tunis who took in laundry. And strays."

Hensley snatched up his glass and took a long drink. He had orchestrated this moment to extract information, not divulge it, but this woman seemed to elicit the most reactionary side of his personality. Made him start arguments uninvited. He should have been on his guard. Or maybe more relaxed.

Whatever it was, he didn't like it. He set down his glass and went on the offensive. "It occurs to me that I have neglected to congratulate you on your windfall. What do you plan to do with the two hundred million?"

Masie continued to stare at him over her wine. From the level in the glass, it appeared that she hadn't taken a sip. He wished he had a cigar, some stage business to camouflage the fact that he was suddenly off balance. Instead he mirrored her posture and tented his fingers against his lips, waiting.

She broke first. "Seems that I'm suddenly unemployed. The first step is to find a job."

"A strange move for someone who just inherited a fortune. Or are you one of those types?"

"Which type is that?"

"The ones who win the lottery and say they're going to keep their job and continue with life as usual."

"I think we both know that—"

A chair landed next to them with a thud, and Davison dropped into it. "What the hell, Hensley?"

Chapter Two: Epiphany

Hensley was glad he wasn't holding the martini, which was housed in a glass admirable for its purpose but notoriously inadequate for containing liquid under the stress of sudden movements.

He took it up now, indulged in a sip, and turned to Davison. "Perhaps you could couch your question in a more explicit form."

"After the last few days, I was fool enough to think things would be different. But you'll never change, will you? "

Masie bristled. "Davison, don't you think—"

"I pick up the tab at dinner as thanks to Harris for bailing us out of this mess and discover the card is maxed out." Davison threw a stack of faxed pages on the table. "One-way plane tickets from Austin to Philadelphia and Philadelphia to Cancún. A room in the hotel in Cancún, clothes from the merchant shops in the resort, and a bar tab for close to a thousand dollars?"

Masie almost spilled her wine. She set it on the table and slid up to the edge of her chair, rifling through the pages.

Hensley popped an olive into his mouth. "The bar tab gained your freedom. And Masie's. A mere fraction of the two million you were willing to pay."

Davison stood. "Welcome to the future. I've cancelled the card and contested all the charges."

Masie pushed up from her chair and studied Hensley. "You stole his credit card?"

Hensley shrugged. "Merely an advance against expenses. To be paid out of the estate."

"How can you be so understanding with a stranger like Julien and so clueless about those closest to you?"

The fire that flashed in her eyes made Hensley envy Davison for the first time in his life. This was a woman to contend with, a woman worthy of the effort. "Have you considered that what you call clueless is actually an expectation that those closest to me, as you say, might display a similar level of understanding?"

"That ship sailed long ago," Davison said. "In a jungle in Angola." He held out his hand to Masie.

"Does this mean I don't need to attend the debriefing session?" Hensley called to their retreating forms.

In the blank space left by the lack of response, Hensley settled back into his chair, admired the sunset, and pondered these things in his heart. He had lived a full life and had many things to ponder, and pondering made a man thirsty.

He snatched Masie's untasted pinot noir from the table. Quite good. He finished it off by degrees.

Hensley considered himself to be of middle age, but the math worked out only if you did your calculations according to the lifespans recorded in the early parts of the Bible. If you calibrated your reckonings according to the Psalms or more recent mortality statistics, he had a couple of decades left to trod the boards. And given his recent experiences in Cancún, mortality was at the forefront of his considerations.

When it came right down to it, as it rarely did if Hensley could avoid it, while spreading light and salt among the far-flung masses, he had failed to establish any solid base from which to operate. That had been by design, and two weeks ago, he would have seen no reason to question the wisdom of that strategy. After all, when life was a con, only a sucker doubled down on a single number and kept playing it.

But that was before he had seen Davison's transformation. His own brother, the ultimate square peg versus the round hole of the world, too sensitive as a kid, too insensitive as an adult. Yet, if Davison's assessment of Masie was accurate, somehow this man of extremes, insensate to the nuances of the language of life as she is spoke across the expanse of humanity, had seemingly stumbled upon a connection to the holy grail of relationships. The real thing. The genuine article.

If such a thing was to be found, and if a man had the good fortune to stumble upon it, well, then all bets were off. You held onto the bronc-rigging for all you were worth, praying to go the eight seconds intact.

But in Hensley's experience, such things were not to be found in this world. They were like the mythical sure thing, oft dreamt of by suckers but as plentiful as unicorns on the front lawn grazing on four-leaf clover.

And yet he had seen it with his own eyes, if such things as eyes were to be believed. Well, to be more precise, he had seen Davison's transformation. If what Davison said about Masie was true, then Hensley had completely missed it.

He nodded and took another sip of wine. That was the problem, the grit of cognitive dissonance that had thrown him off balance all night. The subliminal bur in his saddle.

The unlikely possibility that Davison was right.

After all, if it came down to a contest of who had his finger on the throbbing pulse of the human condition, Hensley would stake Davison half the distance to the finish line with the confidence that he'd break the tape before Davison was out of the starting blocks. Which meant that Davison had to be wrong about Masie.

But what if he wasn't? More importantly, why this sudden bout of self-doubt?

Perhaps it was the fatigue of a week on the run. Or maybe the prospect of a comfortable situation for his twilight years suddenly snatched away.

Hensley shot up from the chair, walked to the edge of the deck, and gazed out across Galveston to the gulf. This was ridiculous. He was much too old for a midlife crisis. On the other hand, some might look upon Hensley's life and conclude that it resembled one long midlife crisis. Bouncing from one place to another. Always looking for the next thing.

An image flashed unbidden into his mind—tossing twigs into the fire pit outside the clinic in Angola, a three-year-old Davison dashing around on the fool's errand of rescuing moths from the flames. On the other side of the fire, his parents sitting in camp chairs, her hand seeking out his, finding sanctuary. Their shared expression of . . . something. Contentment? Confidence? Completion?

The expression Davison had directed toward Masie these last few days. The conviction of the true believer.

In Hensley's world, there was a word for the true believer.

Sucker.

When you lived by your wits on the streets, you couldn't afford the luxury of vulnerability. The consequences for misplaced trust were severe. Poverty. Hunger. Death.

Skepticism was the price of freedom. But now Hensley saw that he was as free as a stray cur in an alley scrapping for a bone. Maybe that latter-day poet and philosopher Kristofferson knew a thing or two about freedom when he said it was just another word for nothing left to lose.

Then another image intruded upon his morose ponderings. Chrystal. Santa Fe. The turn of the millennium. Strange that last month when he got the telegram that brought him back to the States, his first thought had been of her.

While Chrystal had her faults—and who didn't, Hensley would like to know—no one could deny that she went the distance to shore up the bruised reed. If the Father was the first to attend to the fallen sparrow, Chrystal was not far behind, lining a shoebox with cotton and laying in birdseed for the duration.

Of all the women in all the gin joints in all the towns in all the world that he had had the pleasure of knowing, and that number was considerable, she stood out from the crowd like the Statue of Liberty calling to the masses.

Bring me your tired, your poor, your huddled Hensleys yearning to breathe free.

The trick was that at the time, he was under the delusion that he was far from huddled and already breathing free. What if the universe had presented Hensley with the perfect match over a decade ago, and he hadn't possessed the wit to see it? Such opportunities didn't parade by in a never-ending queue, ripe for plucking as the mood struck. They came once and were gone.

He'd missed his one chance. Or had he? Was there actually a cosmic one-shot-in-a-lifetime rule? This was no time to retire the field based on nothing more than speculation and assumptions. Hensley had made a career of creating opportunities from slimmer materials than this.

As the world inched into darkness, Hensley settled on a course of action. He would miss out on a few free meals, and Special Agent Harris would have to manage his debriefing without benefit of the perspective of a citizen of the world, but it couldn't be helped.

Hensley would marshal his forces, march upon Chrystal's fortress in Santa Fe, and plant his flag. Perhaps she had moved on, and if so, he would do the same. But not before making his case for reinstatement to favored-nation status.

However, due to the cancelled credit card, he would have to make certain adjustments. The facts of life in twenty-first century America were that cash couldn't get you a rental car, but it could get you a ticket on a plane.

Hensley threaded through the crowd to the bar to see how Julien was getting along.

He climbed up on a stool and signaled for a refill. When the drink was in front of him, he said, "Julien, my main man, what are you doing in eight hours?"

Julien glanced at the bar clock. "Four a.m.?"

"I can see the years have not dimmed your powers of perspication or calculation." Hensley smiled. "If you have a car, I have a proposition that could tend toward your advantage."

After making arrangements over a final drink, Hensley took the elevator down to the lobby for a quick look around. The protection detail was in evidence, bright-eyed and bushy tailed. Hensley approached him with a broad smile and an open hand.

"My good man, I feel compelled to extend my utmost gratitude for your dedication and perseverance. You are a credit to your profession. Allow me to buy you a hearty breakfast on the morrow as a token of my appreciation."

The agent shook his hand with an air of confusion. Having planted the seed of an expectation, Hensley took the elevator up to his floor, located the service elevator, and returned to his room to hone the finer points of his exit strategy.

DAY 2: FRIDAY

Chapter Three: Oasis

Because he had left Cancún with a certain sense of urgency, Hensley had no luggage, so when the alarm went off at four a.m., he was out the door within minutes. As he waited for the service elevator to arrive, he paused for a mental apology to the agent holding the fort in the lobby for leading him to believe a breakfast was coming to him gratis. Then he descended into the nether regions of the hotel, located the rear exit, and found Julien waiting in the alley as arranged.

The hundred dollars he had promised Julien in return for a forty-five minute ride to William P. Hobby airport in Houston was a bargain any way you looked at it, whether taxi or puddle jumper from the Galveston airport.

On the drive up, they compared notes on how they found the grand carnival some people called life, and Hensley offered a few tips from his four decades of wandering the mercurial climes of the planet as a sentient being.

In the departures lane at the airport in Houston, Hensley elicited a promise from Julien to reconsider the rudderless approach to life he had employed as of even date. Hensley himself had dealt with this milestone in his late teens, but not everyone had the advantage of the Fletcher family code.

Leave the planet better than you found it.

Hensley's own father, Reggie Fletcher, had tackled that goal on a grand scale, creating a clinic for the natives in Angola from whole cloth, and had paid for it with his life. Hensley chose to implement the philosophy on a more modest level, engaging individuals as he encountered them, like a Johnny Appleseed of the soul.

He liked to think that by now he had a grove, if not a small forest, of acolytes spread across the seven seas and nine continents. He could not hope to live to see the fruition of his efforts, but what man could?

Hensley proceeded into the airport and rustled up an agent to sell him a window seat to his destination, paying the exorbitant fee for the short leg from Albuquerque to Santa Fe to save the trouble of finding a taxi to drive the seventy miles.

As the plane banked westward, Hensley's thoughts veered to the first time he saw Chrystal. Just before the turn of the millennium, as a mere kid of forty, Hensley set out from Portland, Oregon, to hitchhike to Times Square. He wanted to be onsite to party like it was 1999 when the numbers rolled over and the ball dropped.

Just outside of Albuquerque, he ducked into a roadhouse to work out his options for the night over a happy hour pint. He walked straight to the jukebox, dropped in a handful of quarters, and punched random numbers. The first song was "Up on Cripple Creek." He took that as an omen. He parked his backpack in a dark corner where he could keep an eye on it, ambled over to the bar for a bottle of the local pale ale, and gravitated toward the pool tables.

Most of the tables featured either guys or couples playing with varying levels of intensity. At the table in the far corner, two women chatted while knocking the balls around in a haphazard fashion. Hensley approached them obliquely like a Weight Watchers devotee might address a bowl of nanner puddin'. He stopped about half a table away and parked an elbow on the foot-wide bar tacked up along the perimeter of the room.

The blonde, who played the game with the confidence and ineptitude of a former cheerleader, kept shooting sidelong glances at him. The brunette, after a single assessing look, studiously ignored him while lining up her shots, but doing no better than the blonde for all her effort.

Hensley nursed his beer, waiting for the psychological moment. When they had knocked in all the balls, in no particular order, the cheerleader faced him head on while the brunette racked them up for another go.

"You going to just stand there gawking, or you going to come over here and play?"

Hensley nodded slightly, picked up his Santa Fe Pale Ale, and approached the table. "I hesitate to intrude, but perhaps I could buy a round of whatever you lovely young women are having and interest you in a small tournament to determine the reigning champion of the back corner table."

The cheerleader snorted a little pig laugh. She had some meat on the bone, probably no more than ten pounds over her prime cheerleader days. Fifteen at the most, and how many could say that halfway between their ten- and twenty-year reunions? Certainly not Hensley, even if he had a reunion to attend. Which he didn't.

A waitress materialized, and Hensley made a small investment into his immediate future.

While Hensley could be as empathetic as the next guy, there were certain exigencies a guy had to take into consideration when sleeping rough from one end to the other of a continent three thousand miles wide. And as Albuquerque was over a mile high, nights could be chilly whatever the season.

What it came down to was sleeping arrangements. In ascending order of comfort and warmth—his tent, a motel room, or something more domestic. These were the parameters of existence for a boy with a dream, living by his wits for two decades and counting.

He was traveling light. A hiker's backpack and a Jackson in his wallet, and two thousand miles to go. Depending on how the game went, the worst-case scenario was an empty wallet and a night in the tent and who knew what would happen tomorrow morning. But no need to think of that now. Sufficient unto the day and all that. Right now there was a pool tournament to consider.

The first bracket featured Hensley versus the cheerleader.

"I defer to you for the break," he said.

She took the shot and missed entirely, the ball bouncing around the bumpers like a geometry problem. "Oops."

"Give it another try," he said.

"Why don't you do it?"

He did. He hit the side to avoid sinking a ball on the break, but the brunette had packed them tight and he sunk a solid and a stripe.

He played another ball, aiming wide, and deferred to the cheerleader. He tried to let her win. He really did. But he knocked in more balls on accident than she did on purpose.

So now it was down to the brunette. The worst thing he could do was to win again. Better to lose and then ask for the best out of three. That would give him more time to triangulate on the best strategy for the endgame.

He turned to the brunette.

She was racking up for the next game. "You want to put some money on it?"

It was the first time she had looked at him since his first reconnaissance. He looked back. She had the lean aspect of a woman who could go the distance. Razor-cut hair in the style of Joan Jett, boot-cut jeans, Tom Waits Rain Dogs t-shirt. This was no cheerleader. No woman who would be hanging with a cheerleader.

But here she was. And so was he. Life led you to places you could never predict, and Hensley had long since quit trying to figure it. He had learned that there was no percentage in questioning fate. Life dealt you a hand at any given moment, and you either played it or folded.

"What did you have in mind?"

"Ten dollars on the game," she said.

"Done." It was half his stake, not counting the drinks, but he was playing the long game. He could lose the game but double down on the rematch and sleep warm tonight. He hit the break head on, and the balls meandered about the table. A loose pack. She had sand-bagged him. Or had she?

She took the next shot and scratched.

Hensley studied her hard. Half his cash and the rest of the night depended on what happened next. He set up a combination shot that would get close enough to sinking a ball to convince even the most suspicious player of his good intentions.

She sunk a solid and missed the next. She was ahead.

He tried to keep it that way, but no matter how he finessed his misses, she missed more. To be fair, she was playing at the same level as before he had engaged them. But he couldn't shake the thought that he was being played.

Despite his best efforts, he won the game. And then she said those fateful words.

"Best of three?"

He looked her in the eye and she looked back. And in that moment, he knew it was on.

"My dear lady, nothing would give me more pleasure."

This time he racked them up. Nice and tight. "Loser breaks."

She sunk three on the break. He played his best game, but he couldn't keep up with her. They were now one and one. The next game determined the winner.

She racked it and nailed him with a gleam in her eye. "Loser breaks."

Hensley had watched her closely and saw the loose pack. He had no chance on the break. It would be all mush and mashed potatoes. He gauged her but could get no solid reading. Should he go for the win or the sympathy play? He decided on the latter and scratched on the break.

Then she missed an easy shot in a corner pocket and avoided his narrowed eyes, chalking her cue. It looked like if he was going to lose, he was going to have to work for it.

It was a hard fought race to the bottom, each outdoing the other in missing shots.

Then the waitress showed up, and it became a question of who was buying the next round. Hensley had already forfeited half of the twenty for the first round. The ten in his pocket was on the game in progress, but it would never do to let this particular fact be known. He bought the round and changed his strategy. A win would give him enough for a night in a bed, which was more than he had experienced in the last month.

But as soon as he sank the first ball in his sights, a solid, with next to no effort, the game was on. The brunette set out to run the table. Even the cheerleader was reduced to silence in this battle of Titans.

Hensley was behind by one when she missed on the last ball before the eight, giving him a final chance to win it.

He had two balls left. He slammed one into a corner pocket and then intentionally fluffed the last one. Anyone within a half-mile could have seen that he could have made the shot. But he had a sudden hunch, and through the years, he had learned to pay attention to instinct.

The brunette raised an eyebrow, tapped in the last stripe, and then turned to the eight ball. It was a straight shot to a side pocket, but she walked to the other side of the table and made a double bank shot that sunk the eight, but also scratched.

"Dang," she said, laid her cue on the table, and pulled a wrinkled ten from her pocket. It hung limp in her fingers as she held it out toward him. When he reached for it, she said, "Winner buys."

The last round left him busted. Once the drinks were delivered, the cheerleader evaporated, and Hensley was left alone with the brunette.

She held up her bottle. "Congratulations."

Hensley returned her salute, not sure if she had intentionally handed him the Pyrrhic victory. On the one hand, she had at least saved him from the ignominy of revealing that he had no cash to cover the bet, but as he admired her impish smile, he got the impression it was more of a mocking grin, that she had guessed he was busted.

"As victor, I request a boon."

"The cash wasn't enough?"

"More than sufficient insofar as it served its purpose but sadly lacking in the most important element."

She cocked her head and waited.

"Something I long to have that you alone possess, and in the giving will make me immeasurably richer without diminishing you in the slightest."

A suspicious frown creased her forehead as the smile melted.

"It is the gift of learning your name."

A nervous laugh of relief escaped. "Chrystal."

"And I am Hensley." He bowed and then stepped aside to make way for a pack of cowboys with pool cues. Hensley stepped to a nearby table and pushed a bunch of empties to one side. "Shall we?"

Chrystal sat down. "You're not from around here, are you?"

Hensley sat and leaned forward. "Judging by your accent, neither are you."

"I think ten years qualifies me as a local."

"That should qualify you as a founding father, or mother, as the case may be."

"And what kind of father, or mother, are you?"

"The best kind." He smiled. "I am a citizen of the world, a denizen *du monde*, riding the tides of time and fortune."

"Riding the road on your thumb and by the seat of your pants, you mean." She took a sip of her Bud Light.

Hensley responded with a sip of his pale ale to buy time. He'd expected an habitué of a desert roadhouse to be a little more pliable and responsive to his charms, but she anticipated his every move, seeming to know what he would do before he did. He followed her glance to his pack and realized she'd had him pegged as soon as he walked in the door.

Chrystal set her beer on the table. "When was the last time you had a home-cooked meal?"

The question took him by surprise, and he became lost in the calculation. "I assume you mean cooked in an actual home."

"Or slept on clean sheets? Had a long shower with steaming hot water?"

The thought of all three luxuries at once overwhelmed Hensley. When he regained the power of speech, he blurted out, "Tempt not the gods with such excess, my lady! We are but mortals."

"Okay, here is the thing. I got two kids at home with the sitter, asleep. You will not wake them up. You will sleep on the couch. In case you get any ideas to the contrary, I sleep with a gun, and I could shoot the eye out of a lizard at thirty yards before I could write." Chrystal finished off her Bud Light and shoved the bottle next to the pre-existing empties. "But if you behave yourself, you can get all three—the meal, the clean sheets, the shower—before you go wherever it is that citizens of the world go."

This proposition was not one of any of the possible scenarios Hensley had played out in his mind. In fact, it was unique in his experience, and he was both delighted and disturbed. But he was in no position to engage in undue inspection of the oral cavity of any extant equines.

"Say no more. I am but your humble servant."

He had stayed the night, got the shower, the clean sheets, the meal. And then he had stayed for another two years.

Chapter Four: Mirage

After a short jaunt in Albuquerque to catch his connecting flight, Hensley landed in Santa Fe in a slight drizzle. Not the weather he was expecting, but the cool air was welcome as he stepped out of the airport.

He snagged a taxi to the Goodwill store on Cerrillos Road and had it wait while he bought a few changes of clothes, some other necessities, and a duffel bag. He scanned his change. A state quarter lurked among the nondescript coinage. Oklahoma. You didn't see those every day. He dropped it in his shirt pocket and shoved the rest in his pants pocket. Then he directed the driver to Chrystal's house on the northwest side of town.

The place looked much as it had twelve years ago, gravel drive that curved through southwest vegetation to the stucco house under the somber stare of the Sangre de Cristo mountains, but without the bikes and toys that had always seemed to be in the yard at the turn of the millennium.

Hensley paid the taxi and rang the doorbell. After a few more attempts, he gave the neighborhood a quick scan. Nothing on the street but a pest control van. He slipped through the wooden gate into the backyard and under the pecan tree to get out of the drizzle.

He found the key to the French doors right where he put it when he left over a decade ago, at the bottom of a planter of salvia hanging from the redwood pergola.

After knocking once more for good measure, Hensley unlocked the door, dropped the key in his pocket, and closed the door behind him. He set the duffel bag on the kitchen island and walked through the house.

A cat brushed against his ankles and threaded between his legs. He scratched it behind the ears. "Home alone, are you? Hello? Chrystal?" It was close to noon on a Thursday. Chrystal was probably at work.

Hensley tried to remember the kids' names. The boy was in junior high when he left, so he was in his twenties by now. Something connected with Dickens. Sidney? Oliver? No, Fagin. That was it. "Fagin? You home?" And the girl . . . something with a C. Or was it an S? Something of the sort. She was probably finished with school too. Possibly on her own.

In the living room, he found a sixty-gallon tank of tropical fish in one corner and a cage of finches in another, potted plants transforming the room into a tropical maze. The cat followed him in an uncharacteristic spirit of camaraderie and exploration, offering feline advice.

The master bedroom, on the end of the house by the driveway, was unoccupied. A cursory inspection of the closet revealed only women's clothes. So she was still single. As he passed the chest of drawers, he caught sight of a photo of himself, Chrystal, and the two kids. He picked it up, and the memory soon followed. A day filled with drama as any excursion involving tadpoles was likely to be. A hike up Picacho Peak with the girl on his back. Santa Fe stretched out behind them in the distance.

Hensley smiled and returned the picture to its place. It was a good omen for a warm welcome.

The two bedrooms on the other side of the house were messy but also unpopulated at the moment. Other than various flora and fauna, nobody was home.

Hensley's stomach reminded him it was coming on lunchtime, especially one time zone over from Texas. En route to the kitchen, he spied a pile of mail under the slot in the front door. He scooped it up and dropped it on the table on his way to the fridge. He'd lost the cat somewhere on the trail, but the species was known for its independence, so he gave it no further thought.

After trolling through various frozen and leftover options, he decided on a sandwich. While the bread toasted, he amassed slices of ham, roast beef, and chicken breast, supplemented with chipotle jack cheese, spicy mustard, and baby spinach. He sprinkled on a little balsamic vinaigrette and a dash of fresh ground black pepper, poured some sea salt chips in a bowl, and grabbed a Red Stripe from the fridge.

As he dined, he perused the envelopes he had gathered from the front hall. Mostly junk mail, a few bills, all addressed to Robin Bumstead, the name her parents gave her.

One of the envelopes was from a mobile service provider. As an old-school bohemian citizen of the world, Hensley had thus far avoided encumbering himself with a digital leash of any kind, but Chrystal was an American citizen with two kids. She could no more avoid a mobile phone than a social security number.

While the contents of the envelope would divulge to him a method of contacting her directly, patience would no doubt produce the woman in question in the flesh within a few hours without the inevitable drama that would ensue if he began reading her mail.

As he dropped it to the table, he heard the slide and click of a key in a deadbolt echo from the front hall. The sandwich dropped from his fingers and splayed out on the plate like a poker hand.

The hour had come. Hensley stepped to the kitchen island and prepared to confront Fagin, or the girl with the name starting with a C or an S, or the woman herself.

A teenaged girl walked into the kitchen, absorbed in rapid thumb play on a smartphone. She dropped her purse on the island, and then noticed the duffel bag. She froze, and her eyes drifted up to Hensley. She screamed and backed against the stove.

"Please, don't hurt me."

Hensley considered placing a comforting hand on her shoulder, but realized that for him to approach her would be far from comforting. After all, when Hensley left, Chrystal's daughter was only two or three years old. There was no way for her to connect that guy back then with the random stranger in her kitchen, a thick, scruffy guy with a healthy goatee, still dressed in Johnny-Cash black, because he had not yet taken time to shower and change into his Santa Fe clothes.

He wished he could remember her name, or had taken the time to scan her room for a clue, but that couldn't be helped now. "No need for concern, dovey. You don't remember me, but I am an old friend of your mother."

If Hensley thought this would calm her, he was severely mistaken. "How do you know my mother?" she squeaked.

"I used to dandle you on my knee in this very room when you could barely walk."

Her eyes grew as big as a super moon. "You did what?"

"You might remember me as Uncle Hensley. I arrived in this house not long after you were born and left just after your second birthday. Cake and candles at this very table." He slapped the table, then bowed his head in deferential regret. "Unfortunately world events prevented me from returning as I had promised. But I have returned at long last."

"Uncle Hensley? I don't have an Uncle Hensley."

"Of course not. Not an uncle of the family tree, but an uncle in spirit nonetheless." He brushed the crumbs from his shirt. "What time does your mother get home?"

"My mother is at home."

Hensley frowned. "In what sense is she at home?"

"She's been at home all day. I just came over to feed the animals."

The puzzle pieces rearranged themselves. He had unforgivably misread the situation. "Ah, dear creature. Please accept my deepest apologies for startling you. I was laboring under a misapprehension. And what might be your name?"

"Uh . . . Toni."

"And you are friends with . . ."

"Saff."

Yes, Sapphire. Started with an S, just like he thought. And a quite apt name, as he remembered commenting when they first met. "But why are you feeding the animals?"

"Ms. Bumstead has gone to visit Fagin."

"He doesn't live at home then?"

"Well, duh. He's twenty-five and a hotshot lawyer in the capital."

"We are in the capital, my dear."

"In DC."

"I'm not surprised. He used to torment me with syllogisms even in grammar school. I understand that his father was a pillar of rectitude and a credit to his race, God rest his soul. Do you know when they'll be back?"

Toni frowned. "They?"

"Chrystal and Sapphire."

"Oh, right. She didn't say."

"Well, then this is exceedingly bad timing for me. I was just passing through and thought I might look in and see how they are getting on."

Toni eyed him as she might an oyster with a pedigree that lacked a month with an R. "How did you get in?"

Hensley turned to reassemble his sandwich. "The door was unlocked." No need to alarm the skittish creature with the knowledge of a secret key.

"I locked it when I left yesterday."

"The back door."

Toni released a doubtful huff but proceeded to open a cabinet door and extract a can of cat food, all without turning her back on him. At the whir of the can opener, the feline materialized and became Toni's new best friend.

Toni gave Hensley a wide berth as she walked to the bowl by the French doors and scooped out the cat food in a most inefficient manner in Hensley's view, using a spoon instead of a butter knife. But experience was the best teacher for the young, who would have no other, so he refrained from casting his pearls in her direction. He had, after all, done his good deed for the week with Julien, who seemed more likely to profit from it.

Hensley finished his lunch while flipping through the mail as Toni distributed birdseed and fish food and closed the front door with what seemed to him unnecessary force. He waited until he heard the snick of the deadbolt and then watched from the living room window as she walked to her car parked at the curb, chatting on the phone all the while like the youngsters were wont to do these days.

If he wanted to connect with Chrystal, he would have to do so in the nation's capital, but that required an address for Fagin.

At the desk in a nook between the kitchen and living room, Hensley searched for an address book but quickly abandoned the project after digging through a few decades of memorabilia, minutiae, and detritus, the only item of interest being a new credit card that still had the activation sticker on it.

He powered up the computer, which thankfully offered no speed bumps in the way of passwords, and searched the web for Fagin Bumstead. It took him a quarter hour to remember that he bore the surname of Chrystal's first husband, Duff, another five minutes to discover that she had spelled it Fagan, and yet another fifteen minutes to find a site that didn't require payment by credit card to divulge that he had an apartment in Georgetown.

Then he searched for flights to Dulles or Reagan National. It turned out that he had already missed any flight that didn't require an overnight layover in DFW, so he recalibrated his timeline. Since the pets were fed and the residents were in DC, as long as he kept a low profile, he could spend the night here and catch an early flight tomorrow.

But it occurred to him that Chrystal's mobile number would come in handy, so he returned to the kitchen and opened the phone bill. Two numbers were listed, probably the first for Chrystal and the other for Sapphire. By now Fagan would be paying his own bills in DC.

He added them to the scrap of paper with Fagan's address and stuffed it in his wallet. He was digging through the freezer for something to thaw for dinner when the doorbell rang.

Hensley froze like a rat when the light is turned on. On the second ring, he dashed to the front bedroom and peered out the window that overlooked the front door.

A tall, muscled guy in a cowboy hat and a well-used cheap suit stood on the porch. He tried the door, but it was locked, thanks to Toni, unexpectedly wise beyond her years. Hensley vowed to put her in his will if he ever had anything worth bequeathing.

After a final shot at the doorbell, the man walked back down the sidewalk toward the street.

Hensley decided this was a good time to find other accommodations for the evening. He grabbed his duffel from the kitchen island, stepped out the back door, and locked it behind him. As he crossed the pergola, the man in the suit rounded the corner, spotted Hensley, and drew a gun from a shoulder holster.

CHAPTER FIVE: APPREHENSION

"Hold it right there," the man said.

Hensley froze. While he was as sanguine as the next guy, and maybe more so, he had great respect for the power of a .38 slug to settle an argument. Permanently.

"Drop the duffel, kick it away, keep your hands where I can see them."

"Is there a problem?"

"Damn straight there's a problem. I don't know you. Turn around. Hands on the door."

Hensley complied. "Forgive me for asking, sir, and I'm sure it's my loss, but how is that a problem?"

"Because I know the people who live here, and you aren't one of them. Plus, you match the description of an intruder that was called in half an hour ago."

Called in. The man must be some brand of law enforcement. He approached, placed a foot against the insole of Hensley's left foot, and began patting him down, confirming Hensley's assessment.

"I'm an old family friend visiting from France."

"How did you get in?"

"Toni let me in."

"That's funny, because she said you were already inside when she got here." The officer slapped a cuff on Hensley's right wrist and pulled it behind him.

Hensley craned his neck around. "It's understandable that you may not know me, Officer. I'm Hensley Fletcher. I used to live here."

The officer grabbed his left hand and pulled it down to his back, cinching it up with the other cuff. "I know who you are." He spun Hensley around. "You're that vagrant that shacked up here in the nineties."

Hensley caught his balance and regarded him coolly. It wasn't the first time he'd been cuffed, and in countries that made him much more nervous than the US. "You say you know me, but I don't know you."

"You didn't have cause to back then, but now you do."

Hensley searched his memory for the face in front of him, but he'd visited every continent in the past decade and met a lot of people. He thought he might be forgiven for forgetting a detective in Santa Fe. "You can look inside if you want to verify I didn't take anything. Other than the makings of a sandwich, for which I will gladly pay at the going rate."

The officer focused a smoldering stare on him for a long time. Long enough, and with sufficient hostility, that Hensley began to revise his earlier assessment of personal peril. The man obviously had some baggage. After all, there was a lot of desert out there, and a person who wouldn't be missed could go undiscovered for years. Decades. Centuries.

And to his dismay, Hensley realized that he was just that sort of person. If this cowboy were to put a slug in his skull, Hensley couldn't name a soul on the planet who would come looking for him.

To Hensley's immense relief, instead of shooting him in the head, the officer grabbed his arm, spun him around, and removed the cuffs.

"Chrystal gets off work at 4:30. You better not be here when she gets back. Or ever."

Hensley stopped himself from blurting out that Chrystal and Sapphire were in DC. Even though the cuffs had been on only a minute or so, he rubbed his wrists. "Current circumstances notwithstanding, I would say that's her choice."

"Oh, believe me, she wants to see you even less than I do." The officer shoved the cuffs back into his belt. "Either way, you're leaving now."

Hensley teased a memory from his ancient past. "Ah. I remember now. You're Deputy Powers."

"Sheriff Powell."

"Congratulations on your success. I'm sure your mother is very proud." Hensley picked up his bag. "Now, if you could recommend a decent coffee shop, I have some work to do."

Powell gave him a final contemptuous glance. "You seem like a clever guy. You can figure that out." He turned to leave but stopped at the edge of the pergola. "How did you get here?"

"Taxi. So it seems we have two options. No, three. You can radio for a cab. Or I can go back inside to call. Either way I'll have to wait around here for a while before it shows up. Or you can give me a ride."

Powell eyed Hensley and stepped past him to check the door. "Come on. The sooner you leave, the better."

They walked around the house. Hensley called shotgun. Powell didn't smile.

Powell pulled away from the curb past the pest control van in silence. The drive out of the neighborhood wasn't a picnic any way you sliced it. It was rare for Hensley to be at a loss for a conversational gambit, not that Powell had offered an opening.

If memory served, Powell had set his cap for Chrystal back in '96 when she became a widow, way before the moment Hensley rolled into town in '99, hitchhiking the US, west coast to east. Not that a cowboy like Powell ever had a chance with a nuanced chick like Chrystal. Hensley was just passing through until he met her and realized she was worth sticking around for.

She had a newborn on her hands at the time, Sapphire, and a ten-year-old, Fagan, and a new job as a court reporter, set up by some judge who had served in 'Nam with her father. Bonds forged in the military were hard to break, especially if they were tempered in combat, and the judge had taken her under his wing when her husband died in the Gulf War. The first one. Both the husband and the war.

Hensley's only regret was that he had never met Duffy, her first husband. Although if Duff had been in the picture in '99, Hensley would have been out and wouldn't be here now, wouldn't have been graced with the opportunity to get to know Chrystal to the degree that had transpired.

Sometimes life was an either/or thing, although it went against Hensley's philosophy to admit it. But that was not the point. The point was that Powell was still carrying the torch for Chrystal, so conversation with him was pointless, and Hensley only engaged in pointless pastimes when they were sufficiently amusing.

The only other reason to draw Powell into conversation was to extract information, but it appeared that Hensley already knew more than Powell about Chrystal's recent movements. So he kept his peace and spent the ride into town pondering where he might spend the night.

He could catch the 5:20 flight out of SAF and sleep in the terminal at DFW, or get a motel room and make the early flight for a quick trip. Since, like Masie, he hadn't spent a full night's sleep in a decent bed for close to a week, he was leaning toward the motel option, even if the establishment had a number in its name, when Powell swerved his Crown Victoria into the parking lot of a coffee shop and skidded to a stop.

"This is where you get off," Powell said. "Next stop, anywhere but here. And don't bother coming back."

Hensley grabbed his duffel and shoved the door open. "It has been a singular pleasure catching up with you, Sheriff Powers. I look forward to another opportunity in the near future."

"Powell," Powell said.

"Oh, yes. My mistake."

"And I'll see you in hell before I see you in Santa Fe, if I have anything to do with it."

Hensley scooted out of the car. "Well, my good sir, if we don't have the happy occasion of the latter, I have no doubt we shall have the opportunity of the former eventually."

He slammed the door. Powell shot out of the parking lot, barely missing the rear quarter panel of a passing Cadillac that honked as it sped past. Lucky he was in an unmarked car, because he might have T-boned a major donor to his reelection campaign.

As Hensley turned to the coffee shop, he heard the sound of wheels on gravel. He jumped to the side and turned to evade what he thought was the return of the sheriff when a white van with a pest control logo skidded to a stop in front of him.

A guy burst out of the shotgun door, slammed the sliding passenger door open, punched Hensley in the gut, grabbed the front of his shirt, and threw him into the van. Then the guy leapt in, directing a well-placed knee into the small of Hensley's back, and jerked the door shut. The van rocketed away from the coffee shop.

Chapter Six: Wingnuts

Before Hensley had a chance to recover from the exhalation of breath, Shotgun was leaning down over him with one hand mashing his right cheek against the rubberized floor and the other pointing a shiv at his left eye.

"Here's the thing," Shotgun said in a voice that owed much to adenoids. "You settle down and lie still, or I'll scoop out your medulla oblongata through your eye socket."

If there was one thing Hensley could appreciate, it was a thug who knew his Latin, even if, from the aroma, he had not showered in three or four weeks. And if there was something he respected more, it was a knife two inches from his left eye in the hand of someone who seemed anxious to wield it.

As his heart rate skyrocketed, Hensley struggled to keep his composure. He took a few deep breaths, not easy when a guy sat atop you leaning on your head.

"Nothing could be further from my mind than resistance, but to what do I owe the honor of this meeting, and whom do I have the honor of addressing?"

"I'll ask the questions. And there's only one question. Where's the drugs?"

Few things could have plunged Hensley deeper into a maelstrom of confusion. "No doubt there are any number of pharmacies in town. I think I glimpsed one across the street just before you invited me to this party."

Shotgun dug his elbow between Hensley's scapula and backbone. It was singularly effective.

Hensley choked down a cry and used all his martial arts training to keep his blood pressure from popping a vessel in some vital part of his anatomy.

Leaning in on his elbow, Shotgun hissed in Hensley's ear. "I'm ready to start scooping, so keep it up."

A low, growling voice came from the driver's seat. "Are you crazy? Stow the knife."

"But he's—"

"Stow it."

Shotgun adjusted his position, flipped the knife closed, and shoved it into a pocket. Then he leaned down next to Hensley's ear. "You know why they don't send donkeys to school, right?"

"Point well taken," Hensley replied. "Perhaps you can provide me with sufficient details to follow your line of questioning."

"I already told you. The drugs. I bet you're the buyer."

"Buyer?" Hensley tried to imagine a scenario in which he could be construed as a buyer of drugs anywhere outside of a pharmacy.

"If you have any ideas of moving in on our territory, think again."

"Believe me, my odiferous friend, I have no intention of moving in on any territory, yours or otherwise. I was just going for coffee."

"That isn't the only place you've been."

"Of course not. I've been to quite a few places in the past few days, none of which had to do with drugs."

"Search him," the driver said.

Shotgun adjusted his stance and pulled Hensley's wallet from his pocket. "Two hundred? That's not enough for this deal."

Hensley was grateful that life had taught him to distribute his holdings.

"Maybe there's more in the bag," the driver said.

Shotgun dropped the wallet, which landed on Hensley's cheek and slid to the floor, planted a knee between Hensley's shoulder blades, and dug through the duffel. After a bit of shuffling through some bills, he said, "Here's another five hundred, but that's still not enough."

"Who is this guy?" the driver said.

"Reginald Hensley Fletcher, according to his passport," Shotgun said. "From Paris."

"That doesn't sound like the cartels," the driver said, hanging a hard right. "Or the Russians."

"That might be because I'm neither," Hensley said.

"What's your game?" Shotgun said.

"He might be telling the truth," the driver said.

"Forget the truth," Shotgun yelled. He leaned into Hensley's back. "Where's the drugs?"

"I came to see a man about a dog," Hensley said.

"What kind of dog is worth seven hundred dollars?"

Hensley had spoken metaphorically, but if they were willing to go with it, so was he. "A pedigree show dog. Champion line on both sides back five generations."

"Pit bull?"

"Shar-Pei."

"What the hell is that?"

"Chinese. One of the oldest breeds in existence."

"The little dogs with the wrinkled faces," the driver said.

"They're worth seven hundred?" Shotgun asked.

"Seven thousand, if you get the right one."

"Dayum," Shotgun said. "Seven grand for one dog. We're in the wrong business, Merle."

"You watch your mouth," the driver shot back.

"That's not for every dog," Hensley said. "Just a few. If you're looking for high profit margins and massive infusion of capital, you're in the right business. On the other hand, going to a kennel to buy a dog doesn't incur the level of risk you might find on a daily basis in your business. Usually."

The pressure between Hensley's shoulder blades reduced slightly.

"If I find out you're lying," Shotgun said. "I will field dress you like a bighorn buck and make sausage from your guts."

The van swerved to the right and skidded to a stop.

"Looks like this is where you get off."

Shotgun crouched next to the door. Hensley took the opportunity to grab his wallet and passport as the doors slammed open and Shotgun shoved him out onto the pavement.

Hensley rolled off the shoulder in a shallow ditch as the van sped away. He struggled to his feet, grateful to have his left eye and his medulla oblongata intact, even if his duffel bag holding his newly purchased wardrobe sped away from him at considerably above the legal speed limit. Not to mention the money.

Brushing the sand off his clothes, he took a look around. The two-lane highway rose to a slight hill either direction, the top of the van disappearing over the hill on his right. In front and behind him, the view extended for miles.

Here and there, a scrubby bush hugged the ground, dirt and sparse clumps of grass dotting the intervening spaces. The only sign of civilization, other than the road itself, was the power lines that ran along what appeared to be the west side of the road, judging by the bright patch in the overcast sky. That meant they had been driving south out of town when they tossed him out.

Distant mountains lined the horizon on most points of the compass. The air was cool and humid, but at least the light drizzle had stopped. Hensley turned toward what he assumed was north and townward and began walking down the long ribbon of road.

Something bothered him. Who were those guys, and why did they think he was buying drugs? A lot of drugs.

Although Hensley cultivated a certain iconoclastic style, a nimbus of untamed hair, an artistic beard, and an opportunistic wardrobe forged by convenience and comfort, he was fairly certain that drug lord was not the ultimate statement of the combination. But they seemed fairly certain that he was in the market. Why?

Hensley double-checked the money belt he kept slung under his clothes below the waist. Satisfied that everything was intact, he topped the slight rise to the north and some low, wide buildings came into view. A few minutes of walking brought him to a sign on the right proclaiming the presence of the Turquoise Trail Charter School. He thought about scaling the three-strand barbed-wire fence and jogging the hundred yards in the hope that he would be able to call a cab from the office, but he noticed that the parking lot was deserted. Not surprising considering it was June.

He continued his northward trudge. The noise of a motor crept up on him. He looked behind. A pickup approached, older, in need of some body work. He stood on the shoulder with hand outstretched, but the citizen behind the wheel didn't even glance his direction, much less slow down.

Thirty minutes or so later, a late-model SUV did the same thing, although the woman did study him intently as she passed, her head swiveling like the turret of a tank. He smiled and waved, and she snapped her head toward the road and accelerated.

Hensley shrugged and continued his trek up another small rise. He hadn't been in the van that long. Couldn't be more than a few miles out of town. And at least it wasn't raining.

As he reached the top of the incline, it started to sprinkle. On the horizon, more evidence of civilization appeared in the form of a substantial set of multi-story buildings set back a quarter mile from the road on either side. Some serious structures.

He neared some signage on the road. First a yellow sign with the silhouette of a cow. Then a large white sign in red and black letters.

NOTICE
DO NOT PICK-UP
HITCHHIKERS
PRISON FACILITIES

That explained a few things, like why he should resign himself to walking the entire way back into town. But nothing explained the hyphen on the sign. Hensley supposed he should count his blessings. At least they hadn't enclosed hitchhikers in quotes.

He reckoned he'd covered a mile or more. A few miles later, the highway sprouted a median and houses appeared. A sign told him he was headed north on Highway 14. Hensley doubted he'd have much luck knocking on doors, so he continued on.

A quarter mile later, he encountered an intersection and a convenience store where he convinced the clerk to dial the number for Capital City Cab. While he waited, he went into the bathroom, slid the latch, and refreshed his wallet from the stash in his money belt. A rookie would have lost the whole nut, but this was not Hensley's first rodeo. Nor his second.

By the time the taxi dropped him off at Goodwill for a fresh wardrobe, it was almost closing time. He threw together a selection from the items that had almost made the cut the first time around, checked his change before dropping it into his pants pocket, and inquired about hotel accommodations. A half mile north, he got a room at the Silver Saddle Motel, which featured a complimentary cowboy continental breakfast.

Like the lobby, the room was studiously kitschy, but Hensley had no objections to laying it on for effect. He deposited his bag and wandered in search of dinner until he found Tortilla Flats across from the Goodwill store. It wasn't the Ritz, but it was good, honest fare. He made do with the guacamole salad, the carne adovado plate with a side of calabacitas, and flan al caramelo with añejo tequila for dessert. These folks knew their stuff. He found a wheat penny in his change and dropped it in his shirt pocket.

Back at the hotel, he took a chair on the deserted breakfast ramada, peeled the cellophane off a cigar he had picked up at the liquor store across the street, and contemplated his situation.

The first thing was to get to DC and reunite with Chrystal. After all, that was the only reason he was here. But getting there would eat up at least a third of his cash reserve.

If all went well, it would last until he got settled in and found something to occupy his time and produce a revenue stream. He'd survived much worse. Many times.

However, he had no desire to test his ability to start from zero one more time. In his twenties, he had spent months sleeping on a half-inch thick mat on a stone floor in the mountains of Guangxi and reveled in the challenge at the time, but a quarter-century on, he was past youthful demonstrations of endurance.

Hensley had come to the age when he wished to relax by the hearth with slippers fetched by an Irish water spaniel, a snifter of brandy in one hand, a briar pipe loaded with Latakia tobacco in the other, and a collection of locked-room mystery short stories in his lap. In fact, the study in the Stone family mansion on the Main Line outside of Philadelphia appealed to him as the perfect setting for the scenario.

That brought up the question of Masie and Davison and the will. Doubtless Davison had acquiesced to the final will that settled the Stone estate on Masie because under the current arrangement he would share in it.

Hensley's problem was that nobody but Ellis knew the conditions of the previous will, and he was such a pillar of rectitude that Hensley knew better than to try to weasel that information out of him.

So it came down to a gamble. He could proceed with the plan of challenging the final will on grounds of mental competence in the hope that the previous will cut him in for some portion of the two hundred million. Or he could hold back and rely on Masie to do the honorable thing and pass on to him some reasonable portion of the inheritance.

Considering Hensley's alienation from the family, which made relying on the previous will a chancy thing, versus Davison's current attitude toward Hensley, which made relying on getting a cut from Masie an equally chancy thing, one would need a micrometer to find an advantage one way or another.

Hensley pulled the wheat penny from his pocket, flipped it, and slapped it on the back of his hand. But instead of looking at it, he took another puff on the cigar and spoke to the empty ramada. "Either I bag a piece of the estate or I don't. Either way, my way forward is clear."

He pocketed the penny and turned his ponderings eastward.

It would be good to see Chrystal again. The two years he had spent with her here in Santa Fe had been some of the best of his life, despite having two kids in the house.

Hensley had no objection to children in principle. It was the actual incarnation of that principle that elicited in him a desire to reformulate society along the lines of the London gentleman's club of the nineteenth century, a place of gentility, restraint, and discretion furnished with an implacable doorman to keep out the untoward disruptions that those under twenty-five invariably introduced.

Primary among the trials of cohabiting with tadpoles was the necessity of quelling their screams by entertaining them with mind-numbing pastimes involving an endless repetition of elemental memes. Hensley recognized the necessity of such building blocks for the developing mind, but he didn't have the constitution to endure the accompanying ennui.

Fortunately for his sanity, during his two years with Chrystal, she had attended to Sapphire's needs, and Fagan was sufficiently advanced to allow for diverting mind games. Hensley had left town before the dreaded teen years, when no remedy short of euthanasia could quell the madness.

He looked back on those times with fondness, but twelve years of radio silence was a long time. He didn't think he had changed materially during the interim, but while a man is the sun, a woman is the moon, with the power to control the tides of men, but equally changeable, and nowhere near as predictable as the actual moon. Surely she had moved on, and if so, where did that leave him?

As he finished off the cigar, he reflected on the thought that the man who could produce a chart to predict the phases of a woman's temperament could rule the world.

But this was the stuff of fantasy. He repaired to his room and the anticipation of the sleep of the just, but visions of Shotgun and Merle danced like sugarplums in his dreams. He awoke thinking that with the sheriff on the one hand and the goons on the other, the sooner he got out of town, the better.

DAY 3: SATURDAY

Chapter Seven: Speculation

The plane touched down at Reagan National with a good hour of sunlight left. Having only a duffel bag for luggage, Hensley beat the crowd to ground transportation, snagged the first taxi, and gave the driver Fagan's address.

DC was uncharacteristically pleasant for the summer, low seventies and low humidity. The boot-cut jeans and light cotton shirt with French cuffs he had scored at Goodwill were perfect. The cabbie showed no inclination for conversation, and that suited Hensley right down to the ground. He had some thinking to do.

He rolled down the window and enjoyed the approaching sunset as they cruised next to the Potomac River along George Washington Memorial Parkway. A few late evening sailboats tacked toward safe harbor.

He'd sought shelter from the storm of life in his time, particularly in the early days right after he had walked away from his father's clinic and into the jungle.

His first sanctuary was the kindly woman in Tunis he'd mentioned to Masie. She guided him on his path as a sixteen-year-old runaway. It was a crash course in the transition from teen angst to survival on the streets of the world, and he had been the beneficiary of her wisdom every day since.

He had found many harbors in the decades since, some serene, some more turbulent than the currents he sought to escape. But those two years in Santa Fe possessed a different quality. A resonance. Like an echo of a time before this time. Before Africa. Back when he had a home.

That afternoon he leaves his bartending gig at the Tinker's Dam to pick up Fagan and take him to his martial arts class.

As he drives up Old Las Vegas highway into town, he reflects on the level of domesticity to which he has become accustomed. Were it not for his gender and the rusted Datsun pickup he'd kept alive through the judicious application of karma and the occasional strategic intervention, his life might be compared to that of a soccer mom. Part-time job. Distributing the kids to their respective institutions on the front side of the day and then picking them up and shunting them to their extracurricular pursuits in the waning hours.

Those who had encountered him throughout his perambulations across the globe would be shocked to see him now, and he has to admit that he is marginally flabbergasted himself.

As he ponders the cause of this seeming stasis in his life, he need look no further than Chrystal, the star that has snagged this wandering comet and pulled him into orbit.

She just makes it too easy. Not that she is a pushover. Far from it. If anything, she is a woman designed to keep a man on his toes. An amalgam of intelligence and compassion, one who brooks no nonsense but at the same time doesn't break the bruised reed nor snuff out the smoldering wick. A worthy opponent and a singular companion.

In some respects, he finds himself contented, but in his lexicon, contentment is for cows. Complacency makes him nervous. The road calls, the ever receding horizon beckons.

And thus it is that when Whyte tracks him down to the high desert, Hensley immediately endorses his plan to do the Andes trail via mountain bike. A grueling five-month trek from Ecuador to Tierra del Fuego. Just the thing he needs to assure himself that he hasn't been completely domesticated.

As he hits traffic, Hensley directs his thoughts to his errand. One never knows what to expect when Fagan enters the frame, although one thing is certain. It will always come in the form of a challenge.

Hensley pulls up to the school and idles at the curb. Fagan flags him down. He has already changed into his gi. He tosses his backpack in the truck bed, reaches through the open passenger window, flicks the handle, and jerks on the door. It opens with a rusty squawk.

Fagan begins talking before he is even in the truck. "So which creature walks on four legs in the morning, two legs in the afternoon, and three legs in the evening?"

Hensley grinds the stick shift into first and lurches away from the curb. "Is it time for Edith Hamilton already?" He casts an appraising eye on the tweenager in the passenger seat. "Buckle up, my youthful sphinx. Shall I speak the answer and precipitate your demise?"

"Aw, man. You know it?"

Hensley snorts. "Imagine you're trapped in a room with no doors. How do you get out?"

"Duh. Quit imagining." Fagan snaps his seatbelt. "I am easy to get into, but hard to get out of. What am I?"

"So it's a duel, is it? In that case, you'll have to step up your game. You can't expect that old chestnut to stump a man of my experience. You're trouble." Hensley negotiates a left turn while delivering his response. "Take off my skin and I won't cry, but you will. What am I?"

Fagan ponders for perhaps three seconds before answering. "An onion, of course." He stares into space for a while. "Okay. I have married many women, but I have never been married. Who am I?"

"You have the unfortunate fate to be a priest. My condolences." Hensley pulls into the strip mall parking lot and coasts to a stop in front of the dojo. "If you have me, you want to share me. If you share me, you no longer have me. What am I?"

Fagan sits in anguished silence for close to a minute. "Time?" he says in a doubtful tone.

Hensley shakes his head.

"Cookies?"

"One can share his cookie and eat it too, I'm afraid."

Fagan ponders. Hensley points to his watch. Fagan sighs and shoves the door open with his shoulder. "Okay, I give up. What is it?"

Hensley shrugs. "I'm afraid that's my little secret."

"Oh. Duh." Fagan rolls his eyes, grabs his backpack from the truck bed, and sticks his head through the window. "What gets broken without being held?"

"Wind."

"Wrong," Fagan exclaims triumphantly. "It's a promise."

"I guess you win."

As Fagan darts into the dojo, Hensley pulls away to pick up Sapphire at the daycare. He retrieves the car seat from the truck bed, secures her in it, and returns to the dojo in time to see the class go through an advanced kata. Of course Fagan executes perfectly while most of his classmates struggle to keep up.

They arrive at the house just as Chrystal pulls in from work. She takes Saff off his hands and hands him a shopping bag. He pulls out one of a half-dozen flimsy, long-sleeved pullovers and looks to her for an explanation.

"Microfiber thermal undershirts. I hear it gets cool in the Andes, even in August."

It is exactly what he needs. A five-month trip requires one to pack light. These six shirts consume less than the space of two traditional thermal shirts.

Hensley bestows a grateful gaze on Chrystal. "As usual, you continue to amaze. In centuries to come the world will study your methods, eager to discover your secrets."

Chrystal remains unfazed by his praise. "Aren't you supposed to cook supper tonight?"

"Quite so." Hensley extracts the bags from behind the seat in the truck and proceeds to the kitchen.

Fagan is already at the kitchen table, up to his elbows in homework. Hensley supplies him with a glass of juice and then opens a bottle of chilled Chardonnay and splashes a bit in two glasses. After a fortifying sip, he sets out some cheese and grapes and turns to the work at hand.

First he unpacks the scallops from the ice, rinses them, and sets them out on a paper towel.

After rinsing and cutting broccolini and putting it on the boil, he throws olive oil and butter in a sauté pan and adds garlic and lemon zest. Then it is time to shock the broccolini in ice water and sauté it.

He slides the result into a serving dish, refreshes the pan with oil and butter, seasons the scallops, and sears them. Within five minutes, he has the table set and ready to rock.

After dinner, Hensley cleans up while Chrystal puts Saff to bed, dispatches Fagan to his nightly bedtime reading routine, and joins Hensley on the patio under the pergola.

He pours her a glass of Chianti and lights a cigarette. They sit in silence, sipping wine, passing the cigarette between them, and watch the sun paint the Sangre de Christo mountains blood-red as it drops behind the world.

Chrystal leans against him, shoulders touching. "What was your first mountain?"

"Kilimanjaro."

"You always go big, don't you?"

"It was close to hand and I needed the money."

Chrystal reaches for the cigarette. "I didn't realize they paid people to climb it."

"More to the point, the people who climb it pay lesser beings to carry their gear."

"You were what, eighteen?"

"Seventeen, but who's counting?"

"The Appalachian Trail?"

"In the eighties. The inaugural leg of my westward trek across the continent."

She holds her glass out for a refill. "What is it about mountains?"

Hensley does the needful. "You have a theory, no doubt."

Chrystal takes a sip and stares at the fading rose of the Sangre de Christos glowing against the deepening blue of the eastern sky. "Back in Maine, when things got too intense at the house, I'd hike the ridge, sit on a boulder, and just listen."

"And what did you hear?"

She sits for a while, as still as a thought. "God."

"And what did he say?"

Chrystal takes a sip of wine. "It wasn't words. More like a . . . an atmosphere. A presence." She glances over at him. "What about you?"

Hensley nods. "There is a certain ineffable quality that pervades the high places. I don't know that I'd call it God. The term is too fraught with baggage for my liking, but there is an undeniable transcendence that greets those who struggle to gain the heights. Something that dwarfs the hubris of humanity."

She passes the cigarette back to him. They sit in silence as the gloom deepens. Chrystal finally breaks the silence.

"Is that why you're going?"

It is a tough question. Reasonable but tough. The truth is that he hasn't subjected the decision to rigorous analysis. Whyte proposed the trip, Hensley accepted instinctively.

"I've never seen the Andes. Seemed a shame to pass on the experience."

Chrystal nods. "When does Whyte get here?"

"Should arrive before midnight. I'll take the next leg, drive through the night. We'll make El Paso before sunrise. Another two weeks to Quito. Give or take."

She draws the cigarette from his fingers, takes a final drag, and crushes it out. Then she slides the patio door open and disappears inside.

Hensley gathers the bottle and the glasses and goes inside. As he makes a final pass through the kitchen, he catches the gentle cascade of the shower echoing through the darkness of the house.

A few hours later, the growl of a vehicle pulling into the driveway penetrates into the master bedroom.

"I think that's my ride."

Chrystal graces him with a final kiss. "Don't get yourself killed out there."

"I'll do my best."

She turns over and snuggles into the blanket. He gets dressed and goes to unlock the front door.

And that was the last time he saw her. He'd had every intention of returning, but the universe decreed otherwise.

The taxi turned off a thoroughfare, drove a few blocks, and pulled to a stop at a set of row houses set back from the street and barely visible in the gloom of approaching night. A light glowed from the front window, a good sign.

Hensley paid the fare with a nice tip, because even cabbies had to put their kids through college, and the way things were in the US these days, the poor blighter would need a lot of overtime just to get his kids a community college degree.

Hensley checked his watch. A few minutes after nine. He smoothed out the white cotton shirt and straightened the cuffs. He was surprised to discover that he was as nervous as a kid on his first date.

As he walked up the steps from the sidewalk, he used breathing techniques he had mastered in Guangxi to settle his heart rate. What was this all about? It was just Chrystal.

But it wasn't just Chrystal, was it? After all, that was why he was here. Because there was no such thing as *just* Chrystal. There was Chrystal. A woman worth tracking down.

Suddenly the past twelve years loomed before him like an open pit. Those twelve years, and especially the last twelve days, had led him to this place, but where had they led Chrystal?

Maybe he had misread the signs back at the house. Just because a man wasn't living there didn't mean there was no man in the picture.

Only one way to find out. Hensley climbed the stairs to the porch, ran a hand over his beard, pushed his hair back from his face, double-checked the address, and rang the bell.

Chapter Eight: Stymie

Chrystal's firstborn opened the door. Hensley saw the slow dawn of recognition rise in his eyes.

"But . . . but . . ."

The boy was obviously speechless with joy, but Hensley could deal with him later.

"Fagan, my man, you are a welcome sight." Hensley clapped a hand on his shoulder, shoved the duffel bag into his hands, and pushed past into the living room.

"But you're dead," Fagan said, standing in the open door.

That sounded a bit off, but Hensley tabled that discussion for later and rounded the corner.

Chrystal sat on the couch, flipping through a photo album, her shoulder-length hair hiding most of her face. She had on a tank top that revealed the tattoo he remembered and a few more he didn't, and the skinny jeans she had always favored.

She hadn't gained a pound since the last time he had seen her. In fact, she'd lost the weight that had hung on for a few years after Sapphire discovered America.

Hensley sensed that he could call her name and she would take his hand, and as his fingers intertwined with hers, the world would disappear, and they would dance like they used to, like every day was the first day of summer vacation and New Year's Eve at the same time.

"Chrystal," he said.

She looked up. When she saw him, she shot to her feet and stepped around the coffee table. "Henz?"

"You are looking as radiant as ever," Hensley said, his arms outstretched as she approached him.

Tears sprang to her eyes as she stepped in close and melted into his arms. He hugged her and swayed, taking in the sandalwood perfume he had given her as a Christmas present over a decade ago.

"You have no idea how much I have missed you," Hensley whispered into the black hair that rested against his lips.

Then her body tensed, and she shoved him away violently. As he stumbled back, she stepped in and slapped him so hard his fillings picked up radio signals from Duluth.

"You better have a good reason for not being dead," she growled at him. "Because if you don't, you're going to wish you were."

While wondering about this disturbingly recurring theme regarding his supposed demise, Hensley tested his jaw to see if a specialist would be required to restore it to full operational status. "My dear, while I don't welcome the eventuality, I could indeed die happy now that—"

"No. I don't want to hear it. Just get out. Now."

Hensley flinched as she raised her hand again, but she used it to point at the door where Fagan still stood.

Chrystal wiped the tears away with the back of her other hand and stepped forward. "You are the last thing I need right now." She pushed him toward the door. "Or ever."

It became apparent to Hensley that many things had changed since they last shared a house and a bed. He wasn't dealing with the woman who had sat across the table from him many a night, the darkness broken by a candle sputtering in a chianti bottle, passing between them a single cigarette and their secrets.

"Give me a moment to get my bearings." He retreated a few steps, splitting the difference between the lioness and her cub. "I am recently arrived in the States from Nepal via Mexico, and my first priority was to seek you out."

Fagan closed the door and dropped the duffel bag on the floor. "How did you know where she was?"

"I don't care how you got here, as long as you leave," Chrystal said.

Hensley focused on the only person in the room who hadn't assaulted him. Yet.

Fagan had always been the clever one. Hensley smiled at him. "It's a long story. Perhaps best enjoyed over a drink." Of all the things in this world, the thing he needed most right now was a drink. Actually, the thing he needed most was the old Chrystal. But since that was not on the menu, understandably, he would have to settle for a drink.

Then he realized someone was missing from the lineup. He scanned the room. "Where's Sapphire?"

"She's run off with Spud," Fagan said.

Chrystal shot Fagan a glare that would have melted the face off the sphinx, with or without the nose intact.

"And Spud is?" When no answer came, Hensley presumed it was a boyfriend with a regrettable nickname. He did the body-language math in his head. "I take it this domestic arrangement was not authorized in advance."

"Also something that is none of your business," Chrystal said.

"Perhaps not, but I am only too willing to provide aid in your time of need."

Every muscle in Chrystal's body seemed to be tensed to the snapping point. "Why are you still here?"

As in their first meeting, none of the scenarios Hensley had run through in his head had taken this turn. He had always looked back on his time with Chrystal fondly and hoped she would do the same, but evidently she had other views on the matter.

"I can appreciate that this is a trying time and that I have arrived unannounced. But I've spent a month and traveled thousands of miles for this moment. Perhaps we could share a glass or two in the reminiscence of days past and stories of life lived in the intervening decade."

Chrystal and Fagan exchanged glances. Her nod was almost imperceptible.

Fagan walked between them to the kitchen. "I have Italian soda, coffee, and tea—green, black, and herbal."

Hensley raised an eyebrow at Chrystal. She shrugged.

"I was thinking of something more along the lines of a celebration," he said.

"Perrier?" Fagan called from the kitchen.

"Do you have anything with more of a kick?"

Fagan peered around the corner. "Grapple?"

Hensley regarded him through narrowed eyes. "Did you say 'grapple?'"

"It's my own invention." Fagan smiled. "One part grapefruit juice, two parts apple. The house specialty."

Words failed Hensley as he contemplated this concoction.

"You just stay there. I can whip up a batch in no time." Fagan disappeared into the bowels of the kitchen.

Hensley turned to Chrystal for an explanation for this unconventional libation.

"Don't get me started." She paced the room for half a minute before dropping onto the couch, sitting on the edge like a feral cat ready to spring. She relegated Hensley to a recliner with a gesture that looked like it wanted a cigarette between the first two fingers.

The room was decorated with the cheap furniture of a first apartment. Hensley sat as directed and gave her a more thorough inspection. It seemed that she hadn't aged since he had seen her last. In fact, she appeared to have shed a few years as well as a few pounds. But judging by the half-moon shadows under her eyes, she had gained a few cares during the interim.

Probably kids in general and Sapphire in particular. That was why he had taken special care to avoid progeny. Not in a W.C. Fields go-away-kid-you-bother-me kind of way. More in a how-adorable-now-trundle-along kind of way.

"First, I must say that while it hardly seems possible, you look even more captivating than you did twelve years ago."

Chrystal snorted her disbelief, but Hensley could see that she was not unmoved by his observation.

"We have only one thing to talk about," Chrystal said. "Why bother to come back now?"

Hensley saw that he would have to start from behind and fight his way to the finish line. "I have recently taken advantage of a unique opportunity to return to the States, and of course my first thought was of you." He smiled. "As have been many of my thoughts in the intervening years," he added.

"Such as in December of 2001?"

"Ah, yes, that." The month he would have returned from the Andes trip, had the twin towers not gone down. Hensley didn't learn of the tragedy until November.

"Yes. That."

Hensley thought himself fortunate that she didn't voice all that was implied in the searing look she focused on him. "Those were perilous times, and there was a bit of a difficulty with my passport."

"Oh?" Her tone conveyed more skepticism than interest.

"As you may recall, at that time I carried a Lebanese passport that passed muster under normal circumstances but was of questionable provenance."

"You mean it was fake. Like everything else."

"Well, not exactly . . . I mean, yes, the passport was a document of convenience, but . . ."

Hensley adjusted to a more comfortable position. Now that he thought about it, she sometimes did have a way of framing things in an inconvenient light.

"It was just that, considering one of the hijackers was from Lebanon, I decided it was in the best interests of all concerned if I didn't put it to the test."

"So you've been hiding out like a Nazi in South America for twelve years?"

Hensley forced out a smile. "It was more like . . . you see, one of the party put in a good word for me at a winery in the Uco Valley, which gave me ample opportunity to explore the life of the mind and the fruit of the vine."

"And of course they don't have telephones or postal service in Argentina."

"Ah." Could it simply be a matter of mismatched expectations? "I see now that I was remiss in the matter of communication. A common courtesy—"

Chrystal jerked to her feet, upsetting the coffee table and scattering magazines. "That's what you call it? After two years together, you go away on a bike trip and never come back, and you think a Dear-John phone call to blow me off would be a common courtesy?" She breathed heavily through her nose like an enraged bull. "I would call it an insult."

Hensley kept a wary eye on her hands, which were balled into fists. "Oh, no, my dear. I meant no slight. It was just the way these things happen in troubled times. Star-crossed lovers and all that. I had every intention of returning. We were merely pawns in a larger game, victims sacrificed in the pursuit of raw power, collateral damage in the chaos of war."

Fagan walked in with a tray holding a pitcher and three cut-crystal glasses. He paused when he saw the magazines scattered on the floor, but recovered, righted the table with his foot, and set down the tray. "Grapple, anyone?" He held a glass out to Hensley.

Chrystal pushed past the coffee table and leaned over Hensley in a menacing stance. "You always did talk sweet, like honey and wine, but you are poison."

She placed a boot heel under the arm of the recliner and shoved violently. It flipped over with a thud, leaving Hensley with his head on the floor and his feet in the air. He rolled out of the chair and climbed to his feet.

Fagan stood with one arm extended, a sweating glass of grapple in his fingers. Hensley faced Chrystal, keeping the chair between them, but she had turned to the built-in bookshelves on the opposite wall.

"I understand your anger. I could have . . . No. I should have handled the situation better. Let me make it up to you. I'll talk to Sapphire and—"

Chrystal swept a whole shelf of books to the floor with a single motion, revealing a wooden box. She flipped it open, pulled out a handgun, a Colt 1911 by the looks of it, and pointed it at Hensley.

"Mom!" Fagan took a step toward her, but she waved him away. He stepped back, still holding the glass of juice.

"Don't even think of Sapphire." Chrystal brought up her other hand to steady her grip. "Don't even think of me, or Fagan, or . . . Sapphire. You lost that right when you walked out on us."

It was the second time in twenty-four hours that Hensley had stared down the barrel of a gun, and he couldn't say he liked it any better for the rehearsal in Santa Fe. His heart rate jumped into triple digits as he searched for the words to defuse the situation.

"Surely we can—"

She raised a boot and kicked the end of the coffee table up. It launched the tray like a catapult, firing two glasses of grapple at Hensley. He ducked behind a forearm, but one hit him in the shoulder and soaked his shirt before bouncing on the wood floor.

Even more disconcerting, her aim never wavered from center of mass during the entire operation.

"Get this straight. There is no 'we.' There is nothing but you leaving, either walking or on a stretcher. And I don't really care which."

Staring down the muzzle of a handgun the size of New Jersey, all words fled Hensley's mind. Surely she didn't mean it, not the Chrystal he knew. He instinctively backed away, stumbled over the overturned recliner, and struggled to stay upright.

As she stepped forward to match his retreat, keeping the coffee table between them, she swung the gun up to his face. He tried to piece together a conciliatory sentence.

"Okay, I can see that I might have been insensitive to your feelings at a time when—"

"In case, after all these years, you have forgotten," Chrystal said in a disturbingly calm voice, "I don't miss."

That much he remembered. Army family. Grew up with weapons like some kids grow up with roller skates. First and second husbands both Army.

Hensley noticed the safety was still on. He toyed with the thought of inching closer and disarming her. She was trained in firearms, but he was trained in martial arts, and this wasn't his first time up against a gun with nothing on his side but his hands and his wits.

Chrystal's eyes narrowed. "Here. Let me settle that question for you." She flipped the safety off with her thumb.

"Look, can't we sit down and talk about—"

"Sure, we could have. Eleven years and six months ago." She kept her distance and the gun steady on him while she used her left hand to wipe her eyes. "Maybe even ten years ago. But now I'm thinking there's only one way I can be sure of keeping you away from my family."

Years of experience had taught Hensley many things, and the one that mattered at this very unpleasant moment was to recognize when words would only make something worse. Instead, he studied

Chrystal, seeing her more clearly than he remembered ever seeing her before.

One of the many things that had endeared her to him was an unswerving sincerity, an intensity that took things to the limit, that hinted at the thrilling possibility of falling over the edge. He had missed those adrenaline-laced moments, but now he reconsidered. There were some edges he had no interest in falling over.

He did his best to ignore the muzzle of the gun staring him down from across the room and instead focus on the woman holding it. And the longer he looked, the more he realized she wasn't bluffing. The more he remembered she had never bluffed.

She operated at one hundred percent, one hundred percent of the time. The best person to have on your side and the worst to go up against. And now he was on the wrong side of that equation.

"Mom, I understand, but . . ." Fagan spoke more quietly this time. But without moving.

He knew too. Everyone knew now.

Chrystal cocked the hammer. "There are some things worth going to jail for."

And Hensley had no doubt she meant it. The only doubt he felt was whether he would make it to the door.

He wondered how it had come to this, to be in fear for his life at the hands of the one woman he thought could save him.

"Chrystal, I can see now that I might have been wrong—"

The gun slipped down a few degrees from the head shot back to the more reliable center-of-mass shot. And strayed a little lower.

"I . . . I *was* wrong." Hensley raised his hands. "I was wrong to come here this way." He shook his head. "To come here at all. You deserved, you deserve better. If there is anything I can do—"

Chrystal's stern expression caused him to repent of this slight attempt at reconciliation. He focused on his priority of the moment—to get out of the door without being ventilated.

"Look, I'll go." He lowered his arms slowly. "Let's just forget I was ever here."

Hensley made a tentative move toward the door. She didn't challenge him, but the gun followed his every move.

He could tell the most slender of threads restrained her trigger finger. The thought of what would happen to Fagan and Sapphire if she let that thread snap. The only reason he was still alive.

"I'll go back into the world, and you can go back to your world, and you'll have nothing to regret."

He edged toward the door and cast a glance at Fagan, who looked back with an expression Hensley couldn't read. Resentment? Regret? Reproach?

He made it to the door, snatched up the duffel bag, and turned back for a last glimpse. Chrystal stood in a wide stance, gun still trained on him, looking drained but determined. He nodded slowly, walked out, and closed the door quietly but firmly.

Pausing on the stoop, he took his bearings. The light had faded and the temperature had fallen into the sixties. The soaked sleeve clung to his right arm, dripping grapple juice onto the pavement.

His heart rate was still well into the triple digits. He took a few deep breaths and proceeded down the street in the direction from which he had arrived. At the first intersection, he stopped, pondering his next move, suddenly adrift and rudderless.

Should he walk away, or should he find a way to make it right? Was that even possible now?

A month ago he would have just moved on, but now he stood at the crossroads of two dead ends. He couldn't go back to Chrystal, that much was clear. But he also couldn't go back to his old life, drifting through the world from one temporary haven to the next. And not simply because he was holding the short end of the chronological stick.

The next move he made would be critical.

Chapter Nine: Rout

Hensley hadn't expected to find himself without accommodations for the night, but such a dilemma was a mere triviality in his world.

If there was an upside to his precipitate departure from Fagan's house, it was that he had executed it in such a fashion as to give him ample time to recover. Philadelphia was a mere three-hour train ride. He could be comfortably ensconced in Uncle Rex's Main Line mansion by midnight.

By promising to share, he persuaded a cabbie to stop by a liquor store. He checked his change, found nothing of interest, and handed it to the cabbie. Each fortified with a flask of borrowed bonhomie, they swapped stories and songs until they arrived at the train station.

That encounter was a sincere but evanescent slice of existence, as had been the case for much of his life, but soon he was alone in a railroad car and wandering back to the days of his youth and a moment in Angola just before the rainy season. He was barely ten and Davison was approaching three. Dad had just finished up in the surgery and Hensley had been helping Mom get dinner together.

The meal was pedestrian for the most part, staples flown in once a month, but Mom had kept some bacon aside and had wrapped strips around the Namaqua dove breasts they had received as payment in kind for services rendered in the clinic.

Dad walked up, glanced at the bamboo skewers Hensley tended above the coals, and turned to Mom, reaching out and pulling her to him in an impulsive but intimate embrace.

It was a simple thing, inconsequential to the casual observer, a moment captured in any number of films during the black-and-white heyday of Hollywood.

Suddenly Hensley became invisible, eclipsed by a shared passion that predated him and would continue without him.

In that moment, he was an outsider, hopelessly alone.

Last week, he had seen Davison and Masie share the same sentiment, what he hoped he would share with Chrystal.

As much as Hensley knew about a lot of things, there was one thing he knew for sure and that was that you never knew about women. No amount of practice made perfect as far as he could tell. Every trip to the plate was like your first time up at bat.

As a freshman in college, Chrystal had defied her career-Army father and married Duffy, a front guy in a punk band. Hensley had to admire a move like that.

But when Duffy fell under her father's spell and enlisted, instead of walking out, she doubled down. Fagan was born while Duffy was deployed in the first Gulf War.

This wasn't a woman to lightly toss a soul mate aside.

And to be fair, she hadn't lightly tossed Hensley aside in DC. She had thrown him out with great force and passion. But perhaps he could turn that passion to his advantage.

Engaged in such thoughts, at the 30th Street station, he transferred to the Thorndale line out to Villanova and took a cab to the Stone estate.

Even though it was midnight, the housekeeper let him in as if she were expecting him, deposited his duffel bag in a bedroom, set him up in the kitchen with pasta primavera, a selection of cheeses, and a bottle of white wine, and disappeared.

Evidently, despite the demise of the lord and master, things were running on autopilot at the Stone estate and probably would be until the new owner assumed control. Tomorrow he would head downtown and determine the likely identity of the successor.

Hensley finished off the pasta and the glass of wine, corked the bottle, set the plate in the sink, and strolled through the silent mansion to the study, where he liberated a Cuban cigar and a superannuated whisky.

Amongst the leather-bound books and wood paneling, he considered life in a mansion unencumbered by anything other than property taxes and utilities. In fact, if things had turned out differently, he might now be setting up house, perched next to the housekeeper in the kitchen with a bottle of wine and the household accounts before them, getting up to speed on his new home.

Some might scoff at the thought, but that would be the some who weren't in full possession of the facts of the matter.

Point one: Hensley was the oldest surviving heir of the Stone family.

Point two: Before Hensley had been whisked away into the heart of the dark continent, a hostage of the relentless altruism of his parents, Uncle Rex had showered him with attention. In point of fact, for the first nine years of his life, Hensley had spent at least twice as much time with Uncle Rex as with his own father, much of it in this very study.

Conclusion: In a parallel universe, there was likely a Hensley who had not been alienated from the affections of his uncle and was now in possession of the estate.

Hensley inches his way up the stairs with his Apollo Saturn rocket model, simulating a launch from Cape Canaveral. The night before, he had sat up until the wee hours with Uncle Rex. When a grainy, black-and-white Neil Armstrong jumped off the last step of the ladder onto the surface of the moon, Hensley jumped off the couch and cheered.

Now he maintains a steady roar through clenched teeth, punctuating it with booms to mark the separating stages and dropping the spent hulls to clatter down the stairs to the entrance hall where the maid snatches them up.

He's halfway to the landing when he drops the last stage. He reduces his roar to a soft hiss as the capsule glides up the stairs, past the turn in the landing, and upward to the moon, which in this scenario is the balcony at the top of the stairs.

A pirouette simulates moon orbit, and then Hensley slowly lowers the capsule, which must serve for the lunar landing module since the model pre-dates the moon mission. After planting the flag, Hensley launches the capsule back into orbit.

His last act is to attach a parachute improvised from a bit of string and one of Uncle Rex's handkerchiefs and drop the lot from the balcony to splash down in the entryway below.

It bounces and rolls before the maid can get to it. Hensley races down the stairs to rescue the model for a second moon mission. As he rounds the corner, he runs into Uncle Rex.

"Young Hensley, I see you have recovered from our foray into the advanced hours." Uncle Rex guides him toward the study with a hand on his shoulder. "I have something to show you."

Hensley glances over his shoulder at the maid recovering his downed capsule and reluctantly allows himself to be ushered into the study.

Uncle Rex seats him in the chair behind the desk and focuses a gooseneck lamp onto a set of coins in a plastic case. "What you see before you is a deep cameo 1967 proof set from the San Francisco mint."

Hensley inspects the coins. They're shiny, but as far as he can see they're just money. Ninety-one cents, to be exact. "So?"

"The Kennedy half dollar is forty-percent silver clad. The Washington quarter and the Roosevelt dime are copper-nickel clad. The Jefferson nickel and Lincoln cent are of traditional composition—copper-nickel and copper-zinc, respectively."

Hensley studies them again. "Is that good?"

"Not as good as the 1964 silver Kennedy half dollar, but that's not what makes these special."

So they are special. Hensley looks again. They're shiny, but they're new, evidently never used, so that isn't surprising. He peers closer at the half dollar. The background is shiny, but President Kennedy isn't. Now that he thinks about it, he's never seen a coin quite like this one.

He picks up the case and turns it to catch the light of the lamp.

"Yes," Uncle Rex says. "The deep cameo proof is rare. Not as rare as a moon landing, but rare enough in numismatic circles."

Uncle Rex takes the proof set from Hensley and sets it in a box with similar cases. Then he turns to a different box and pulls out another set of coins in a plastic case and sets it on the desk.

"Have you seen one of these before?"

These coins couldn't be more different. They are dull and worn. The heads have a crown of leaves on them and the letters look strange.

Hensley shakes his head.

"These coins were thousands of years old when the shot heard round the world was fired in Concord. Some were minted before the Romans executed a man named Jesus for causing trouble in a little backwater province governed by a third-rate prefect."

Hensley recognizes the figures from his history book. The Caesars. He picks up the case gingerly and examines the coins. This is something indeed. Hundreds of lifetimes have passed since these men were alive, and here he is holding their pictures in his hands. They were still alive when these were made.

He looks up at Uncle Rex. "How many different Caesars are on coins?"

"Perhaps a dozen."

"And how many people are there in the world?"

"At this moment?"

Hensley nods.

"Three or four billion."

Hensley struggles with some math and eventually decides that trillions of people have lived since then, all but a mere handful forgotten. But these few men are still known two thousand years later.

He points to the first coin. "Who is that?"

"Julius Caesar."

"This one?"

"Julius again."

Hensley points.

"Augustus. He was Caesar when Jesus was born. And that is Tiberius. He was Caesar when Jesus died."

"You think they'll put Neil Armstrong on a coin?"

Uncle Rex chuckles. "Not likely. That honor is usually reserved for presidents."

"But Benjamin Franklin was never president, and he's on the hundred dollar bill."

"Neither was Hamilton. Or the Indian on the wheat cent piece. Or the buffalo on the old nickel. But those are rare exceptions."

Hensley stares off into the vastness of the study, dreaming of the feats he will accomplish to get his face on a coin. He'll walk on the moon, of course. No, he'll walk on Mars. And then he'll become president. The best president there ever was. And they'll put him on a silver dollar and make deep cameo proofs, and centuries from now a kid will look at a coin and say, "That's Reginald Hensley Fletcher, the president who walked on Mars."

Uncle Rex returns the plastic case to the box. "How would you like to start your own coin collection?"

"Sure!"

Uncle Rex sets a stack of folders, some green, some red, on the desk and opens the top one. It folds out into three sections with round holes for coins, five across and six down.

"This one is for Lincoln cent pieces." He opens the next one. "Jefferson nickels. You get the idea."

"Thanks!"

Hensley gathers up the albums and dashes out of the study up the stairs to his bedroom, where he pulls his cigar box out from under the bed and dumps the contents on the dresser. He extracts the two buffalo nickels and the three wheat pennies he has squirreled away, flips open the appropriate folders, checks the dates, and snaps them into place.

From this day forward, he will check his change until he fills all the folders. Then he'll start collecting Caesars.

Hensley's cigar had gone out. He resurrected it, blew out a cloud of smoke, and peered into the swirling mass for a vision that would make sense of everything.

It was more than four decades later, and he hadn't walked on Mars. Hadn't even become president. His dreams of greatness had been shattered when he had been dragged off to a jungle in the middle of nowhere and pressed into service as an orderly.

He had long since abandoned those dreams and settled for living life on his own terms. And after all, how many men could claim such an accomplishment? Precious few, Hensley was willing to wager. Not even presidents.

In that regard, like the Caesars, he had achieved resounding success, even if he didn't have his likeness stamped on a bit of metal in circulation amongst the masses, kids and collectors searching for the odd coin to fill the final slot in their folder.

He refreshed his glass and took a sip to focus his thoughts. All things being equal, if Masie hadn't come along, it was better than even money that Uncle Rex would have provided for Hensley in a manner sufficient to sustain even the most extravagant dreams.

Perhaps not the lion's share. As things turned out, Davison had supplanted Hensley as the apple of Uncle Rex's eye. But Hensley would be in for a goodly portion, without a doubt.

And there might still be an angle he could play. What if he could convince Masie to take the money and leave him the house? And what if he went to Chrystal and offered her a life in a mansion? Could that soften her rage?

In less time than it took to take a sip of scotch, he realized Chrystal was not a woman who could be bought, not even with something as substantial as being set for life in a mansion. She'd proved that to everyone when she skipped her high school graduation and fled as far away as a college scholarship could take her, to the University of New Mexico, the flames of her burning bridges visible for two thousand miles.

He poured another two fingers of scotch as fine as the small print on a codicil and replayed the scene in Fagan's living room. Chrystal's reaction to his arrival was unexpected, both in substance and intensity. It occurred to him now that if she had simply forgotten him, she would have been puzzled by his presence. But she moved right past puzzled to enraged. That could mean something, couldn't it?

Perhaps he was right after all. If he had meant nothing to her, would she be so angry now? And if the passion still flowed, he might be able to ease that river back into its former course.

But not with money. Not with a mansion. With something that actually meant something to her.

Sapphire.

Despite her final words, Hensley was sure that if he were to reunite mother and daughter, sans the odious Spud, Chrystal might see him in a new light. Or the old light in which she used to see him.

After all, how hard could it be? He'd dealt with murderous drunks, outsmarted devious con men, played the players of every continent. What was a sixteen-year-old girl compared to that?

DAY 4: SUNDAY

Chapter Ten: Karma

As one would expect from an old-school family retainer, Ellis agreed to meet Hensley on Sunday afternoon. Not that Hensley realized it was Sunday until after he made the call.

It was a beautiful day. Sunny, mid-eighties, light breeze, a perfect Sunday to spend in Fairmount Park. A doorman let Hensley into the office building, and he wondered if Ellis had rousted the poor functionary from his home just for this occasion. Not that he needed sympathy. He was probably well paid for his efforts, possibly billed to the estate. Ellis might be faithful, but like Hensley, he was no fool.

Both the outer and inner doors were open, so Hensley strode into the sanctum sanctorum. It was the legal equivalent of Uncle Rex's study, all polished wood and leather chairs, an enormous desk the focal point, backed by a wall of law books.

"Ellis, my main man, what's the haps?"

As he had done two weeks ago, Hensley pushed aside the wooden chairs in front of the desk and dragged over a low-slung overstuffed armchair from the coffee table by the window.

If the rearrangement of the furniture bothered Ellis, he betrayed no trace of it. "I trust this pleasant day finds you well."

"Ellis, you have caught the nub of it. An excellent dinner. A serene night's sleep. A peerless breakfast. A pleasant train ride into town. And now some good news." It never hurt to be hopeful. In guarded doses.

The fossil on the other side of the desk opened a drawer, pulled out a portfolio, and opened it. "I have news, at any rate. The goodness of it I will leave for you to judge."

"One thing. While looking into the matter of Rex's death and the questionable activity regarding the will, I incurred certain expenses that I took the liberty of putting on Davison's credit card."

The frown of disapprobation in the old man's eyebrows was muted but perceptible.

"Unorthodox behavior, I confess, but the heat of the moment didn't allow for consultation and discussion. I assumed that the charges would be paid out of the estate."

After a strained silence, Ellis responded. "I'm afraid you were not acting as an agent of the estate or under our authorization."

"So that would be a no then?"

"Correct."

So much for good intentions. "I see. Then let's hear the news." Hensley wondered how old Ellis was. Could be anywhere from late seventies to early nineties by the looks of him. And he had no doubt the man was as clean-living a specimen as ever walked the planet, an acolyte of Franklin's principles of self-improvement, so the odds were toward the higher end.

How many clients could he have left? The Stone estate could be his only brief.

Ellis flipped through the papers. "On the one hand, Rex had the presence of mind to do everything by the book on the new will. From the point of view of process, it's unimpeachable."

"Peachy."

Ellis paused for a moment, one eyebrow twitching at the interruption. "On the other hand, given the medical evidence, there are certainly grounds to support a challenge to the will."

"But he was of sound enough mind to cross all his Is and dot all his Ts."

"Yes. And Davison has forwarded me his deposition."

Hensley let out a long sigh and melted into the chair like a deflated balloon. For the merest fraction of a second, Hensley entertained the possibility of an uncharitable thought toward his younger brother. They had been at odds for close to four decades, and the last two weeks had done little to bridge the chasm.

One thing restrained Hensley from clearing off a space and invoking a curse upon Davison—the fact that he had abandoned Davison long before Davison had chosen Masie over him. And who could blame him? Masie appeared to be a better person than Hensley could ever hope to be, even on his best days, and those came only once or twice a year, whereas Masie was 24/7/52. Plus one on leap years.

So Hensley stepped back from the uncharitable thought. It seemed every religion had a golden rule, a concept of karma. In the immortal words of the revered philosopher known as Daniel-san, what goes around comes around. And now it was coming around. In spades. With knobs on.

After a bit, he leveraged himself to a standing position and held out a hand to Ellis.

Ellis stood and took his hand. "Don't lose heart."

Hensley laid a second hand on top of the old man's claw. "In the end, we get what we deserve."

"I pray that it is not so, or else we are all doomed," Ellis replied.

It was a nice thought, but Hensley couldn't put any stock in it. There might be a world where a man could hope to escape the consequences of his actions, but he was pretty sure this wasn't that world. It had taken almost four decades, but karma had finally caught up with him.

The first time Hensley had hitchhiked across America, back when he was in his twenties, he had stumbled upon a tent revival in the panhandle of Texas where he stopped for the shade and the fried chicken dinner. The three points of the sermon had stuck with him long after the taste of the chicken had faded.

You reap what you sow. You reap later than you sow. You reap more than you sow.

If he had known then what he knew now, he would have stood to testify. He had abandoned Davison. He had abandoned Chrystal. He had sown the wind and was reaping the whirlwind.

Two hundred million dollars was a mighty high price to pay, but as Hensley thought back, it was no more than he deserved. The loss of the money stung, but the loss of Chrystal stung more.

A few weeks ago, such thoughts would have never occurred to him. Maybe this was progress, but it was hard won and past its sell-by date.

Who was he fooling with all his late-night contemplations and scheming? The woman had pointed a cocked gun at him, as clear a statement of intent as possible. Even if he could find Sapphire, interfering would serve only to further enrage Chrystal, not win her back. And it was all his own damn fault. It was time to cut his losses and ride into the sunset.

He took a moment to return the room to its original configuration. Then he directed a final nod to Ellis and left.

He had one task left, and then he would leave with a duffel bag and a few hundred dollars in his pocket. It wasn't much, but it was a better stake than he had started out with thirty-seven years ago, and he had Davison to thank for it. That was something, wasn't it?

CHAPTER ELEVEN: LEGACY

Hensley took the train back to the Stone estate to pick up his duffel and strategize his next adventure. Although he fancied a few months in Europe, he was leaning toward South America, where he could stretch his cash. But when the train passed over the Schuylkill River, memories from fifteen years back ambushed him, and he found himself getting off at the Merion station.

He took a taxi to the cemetery overlooking the river. He'd been here only once before. The day they buried his mother.

The memories were sketchy due to the pub crawl with which he had medicated himself after the funeral, but they rushed in, surprisingly raw. As the cab neared the spot, Hensley pulled the flask from the night before out of his back pocket and finished it off.

Even thus fortified, he didn't trust himself to speak, so he signaled the driver to wait. He hiked through the graves, veering back and forth in a general northward direction until he found the Stone family crypt with the family motto engraved above the door.

I shall not be moved.

Only one urn had been added since his mother's funeral, that of Uncle Rex, her younger brother and last to bear the family name.

Hensley had remained completely composed when he returned to Angola for his father's funeral after wandering the planet for nine years. After all, the old man was the reason he had left in the first place. What did he owe a man who would rip his own son up by the roots from civilization, drag him half a world away and several centuries back in time, and then press him into service as if he were some vassal on his estate?

And the old man knew what he thought. Hensley had made sure of that.

Hensley walks through the jungle back to the compound, fancying himself a latter-day Natty Bumppo. If his gang back in the States could see him now, they wouldn't recognize him.

Of course they are just starting high school back in Pennsylvania. Having worked their way through junior high, they are gearing up for a four-year tour of duty in the art of navigating the land mines of the cutthroat social games of society, while he is engaged in the fifth year of a self-study course in learning the ways of the jungle.

Hensley wonders if the two worlds are really that far apart. Obviously they observe different dress codes. He doubts his ratty t-shirt, cargo shorts, and tire-tread sandals would serve in the halls of a prep school, but he suspects the civilized world is just a different kind of jungle. Surely the skills he's acquired in the past five years—watching quietly, gauging his prey, learning its ways, its preferences, its blind spots, exploiting this knowledge to gain the upper hand—must be transferable.

He has no doubt that, if by some lucky turn of fate he found himself back on his home turf, he would regain his position as leader of the pack in no time.

Smiling at the thought, he enters the clearing, avoiding the clinic on his way to the deal table behind the house, and sets down his game bag. He goes to the fire pit, builds a tent of sticks, and gets them going. Then he grabs a bucket and retrieves water from the stream at the bottom of the hill.

Back at the table, he sets the bucket to one side, pulls a hunting knife from his belt, and begins dressing the half-dozen Namaqua doves he bagged using nothing more than a slingshot and his native skill.

Hensley drops the last dove breast in the water as the rifle-shot of the clinic door echoes across the clearing. He glances over his shoulder. His father approaches, Davison close on his heels. He tries to imagine Davison in a second-grade classroom. The poor kid would lose his lunch money on the first day. And every day after.

Shaking his head, Hensley threads a sungazer lizard onto a skewer, sets it aside, and picks up another lizard.

His father stops next to the table and watches him skewer the second lizard. "We could have used you in the clinic this afternoon."

Hensley shrugs. "I was out getting dinner."

"Your brother can already roll a bandage better than you, and he's only seven. Half your age."

"Sure he can." Hensley thrusts the stick through the lizard, ripping it open. "But can he take out a sungazer with one shot? Because that's all you get. You miss, you go hungry."

"We have plenty of provisions. And we can barter for dinner if we want game."

"And you can train a monkey to roll bandages if Davison can't keep up." Hensley snatches up the lizards and grabs the handle of the bucket.

"It's a matter of priorities. We're here for a reason."

For the first time in the conversation, Hensley looks straight at his father. "You're here for a reason. The rest of us are just hostages."

He glances at Davison as he pushes past them toward the fire pit and realizes his monkey remark has found the wrong target. He hesitates but is too angry to form an apology. If there is one thing he's learned, it's to show no weakness in front of his father.

The sticks in the fire pit have collapsed into a mound of coals. Hensley places larger branches on the fire and begins skewering the dove breasts.

What if they had never left civilization to save the benighted natives of Africa? What would he be doing right now back in the States? He can't even imagine it. But he vows in his heart that one day he will find out.

Hensley was certain that when he ran away, the old man had shed no tears. They had no use for each other at the time, and upon returning for his funeral, Hensley had seen no reason to pretend otherwise.

But when he traveled from New Zealand to Philadelphia for his mother's funeral thirteen years later, it was a different story. He'd been blindsided by a confusing wave of loss. He had always thought of Mom and Dad as a team with the home field advantage up against him and Davison.

Then six days ago in Mexico, he had held his mother's necklace in his hand—a silver chain with the Rock of Gibraltar hanging from it and the Stone family motto engraved on the back. The first time he'd seen it in thirty years.

Hensley realized that was why he was here now. For decades he had seen Davison as the primary victim of his betrayal when he ran away. But now he considered the question that had sprung to his mind at the sight of her necklace. Had he indeed broken his mother's heart when he left? The woman who had welcomed him back at her husband's funeral without a word or look of reproach and watched him leave the next morning, probably guessing she would never see him again?

The woman who came to mind when he saw Davison look at Masie. Who now came to mind when he thought of Chrystal.

"Did you forgive me?" he whispered into the silence of the crypt, but he knew the answer before he asked. And that prompted a second question. "How did you forgive me?"

He leaned back against the wall and slid down to the floor, sitting with his knees up, arms resting on knees, head resting on arms, eyes misting.

Hensley rarely encountered a reason for tears. His lifestyle couldn't afford it. In fact, he hadn't shed a tear since her funeral fifteen years ago.

And despite the question, he knew how she had forgiven him. Because that was how she lived, holding nothing back, believing in the good in this world, creating the good, becoming the good. Even when random, senseless violence took her husband. Even when a case of inoperable pride had taken her eldest son, and the old-money family she had forsaken took her youngest son.

Hensley didn't believe in spirits, in ghosts, in voices from beyond the grave. But now, in this vault surrounded by the ashes of his ancestors, he heard his mother's voice.

Leave the world a better place than you found it.

The family motto not of the Stones but of the Fletchers. It echoed in his head.

Whatever he thought of his father, Hensley was as much a Fletcher as he was a Stone. And in his own way, he had done his bit to improve on the world as he found it. He was no Mother Theresa, but he wasn't Hitler either.

Leaning against the chill wall of the family crypt, he recognized this rationalization for what it was. A deflection. A copout.

Here he was, licking his wounds after losing both Chrystal and the estate, but when you took the longer view, what was the difference between Hensley right now and Hensley a month ago?

Expectations. A few months ago, he was in Nepal living off a few dollars a day, and he was as happy as a pig in mud. Today he was in Philadelphia with a grand in cash and the infinite possibilities of the universe stretched out before him, and he was desolate because he'd lost his shot at the inheritance and the possibility of reuniting with Chrystal.

Amazing how much one's perspective could be warped by expectations. It was as if he'd learned nothing from his years in Guangxi. Desire was the source of suffering. No expectations, no disappointment.

Hensley regulated his breathing, focused on a place deep inside, dialing down to a single atom. Once it was fixed in his mind, he stripped away the electrons, dismissed the protons one by one, until all that was left was the emptiness of the open hand.

No expectations. No agenda. No pretense.

He would open his hand and his heart, let go, and venture forth into the world as he had done these many decades past, receptive to what the universe would bring to him. Let the cycle begin anew.

But still a whisper of the Fletcher motto echoed in his mind. Leave the world a better place than you found it.

Why not? He could do this one thing, find Sapphire, talk sense into her, reunite daughter and mother. His path to the next thing might as well run through Santa Fe as any other town. And it shouldn't take long.

Hensley pushed himself to his feet, kissed his fingers, and laid them against his mother's urn for a few seconds. Then he walked out into the sunshine, blinking and searching for the taxi that would ferry him to the launching point of this quest.

DAY 5: MONDAY

CHAPTER TWELVE: PURSUIT

If anyone needed proof that Hensley was serious about spreading love and joy, the fact that he left the Stone mansion well before sunrise Monday to catch an early flight to Santa Fe would have removed all doubt.

He spent the flight scheming the best way to track down Sapphire and her companion of dubious name and virtue, Spud. It occurred to him that if a grizzled man in his fifties went around town inquiring into the whereabouts of a girl of sixteen, the best he could hope for was free room and board for at least one night courtesy of Sheriff Powell. The worst was a free trip back down NM-14 in the trunk of a car to an unmarked grave out in the desert.

He had to leverage his assets. Who might know where Sapphire had got off to? Toni was a prime suspect, but pursuing that lead had many of the same drawbacks as the first plan. Plus she evidently had Powell's number on speed dial.

Then he had a flash of brilliance. Sapphire's father might have some ideas on the matter. Too bad his name was a mystery. Hensley was sure he must have heard it at one time or another, but a short stroll through the alphabet produced no candidates.

The only thing he could remember about the guy was that Chrystal wanted no piece of him at any price. In fact, she was allergic. Perhaps not as allergic as she was to Hensley at the moment, but as close as made no difference for those keeping score in the bleachers.

If he remembered correctly, the guy was one of those black helicopter types, overflowing with conspiracy theories and doomsday scenarios.

A picture sprang to Hensley's mind of a stocky guy of about six feet wearing camo and an air of profound disappointment that civilization had survived the Y2K holocaust with nothing more to worry about than a VCR that kept blinking 12:00:00 no matter how many buttons you pushed. Survived on twigs and berries and such and lived in a cabin out north of town somewhere in one of the half-dozen national forests that littered the landscape in those parts.

And if indeed Chrystal was still as allergic to this gargoyle as Hensley remembered, then Sapphire might very well have turned to him in her hour of defiance.

But for all these epiphanies, Hensley found himself again staring at square zero with unwelcome recognition. He had no more idea of how to locate the father than the daughter. Less, in fact, since he didn't even have a name.

Lanny something! That was it. No, Lenny. Or Lemuel. Too bad Hensley had woken up on the wrong side of Sheriff Powell. That was a cop who surely knew Chrystal's ex right down to his shoelaces, including his rap sheet, assuming he had one, which he probably did if Hensley was any judge of form.

Lamm! Buh . . . Buh . . . Bobby Lamm. Or some such.

As the pilot came on to announce their arrival in the Land of Enchantment, Hensley had a brainstorm that caused him to fasten his seatbelt and return his seat back and tray table to their upright and locked positions. The judge.

Chrystal's godfather. Served in 'Nam with Chrystal's father. Pulled strings to get her the job as court reporter after she kicked out Lamm or Lenny or whoever. He would know everything. And best of all, the judge had no reason to hate Hensley. As far as he could remember, anyway.

Unfortunately, the judge shared one characteristic with Chrystal's ex. Hensley didn't know his name. But he figured it would be easier to locate a judge in Santa Fe than a militia wacko in the mountains.

From the airport, Hensley took a cab to a tonsorial parlor and ordered the works, opting for a buzz in the interest of bathing efficiency. If he was going to start hunting down a minor, he had to look respectable, something he had done many times in his life as required by exigent circumstances.

The Hensley who emerged was the same on the inside but transformed almost beyond recognition on the outside. He had lost two pounds without breaking a sweat, looking less like Jerry Garcia and more like Jerry Douglas, only without the dobro.

He stopped by Goodwill, said hello to his favorite clerk, and picked up a sky-blue Oxford button-down and a charcoal-grey sports jacket. He figured the jeans and boots would pass muster for business attire this far out west.

Out on the sidewalk, Hensley discovered the weather had somehow forgotten this was Santa Fe and not Texas. The temps were in the nineties, which was practically against the law in New Mexico. At least it wasn't drizzling on him like Friday.

Hensley slung the jacket over his shoulder and waited at the bus stop. He'd don the finery when the psychological moment arrived.

A little after eleven a.m., he jumped off the bus downtown and strolled around until he found the Santacafe, an elegant little place just east of the courthouse. The hostess led him to a small table in a corner, where he studied the menu as if the final exam was imminent, being particularly drawn to the appetizer section.

As he was thus engaged, a young woman with shoulder-length corkscrew curls and an order pad materialized.

"My good woman, you can help me settle a question that has been plaguing me these last few minutes. Which would you say is to be preferred—the shitake and cactus spring rolls or the shrimp and spinach dumplings?"

"I think it would be a mistake to miss either of them."

Hensley set the menu down. "I see you are gifted with wisdom far beyond your years. No doubt your parents named you Sophia."

"No, just Michelle. We have an excellent chardonnay that pairs quite nicely."

"Tempting, but I must keep my wits about me for the next few hours. Tap water will do."

After all, he was about to go toe-to-toe with a Vietnam vet. Which reminded him of the small hitch in his plan.

"Say, Michelle, I'm looking for a gentleman I met a few years back. Don't recall the name, but I do remember he's a judge, African American of the large, economy-size version, and brooks no nonsense." A potential complication suddenly occurred to Hensley. "He might be retired by now."

"Oh, that's Judge Cox. He's still going strong. Says they'll have to carry him out feet first. Walks down for lunch every Friday. A Reuben and a Santa Fe pale ale."

"So he's in the federal court building?"

Michelle nodded. "Right across the street."

Hensley discovered that his instincts had not led him astray. The appetizers were unparalleled. He made quick work of them and crossed Washington Avenue to the courthouse, hoping to catch the judge before he left for his regular Monday watering hole, wherever that was.

Chapter Thirteen: Gauntlet

Hensley donned the sports jacket and stepped into the courthouse. He was immediately confronted by a metal detector.

The security guard eyed him. "Do you have a cell phone?"

"I'm afraid not. But could you direct me to Judge Cox's office?"

"Do you have an appointment?"

"As it happens, I'm in town on business and thought I'd drop by to say hello. It's been a few years. If he doesn't remember my name, just tell him that I met him at Chrystal's house back at the turn of the millennium."

"Wait here." The guard made the call, waited as the message was relayed. He hung up and handed Hensley a tray for metal articles. Hensley contributed his watch for the cause, retrieving it on the other side.

The guard pointed. "Down the hall, up the stairs, left to the front of the building, last door on the left."

Hensley found his way and was buzzed into the office. Despite his newfound, fresh-as-paint respectability and the advance notice, the secretary peered at him as if she were a governess protecting her charges from a reincarnation of Rasputin and withdrew into the judge's chambers. After a minute, she emerged and gestured him in, closing the door behind him.

US District Judge Simon Cox looked up from a brief on his desk and impaled Hensley with a steely gaze. His close-cropped hair had not receded, but it had lost the battle of the black and the gray. Even so, anyone could see that, Cox's height and bulk notwithstanding, there was not an ounce of fat on him.

Despite Hensley's martial arts background and the advantage of being twenty, perhaps thirty years younger, he had no doubt that Judge Cox could pound him into a PB&J sandwich without breaking a sweat and would then ship his remains off to a rendering plant to make glue or dog food or whatever it was they did with unfortunate souls who happened to run afoul of a US district judge.

And as he approached the desk with his most winning smile turned up to a thousand lumens, Hensley got the impression that Cox would like nothing better than to do that exact thing, right down to the rendering plant or the unmarked grave. He began to suspect that he had made a serious miscalculation in coming here, much as he had done in DC.

Cox preempted Hensley's greeting with a growl. "I see the reports of your demise have been greatly exaggerated."

"Ah." Hensley lowered the arm he had begun to extend. "So you remember the first time I passed through your charming little burg."

"Yes, but I remember your failure to return much more clearly." Cox nodded to a chair. "Sit down and tell me why I shouldn't risk my retirement by horsewhipping you right now out in front of the courthouse."

Hensley took the seat, not doubting in the slightest that Cox kept a rawhide whip in the armoire that held his robes. "I'm not saying you wouldn't be within your rights to do so, sir, though I must assure you that I feel my transgressions most keenly without resort to the administration of the swift and sure hand of the justice of the West."

At this point, Hensley regretted the failure to buy a hat along with the boots, for no other reason than that it would allow him to turn it in his hands by the brim to lend credence to his sincerity. And oddly enough, he realized that he actually meant everything he had said. He had done Chrystal a great disservice, no, an inexcusable insult, and he felt that enduring some singular act of penance would not be amiss. However, he hoped it would fall short of a public whipping, as much for the sake of his hide as his pride.

"However, be that as it may, I come not on my own account but for the sake of Chrystal and her current distress."

Cox frowned. "What distress?"

"The matter of Sapphire."

"Get to the point."

It appeared that those who knew Chrystal best knew nothing, and Hensley, who had been absent for over a decade, held the high cards, thanks to Fagan's lack of impulse control.

"The latest intel is that she has run off with a lad bearing the unfortunate name of Spud."

The searing look Cox had bestowed on Hensley at his entrance was nothing compared to the expression that clouded his face now. "What are you talking about? I saw Chrystal on Memorial Day. Sapphire was there."

"That was two weeks ago. I learned of it this weekend when I visited Chrystal in DC."

Cox's left eye twitched as he absorbed the implications of these two sentences. A moment later, his gaze focused back on Hensley, but he said nothing.

Hensley nodded. Cox had not achieved his position by requiring that everything be explained to him. The man was already up to speed. The relief of not having to connect the dots filled Hensley with joy, and he respected Cox's time and ability by cutting to the chase. "What do you know about Sapphire's father?"

Cox shook his head. "He didn't have anything to do with this. D.B. has no use for the Tatum clan. Mortal enemies, in fact."

Yes. Just as he had remembered. D.B. Lamm. "But if she defies her mother, might she not run to her father, the one person Chrystal will have nothing to do with?" Well, maybe not the only one, but Hensley's problems were not germane at the moment.

He almost smiled at the rarity of that last thought. Not that he never gave thought to the needs of others, but at best they might share equal billing with his own concerns, if they made it on the marquee at all.

But he was in the way of addressing that very flaw at this very moment. That notion caused him to smile, if only a little.

Cox raised an eyebrow.

Hensley corralled his smile. "It wouldn't hurt for me to pay D.B. a visit to find out what he knows, would it?"

"Who was with Chrystal in DC?"

"Fagan, of course. She was at his house."

"And that was all?"

"Of course. Sapphire is with Spud Tatum. Who else would be there?"

Cox settled back in his chair and regarded Hensley with a detached air that elicited a frisson of concern. "Did Chrystal ask you to help find Sapphire?"

Hensley considered his response carefully. He wasn't dealing with Sheriff Powell anymore. "Not in so many words."

"I assume you mentioned the possibility. How exactly would you characterize her response?"

"I wouldn't care to speculate."

Cox almost smiled. The effect was far from heartwarming. "But you will, regardless."

Hensley didn't bother with pointless protestations. When you saw checkmate in five moves, you flicked over the king instead of going through the tedious motions. "She was less than enthusiastic at the prospect."

"I think you mean to say that she offered to remove your head and relocate it in a more southerly hemisphere. Well out of direct sunlight." Cox inclined his head toward Hensley. "I would be so bold as to say that she suggested the possibility of providing you with a pulse-free future."

The man certainly knew his goddaughter. It was like he was in the room when she produced the Colt. He wondered if Cox had known everything all along, but his surprise at learning Sapphire had run off seemed genuine.

It violated Hensley's core principles to show his hand, but when your opponent had already named every card you were holding, taking the coy approach was self-defeating.

"You will not be surprised to learn that Chrystal did not welcome me with open arms. Quite to the contrary, she welcomed me with a 1911 model Colt .45, if 'welcomed' can be used in such a context."

From the smile that crept onto Cox's stone mask, it would appear that he was proud of his goddaughter, but he made no comment.

"Be that as it may, and I don't dare suggest that I didn't deserve every terror-inducing moment, I would like to lend a hand in reuniting mother and daughter."

"Because . . ."

"Because she deserves better. Better from her daughter. Better from me. Better from life." Hensley took a deep breath and leaned forward. "I can't deny that I am late to this party of seeing Chrystal in a proper light, or that I would like nothing better than to pick up things where I foolishly left them a decade ago, but I do not make that a condition of my involvement. I say we take on the task of saving Sapphire from herself and let the chips fall where they may."

Cox studied Hensley for a long time. Hensley was inured to long silences. He hadn't spent three years in a monastery in the mountains of Guangxi for nothing. But long silent hours with the monks didn't compare to five minutes of Cox staring him down as he waited for Hensley to break. In the right context, five minutes can be an eternity. Like when someone held your head under water.

But he would not break. Not now.

Perhaps Hensley hadn't endured the soul-crushing reality of years as a soldier on the ground in a thankless war in southeast Asia half a century ago. Hadn't spent the last several decades holding the fort on an entrenched beachhead in the American West, defiant in the face of societal and cultural decay. He would give Cox that much.

But Hensley had a mission, a vow to fulfill. He would leave the world a better place than he had found it, dammit, and this was the only way he knew to accomplish that goal. And he would do it if he never saw the back of his head.

And Simon Cox would not stop him. Yes, the judge had a résumé, but Hensley had a résumé of his own. He had survived in defiance of all odds, kept body and soul together and done a measure of good along the way. Sure he had made his mistakes, but if Hensley was any judge of horseflesh, Cox had his share of regrets to haunt him in the midnight of the soul.

Hensley squared his shoulders and took a good long look at Cox. Within five seconds, he instinctively knew two things: that Cox had a bottle of fine scotch in his desk and that before Hensley left this office, they would share a glass of it.

Confident in this knowledge, Hensley let out a long breath, settled back into his chair, and allowed himself a private smile.

The judge's eyes narrowed for a moment. Then he reached for a drawer without breaking eye contact, extracted a bottle of Bruichladdich, set it on the desk, and set a single tumbler beside it. "So, here's how it will go down." He turned to the bottle and twisted the cork out.

Hensley waited as Cox poured two fingers of scotch into the glass, paused, and then added a third. Cox took an inaugural sip.

"I'll stake you the nerve of coming in here shorn and draped like the favorite son, but you're going to march your candy ass out of here and catch the next stage to the sunset and leave Chrystal and hers alone. And that includes D.B. Lambert and his band of bozos."

Ah, yes, D.B. Lambert. That was the name, just as he had remembered. Hensley cocked his head to the left. While he could not fully endorse this approach, he could appreciate the man's perspective.

"Judge, I sense a latent hostility, but I fail to recall a moment when I might have had the opportunity to incur your displeasure."

The judge remained impassive as he took another sip, but it seemed that every muscle under his command ached to rearrange Hensley into a Picasso reject.

There were times to ease the friction of silence with the ready word and the welcoming smile, but Hensley could see that this was not that time. He had what he came for—the name of Chrystal's ex—so he settled into the chair and waited out his opponent.

Finally Cox relented. "It's for your own good. D.B. is within a frog's hair of being raided."

"By whom?"

"Dealer's choice. FBI, DEA, ATF, Homeland Security."

D.B. had upped his game in the intervening years. "No point in me getting tangled up in that. What can you tell me about Spud Tatum?"

Cox studied him for a moment. "How does that concern you?"

Hensley shrugged. "Just filling in the blanks before I leave."

The judge relaxed into his chair, evidently satisfied with the response. "Most recent in a long line of two-bit lowlifes. Regulars in the lower courts. I've never seen any of them at the federal level."

"Bar fights, B&E, DUI, small-time drugs?"

Cox nodded.

"How did Sapphire get mixed up in that?"

"The life of a single mother is not an easy one. And the life of a girl with no father to speak of, living in the shadow of a precocious older brother, is hardly a cakewalk. So easily led astray."

Hensley considered this proposition. He would put up his dysfunctional childhood against all comers. Take being whisked away when you are nine to the jungles of Angola, into the middle of a civil war, old enough to feel the loss of civilization but too young to do anything about it.

On the other hand, if he had learned anything in his travels of the past four decades, it was that there exists no objective scale against which to measure suffering. Pain is pain. The angst of a suburban American teen may be trivial in the larger context of things, but what teen had a global perspective?

Hensley wondered how different Sapphire's life could have been if her father hadn't bailed and retreated to the hills.

Cox broke into his ruminations. "What if Chrystal had met someone willing to stick around for more than a year or two? To take the place of the father Sapphire never had?" He downed the rest of the tumbler in a single throw and slammed it down on his desk. "But no sense in wasting time speculating about things that didn't happen. We're done here."

Hensley recoiled at the insinuation. It was hardly cricket slapping him with such a thinly veiled accusation after he had come here of his own free will to lend a hand. Easy for Cox to judge from his position of ease and power, his regular routine, Reuben sandwich every Friday like clockwork, and who knew what else.

There was no need for empathy in Cox's world, for riding the ever-breaking wave of humanity, sensing the brokenness of others, people like Julien at the rooftop bar in Galveston, wayward sheep who needed the nuanced nudge to power over the speed bump into a better life.

In the world of a judge, it was all black and white, wasn't it? All checkboxes and coloring inside the lines. What else could you expect from a guy with a military background?

He was ready to lurch from his chair and storm out, when he realized he had to let it go for the greater good. For Chrystal.

"I like to think that we all play the hand we've been dealt the best we can." He stood. "I thank you for your consideration."

As Hensley left the inner office, he stopped at the gorgon's desk. "Could you direct me to the closest library?"

"Turn right on Washington. You'll see it." She picked up a pen. "What's your cell number?"

"I'm afraid I am neither blessed nor cursed with that bane or boon to modern existence, depending on one's perspective."

She eyed him with even greater suspicion than before. "You don't have a cell phone?"

"You surmise correctly."

She readied her pen again. "The number of where you're staying then."

"Once again I fear I must disappoint. I just arrived this morning from the coast and have not yet established a base of operations."

"Then how will the judge contact you?"

Hensley laid his hand on his heart. "The onus is uponus to maintain communication."

In response to her dissatisfied scowl, he smiled and took his leave.

Chapter Fourteen: Bivouac

At the library, Hensley signed up for thirty minutes on the computer and discovered that D.B. had a place just across the Colorado state line near Pagosa Springs. A three-hour drive if it was a minute.

Hensley printed out the map and checked the time. Just a few minutes past noon. Still eight hours of daylight left.

He'd need a car. A rental. And that meant a credit card. He floundered for a good ninety seconds before his memory threw him a life preserver.

Chrystal had a brand new, unactivated credit card under the name of Robin Bumstead sitting in her desk drawer. He could borrow it and then reimburse her later. Fortunately, he still had the key to her back door.

As he walked to the bus stop, he reconsidered his plan. Quite legitimately to his mind, he was merely borrowing the use of the card. If he had the alternative to pay cash, he would do it gladly, but that was not an option. And he had the funds on hand to pay off the card before the charge was even billed. Practically, there was absolutely no impact on Chrystal or her finances.

However, technically he was committing fraud, identity theft, essentially stealing her credit card. Hensley was more a spirit-of-the-law kind of guy, but he realized most of the population lacked the flexibility to see his perspective. That was the curse of living in the skinny part of the curve.

The bus pulled up, and he boarded. Once again he found himself forced to think tactically with no time for pre-authorization. And once again he opted for the greater good. By using Chrystal's card, he might be eliminating the slim chance he had of regaining her favor, but if his felonious activity served to rescue Sapphire from her bad decisions and return her to the bosom of her family, he was willing to take that risk.

Half an hour later, he was in Chrystal's house. The cat welcomed him as a long-lost member of the fraternal order. From the looks of things, Toni was still on the job. Hensley would have to be in and out quickly to avoid running into her again.

He located the card, dialed the 800 number, punched in the code, and got the acknowledgment. Then he peeled off the jacket and the button-down, stuffed them into his bag, changed back into the French cuffs, and was back in the taxi before the driver had the time to turn the page on the comic he was reading.

One obstacle remained to acquiring unlimited mobility—a driver's license. He directed the cabbie to The Tinker's Dam, a sketchy establishment a few miles out of town on Old Las Vegas Highway.

While it hardly seemed possible, Tinker's looked even less reputable than it had the last time he had seen it a dozen years ago. The corrugated metal siding had rust stains at the rivets like mascara after a good cry. One of the windows was covered in graffiti-laden plywood.

Even though it was barely one p.m. on a Monday, the parking lot was packed with motorcycles, pickups, beaters, and a riding lawn mower.

Hensley grabbed his duffel, dismissed the cab with a decent tip, and assessed his dwindling stake. The thugs had cut his two grand nearly in half, and travel expenses had done the same to the balance. A license shouldn't put too big a dent in the reserve, but before long he would need an infusion of capital, which would be difficult to come by while in search-and-rescue mode.

A half-dozen locals stood outside the door smoking next to a No Smoking sign. Hensley nodded in passing and plunged into the perpetual gloom of Tinker's without pausing to let his eyes adjust, a gesture that informed anyone who was looking that he was no tyro.

He navigated the shadows and silhouettes of the local fauna congregated around pool tables, dropped his bag on a stool, and slapped a twenty on the bar.

"Tink, my man, set me up with an Irish boilermaker and treat yourself to one on me for old time's sake."

The giant behind the bar had the build of a natural-born blacksmith. He scowled like a bear with a sore tooth and squinted at Hensley for a good five seconds. Then, without changing expression, he slammed two pint glasses on the counter and opened a can of Guinness. "You cut your hair."

Hensley inspected the bartender's 'do, which was buzzed on the sides and a wiry mess down the middle. "I see I am not the only one."

As the Guinness did its cascading carbonation dance, Scooter Bell, known as Tinker Bell to his friends, filled two shot glasses with Irish whiskey, and then shoved one of them, along with a pint glass, across the bar.

Hensley held up the shot glass. "To old friends and older whiskey."

"Fast women and faster horses."

They both drank their shots and chased them with the Guinness.

Hensley pulled two cigars from his bag and offered one to Tink. "How's bidness?"

Tink took the cigar, dropped it into the drawer of the register, and slammed it shut. "Can't smoke that in here."

"Surely you jest, my fine feathered friend." Hensley scouted the room. No ashtrays. No smoldering cigarettes on the edge of a pool table.

"Been illegal for six years. And they mean it. They'll shut you down in a heartbeat and never shed a tear."

Hensley shook his head and slid his cigar into his pocket. "And this used to be a respectable establishment. You step out for just a minute and they change everything on you."

Tink grunted and cleared the empties.

"Bartleby still around?" Hensley asked.

Tink nodded toward a door to the right of the bar.

"Keep it frosty." Hensley grabbed his bag and stepped through the door.

The back room housed half-a-dozen booths in little alcoves, bead curtains affording a measure of privacy, all occupied. Hensley noted the figure in the third one on the right and approached. "Hello the table."

"Hello the room."

Hensley pushed the beads aside and slid in. Bart had not changed in the intervening decade. Gaunt, almost wraithlike, with stringy brown hair just touching his shoulders. As ever before, his eyes never left the screen of the laptop in front of him.

"Bartmeister, I am once again in need of your services."

Bart appeared to pay him no mind.

"New Mexico driver's license to match this credit card." Hensley slid a scrap of paper with the particulars in his direction.

Bart clicked the mouse. The LED on a camera above his head glowed red. "Try not to smile."

Hensley straightened his posture, leaning his head against the green screen that hung across his side of the booth.

Bart positioned the laptop and clicked the mouse. "Good." He began working.

Hensley set five twenties on the table. "By the way, I'm in search of D.B. Lambert. Can you tell me anything about him?"

"I would prefer not to," Bart replied, without looking up from the screen.

"I hear he might be moving beyond conspiracy theories to actual felonious transgressions."

The living *Dia de los Muertos* figure across the table made no comment.

Hensley dropped another twenty on the stack. "What have you heard?"

"I would prefer not to comment."

Another twenty. "Surely you've heard something."

Bart said nothing and made no move other than to continue working on the ID.

Hensley sighed and slid out of the booth. "I shall await your pleasure at the bar, should anything occur to you."

He slipped out to the main bar and settled on a stool. "How much for refills?"

Tink set up another boilermaker without comment.

"I'm looking for temporary quarters." Hensley sipped the whiskey. "You still got that Airstream out back?"

Tink nodded.

"Is it available?"

Tink nodded.

"Also need to build up a stake. Need any help around here?"

Tink looked him over. "Ain't exactly a spring chicken."

"Lucky for you, since chickens aren't much help in loading a keg, whether of the spring or autumn variety." Hensley sipped the beer. "Or talking drunks out of fights. Or knocking a few heads together if they don't succumb to more gentle inducements."

The skeptical air with which Tink regarded Hensley got his back up. "Two weeks ago I ran across an argumentative fellow approximately twice your size and rang his bell to such extent that the local authorities cited him for violating the noise ordinance." Hensley didn't mention that he had done so from behind with the aid of a fire extinguisher. The relevant points of the story were there.

Tink softened slightly. Hensley could tell by the way the lines on his forehead decreased by one.

"But I must warn you that I'll need a certain flexibility when it comes to the hours. I have a little side project going."

Tink shrugged and resumed restocking the cooler behind the bar with beer, which was as good as a handshake in Hensley's book.

He grabbed his duffel bag and tossed it behind the bar. "You see Chrystal much these days?"

Tink glanced up. "That why you're back? Scouting a meal ticket?"

"You wound me most unjustly, my friend." Hensley shook his head and sipped the beer. "She seeing anyone these days?"

"After you left, she swore off men." Tink slammed the cooler shut and tore down the box with a swift twist of his meaty fists. "First D.B., and then you. That sealed the deal, I reckon."

"How is the old infantryman? Still fashioning hats from tin foil and keeping a weather eye out for black helicopters?"

"He don't come down here much. Never was one for drinking."

Hensley nodded and dropped it. No need to raise suspicions.

"But his boys stop in here sometimes for a few games during happy hour."

"Boys? I thought he had just the one girl. Did he get remarried?"

"Naw, his crew. Militia types."

"So he has a crew now, does he?"

Tink grunted. "Just a few guys playing army up in the mountains." He scanned the room. "Keep an eye out." He disappeared through a door into a back room.

Hensley turned on his stool, elbows back against the bar, and assessed the room. Everyone seemed to be behaving themselves.

One doughy kid approached from a pool table. "Hey, where's Tink got off to?"

Hensley sprang from the stool and vaulted behind the bar. Too bad Tink wasn't there to see this validation of his résumé. "He's off to the trading post for supplies. What can I do you for, my corpulent young friend?"

The kid blinked. Looked barely into his twenties, and Hensley was betting he had not been valedictorian of his graduating class. Assuming he had graduated.

"Huh?"

"Hensley Fletcher, itinerant bartender at your service. Pick your poison." He gestured to the shelf of beer bottles that indicated the available brands.

"Four Buds."

Hensley slid the cooler lid open, located four cold beers, and opened them as he set them on the bar. "You have a tab?"

"Nah." He pushed a wrinkled ten across the bar and grabbed two of the beers with his left hand.

Hensley dropped the bill into the cash register and slammed the drawer closed.

The kid stood there staring.

"Was there something else? A pickled egg perhaps?"

"It's happy hour."

"Of course it is."

"So the Buds are two dollars."

"Ah, so they are." Hensley opened the drawer, withdrew two ones, stuffed one into the carafe that served as a tip jar, and pushed the other one back to the kid.

The kid picked up the dollar with his right hand and glanced at the other trapped in the tip jar.

Once again it was time for a life lesson, and fortunately Hensley was there to impart a measure of wisdom to this representative of the next generation who are our future.

"What did you say your name was?"

"Tyler."

Hensley held out his hand. Tyler shoved the dollar in his shirt pocket and shook Hensley's hand with a frown of confusion.

"Now listen closely, Tyler, because I can see you are just starting out in life and this is a moment with the potential to guide your future, either to success or to disappointment."

"Okay." Tyler glanced over his shoulder at his buddies, two of whom were involved in a pool game. A third looked over at the bar, impatient for his Bud. Tyler looked back at Hensley and then at the dollar in the tip jar.

"Tyler, I can see you are a man who works hard for his money and expects to get full value for it."

"Sure."

"As am I. But I can see that, like myself, you are not a cynic. You have an appreciation for the things that make life worth living."

"Okay." This response had the upward inflection of a man completely at sea in his current circumstances.

"A cynic knows the price of everything but the value of nothing. Life, a life worth living, is not about price. It is about value."

The buddy approached, a stringy guy in his late twenties who appeared to spend his days in the sun performing manual labor. "What's the holdup?"

Hensley grabbed the two beers on the bar and passed them to the newcomer. "Here you are, sir. Enjoy."

The newcomer studied Hensley, then Tyler, shrugged, and left with the two beers. Hensley turned back to Tyler.

"A man who goes through life hoarding every dollar he manages to acquire has failed to learn the universal law of reaping and sowing. But you probably know this already."

Tyler angled his head like a puppy waiting for his master to quit talking and hand him the bone.

"Riddle me this, Tyler. What do you do when you want corn?"

"Go to the grocery store?"

"You're on the right track, but let's peel it back a layer or two. You're a farmer. You harvest your corn. But do you eat it all? No, you save some to plant. Now why do you do that? Because you know that for every kernel of corn you bury into the earth to die, you will be rewarded with hundreds of kernels in the fullness of time."

"Okay." Tyler's attention wandered back to the tip jar.

"This dollar you have placed in this jar is the seed corn of karma. As you go through life, sowing generosity, you are preparing for yourself a harvest of riches. Because we know three things about sowing."

Hensley drew in a deep breath and held up a finger. "You reap what you sow." A second finger. "You reap later than you sow." And the final finger. "You reap more than you sow."

Despite this feast of wisdom, Tyler appeared more confused than convinced. And more impatient than either.

It was time for the bold statement. Hensley pulled out his wallet. "To show you how important this principle is, I will join you in this investment in your future." He extracted a twenty and stuffed in the tip jar. "There. The seed has been planted."

Tyler watched this practical demonstration of Hensley's life philosophy with all the appreciation of a hockey player attending a performance of *Swan Lake*.

"But that was Brian's ten."

The newcomer returned. "What's the problem here?" He grabbed a beer from Tyler. "Where's my change?"

Tyler pulled the one from his pocket.

Brian grabbed it. "Where's the rest?"

Tyler nodded at the tip jar.

"You giving this guy my money?" He reached for the carafe.

"He was merely paying it forward on your behalf," Hensley said.

"Screw that." Brian fished out his dollar. "I didn't take you to raise."

Hensley watched the dollar disappear into Brian's pocket. "Well said, sir."

As Brian and Tyler returned to the table, Hensley inserted two fingers into the carafe to rescue his twenty.

Tink busted through the door with two more cases of beer. "Helping yourself to an advance on wages?" He slammed the boxes on the bar.

Hensley shoved the bills down into the carafe. "Tip from the foursome at the corner table." He set the carafe on the bar.

Tink squinted from the twenty to the pool players and grunted with an inflection that conveyed equal parts surprise and skepticism. He grabbed an envelope from the top of the boxes and tossed it at Hensley.

Hensley opened it and extracted an excellent facsimile of a New Mexico driver's license in the name of Robin Bumstead, complete with hologram. The envelope also contained a few folded pages, but before he could inspect them, Tink pulled a key from his shirt pocket and set it on the bar.

Hensley grabbed his duffel bag. "I have a few errands to run. Where's your phone?"

Tink pointed to it with a beer. Hensley called for a cab and then went to stow his gear in the trailer, which appeared to be older than Hensley.

Just inside the door to the right, a couch with plaid cushions stretched the width of the trailer. Directly ahead a blue-checkered tablecloth covered a small fold-out table. On his left a stove, fridge, and sink, and beyond a bedroom with two single beds separated with a nightstand and a vintage lamp.

He installed his worldly possessions inside, locked the door, and proceeded to the front to wait for the cab.

The crowd of smokers still congregated around the door. Or maybe a different crowd. Hensley shaded his eyes from the sun and squinted northwest toward town. The heat was climbing through the mid nineties. Might even break one hundred before the day was done. But at seven thousand feet, Santa Fe was high and dry, and the mid-nineties here was a lot easier to bear than the mid-eighties in Galveston four days ago.

Hensley pulled out the envelope from Bartleby and flipped open the folded pages. An FBI dossier on D.B. Lambert and his little cell of militia types.

In 1999, just a few months before Hensley arrived on the scene in Santa Fe, D.B. had bought a miner's cabin up in the San Juan mountains north of Pagosa Springs and put some metal buildings on the lot. Probably stocking up to wait out the millennial race wars and the disintegration of civilization. When that failed to come off, he'd evidently branched out into meat processing, taxidermy, and critter control to keep the lights on. Nothing to raise a red flag other than the possible cross-pollination of the meat processing with the critter control business.

Hensley flipped through the pages as the taxi pulled up, and then shoved the envelope in his pocket. He directed the driver to a car rental agency downtown.

As far as Hensley could tell, other than some questionable firearms purchases, D.B. had kept a low profile. Not even a parking ticket. However, some of his running buddies weren't as fastidious. Various DUIs and drunk and disorderly charges shared between them.

Nothing that would have an alphabet soup of federales swarming in. Which made one wonder what the judge knew that the FBI didn't. Maybe Cox, knowing Hensley's disinclination to hobnob with the authorities, was just trying to scare him off.

Either way, he'd have to keep his wits about him. For all he knew, D.B. could have gone ballistic when he found out his daughter was running off with a Tatum.

Chapter Fifteen: Compound

Hensley drove off the rental lot in a black Jeep Grand Cherokee and headed up US 84, working out his approach.

As Hensley remembered him, D.B. was as serious as they come. Next to him, Judge Cox was a regular kidder.

At the famous Memorial Day cookout where he had met both Powell and Cox, Hensley had found himself cornered by D.B. ranting about how the government had concocted the entire Y2K hoax to force the sheeple to upgrade their electronics. The government having secretly introduced stealth surveillance circuitry into the Y2K-compliant chips. Of course.

Although it went against Hensley's instincts, in a situation like this it seemed best to lay his cards on the table. A guy like D.B. would be suspicious of, and impatient with, small talk and pleasantries. Going down that road would be about as productive as poking a bear with a stick.

A few minutes after six, east of Pagosa Springs, Hensley took US 160 up into the San Juan mountains. After half an hour and a few switchbacks and wrong turns, he found the gravel road leading to the compound. As he gunned the Cherokee up the grade, he caught a glimpse of a log cabin through the pines. Then he rounded a hairpin curve, and the next thing he knew, he was accelerating up to the cabin in question.

The place appeared to be deserted. No vehicles, no humans milling about. Hensley pulled within ten yards of the steps leading up the porch, put the Jeep in park, punched a button to roll down the windows, another to open the sun roof, and killed the engine.

Hensley reckoned he was up to ten thousand feet, the air thin and pleasant in the mid-eighties. He planned to spend a few minutes in the car to give the residents time to get used to his presence. Not that D.B. was dangerous, but his running buddies seemed to be a fractious lot, and there was no percentage in startling the herd.

He wished he had possessed the foresight to pick up a cigar or two to pass the time, although smoking in the rental would cost him a packet.

From the looks of the place, the cabin had been extended to a considerable degree since the original miner had built it. It stood on a steep grade that sloped up to the back and looked to be forty to sixty feet across the front, not counting the wrap-around porch.

From a tactical standpoint, it gave the occupants the high ground against those coming in from the drive. Had to admire that, no matter what you thought of the man's politics.

Beyond the screen door of the cabin, darkness awaited, indicating the inside door was open, which was no surprise given the excellent weather. A slight breeze wafted through the Jeep.

It was coming on seven p.m. and up here on the ridge, there was still plenty of sunlight. Behind the cabin, the ridge sloped up to the left, which was north as best as Hensley could make out from the shadows. As the ground fell away to the right, he could see past the ridge to other peaks toward the east.

It was a rugged land, but it had an accessible, seductive beauty, a siren call that whispered to the soul of a man, beckoning him to test his mettle against the planet, to immerse himself in an ascetic, solitary life of the body and the mind, cultivating a oneness with the universe.

Tempting for some, but Hensley was no ingénue. He knew what it was to live without the creature comforts of the West through winters in climes much more spartan than this. That was a young man's game, and Hensley would have no part of it. He scanned the compound.

Solar panels on the cabin roof. A medium-sized, green house downgrade from the cabin. Two large metal warehouses upgrade, two 500-gallon propane tanks alongside. No doubt a gasoline generator or two for backup. Whatever else he might be, D.B. was no fool.

Hensley reassessed his situation. His view of D.B. was based on one tedious conspiracy-theory conversation thirteen years ago, more crackpot than threat, but the mind that brought this plan together was not to be dismissed lightly.

A glance at his watch told him he'd been at this second-guessing for five minutes. He cracked the door open, slipped out, and rested his right arm on the open window.

The screen door slammed against the logs, and a man sauntered out onto the porch. He was of a goodly size, six-feet at least and solid. As lean as prime USDA grass-fed beef on the hoof and just as focused on the stranger. He stopped at the top of the stairs and leaned against the column.

Hensley waited another moment before speaking. "I'm here to see D.B."

"You wasted a trip."

"I can wait."

"That's where you're wrong."

"How can I contact him?" Hensley gave it a good five seconds before continuing. "It's about his daughter."

A flutter of the eyelids before answering. "What about her?"

"Well, now, that's between me and him."

The guy pushed away from the column and took a wide stance. "What do you know about it?"

The screen door opened, and a woman stepped out. She had on a pair of worn jeans and a red spaghetti-strap tank top, filling out both in a manner designed to get and retain a man's attention under the most extreme of circumstances. Her shoulder-length, glossy black hair was restrained with a bandana do-rag. She held a cigarette in one hand and a tumbler with ice, lime, and an undisclosed clear liquid in the other.

She eyed Hensley through slits that betrayed more interest than suspicion. "Who's this, Merle?"

Merle dismissed her with an impatient jerk of his chin. "Get back inside, Ronnie. This ain't no concern of yours."

Merle? He'd heard that name recently. Hensley straightened up for a better look and in so doing caught sight of movement in the side mirror of the Jeep—a scrawny guy with a shotgun clearing the back of the vehicle.

Hensley's pulse quickened. Perhaps he should have given more weight to Cox's warning and less to Tink's dismissive appraisal. He shifted his weight to the balls of his feet and studiously ignored the man behind him while keeping tabs on his position from the corner of his eye.

"How gratifying to see you again, Miss Ronnie."

Ronnie's eyes opened wider. "How did you know my name?"

"Have you forgotten already?" Hensley asked. "My dear lady, you have cut me to the quick and laid waste all my foundations."

A flash of movement in the side mirror prompted Hensley to spin, catching the attacker with a well-placed kick to the sternum as he rushed to club Hensley with the butt of his gun.

Hensley stepped forward to retrieve the shotgun but desisted when a blast sounded behind him and the windshield of the Jeep disintegrated.

Hensley turned slowly as Merle racked a shell into the chamber of the shotgun he had evidently placed behind the pillar earlier as insurance against future complications. They seemed to be well prepared for all contingencies here at Chez Lambert.

As ever, Hensley had a deep respect for the persuasive power of a loaded firearm of any variety, but the warning shot through the windshield gave him some hope that Merle was merely unsociable rather than homicidal.

Hensley glanced at the Jeep. He had paid extra for the insurance but doubted that it covered assault by militia henchmen.

"Now see here," Hensley said. "You can try to dry-gulch a man, and if you can get away with it, who's to know, although it's not quite cricket on either side of the pond, but shooting out the windscreen of a rental, that's just bad form, old man."

From the noise behind him, Hensley gathered that the scrawny guy had scrambled to his feet and retrieved the shotgun.

"Merle, it's him," the guy said. "From Chrystal's house. Just got a haircut."

Hensley would recognize that adenoidal voice at any altitude, latitude, or longitude. It was Shotgun, the guy who had placed a bony knee between his shoulder blades in the back of a panel van. The guy who had requisitioned seven hundred dollars of Hensley's stake three days ago out on Highway 14. And the guy on the porch was Merle, the wheelman of said van. What were they doing here?

Instead of an answer, he received a swift blow to the back of the skull, courtesy of one Shotgun the Henchman.

Stunned, Hensley staggered forward, snagged his shoulder on the driver's side mirror, spun around, and fell.

Before he could react, Shotgun had a knee between his shoulder blades and cold metal against his ear.

"Out here, no one can hear you scream."

CHAPTER SIXTEEN: TÊTE-À-TÊTE

The next time Hensley had a coherent thought, he was lying on his back in the dark. A quick inspection by the available light revealed that his left hand was secured to a bedpost with handcuffs, and an attempt to sit up revealed, via a sharp pain to an already painful head, that he was in the lower bunk of a set of bunk beds.

After a short recovery period of anywhere from two minutes to two hours, Hensley made a second attempt, this time turning slowly to his left and crouching into a sitting position. An assessment with his right hand revealed a trickle of blood running down his face from a cut on his forehead. He wasn't certain as to whether it was delivered courtesy of his captors or self-inflicted by sitting up too suddenly on the bottom bunk.

Hensley took the opportunity to assess the potentiality of the room. Two sets of bunk beds, a few other items of furniture, a set of folding doors that indicated a closet, and a door through which a sink was visible.

Shucking a set of handcuffs was no feat for a Hensley in possession of a small bit of metal featuring the required properties, but that was the one ingredient Hensley was fresh out of. And even if he had the proper implements, the fading light falling through the window revealed a set of wrought-iron bars.

The luminescent dial of his watch told him it was coming on eight p.m. and the heated conversation riding on the light bleeding through the crack under the door told him that he would have to fight his way out in that direction.

But first, some rest and reflection was in order. He had obviously misunderestimated the situation. He was prepared to win his way past the reluctance of an uncooperative father and his antisocial running buddies to form an alliance, however uneasy, focused on rescuing Sapphire. A challenge, perhaps, but obviously within the realm of his expertise.

However, he had lacked a critical piece of information—that his erstwhile captors were at least associated with D.B. and possibly working under his orders. And of course the burning question: where was D.B.?

And the other burning question: how loose were these screwballs?

Hensley gave further consideration to the handcuffs. Regulation issue. He examined the bunk beds. Stackable. He pushed up the top bunk with his shoulder and slipped the cuff off the post. Whoever had interned him hadn't been cursed with a superabundance of operational brain cells. Hensley's money was on Shotgun.

Keeping an ear tuned for any change in the conversation outside the door, Hensley crept to the closet and glanced inside. Fleece-lined parkas, backpacks, snow boots, and some moving boxes. The backpacks and boxes would bear investigation, but he couldn't take the time to do it now. He made delicate inquiries of the door. Locked from the outside.

Thus informed, Hensley restored himself to his captive position on the bed. The fact of his ready mobility was not widely known, and he was unwilling to grant his captors even the slightest of advantages. Life was a chancy thing at best. No point in shortening the odds for the opposition.

It appeared that in his present circs, there were wheels, and then there were wheels within wheels, and perhaps even wheels within those wheels that were in other wheels.

If he were to take events in the order in which he had experienced them, first there came Shotgun and Merle staking out Chrystal's house in a pest control van and interrogating Hensley about missing drugs under rather unpleasant circumstances.

Then twenty-four hours later there was Fagan revealing that Sapphire had run off with Spud.

Then eighteen hours subsequent, Judge Cox intimating that a host of federal agencies, including the DEA, were interested in D.B.'s activities.

And a few hours later, the FBI report Bartleby had slipped into the envelope with the driver's license, the one that said D.B. and his crew were relatively benign.

In this vortex of information, Hensley rearranged the timeline and connected two points. Sapphire ran away with Spud, and then Merle and Shotgun showed up at Chrystal's house looking for stolen drugs. It didn't take Stephen Hawking to draw a picture in this case. And in the light of this analysis, the imminent raid seemed more likely.

But such cogitations made a man thirsty, not to mention the fact that it was long past suppertime, and a growing boy needed his nourishment. Particularly considering he had taken an early, if peerless lunch.

He sampled the air with a discerning olfactory system. It seemed that someone had fired up an oven. He seconded the motion. Such measures were long past due.

Hensley took a deep breath. "Pardon the interruption, but what does it take for a guy to get a crust of bread around here?"

The murmur of discussion leaking through the crack under the door ceased.

"Merely a matter of inquiry from an interested party. Feel free to reply at your earliest convenience."

A muted commotion ensued that Hensley hoped indicated an interested party was hustling up some grub. The door burst open. Hensley spied a rough plank table with half a dozen chairs and a kitchen counter beyond where Ronnie stood with her back to him, slicing a cut of meat with an impressive knife.

Then Shotgun strutted through, flipped on the light, and slammed the door behind him.

Hensley regarded Shotgun as he might a forgetful bellboy. "Ah, my dear fellow, there is a little matter of seven hundred dollars I'd like to discuss with you."

"What?" Shotgun eyed Hensley for a moment before he snapped to the situation. "Oh. That there is what we call your tuition in the school of hard knocks."

"Then perhaps you could provide me with a receipt for tax purposes."

"If you're so smart, why is it you're the one chained to the bed and I'm the one with the key?" He took a step closer. "Tell us where Sapphire is and we'll let you go."

Hensley slid to the edge of the bed, careful to clear the upper bunk. "That is exactly the information I came here to acquire. Her mother is worried sick about her."

"Chrystal ain't around neither."

"Of course not. She is wandering hither and yon like a mother hen frantically searching for her helpless baby chick."

Shotgun snorted. "Sapphire? She's about as helpless as a baby rattlesnake."

The comment gave Hensley pause. His opponent might be as dense as a black hole, but on the subject of Sapphire he seemed to speak with the voice of experience. But Hensley could explore that topic after he had secured Sapphire's safe return.

"I'd like to consult with D.B. posthaste. When do you expect him to return?"

"Now see here, this is the thing. I'll be asking the questions and you'll be giving the answers."

"Fire away, my crepuscular companion."

"What were you at Chrystal's house for?"

"Merely seeking to reestablish an old connection."

"You're her connection? Where's the drugs?"

This seemed to be a perennial point of contention with the Shotgun. He had asked the same thing in the van to no effect. Hensley sighed and leaned against the bedpost. "If you could describe your ailment, perhaps I could suggest a few holistic remedies. Piles, perhaps? Incontinence? Irritable bowel syndrome? Terminal flatulence?"

Shotgun's eyes narrowed as his lip inched up on one side. Cold, predator eyes. Thin, reptilian lips. He cocked his head and regarded Hensley with one eye like a lizard. "You're one of those types all right."

"Which type is that?"

"Too smart for your own good. But I got just the thing to crank you down a notch or two."

He turned to the closet, stepped up on a box to compensate for his diminutive stature, and pulled something from a shelf Hensley hadn't noticed.

It was a worn wooden box with a handle on the top, a crank on the side, and a pair of cables. The kind of thing Hensley had seen in old western movies. The ones they used to fire up the dynamite. Or in gangster movies. The box they used to convince the patsy to talk.

It was the nineteenth-century equivalent of the Taser. Hensley's first reaction was to wonder why they didn't simply invest in a Taser. His second was to consider that he might have seriously misjudged the situation.

Shotgun set down the box and grabbed a cable. "Now let's get them boots off."

"I regret that I must decline your invitation."

Shotgun flexed the alligator clip on the cable. "This here is in the way of what we call a mandatory requirement."

Hensley considered his options. It would be but the work of a moment to slip the cuff off the bedpost and incapacitate Shotgun, but the noise would bring Merle, doubtlessly armed, and Hensley's one advantage would be gone.

If he was going to let loose the fabled Hensley mojo, he needed both targets in close proximity, preferably sans firearms.

"I'd like to get a second opinion."

Shotgun grinned his oily little grin and waved the cable. "I got your second opinion right here."

Maybe if Hensley got the two of them right in front of him, he could tip the top bunk over on them both. "Ahoy the kitchen! Merle, could you be so good as to join us for a consultation?"

"Never mind," Shotgun yelled. "I got this."

"I'm afraid I really must insist," Hensley shouted louder.

The door opened and Merle, wheelman and wielder of hidden shotguns, stepped into the room, armed with his favorite weapon. He looked from Hensley to Shotgun to the cable in his hand and the box on the floor. "Arch, what the hell are you doing?"

"D.B. said to find out what he knows about Sapphire and Spud."

"So ask him."

Arch blew out an exasperated breath. "You think I haven't done that already? He ain't answering."

"Put that back up, you maroon." Merle turned to Hensley. "What do you know about Sapphire and Spud?"

"Merely that they have run away together. I'm here for one purpose and one purpose only, and that is to reconcile mother to daughter. Whatever else is going on up here in your remote aerie I neither know nor care."

"Is that so? And what about the drugs?"

"Perhaps you can explain your impression that I am somehow connected with drugs."

"Come on. We're not stupid," Arch said, the cable still in his hand. "If you didn't know about the drugs, you wouldn't be here."

"I just came for the girl."

Arch barked a scornful laugh.

"I think he might be telling the truth," Merle said.

"Precisely. Since you have no information regarding Sapphire's current location, I'll be on my way."

"Like hell you will," Arch said.

"Yeah," Merle said. "You leave when D.B. says you leave." He walked out of the room.

"Then let's get him on the horn," Hensley said to Merle's retreating back.

"He's unavailable for comment," Arch said. Reluctantly, he picked up the generator and returned it to the shelf. He graced Hensley with a final smile. "You just hang tight."

He flipped off the light, slammed the door, and shot the bolt on the lock.

Chapter Seventeen: Succor

Hensley sat in the dark, the sun having set while he was otherwise engaged, and considered his situation. Little had changed. He had learned that Arch was unhinged, and that evidently nobody knew where Sapphire was. And that if Merle kept Arch on a leash, he might have a fighting chance of wriggling out of this thing.

As he was thus engaged, footsteps approached, the chattering of locks echoed in his head, and the door opened, revealing the silhouette of a woman. She flipped a switch, and Hensley squinted in the sudden illumination.

Ronnie rushed forward and set a tray on the bed. "What happened to your head?" She turned and skittered out of the room.

Hensley took the opportunity to inspect the local fare. Three slices of pizza, not takeout by the looks of the scorch marks. He managed to snag a slice from the plate. Not bad for homegrown, but the meat was a bit tough.

Ronnie returned with a wet washcloth, knelt beside him, and dabbed at his forehead.

"What is this?" Hensley asked, holding up the slice.

"Venison pizza." Ronnie paused in her ministrations. "Don't you like it?"

"I've never had anything like it," Hensley said, having studied for years in the art of the pleasingly ambiguous response.

Ronnie smiled. "It's my own recipe."

"You amaze me." He took another bite and gamely chewed away.

She resumed her nursing duties. "D.B. swears by it."

Hensley was very nearly moved to swearing himself, but at this point he was willing to ingest practically any organic matter to keep the old machine running.

"Perhaps you could help me understand how things stand." Hensley wrestled another bite down the hatch and resumed. "I drove up here to talk to D.B. about Sapphire running off with Spud, and the next thing I know I'm chained to a bed and interrogated."

"Oh, you done stirred up a regular hornet's nest, and God help you." Ronnie made a last pass with the washcloth at Hensley's face and sat down on the bed next to him. "They don't know whether to spit or go blind." She nodded at the door. "They've been calling D.B., asking what to do with you. And D.B.'s fit to be tied, cursing up a blue streak at them for snatching you in the first place. And now that you're here, he don't have any better clue what to do than them two, and them not even able to find their own butts with a GPS and an ugly detector."

This rush of words, delivered in a single breath, took Hensley's breath away. He finished off the third slice and pondered these things in his heart.

"It's all Percy's fault. Trying to impress D.B. and messing everything up."

"Percy?"

"Percival, I mean. Good thing he's not around to hear me or he'd give me a licking, if D.B. would let him, which he wouldn't, and he better not try if he knows what's good for him. He don't like being called Percy, but what civilized person has the energy to say Percival every time you want a body for something?"

"Indeed." At this point, Hensley felt the need for something with which to wash down the pizza. "Could I trouble you for—"

"He's the one that brought in those drugs in the first place and without asking a soul before he done it. If he hadn't done that, none of this would have happened. And Lord knows nobody up here wanted anything to do with that kind of thing, so where he got off with that harebrained scheme is anybody's guess and nobody knows."

"Drugs?" He might at last get a straight answer about the drugs.

Ronnie slowed down long enough to face him full on, eyes flared open and face flushed with wonderment. "Oh, you don't know the half of it."

As she launched into a full account, Hensley listened with half an ear while he got his first good look at her as illuminated by the light kit on the ceiling fan. The black hair cascading from under her do-rag and pushed behind small, elfish ears was so dark it seemed to glisten with midnight blue highlights.

Hensley rallied with the sense that perhaps he might escape this fresh hell with body and soul intact.

Ronnie's eyes, wide with energy, were a shade of hazel that made one think of the isle of Erin. They were set a bit too close for Hensley's preference, but along with the ears, they conferred a certain whimsical aspect that no doubt many found appealing. Further inspection confirmed that she had been put together by nature in such a manner as few would find objectionable.

He reviewed the substance of her peroration, the gist of which was that Percival, D.B.'s ambitious second, had engaged in certain unauthorized extracurricular entrepreneurial activities with an itinerant meth dealer outside of Albuquerque, doing so with the view of providing a swift infusion of capital for the purchase of weapons or fortifications or a satellite hookup or something of the sort.

But evidently Sapphire or Spud or possibly both, she wasn't clear on this point, had got wind of the transaction and appropriated the stash, which had a street value upward of six digits, to finance a new start on a new life in a new location as yet undisclosed, to the universal consternation of all parties concerned, and particularly to Hensley as he slumped against the headboard of the bed, his legs aching, his soul yearning for a beverage to compliment his meal, doing his best to refrain from clubbing himself into unconsciousness with the empty pizza pan to stop the noise as Ronnie waxed eloquent on her chosen theme.

When Ronnie paused in her frantic narrative for a nanosecond, Hensley raised a finger on his available hand. "This is very illuminating, but could I interject to request a fine ale or other suitable libation to accompany this excellent meal?"

"Oh, no," Ronnie breathed. "D.B. don't allow beer up here, fine or not."

"Then an aged bourbon or rye. Neat is fine."

"He don't allow alcohol of any kind."

Hensley frowned. "What was it I saw you with earlier? The tumbler with a twist of lime?"

"Sparkling mineral water. D.B. trucks it in on pallets."

"That will serve marvelously."

Ronnie left to fulfill his request, and Hensley considered the implications of this new information. The question foremost in his mind was that of how much of this story Chrystal knew? She knew about Spud, but did she know about the drugs? And who had concocted this ridiculous plan—Sapphire or Spud? How did they find out about the stash? Where did they take it? And how did they hope to convert it into cash?

Casting further afield, how much did Judge Cox know? Or Sheriff Powell? Hensley was confident Powell was clueless as a newborn colt. Cox had implied some nefarious game was afoot up at the compound, but Hensley would wager his eyeteeth that the good judge wouldn't have been so blithe if he had known about Sapphire.

Ronnie returned holding a glass tinkling with ice.

Hensley feigned an attempt to take it with his left hand, then shrugged and accepted it with his right.

"Don't that chafe somewhat?" Ronnie inspected his wrist, which was flushed by the ordeal.

"Quite." Hensley jangled his left hand around. "And quite pointless, since the door is kept locked and the window is barred. I don't know what they're concerned about."

"Oh, you poor dear," Ronnie said. "They really got no cause to pen you up like a dog with hydrophoby. I mean, what are you going to do? It's clear as varnish that you don't have a piddling thing to do with anything, just trying to help a poor mama find her baby girl, and they got no cause to go shooting out your windshield, especially it being a rental and all, but they're just plain scared down to their socks, plus Arch being mean as a snake to boot, so what can you do in a case like that?"

Hensley took a fresh look at Ronnie in the harsh overhead light. "You seem an unlikely candidate for conspiracy theorist of the year, if you don't mind my saying so."

"Oh, I don't care none about any of that. I'm just visiting my brother for the summer."

"Which one is he?"

"Arch. The little sawed-off one."

"That crea . . . homunculus is your brother?"

"Different daddies. His was from Alabama."

Hensley nodded as if this explained everything. "And I take it you hail from fairer climes?"

"Georgia. Outside of Savannah."

"Well, that makes all the difference, I should think."

"I like to think so. But it ain't no place to be in the summer. And my fiancé was getting on my last nerve."

Ronnie rubbed her hands along her thighs as if smoothing out her jeans, although as far as Hensley could see, their form-fitting nature prevented wrinkles along the smooth curves of the anatomy.

She leaned toward him with a conspiratorial whisper. "Tell you what I'll do. You seem like a man of honor, and they got no cause to treat you otherwise. I know where Merle keeps some shine stashed out in the taxidermy, no matter what D.B. says. Give me till midnight, and I'll be back in here with the key to them cuffs, and we'll see what we can do about getting you out of here."

Hensley held up his right hand wearily. "I must protest you putting yourself in any danger on my account. I drove up here with my eyes open, and I'll leave under my own steam. But could I trouble you for one last thing?"

She nodded.

"What is Percy's last name?"

"Fisher."

"And one final detail. Do you have the number of D.B.'s cell phone?"

Ronnie patted his leg. "Bless your heart, I knew you for a gentleman the moment I set eyes on you." She pulled a phone from a pocket, walked into the bathroom, moistened a finger, and wrote an invisible number on the mirror.

Then she returned to the bedroom. "Now don't you fret about me. They ain't nothing Veronica Lodge can't handle."

There was something about Ronnie that stirred an immediate sense of admiration in Hensley. Here was a woman who knew her limits, but what was more, knew her power, and she used it when it counted in the service of the greater good of humanity. He wished he could tarry to commune with this kindred spirit, but he was, after all, a man on a mission.

"I don't doubt it in the least, but I can't in good conscience jeopardize your safety. Give no thought to the key to the cuffs. If you tend to the gnomes, I shall see myself out at my earliest convenience."

Ronnie studied him for a long moment as if considering whether he could be trusted to accomplish the task under his own steam. "I never got your name," she finally said.

"Hensley Fletcher, forever in your debt." He held out his hand.

She took it, but not to shake it. Instead, she turned it palm up and traced the lines she found there. Then she looked up at him. "You'll be fine, Hensley Fletcher."

She turned and walked to the door, stopping just beyond the threshold. "But if you find yourself down in Savannah, be sure and look me up."

Hensley affected an abbreviated bow from his position seated on the bed. "You have my word." He blew her a kiss. "Could you get the light? I'd like to get a few dozen winks, give or take. And don't forget to lock the door."

Ronnie smiled, flicked off the light, and pulled the door to. The lock thudded loudly as she snapped it.

Hensley let his eyes adjust to the gloom. Then he gathered the pillows from both bunks, arranged them into a comfortable position, and relaxed, propping his left arm to relieve the pressure from the cuffs. If things went awry and one of the gnomes rushed in, he didn't want to be caught untethered.

He listened to the muffled drone of conversation from the main room and considered his next steps. Despite his preferences, and even his instincts, it looked like he would have to collaborate with Powell. Hensley didn't have the infrastructure to track down interstate drug connections.

Of course Davison did have those connections, but considering how they left things in Galveston, Hensley doubted his brother would be willing to call in any favors on his behalf.

The conversation in the next room died down, and a door opened and closed. Hensley relaxed, waiting to see if Ronnie had gone to fetch the moonshine or if she had taken the party up the grade to the shop he had spotted when he first pulled up to the cabin.

He didn't have to wait long before he heard the door and the clinking of ice in glasses. He gave it another half hour as the volume of conversation gradually increased in proportion to the blood alcohol content of D.B.'s crew.

By then he had approached an approximation of the old Hensley universally loved and admired by all right-thinking citizens. He swung his legs over the edge and groaned into a sitting position. Then he rose gingerly, pushed up on the top bunk with his shoulder, freed the cuffs, and padded into the bathroom, closing the door behind him before he switched on the light.

He leaned over the sink toward the mirror and memorized the phone number one breath at a time. Then he opened the bathroom door slowly. The celebrants had cranked up some music, some kind of frenetic southern rock. Hensley guessed that was Ronnie's doing. He smiled, retrieved a backpack from the closet, and returned to the bathroom.

As he suspected, it was a go bag. Inside he found all kinds of articles one might find useful when fleeing from the feds out a back door at a moment's notice. Such as a Leatherman with which he freed himself from the cuffs. He extracted a small, black metal flashlight slightly larger than a shotgun shell, covered the lens with his hand, and killed the bathroom light. Then he flicked on the flashlight and spread his fingers to allow a sliver of light to illuminate the floor. It was surprisingly bright for its size.

Thus armed, he began his search for the other thing he expected would be a feature of not only this bedroom but every room in the cabin. He started with the ceiling, particularly above the beds, shining a ray of light across the boards, looking for a seam. When that failed, he searched the floor. He finally found what he was looking for under the other bunk bed. A trapdoor.

He switched the flashlight off and shoved it into his pocket. It took a few minutes of slow-motion painstaking work, but he got the mattress propped up against the wall, a few slats set aside, and the trapdoor open without making any noise that would be noticed over the din of the party in the other room, where Ronnie seemed to have goaded Arch into singing "Sweet Home Alabama" by starting off with "Georgia on My Mind."

Hensley retrieved the backpack and dropped it into the crawl-space below. Then he lowered himself down, his feet touching ground when he was waist-deep.

With a final salute to his patron saint in the other room, he tilted the mattress until it leaned on the top of the trapdoor, put the slats back into place, and then lowered the door until the mattress came to rest on the bed and the door settled into place.

Then it was out with the flashlight and a general survey of the area, typical pier and beam construction, taller west toward the front of the house and more constricted to the east. He decided to split the difference and head northwest, which had the advantage of giving him more headroom while leading away from the party.

He crawled through a varying landscape of rodent carcasses and discarded rattlesnake skins, eventually found a screened access panel on the north wall, and kicked it open. The sound of the party probably masked the noise, but still he doused the flashlight and sat in the dark of the crawlspace for a few minutes.

The music bleeding through the floorboards at the other end of the building morphed to The Chieftains. Sounded like "I Tell Me Ma."

Hensley poked his head out of the opening. He was at the northwest corner of the wraparound porch. He peered up over the edge at the parallelograms of light spilling out of the windows and spanning the distance from the cabin to the railing.

Satisfied that Ronnie had everything under control, Hensley grasped the edge of the porch, pulled himself to his feet, and took a few tentative steps.

His feet were tender and his legs ached, but he thought he could make it to the Jeep. He stepped out from the shadow of the porch, stumbled on the grate he had kicked out, and staggered into a diminutive dark form that had chosen that moment to round the corner of the cabin.

Chapter Eighteen: Fisticuffs

Hensley's forward momentum knocked the intruder on his back. Hensley landed belly-first on top of him. He flicked on his flashlight. A glassy-eyed Arch squinted up at him.

Something hard rested between them. Hensley flicked the light down. The whiskey bottle, which Arch nestled against his chest in the crook of his arm.

"Hey," Arch shouted. "How did you—"

Hensley slapped a hand across the little man's mouth. "It's Archie, isn't it?"

Archie's eyes bulged. He nodded.

"Well, it may be occurring to you right about now that you failed to cover all your bases. Like checking me for weapons."

Hensley snapped off the light, reached to his waistband in the small of his back, flipped the flashlight around in his hand so that the butt end now pointed out of his fist like the barrel of a gun, and swung it up and placed the cold metal against Archie's temple.

The breath rushing over Hensley's hand doubled in intensity and frequency, billowing out from Archie's face in a small cloud. For the first time, Hensley noted that the temperature had dropped significantly. Quite refreshing.

"Archie, my repellant young hoodlum, you are now faced with the most important choice in your career. As you contemplate your next move, take into consideration that although I have no desire to terminate your employment with extreme prejudice, I will not hesitate to do so if your job performance fails to meet my exacting standards."

In the weak light, Hensley fixed his gaze on Archie. "Do we have an understanding?

Archie nodded as best he could.

"Excellent. First, as recompense for the trouble you've caused me, you're going to set that whiskey bottle aside for my future use."

Hensley pushed himself up with the hand clamped over Archie's mouth. The terrified anarchist set the bottle on the grass.

"Now I'm going to let you up. If you make even a small sound, I'm going to make a very big sound. To clarify for your benefit, things will happen that will probably make the six-o'clock news tomorrow, but you won't have an opportunity to watch it."

Hensley raised an eyebrow for emphasis. Archie nodded vigorously.

"I'm placing my trust in you, Archie. Don't disappoint me." In a quick motion, Hensley rolled away from the porch, placing Archie between him and the cabin, struggled to his knees, and stood.

Archie lay there for a second, watching Hensley with a distrustful squint. He pushed into a sitting position and crawled to his feet.

He was silhouetted by the light from the windows, so Hensley couldn't see his face, but the motion of Archie's head as he stared at Hensley's "gun" hand was unmistakable.

"Hey, wait a minute!"

Hensley swung up the barrel of the flashlight and stepped forward. Archie backed away instinctively.

"Archie, I thought I was clear about you not making a sound."

In the split second of Archie's indecision, Hensley threw the flashlight at him and grabbed the whiskey bottle. Archie charged. Hensley applied the bottle to Archie's head with a satisfying thunk.

He dropped the bottle, spun the dazed Archie around, and locked him in a strangle hold while backing away from the cabin.

Archie's feeble attempts to break the hold faded quickly. Hensley looked around for a place to stow Archie's unconscious form. He spotted the Jeep, which had a front seat full of windshield.

Hensley dropped Archie to the ground and rolled him under the Jeep. He would keep until Hensley found alternate transportation, and if he did awaken, Hensley would hear his struggle and return him to oblivion as required.

After a short search, he found the flashlight. It still worked. Hensley headed up the hill in the direction Archie had come from. In the metal barn he'd seen earlier, he found a white panel van with "Patriot Pest Control" stenciled on the side. The same van he'd been tossed out of three days earlier.

He pointed the flashlight at the ignition, but it was bare. Then he flipped down the visor. A set of keys dropped into the front seat. Perfect.

Hensley jumped behind the steering wheel and shoved the key into the ignition, but paused. He should get a mile or so down the hill before firing up the engine. And he should give himself as much lead time as possible by restraining Archie.

Finding the required materials in the barn was a cinch. He tossed them in the passenger seat, put the van in neutral, and pushed it slowly forward until the front wheels cleared the slab and hit the incline. Then he jumped in and used the brake to ease down to the cabin, stopping in front of the Jeep.

As he got out of the van, he glanced at the cabin windows. The playlist had changed to Hank Williams Jr., but otherwise everything seemed copacetic. The whiskey bottle glinted in the grass. Hensley picked it up. Powers. Hensley smirked, grabbed a roll of duct tape from the van, and proceeded to the Jeep.

He found Archie right where he had left him, sleeping the sleep of the just. He dragged him out, wrestled him behind the driver's wheel of the Jeep, taped his hands to the steering column, and then applied a section to his mouth for good measure.

On a whim, Hensley wriggled Archie's wallet from his back pocket and inspected the contents with the flashlight. Three hundreds and some odd twenties and such. Hensley appropriated the cash, leaving behind a few ones as a memento of their good times together.

Then, for the crowning touch, Hensley opened the bottle of Powers, took a swig, poured a goodly amount on Archie's shirt, and then set the bottle between the man's legs.

As he turned toward the van to make his exit, the floodlights on the porch flared, illuminating Archie behind the wheel of the Jeep. The screen door slammed.

"Arch, what in Sam Hill are you doing?"

The van blocked Hensley's view, but he knew the voice and it failed to set him aquiver with joy and anticipation.

As heavy footsteps thudded down the porch stairs, Hensley darted to the shadows of the van, opened up a back door, and grabbed the first thing he could turn into a weapon. It was a lug wrench, the cross-bar type with four socket sizes. He peered around the driver's side, which was illuminated by the porch light, just in time to see Merle slam the driver's side door and walk around the front of the van.

Hensley slipped to the other side. Merle looked around in the shadow of the van, glanced at the Jeep, and caught sight of Archie.

"I see how it is," he yelled. "Hogging the good stuff all for yourself." He strode to the window and reached in, but snatched his hand back without taking the bottle. He spun around in an awkward pirouette, catching his balance with a hand against the hood of the Jeep, and spied Hensley behind the van.

With a roar, he charged. Hensley fired the lug wrench at him like a shuriken. It caught Merle on the right shoulder and bounced off his head as it whirled past and slammed against the front fender of the Jeep.

Merle staggered sideways and stopped with his hands on his knees. He stood, raising his right hand to his head, but winced and used his left hand to check for blood.

Hensley turned to the van for another weapon. Something with a longer reach. He snatched up a set of jumper cables and twisted the alligator clamps so the ends didn't meet. Then he darted into the shadow of the van.

The floodlights from the porch glared down on Merle like spotlights from a prison tower. He glanced at his left hand for blood, then used it to shield his eyes. He started toward Hensley with a growl.

Hensley kept to the shadows. He adjusted the cable so that a three-foot length hung down from either hand.

As Merle neared, Hensley stepped away from the van and swung the ends of the cable on either side like a paddle wheeler. One clamp caught Merle under the chin, the other hit him under the wrist of his left hand.

Merle's head snapped back. He howled in pain as he staggered sideways. He probed his chin with his left hand, his fingers coming away bloody. He raised his left arm and stared at the blood running from a gash in his wrist and dripping off his elbow. Then he glared at the one responsible.

Hensley pulled back into the shadow of the van to await Merle's next move. He kept the cables twirling in a slow loop like he was jumping rope.

"I do apologize for the inconvenience, old boy, but I'm afraid I'm going to have to ask you to get into the Jeep and tape your left hand to the steering wheel. If it's any consolation, it will help stop the bleeding." Hensley nodded at the roll of duct tape on the hood.

"When I'm done with you, you're going to need that duct tape to put your head back on."

"Wrong answer, I'm afraid." Hensley swung the cables above his head like two helicopter blades spinning in opposite directions.

Merle charged. The first clamp hit him flat on the left side of the head. He staggered but kept coming. Hensley aimed the other cable lower and wrapped it around Merle's neck, the clamp catching his Adam's apple.

Merle let out a roar and grabbed at the cable. He looped it around his right arm and pulled Hensley closer.

Hensley spun the other cable up to speed, wrapped it around Merle's neck, and jerked with all his weight.

Gasping for air, Merle pulled back on the cable. They stood poised in a macabre tug of war for an instant. Then Hensley charged at Merle.

Suddenly off balance, Merle staggered backward. Hensley leapt up, planted a foot on Merle's chest, and slammed the giant to the ground on his back.

Hensley allowed his momentum to carry him past Merle's head. He spun around and pulled the cables tight, dragging Merle by the neck, inch by inch, toward the Jeep.

Face crimson and eyes distended, Merle managed to scramble to his knees, get one foot on the ground, and lunge. He got his arms around Hensley's waist and drove him backward against the side of the Jeep.

Hensley's head bounced against the center pillar. He was blinded by the pain for a second. Long enough for Merle to begin clawing his way up Hensley's body to a stand. Hensley reached back into the driver's window, grabbed the whiskey bottle, and splashed some into Merle's face.

Merle let go, and Hensley clubbed him with the bottle. Merle dropped to his knees, tried to stand. Hensley hit him again, and the giant finally fell.

"What does a girl have to do to get a drink around here?" Ronnie stepped around the van holding a tumbler of ice in her right hand. She looked from the whiskey bottle in Hensley's fist to the bruised and bleeding Merle lying on the ground, panting. "If I was you, I'd cut him off. Just saying."

Hensley straightened up, staggered to Ronnie's side, and awarded her with a generous pour.

She held the glass out to him. "Looks to me like you could use this a whole lot more than me."

"I never drink whiskey on the rocks." Hensley turned the bottle up and drank enough to soften the pounding of his head.

Ronnie took a sip of her whiskey and surveyed the damage. "Think you could give me a ride to the airport?"

Hensley shrugged. "Sure." He nodded at Merle. "But first, can you help me get him into the Jeep next to Archie?"

Ronnie frowned. "Why?"

"I have a thing about symmetry."

Together they guided Merle to the passenger seat. Hensley used his talents to render him unconscious and then duct-taped his left hand to the steering wheel. He rolled down the window and taped his right hand to the side-view mirror. On a whim, he retrieved the rental contract from the glove box.

"That should give us a good twelve-hour head start." He turned toward the van but had a thought and stopped. "Could I trouble you to retrieve Merle's wallet?"

"Why?"

"The first time I met this comedy act, they caught me at a disadvantage and relieved me of a third of my operating capital. I'd like to replenish it if possible."

Ronnie shrugged and did the needful. "Two hundred and seventy-three dollars."

"Close enough. Leave the ones."

She tossed the wallet onto Merle's lap and held out the cash to Hensley.

He stuffed the money into his pocket and suddenly felt the impact of the full slate of indignities to which he had been subjected over the past few hours. He laid a hand on Ronnie's shoulder to steady himself as he guided her to the van. "If you could be so good as to take the wheel for the first leg of the journey, I shall be forever in your debt."

She climbed into the driver's seat. "You'll have to hold my drink."

As they bounced down the gravel road to the highway, Hensley took time to reevaluate his most recent life choices. He had taken on The Case of the Absconding Daughter as a favor, the brief detour of a good Samaritan, but the situation had escalated from an elopement to a felony.

It was one thing to subdue a randy teenager and talk sense into the daughter of a former love, but quite another to do so while fending off a militia wing nut desperate to retrieve his stolen drugs.

Hensley glanced at Ronnie, whose face glowed green in the light from the instrument panel. "What sort of fellow is the gallant Percival?"

"Ex-military, like D.B., but like, kind of young for his age."

"Somewhat impulsive? Ambitious would you say?"

"Oh, you can say that again. The best thing to do around Percy is to keep your mouth shut. One wrong word and you're done. He can rant for hours without taking a breath about the Patriot Act and the military-industrial complex. I wouldn't be surprised if his closet is full of tinfoil hats, at least one for every day of the week."

"Is he the violent type?"

"He's got a temper like a rattlesnake. Rattles a lot, but I never saw him strike." She shrugged. "On the other hand, I haven't never seen him provoked with something like this before. Don't know where he got the cash, but he's out a lot of money. More than I'm likely to see in a stack all in one place. He blew out of here like that thing in the cartoons that looks like a tornado."

"It's been a while since I've shared a drink with D.B., but he seemed like a man who could take care of himself."

"I wouldn't worry your head about D.B. He's three times the man Percy is."

"What about Spud?"

Ronnie frowned. "I only saw him once. Reminds me too much of Arch."

Hensley settled back in the seat and closed his eyes. In his considered opinion, the best path forward was to entrust the rescue of Sapphire to D.B. Instead, Hensley would work at The Tinker's Dam for a while to pay off the credit cards, Davison's and Chrystal's, and rebuild his stake. But it might be a good idea to brief Cox on the developments.

He woke up when Ronnie pulled off the road on the north side of town for gas. He took over the driving duties, made sure she was settled into a room in a motel near the airport, and then turned the nose of the van toward the outskirts of town.

Just before two a.m., Hensley pulled into the parking lot of The Tinker's Dam. It was packed.

It was doubtful that anyone would come looking at a dive bar for a Patriot Pest Control van, but to be on the safe side, he parked behind the Airstream, which was behind the building.

He flopped out of the driver's seat like a soggy beach towel slipping off a deck chair and took a moment to stretch his legs, then his arms, his neck, and his back.

Hensley was a man who could take it as it comes, even when it came hard and fast directly to the chin. A good night's sleep would go a long way toward reversing the effects of an evening's entertainment with Merle and Archie.

Even so, he couldn't help but reflect that a mere twenty-four hours ago he was in Philadelphia sampling Uncle Rex's scotch collection and mapping out the plans that ultimately led him to this spot.

He locked the van and walked into the bar through the back door just as Tink rang the bell for last call.

"Just in time," Hensley said as he sat down on a stool. "Set me up with a double shot of the good stuff."

Tink scowled. "If this is how it's going to be, you're going to have to pay for the room up front."

"Had to see a man about a dog."

"Clear the room and we'll see about the whiskey."

Hensley slid off the stool. "Do I get an employee discount?" He took it slowly, making one round with a trash barrel, then another setting chairs on tables and setting things in order.

When the last cowboy staggered outside, Hensley barred the door, turned off the outside light, and returned to the bar.

Tink was counting the till, so Hensley went behind the bar, located a dust-covered bottle of Laphroaig 10 and a glass, perched himself on a stool, and poured a generous shot.

After a contemplative sip, he emptied the tip jar and shoved the lone twenty toward Tink. "Take it out of my tip."

Tink stuffed the twenty in his shirt. "That won't cover it."

Hensley shrugged. "I'll work it off tomorrow."

They fell into a benign silence as Tink counted the money and slipped it into a bank bag. Then he poured himself a shot from the bottle and drank it in one go.

"Master Tink, I must say that I found the hospitality of your garden-variety militia wing nut to be more demanding on the physique than I had anticipated."

Tink set the glass on the bar and looked at Hensley. "That reminds me. The sheriff came asking about you right after you left. 'Bout as cheerful as a grizzly with a sore tooth."

DAY 6: TUESDAY

Chapter Nineteen: Feint

Hensley emerged from the trailer at the crack of noon, the worse for wear but ready for another day of fighting the good fight. He wore the button-down shirt, jeans, and boots, and he carried the jacket, because the weather still hadn't figured out which zip code this was.

He nodded at Tink, who sat behind the bar drinking orange juice and reading *The New York Times* on his tablet. "Just going to make a quick call."

Tink grunted.

Hensley closed the door to the office and called the 800 number on the rental agreement. It took a few buttons to get to a human. "I would like to report a stolen car."

It took a few more minutes to quell the consternation on the other side of the line. He provided the requisite information from the contract and improvised a pub crawl in Pagosa Springs, the dismaying discovery of a missing Jeep, and the subsequent ride back to Santa Fe with an accommodating trucker. After assuring them that he would file a report with the local authorities, Hensley rang off, waved to Tink on the way out, and pointed the van toward town.

Last night when Tink revealed that Powell was looking for him, Hensley was far from alarmed. Despite his natural lack of affinity for the Boy Scout in question, he had already formed a plan to seek out the sheriff and pass the torch to him.

While Hensley could think of few parties that would be enhanced by the arrival of the authorities, the calming influence of a duly-elected representative of the law might be the perfect antidote to what otherwise appeared to be a large pot of disaster stew in the making. Especially considering the mixed bag of nuts currently in orbit around Sapphire.

He jumped on I-25 and jumped off at Highway 14, the same road where four days earlier he had been ejected from this very van in an inexcusably undignified manner.

At the sheriff's compound, Hensley tumbled out of the van, donned the sports coat for effect, and walked through the heat to the front door.

Inside, he located a reinforced glass window to the right of the entrance, alerted the receptionist to his presence, indicating that he was expected, and learned that the good sheriff was not available for consultation.

As it was now well past lunchtime, a quick repast was in order before he tackled the next candidate on his list. He arrived in downtown on the tail end of the lunch rush, stashed the van on the roof of a parking garage to minimize the risk of it being spotted, and walked the half block to Tia Sophia's. He managed to snag a booth in the back and waved away the menu. There was only one thing to order at Tia Sophia's.

"Christmas burrito, egg over easy. And coffee."

The waitress nodded. Less than a minute later, a man approached with a cup of coffee. "Best I remember, you take it black."

It took mere seconds for Hensley to scroll back a dozen years and dredge up a name. "Carl, your steadfastness is a beacon to us all." Hensley stood and shook his hand. "Still pulling for the Packers?"

"We'll give it a go."

"Do you have another Desmond Howard lined up?"

"Long odds don't scare me. Bring it."

"You are justly famed for your quixotic nature."

"Well, you know what the monkey said when they cut off his tail."

Hensley waited.

"I guess it won't be long now."

Hensley nodded. Carl returned to his duties and Hensley returned to his seat and his ruminations.

Given Powell's ignorance of Chrystal's departure to DC, Hensley was willing to bet that he knew nothing of Sapphire and Spud and the magical cache, nor of Percival's perfidy, nor D.B.'s pursuit. Most likely the next name on his list, Judge Simon Cox, was equally ignorant.

But both clearly placed the welfare of Chrystal and her cubs at the highest of priorities, and when it all went down, having a cop or a judge in the mix to safeguard the interests of the clan couldn't hurt.

In due course, the waitress deposited the award-winning burrito on the table for his consideration. It was about the size of the user manual for the Jeep Hensley had left behind on a mountain in Colorado, but there the similarity ended.

Unlike the manual, the burrito was drenched in melted cheese and circumscribed with red and green chile in a yin-yang configuration. A fried egg topped the concoction, its captive yolk quivering with anticipation. Inside, scrambled eggs, bacon, and hash browns. The aroma of chiles, cheese, and crispy bacon wafted up.

Hensley's eyes rolled up to the waitress. "Transcendent, as expected."

She smiled and left him to absorb the experience. He took the first bite from the red side, savoring the tang of the sauce and the crunch of the bacon. Next, a bite from the green side, where the chiles bit back. Then he ripped the yolk open with a tine of the fork and let it run.

For the next twenty minutes, the cares of the world faded as Hensley communed with the burrito, supplementing it with the occasional sip of coffee.

When he emerged from his epicurean trance, he dropped some cash on the table and bade farewell to the effervescent Carl.

Ten minutes later, he was through security and laying his case before Cox's gatekeeper. A few sentences in, her phone rang. She answered, listened, and looked at Hensley. "Yes, it is." Another pause. "Yes, sir." She hung up the phone and focused her steely gaze on Hensley. "The judge would like to see you immediately."

"Capital." Hensley strode into the judge's chambers.

In a chair across from the judge, Sheriff Powell twisted around to inspect the new arrival. Hensley flinched a micron or so but recovered instantly.

"How fortunate to find you both gathered in one place." He availed himself of the empty chair next to Powell. "I come in regard to a matter that concerns us all."

"The only thing that concerns me is why you're still in town," Powell said. "I made myself clear last Friday."

"Quite so, as did the judge yesterday, and I did not treat either suggestion lightly. I departed less than twenty-four hours after we parted ways and two hours after receiving the judge's advice."

"And yet, twenty-four hours later here you are again a third time," Cox rumbled. He looked to Powell. "I think he might take a little more convincing. Any ideas?"

As Powell settled in his chair to propose a course of action, Hensley stood to make his case.

"Gentlemen, please set your minds at ease. Once this conference is concluded, I have purposed in my heart to leave this beautiful town with no plans to return." After all, the Tinker's Dam qualified, as it was outside the city limits. Or at least he thought it was. "But I have recently come into some intelligence that requires the touch of the professional, and thus I seek to enlist the assistance of two members of that class who inhabit the rarefied air at the top of their profession, and what is more to the point, who share my deep interest in the welfare of Chrystal and those within her care."

Hensley detected a deep-seated growl from the general vicinity of Powell, but Cox was more expressive.

"Maybe you could cut the crap and get to the point before we run you out of town on a rail."

"Ah." Hensley inclined a knowing index finger in the direction of the judge. "You spur me on, and I am eager to follow. Allow me to lay before you the essential details of the matter at hand." He took a deep breath to emphasize the dramatic pause. After all, he was about to gently lay before them a bombshell. Common decency dictated that he give them a moment to compose themselves.

"I have it on the best authority that Spud and Sapphire have absconded with an embarrassing quantity of methamphetamine, upward of six figures, doubtless for good reason. But I fear the authorities at hand will lack sufficient context to extend leniency should they be the first to the scene." He spread his hands in apology. "The authorities outside this room, I hasten to add."

Cox leaned forward, hands on his desk, veins bulging from his neck. Powell shot to his feet.

"What?" Powell looked from Hensley to Cox. "You said they eloped."

"And he was correct insofar as his understanding extended," Hensley said. "I have come by this information within the last twenty-four hours through confidential channels, at considerable risk to my wellbeing." He rubbed his wrist, still feeling the effects of the cuffs. "Please take a seat, and I shall fill in the details."

Powell dropped back into his chair.

Hensley directed a meaningful gaze at the drawer that housed the Bruichladdich. "Although a wee dram would aid in the delivery."

"Get on with it," Cox growled.

"Quite right, sir." Hensley laid the whole story before them— of Percival's overweening hubris, of Spud's devious machinations, of D.B.'s righteous pursuit—making the most of the inherent pathos while eliminating any reference to his trip to the compound. After all, this wasn't about him. Not to mention that such details were available strictly on a need-to-know basis, and the subjects in question weren't cardholders in that elite fraternity.

"And so I will fade into the background, resting the matter in the capable hands of those most suited to the task that lies before us. Or, as I should say, the task that lay before the two of you, since I will take my leave as directed."

As Hensley uttered those words, a silence descended on the room. He stood in anticipation of some sort of response, but none was forthcoming.

"Okay, then. I entrust you with this sacred quest. Should fate deem that our paths cross again in the future, I shall look forward to the story of your success."

He walked out of the room without a backward glance, past the guardian in the antechamber, and into the sweltering afternoon.

One task remained before he returned to his peripatetic life.

CHAPTER TWENTY: CLAYMORE

Hensley backed the Patriot Pest Control van deep into Chrystal's driveway to avoid prying eyes, and retrieved the key, entering through the French doors as he had done before.

The cat greeted him, and he stooped to give it a scratch behind the ears. He had always been partial to cats, how they maintained an aloof independence while availing themselves of the resources of their hosts.

He walked to the nook between the kitchen and the living room, extracted the credit card from his wallet, and set it on the desk.

The daily rate for the car rental was negligible, and he had possessed the foresight to take out the insurance. A Benjamin would be more than ample to cover the cost, but there were considerations. He pulled out all the bills he had recovered from the thugs at the compound and set them on top of the card. It came to over twenty times the daily rate of the car he had rented one day ago, but who was counting? Certainly not Hensley.

He turned to go but couldn't bring himself to take a step to the door. To leave was to leave forever. To close the door on the possibility of what could be.

Granted, the woman he considered the premier candidate for soul mate had drawn a gun on him just three days ago, had deliberately flicked off the safety and cocked the hammer, had driven him from the house and threatened him with worse if he should possess the temerity to cross her threshold at any time in the future.

Hensley was willing to concede that point, but not the death of the dream. At the same time, he had no choice but to acknowledge that Chrystal had left little to interpretation. Leave he must, but he would not leave without some memento of what could have been.

He strode to the master bedroom and located the photo of the foursome on Picacho Peak—Hensley, Chrystal, Fagan, and Sapphire—the lot of them happier than any human had a right to be. In this world at any rate, and who knew if there was another world, another chance, another way to make it real. He slipped the photo from the frame and into the inner breast pocket of his jacket.

It wasn't until he was out of the sliding door, reaching to restore the key to the bottom of the potted plant that it hit him.

Never before had Hensley sought out a souvenir to remind him of a place he had left behind. A token of what he had lost.

From the moment he left the clinic in Angola, he had never taken a backward glance. It was always about the open road. The infinitude of possibility that lay just beyond the horizon.

He had lived a life without regret. Until now.

Until the moment he realized that the infinitude of possibility lay not beyond the horizon but in the photograph. He could rip it from his pocket, tear it into a thousand pieces, but he couldn't excise it from his memory.

And that was what it would remain. A memory. It was out of his hands. He secured the key in the pot and turned to go.

Halfway to the van he stopped. Chrystal had kept this photo for a reason. Had he any right to appropriate it for his own? He retraced his steps, retrieved the key, and returned the photo to its rightful place. He had no further use for it. It wasn't likely a scene he would forget no matter how many drinks he ingested in the effort.

He owed her that much. No, he owed her much more. But what more could he do? He had delivered relevant information to those better suited to bring the whole mess to a satisfactory conclusion. Or had he?

Everyone knew that Sapphire had taken a powder under the spell of the dubious Spud, but nobody knew to where they had fled. A critical bit of information. Perhaps he could turn it up for them.

Hensley checked the clock on the stove. Mid afternoon, close to the time Toni had come to feed the menagerie on Friday. As the cat did figure eights around Hensley's ankles, he checked the feeding dish with a swipe of a finger, revealing a crusty veneer of canned food. He wiped the residue on a paper towel.

It had been twenty-four hours since the feline last fed upon the spoils of the Purina Corporation. Hensley had merely to occupy the premises for a few minutes, perhaps an hour, to have the opportunity to siphon information from the person best placed to know Sapphire's most recent movements. In the interim, he would glean what he could from Sapphire's personal effects.

Hensley moved to the lesser bedrooms. The back bedroom featured a collection of Transformer action figures and a closet full of boy's clothes. A photo of a soccer team sat on the dresser, a gang of prepubescent munchkins squinting into the lens.

Puzzling. Chrystal had made no mention of a third tadpole. He picked up a spiral notebook from the desk by the back window and glanced at the front.

Subject: History

Name: Reggie Bumstead

Chrystal's maiden name. The name she returned to when she divorced D.B. He frowned, dropped the notebook onto the desk, and stepped back to the photo.

Had she adopted a kid, and if so, why? He scanned the boys in the photo but didn't see any with Chrystal's jet-black hair or fair Irish complexion.

It was a mystery, but not the one he had come to solve. In the front bedroom, he found the feminine clothes he expected. He wandered around the room, spotted a spiral notebook on the nightstand, and flipped it open. Interspersed with notes on the sinking of the Lusitania, he found "Mrs. Sapphire Tatum" scrawled repeatedly in voluptuous purple ink. A confirmational detail, but hardly revelatory.

A cursory inspection turned up little of value. Hensley surmised that if a youth of the twenty-first century had a diary, it would be in the cloud, not under a pillow or on the nightstand.

He returned to the kitchen, scouted out options for an afternoon snack, and discovered a roll of tollhouse cookie dough in the fridge. Forty minutes later he had a plate of cookies ready. He made a cup of tea and sampled the provisions.

As Hensley reached for a third cookie, he detected the snap of a deadbolt. The swing of the door followed, and then a query. "Ms. Bumstead?"

Toni appeared, her questioning gaze alighting first on Hensley standing behind the island, then on the plate of cookies, and finally back on Hensley. "Who are you?"

Hensley smiled. "Given the drastic alteration in my appearance, I'm not surprised you failed to recognize me, but I remain Uncle Hensley at your service. Please avail yourself of a cookie. I prepared them in anticipation of your arrival."

Toni's confusion lasted only a few seconds. "Wait. You're that guy."

"Yes, I am indeed that guy. Friend of the family. I just returned from the nation's capital where I consulted Chrystal on the matter of Sapphire's disappearance. To say that she is concerned would be an understatement."

Hensley stepped to a cabinet and extracted a glass. "But first we must attend to the matter at hand. Do you prefer milk, tea, or coffee with your cookies?"

"Uh, Diet Coke," Toni blurted out before she gathered her wits. "But what are you doing here?"

"I am attempting to save Sapphire from herself." Hensley stepped to the fridge, filled the glass with ice, snagged a soda from the interior, and poured it. He gestured to a stool. "Have a seat and a cookie."

Toni studied him for a good fifteen seconds, then climbed on the stool. "I remember you. You dressed up like a clown at Saff's birthday party."

Hensley had long purged that memory from his consciousness, but now it came flooding back in Technicolor. Had he really been that prosaic back in the day? The evidence seemed to suggest so.

"Guilty as charged, I'm afraid." He availed himself of a third cookie. "Those were happier times, but we must address the issue of the moment. The last time we talked, you gave me the impression that Sapphire was with her mother in DC, but we both know that is not the case. I understand Sapphire feels she has found her soul mate, but her mother has practically turned inside out worrying about her only daughter."

Toni nibbled nervously on a cookie. "I don't know where they went."

"And by 'they' you mean Sapphire and the young Tatum."

"Uh, yeah."

"Your best friend ran off with her boyfriend and told you nothing?" Hensley focused his most penetrating gaze upon Toni. "Surely you don't expect me to believe such an absurd story."

Toni took a bigger bite of the cookie, chewed it thoroughly, and washed it down with a gulp of soda. Hensley leaned his head forward and directed a measured frown at Toni. They sat in silence for a period of time that Hensley suspected would feel like hours to Toni, although it was barely fifteen seconds.

"Seriously," Toni blurted. She took a deep breath and blew it out with the sound of defeat. "Okay. I tried to talk her out of it. I mean, she's not even old enough." She took a gulp of soda. "I told her they would come after her, and Spud could end up in jail."

"He's over sixteen, I take it."

"He's a senior. Or would be if he was still in school."

Hensley considered this for a moment. Based on what he had seen in the notebook, Sapphire was bent on marriage. And based on Toni's comment, he surmised that sixteen fell below the age of consent. A dangerous combination for a young woman with a mind of her own. But he kept coming back to a pronoun.

"They would come after her? Who is this 'they' of which you speak?"

"Duh. D.B. He hates Spud more than Ms. Bumstead does, and that's saying something. He said if Spud messed with Sapphire, he would nail his—" Toni caught herself and regarded Hensley with narrowed eyes. "Why do you care anyway?"

Hensley stepped to the stove for more tea. "The way I see it, there are only two ways for this to play out." He filled his mug, returned to the island, and took a sip before setting the mug down and arresting Toni's attention with a focused stare. "The best case scenario is that Sapphire goes to jail. For a long time. Assuming the authorities get to her first."

Toni frowned. "Why would Saff go to jail?"

"That's what usually happens to someone caught in possession of a half-million dollars of crystal meth." Hensley didn't know the exact amount, but neither did Toni, so he chose the number for its shock effect. And it did the trick.

Toni jumped off the stool, knocking her glass over. "She would never—"

"Oh, but she did." Hensley stepped to the sink and snagged a roll of paper towels. "You didn't know?" He tore off a dozen and dropped them on the spill.

"No! I mean, Saff would never be involved with drugs."

Hensley nodded. "That's how it works. They never are right up until the moment they are. And then they are." He soaked up the spilled soda and tossed the paper towels into the sink. "After all, it takes a little capital to run off and start a new life together."

Toni squinted at Hensley. "You're making this up."

"Believe me, nothing would give me greater pleasure than to shout 'April Fool' and share a good laugh, but I have talked to the people to whom the drugs belong, and I can assure you that no one will be laughing if they find Sapphire before we do." Hensley poured Toni more soda. "That is the other scenario. The worst case. And we decidedly do not want to think about that one."

"No. I can't believe it."

Hensley slid the glass toward her. "Take a long drink, settle yourself on the stool, and give me another sixty seconds."

Toni pondered for a good fifteen seconds before returning to the stool, but she didn't pick up the soda.

Hensley planted his palms on the island and leaned forward. "Do you remember what you did after the last time we talked?"

Toni nodded. "I called Uncle Bobby."

That explained a few things about the rapid response four days ago. "Who is, as we know, the sheriff of Santa Fe County."

Another nod.

"And who paid me a visit, and through various inducements and persuasions, urged in the most emphatic terms that I should not return to this town, much less to this house, upon pain of imprisonment or worse."

Hensley took a sip of tea. "Now, my young friend, you know little about me, but rest assured that when a man with a gun tells me I should take the opportunity to enjoy the climate of another time zone, I listen closely and attend with the utmost respect."

To let that information marinate, he paused for another sip. "A scant twelve hours later, I was on a plane flying east with no intention of returning. Since then I have spoken to Sapphire's mother and her godfather. I have been held captive by the thugs her father left behind at the compound while he went in search of her, which is how I know the gruesome details of the drugs."

Hensley considered telling her that he was working with Powell, but he didn't want to say anything that would give her the idea to call her uncle for confirmation.

"Nothing less than the safety of Sapphire would have induced me to return to this house and risk incarceration. I came with the express purpose of enlisting your aid in tracking down Sapphire before the worst happens."

Toni pulled a cell phone from her pocket.

"What are you doing?" Hensley asked.

"Calling Uncle Bobby."

Hensley snatched the phone from her hand before she could hit send.

"Hey!" Toni lunged across the island.

Hensley dodged her hand. "Let's finish our conversation first. If I am going to be of any help, I need to be clear of this house before you call." He set the phone on the counter behind him. "Give me a few minutes, and then you can do what you feel you must with no objection from me."

She didn't like it, but she settled back down on the stool, pouting.

After taking a deep breath, Hensley plunged forward. "I believe you when you said you didn't know about the drugs. For all we know, Sapphire wasn't aware of them either. Spud could have masterminded the whole thing without telling her. But either way, she's now on the run with a small fortune in Class A pharmaceuticals. You knew they were running off together. Did she say where they were going?"

Toni shook her head slowly. "She didn't know. Exactly."

"Did she mention options?"

Wrinkles appeared on her forehead as she considered this question. "Well, Saff said Spud had some cousins up in Portland they could stay with for a little while."

"Maine or Oregon?"

"There's two Portlands?"

"They're three thousand miles apart, so it's important to start looking in the right one."

Toni shrugged. "I don't know." She reached for the soda and then stopped. "She said there were mountains. A cabin."

"Mt. Hood. Oregon."

"Sure. I guess."

That gave him something to go on. They couldn't fly, not with ten pounds of meth, maybe more.

"Does Spud have a car?"

Tori snorted. "Well, duh. If you can call it that."

"What kind?"

"Brown. Ugly. Ozone killer."

"I'm going out on a limb here and guessing that 'Spud' is not the given name of the Tatum in question."

"Huh?"

"Do you know Spud's real name?"

"Wilber."

"Wilber Tatum?"

"It's really Wilberforce, but nobody calls him that."

"I shouldn't wonder." With the full name, he might be able to ascertain the make and model of Spud's car, assuming it was registered in his name and not stolen.

They had a head start of a week, more than enough to make the thousand-or-so-mile drive even if they went slow and laid low. But it was also possible that they were still en route. Could have encountered car problems, and they may be drug rich, but that didn't mean they had cash.

"Did she say what they were doing for money?"

"She just said Spud was taking care of that."

Which could mean he was counting on the drugs to solve that problem, but it wasn't easy to turn meth into cash if you weren't already a player, and if Spud or his family had been players in that game, they wouldn't have been strangers to Cox's courtroom.

Hensley would pass this info on to Cox once he was back at The Tinker's Dam.

He picked up Toni's phone and handed it to her. She scrolled through her contacts.

"One thing you should consider," Hensley said. "Telling your Uncle Bobby now that you knew about Sapphire's plans a week ago might not turn out well. And he has no jurisdiction outside of the county, so he can't do anything about it anyway." He shrugged. "Just something to think about. But you do what you think is right."

Toni stared at him for a moment, then slipped the phone into her pocket. "I have to feed the animals."

Hensley snatched a cookie for the road. "Be sure to take these with you. I made them just for you." He turned to leave out the back door but paused and turned back. "Toni."

She looked up from the cabinet from which she was retrieving a can of cat food.

"Thank you for your help. I appreciate it, and I know Chrystal does too. And eventually, so will Sapphire."

Toni winced. "I doubt it." She stuck the can in the opener and the cat materialized as if from a teleporter.

Then Hensley remembered something. "One more thing. The back bedroom?"

Toni grabbed a spoon from a drawer. "What about it?"

"Who is Reggie?"

"Well, duh. Sapphire's little brother."

"Adopted?"

The smirk combined with the furrowed brow conveyed the thousand words of her contempt for his ignorance.

The situation puzzled Hensley. Reggie hadn't been in evidence at Fagan's apartment. And Chrystal hadn't said anything about another husband. Of course, she'd had a few other things on her mind, such as, reading from left to right, the disappearance of Sapphire and the reappearance of Hensley. But no one else had mentioned it either. Not the sheriff. Not the judge. In fact, Tink said Chrystal had sworn off men after Hensley left.

On the other hand, the kid had her maiden name, so that meant a lot. But what exactly?

"How old is he?"

Toni paused in dishing out the food into the cat's dish. "I thought you were a friend of the family."

"Yes, but matters of interest in other hemispheres have prevented me from staying in touch the last decade or so."

"He just turned eleven last month."

He took a moment to do the math. Reggie was born the May after Hensley left for the Andes trip. Nine months after.

A glacier coursed down Hensley's spine, transforming the landscape of his life. The distinct flutter of dark wings beating above his left shoulder combined with the knife of an alarm bell, and his knees suddenly refused to perform their required duties. He grabbed the island for support.

"Who is his father?" he choked out.

Toni turned back to the feeding of the cat. "He's dead."

Chapter Twenty-One: Bombshell

But you're dead.

That's what Fagan had said when he saw Hensley on the doorstep of his apartment.

Not *supposed to be dead.* Just *dead.* Like it was a fact. Like it explained to everyone why he had never returned to assume his fatherly duties toward his son.

"How did he die?" Hensley asked.

Toni opened the top of the fish tank. "Fell off a mountain down in Mexico or somewhere. Never found the body."

"That's too bad. Where is Reggie now?"

Toni slammed down the lid of the fish tank, causing the occupants to spasm around the interior. "In Washington. With Chrystal." She shook her head. "I thought you went there."

"It was late. He was probably in bed. I didn't stay long."

Toni turned away and dipped a scoop into a bag of birdseed.

Hensley lunged to the front door. "Thanks for your help. Bye."

Toni's car was out front, facing north. He staggered down the walk and headed south. He dropped onto the curb behind a sprawling agave plant and kept an eye on Chrystal's house as he gathered his wits.

If Toni was to be believed, all indicators pointed toward the possibility . . . No, the likelihood . . . that Hensley was father to an eleven-year-old soccer player named Reggie.

But it was an impossibility. Hensley knew this because early in his career he had realized, and quite rightly, that his nature did not contain the stuff of which fathers were made, and he'd taken measures to assure that such an eventuality would never transpire.

The ancient philosophers all agreed that the only certain things in this world were death and taxes, and from what Hensley could see, they were right on both counts, but coming in at a photo finish for third was the vasectomy. The failure rate was two hundredths of a percent.

At the time, it had seemed like unbeatable odds, but now that Hensley took a moment, it worked out that out of every five thousand men who went under the knife, life would find a way to persevere for one poor schmuck.

One out of five thousand were long odds indeed, but nowhere near as long as for the lottery, which came in at one in fourteen million, and people bought lottery tickets every day hoping to beat those numbers.

Hensley jerked to his feet. No. It could not be. He turned to walk back up the street, saw Toni come out of the house, and dropped back down behind the agave plant, peering through the tangle of leaves until her car disappeared around a corner.

He hurried back up the sidewalk and up the driveway, past the Patriot Pest Control van, into the backyard, and to the French doors, which he found locked. That Toni was a clever girl, but no match for Hensley. He retrieved the key and was inside three seconds later, ignoring the advances of the feline as he strode down the hall to the back bedroom.

He went directly to the team photo and scanned the rows, looking for a familiar face. He searched a second time and a third.

He looked in the closet. Nothing but clothes and shoes and baseballs and gloves and assorted sports paraphernalia. He turned to the desk. He pulled open the drawer and found a bald eagle staring back at him from the cover of a folder housing a collection of state quarters.

Suddenly Hensley found it difficult to breathe. He dragged the chair back, dropped into it, pulled the folder from the drawer, and placed it on the desk. When he flipped it open, he saw that all the slots were filled except Oklahoma, Vermont, and Kentucky.

But lots of kids collected coins, didn't they? In fact, when he departed on his cycling trip, he left behind a jar with the thirteen state quarters that were released before August 2001. He had planned to fill in Vermont and Kentucky when he got back.

It looked like someone had picked up the torch and collected all the quarters for the next seven years, but no one had gone back to fill in the coins from the second half of 2001.

And that jar explained it. Just because the kid collected coins, it didn't mean he was a Fletcher, son of Hensley the wanderer. It just meant that somebody got him an album for the coins that Hensley left behind.

Hensley pushed away from the desk and traversed the house to the master bedroom. There were other photos on the dresser besides the one from Picacho Peak. On the far end, he found a shot of a kid in a soccer uniform standing on the field with his foot on a ball. Hensley picked it up and held it to the window to catch the light.

That was when he caught the final kick to the gut. The face that squinted into the noonday sun could have been any kid on the planet, but it could also have been taken from his own mother's photo album just before they left the States for Angola. Only it would have been a photo of Hensley with a baseball bat over his shoulder.

With a protracted groan, Hensley staggered back and dropped onto the bed. The implications swarmed his brain in an undifferentiated mass, as if he had just kicked over their nest.

Just the one thing I don't . . . But why didn't Chrystal . . . And why didn't anybody else say . . . Then again, who else knew about . . . Cox knew, I'd stake my stake on it . . . So what does that mean for my chances with . . .

Then it all resolved into a single question.

What am I going to do with a kid?

Hensley sprang from the bed. Who said he had a kid? You couldn't base anything on a slight resemblance. That's what DNA tests were for. After all, it wasn't like his name was on the . . .

Birth certificate!

He tossed the photo on the bed and dashed to the nook and the computer. There was a filing cabinet to the right of the desk. It took a good ten minutes to track it down.

Name of Father: John Doe.

Hensley stared at the blank in the form. John Doe? Who puts John Doe on a birth certificate?

He slammed the drawer shut, found the cell phone bill in the pile of papers on the desk, picked up the receiver of the phone on the desk, and dialed Chrystal's cell phone.

She picked up on the fourth ring. "Hello? Toni? Is something wrong?"

Hensley decided to play against type to throw her off her game. "When were you going to tell me about Reggie?"

"Henz? What are you doing in my house?"

"Or were you going to tell me about him at all?"

A short pause. "Up until a few days ago, you were dead as far as anyone knew."

"You couldn't have told me when I was there? Let me meet him?"

"What? Reggie's not . . ."

Hensley waited for the end of the sentence. Not there? Not well? Not his? "And Reggie's not the only thing you weren't straight with me about. You failed to mention the drugs Sapphire and her boyfriend stole."

There was a longer silence, during which Hensley imagined Chrystal wishing he was in the same room so she could point a gun at him again and finish the job.

"There's a reason for that," she finally said. "Because none of this is your business."

"Genetically speaking, Reggie is fifty-percent my business."

"Eleven years is long enough to make a case for abandonment. You petition the court for joint custody and you'll get laughed out of New Mexico."

There it was. Hensley took a deep breath. "So I am the father."

"You're . . . Of course you're the father! You even have to ask?"

Hensley closed his eyes and let out a long breath. The words sank into his innermost parts like a citrus marinade. He knew the moment he saw the photo, but looks aren't proof, and there was always the possibility of a loophole.

Most men were thrilled to have a son, but Hensley wasn't most men. Not by a long shot. A very long shot. With knobs on.

He wasn't the kind to toss the ball in the backyard every weekend and go to games and have a talk with the kid when he got crossways with his teacher. He was more the kind to give the kid a twenty and tell him to do his best to stay out of jail.

But it seemed like he should at least get a look at the kid. Maybe something would click. Was that what he wanted? He owed it to himself, and the kid, to find out. "I have no desire for custody, joint or disjoint, but we should at least set eyes on each other."

"Okay, riddle me this, Einstein. Which is worse? For Reggie to think his father died while mountain climbing or to learn that his father didn't want him?"

"I didn't know about him."

"And why was that?"

"I told you—"

"Oh yeah, that story about nine-eleven and the Lebanese passport and the winery. That will make a lot of sense to an eleven-year-old."

Maybe she was right. After all, what did Hensley know about eleven-year-old kids? He wasn't even sure that he had ever been eleven. And maybe she was right about the other thing. What if, in the throes of the psychological moment, Hensley found himself unmoved, just as undesirous of fatherhood as before?

The last thing he wanted to do to the son he never had was to traumatize the poor tadpole just before he walked out of his life forever.

But he still wanted to see him, be in the same room, wait for the lightning that might come. "I propose that I return to your location. You can—"

"No. Absolutely not. You show up here, I'll call the cops."

"But I won't be returning as the long-lost father. Just introduce me as an old friend of the family. Uncle Hensley if you like."

"Don't waste your time. He's not even here."

Hensley frowned. "Staying with friends here in Santa Fe?"

"Lose my number. And get out of my house. I'm calling Bobby right after I hang up."

If she could have slammed down a mobile phone into the cradle, Hensley had no doubt that she would have done so. He also had no doubt she was calling the good Sheriff Bobby at this very moment. And she had every right.

Hensley set the phone down and began the process of erasing evidences of his presence in the house, beginning with the mess in the kitchen. As he scrubbed the cookie sheet, he considered what to do about the search for Sapphire.

The whole point of the project was to demonstrate to Chrystal that he was a changed man, but that no longer mattered. He could see that no amount of goodwill he might generate from restoring Sapphire to the bosom of her family would trump Chrystal's burning passion for assuring that Hensley and Reggie would never occupy the same zip code.

It was over.

As he straightened up the kitchen in preparation for his departure, the phone rang. He stepped to the nook and stood over it, almost letting it go to voicemail, but thought better of it and answered.

"Bumstead residence."

"Hey," Fagan whispered over the noise of running water. "Mom's not lying. Reggie isn't here."

"Does it matter?"

"Percival snatched him on the way home from school."

"The Percival who recently lost a large quantity of Class A pharmaceuticals?"

"Affirmative. Evidently he's using Reggie as leverage to get the drugs back."

Reggie kidnapped? "Did Chrystal go to the authorities?"

"D.B. came by and told us about it, said he would track down Reggie and Saff and get them back. He said if we called the FBI, Saff would likely be arrested for trafficking drugs, and given the quantity . . . well, you can see how that would turn out."

"What about Powell?"

"That was the one lie she told. Calling Powell would be worse than calling the Feds."

Fagan always was the clever one. "Judge Cox?"

"Keeping him out of the loop was tougher, but we couldn't take the chance."

"So Sapphire is on the run, Percival is after her with Reggie as a bargaining chip, and D.B. is the only one on the case."

"That's why I called. You're not exactly . . . inexperienced with situations that require . . . flexibility. And you can hold your own in a fight."

"But—"

"Just don't tell Mom how you found out. Now I have to get wet and shave so it looks like I really did take a shower."

"Just so you know, both Powell and Cox know about the drugs." Silence. "Fagan?" Hensley set the phone in the cradle, checked the caller ID, and wrote the number on the paper in his wallet. For good measure, he wrote down the number for D.B. he had memorized from the bathroom mirror at the compound.

On a whim, he dialed Sapphire's number, preparing a greeting, but it went straight to voicemail. He hung up and stepped to the patio door.

Hensley doubted that Toni would call Powell, out of an instinct for self-preservation if nothing else, but he had no interest in pushing his luck.

He took a final look around. No matter how things turned out, there was a very good chance he would never be in this house again. He opened the door, hesitated, and then trotted to the master bedroom.

The photo of Reggie lay right where he had tossed it. He flipped the frame over, popped the back off, and extracted the four-by-six print.

Back in the Patriot Pest Control van, he tossed the photo into the glove box and pointed his trusty steed toward The Tinker's Dam. He had to tie up a few bows before he set out in search of the son he never knew he had.

CHAPTER TWENTY-TWO: CRUX

Given the weather, Hensley stopped by Goodwill for a Tommy Bahama aloha shirt and a pair of board shorts. He found a buffalo nickel in the change and dropped it into his shirt pocket, shoving the rest in his pants pocket.

On the drive back, he tried to quell the raging machinery in his mind. He had a son. He should have guessed when he saw the first name, the same as his own first name, but he cut himself some slack. When the obvious was impossible, one dismissed it. If he remembered correctly, Sherlock Holmes had said the same.

The bottom line was that he had no choice but to pursue the leads he had gathered and retrieve his son from the locus of danger. He'd gather his wits, rest up for the marathon drive to the west coast, and pull out at sunrise.

At The Tinker's Dam, he once again hid the van behind the Airstream, made a quick change to temperature-appropriate clothing, and entered the bar by the back door.

Barely six p.m. on a Tuesday and the place was three-quarters full, all the pool tables occupied and hopefuls lurking.

Tink was pouring a bucket of ice into one of the coolers. "Good work if you can get it."

"How much custom do you typically get before the proles clock out?"

Tink dropped the bucket on the cement floor and slammed the cooler lid. "You been here before, right?"

He had a point. Even back at the turn of the millennium the place was never less than half-full, regardless of the hour.

Hensley stepped up to the bar, grabbed a towel, and dragged it around on the pristine surface. "Take a moment for yourself. Perhaps a cucumber facial with aromatic candles and zither music. Come back tomorrow. Tonight I shall take all comers and acquit myself with honor."

Tink grunted, snatched up the bucket, and disappeared out the back door. Hensley leaned on the bar with a practiced slump and gazed out onto the narrow slice of the local demographic that presented itself at The Tinker's Dam. Largely male, ranging from the cusp of drinking age to upper thirties, exclusively blue collar. Or no collar, as the case may be. His people.

While his vocabulary, accumulated through a self-imposed reading program that began before his first day of elementary school and continued throughout his life, might give the casual observer the impression of a formal education, his parents had evidently not felt the need to provide their sons with such a course of study. Or rather, not until Hensley adjusted their understanding by disappearing at age sixteen. Their course correction resulted in providing Davison with the educational opportunities denied to Hensley.

Not that he begrudged his brother the opportunity. It was his and welcome to it. Between the two of them, Hensley was more suited to the life of the autodidact. He had parlayed his modest stake into an audience with a king and had shared a glass with the lowliest of the realm. In the same day.

While he had held his own among the frothy superstructure of society on more occasions than he could count, Hensley was most at home with the great unwashed, the cogs that kept the machine turning. And it was those people he saw before him tonight.

Hensley nodded with appreciation. Tink had done a fine thing here keeping this place going all these years. But he could do even more, given the right guidance.

For example, here it was late in the afternoon, coming on dinner time, and no doubt an exodus was imminent. The available comestibles were limited. Pickled eggs, jerky, beer nuts. Give these poor working stiffs a few options and they would hang on even longer.

Tink wouldn't even have to invest in a kitchen. He could invite a food truck or two to set up shop for a few hours in the afternoon on weekdays. Maybe all day on weekends. Set up a volleyball net outside. Horseshoes. The possibilities were endless.

Hensley started working out a percentage deal for incremental revenue based on his innovations when he realized he was just playing mind games to keep himself distracted from the matters at hand.

Despite his best efforts, he was a father. What did he have to offer a nascent citizen of the world? Sure, he had a few life sessions tucked up his sleeve, but when it came down to it, he was about as useful to a prepubescent tadpole as a severe case of acne.

Yes, he had lobbied with Chrystal to grant him an audience with the subject in question, but she had shown the trademark uncommon common sense of her gender by refusing his request in the most severe of terms.

Hensley sold a couple of beers to the laborers who presented themselves at the bar.

Now that he had the luxury of a few hours to achieve a level of perspective, he realized that Chrystal was right. Who did he think he was fooling with all this "show up and wait for the lightning" nonsense? He had never been a fan of halflings, even when he was one. Was there any reason to expect that his nature would be contravened simply because the munchkin in question shared fifty percent of his DNA?

He snorted a bitter laugh. He had allowed himself to be seduced into a delusion. He had been fashioned by nature, or nurture, who knew or could ever know, as the consummate drone. As such, there were aspects of the human experience denied to him, things he had never missed. Why should he start yearning for them now?

A rogue thought swerved into his consciousness. Son of his or not, the kid had been kidnapped by a desperate would-be drug dealer. Was not this a cause worthy of his efforts?

As he attempted to wrap his rationalizations around this idea, a dumpy kid approached the bar. He'd seen this kid before.

"Four Buds." The kid dropped a twenty on the bar.

"Tyler, my main man, what's the haps?" With a sense of relief, Hensley dropped back into a familiar script. He snagged four beers from the cooler, snapped up the twenty, and returned a ten and two ones.

Tyler stared at the change.

"Is something amiss, my reticent friend?" Hensley said.

"That's too much. It's not happy hour anymore."

"Would that Diogenes were here, he could call off the hounds, cancel the alarm, and rest from his labors."

"But . . ."

Hensley smiled at Tyler's confused expression. "For such distinguished guests as you and your party, we make allowances. Wear it in good health."

Tyler's focus bounced from the beers to the clock to the change in consternation. Then he locked eyes with Hensley and took a deep breath. With a deliberate motion he stuffed the ten in his shirt pocket and dropped the two ones in the tip jar. "Thank you."

A warm glow spread throughout Hensley's being. "Oh, no. Thank you, sir."

Tyler gathered up the beers by the neck, two in each hand. Hensley watched him return to the pool table with the swagger of a man who has done his duty.

Hensley regarded the two bills in the tip jar with pride. He had no intention of adding them to his modest cache. In fact, he decided that the thing to do was staple them to the column at the end of the bar as a testament to the latent charity that lay dormant in the soul of every man.

As Hensley dug into the tip jar to extract them, Tink returned, bearing a brown paper sack.

"Running short on rations, are we?" Tink said.

Hensley held the two bills aloft like an Olympic torch. "Far from it, my stalwart friend. This is a testament to the transcendent potential of the human race. Do you have a stapler handy?" He sampled the aroma emanating from the bag in Tink's hand. "Do I detect cumin?"

Tink dropped the bag on the bar. "Keep this up and you'll owe me before the end of the week." He pulled a foil-covered paper plate from the bag, peeled up the foil, and extracted a taco.

Hensley pulled the foil farther back and snagged a taco for himself. He took an exploratory bite and decided it was likely the most luscious carnitas taco this side of Jupiter. Tender braised pork, lush with spices, and just enough kick to let you know it meant business.

He stepped to the French press to make some coffee. "I shall forever be in your debt for this, my hirsute companion."

"That's what I'm afraid of," Tink said between bites.

"Where did you find these peerless contributions to culinary pantheon?"

"El Chile Toreado."

The coffee deepened the flavor, and Hensley decided that if he got a piece of the inheritance, he'd buy El Chile Toreado. They finished off the tacos in silence, serving the occasional patron as required. Then Hensley covered the front while Tink caught up on paperwork in the office. After last call, Hensley had the stragglers out and everything buttoned down by two.

Back in the trailer, he took a seat in the open doorway, decanted a tumbler of Irish whiskey from the bottle he had procured in town, fired up the cigar he had tried to smoke the day before, and pondered the matters at hand. Should he or shouldn't he?

On the one hand, every known authority on the planet agreed that the more cubic miles of dead air that Hensley put between himself and Chrystal, and by extension Reggie, the better. And Chrystal, knowing that Reggie had been kidnapped, remained steadfast in her opinion that Hensley should remain steadfast in his absence.

On the other hand, if he was honest, which he frequently was when circumstances dictated, Hensley could see their point. On what basis could he argue that the burning need in Reggie's life was the immediate and continual presence of more Hensleys?

Hensley knew about as much about fathering as he did about zero-gravity hydroponic farming. Less, actually, since he at least had some vague sense of what was involved in hydroponics.

His own father had seemed to be equally clueless. He was in medical school when Hensley was born, and then moved on to a residency, which meant Hensley was rarely in the same room with his father before he moved the family to Angola to build a clinic.

But the near constant proximity they enjoyed in Angola had no appreciable impact on their relationship, except for plunging Hensley into indentured servitude in the clinic. If Hensley could add up all the conversations that had passed between them—and by conversation he meant any communication that concerned something beyond the mechanics of clinic operations—the number would total half a dozen at most.

When it came to Hensley and the whole fatherhood thing, all indications pointed to endorsing the cease-and-desist policy advocated by the general populace.

On the other other hand, there was Fagan, who seemed to think that in the matter of Reggie's abduction, Hensley should model his response along the lines of Liam Neeson. But he was outvoted three to one by those older and possibly wiser.

While Hensley couldn't deny that he felt a certain stirring within the inner depths when he learned of Reggie's existence, what right did he have to disrupt the life of the son he had never wanted?

Leave the world a better place than you found it.

Very possibly Reggie's world was better off without Hensley. But something nagged at him. In his experience, the complexity of living in the world couldn't be reduced to a bumper sticker slogan.

If he walked away, caught the next train or plane or rental car to South America, could he live with himself?

Maybe. Hensley had found ways of living with himself in all manner of circumstances, situations that would defy the imaginations of these with more prosaic minds. One did what one must to survive, and who was to judge?

But no man could escape the judgment of his own soul. Hensley's thoughts were drawn back to the father who had abandoned him without ever leaving.

Reginald Fletcher had left the world better than he had found it. In his own way. At the cost of his own family.

Hensley had bailed out at the tender age of sixteen, choosing to make his way alone in the world rather than serve the uncompromising demands of his father's vision.

Even Davison, the consummate follower, had been forced to build his own life from the ground up. The folks had shipped him to the States for an education that would qualify him to continue the work at the clinic, but he had gone so far as to join the Secret Service to declare his independence.

As in many other things, it wasn't really an either/or proposition.

Hensley lacked the transcendent vision that drove his father to ignore everything, even his own flesh and blood, in service to the greater good. It might be a failing, but Hensley couldn't think of anything greater than delivering one small boy from the clutches of a maniacally ambitious militia wing nut.

The next step was clear, and it didn't lead to South America.

It was time to double down, to combine the motto of the Stone family with the motto of the Fletchers.

Leave the world a better place and refuse to be moved.

A lessening of the darkness behind the trailer indicated that dawn was not far off. In Hensley's view, the best time to enjoy the sunrise was on the way to bed rather than from it. In fact, he had chosen this particular temporary job for that specific reason, among others.

He took another draw on his cigar and realized it had expired, reached for the whiskey bottle, discovered it was half empty, and concluded it was time to get horizontal and allow sleep to knit up the raveled sleeve of care. Fortunately it was a short commute to the bed.

As he drifted off, Hensley dismissed the doubts that had plagued him the last few hours. It made sense to leave the job to D.B. and the pros when Sapphire was the target, but Reggie was Hensley's son, the missing link that established once and for all his connection with Chrystal. For the first time in his life, Hensley not only had a chance to play the long game, he wanted to give it a go.

All that stood in his way was the sheriff, the judge, and a Colt 1911 in the hand of his soul mate.

Tomorrow he would defy them all.

DAY 7: WEDNESDAY

Chapter Twenty-Three: Hiatus

After what seemed like three to seven seconds of bliss, Hensley was aroused by a banging on the trailer door. He checked the clock radio. Seven a.m. Two hours of sleep. Despite the solitary debauchery of the preceding hours, he was awake in an instant, scrolling through the list of possible assailants.

Sheriff Powell and Judge Cox were the premier suspects, but to Hensley's knowledge neither of them knew his whereabouts. On the other hand, they were of an indigenous species and in a position to have eyes and ears in the most unlikely places.

A veteran of expedient departures, the first thing Hensley had ascertained upon move-in was an exit strategy. If circumstances required, he could wriggle out the rear window, but it would be a toucher, and he had no desire to submit himself to that indignity if a more congenial exit could be engineered. And in Hensley's world, a congenial exit was the most likely outcome of any situation, ticklish or otherwise.

Hensley slid off the bed, dragging the sheet with him, and veered toward the door while arranging his improvised toga. He pulled the door open to behold Tink, bright-eyed and bushy-tailed, lurking on his threshold. "Tink. This is unexpected, not to say unwelcome."

"Mama has a doctor's appointment in Albuquerque. You'll have to open up." He tossed a set of keys at Hensley.

"It's barely seven," Hensley observed as he snagged the keys.

"Opening time in New Mexico. We're not as liberal as Arizona."

Hensley nodded. He could delay his departure for a few hours. Plus, he had something to ask of the noble Tink, so best to have him at his most congenial. "Nothing would give me greater pleasure."

Tink grunted and walked away.

"You didn't happen to procure breakfast comestibles," Hensley called after him.

"On the bar."

"Good man," Hensley muttered.

He took ten minutes to prepare himself for the outside world, eight of it in a scalding shower and most of that just hanging onto the showerhead and groaning. It would have been twice as long, or longer, but the Hensley sans-hair incarnation was toiletry-optimized.

It was cool out, in the sixties, but Hensley knew the day was destined to deliver temperatures in the high nineties, so he donned the board shorts and the aloha shirt.

Reaping the benefit of his closing-time work the night before, he took a few seconds to verify that all was in order, unlocked the front door, flicked on the "Open" light, and set up shop behind the bar.

The first order of business was to grind beans for coffee. The Tinker's Dam might look like a dive, but . . .

Okay, who was he kidding. It was a dive with a capital V. But Hensley had sought out Scooter Bell in his time of need for more than one reason.

Yes, Scooter was a perennial fixture in the landscape and provided to the cognoscenti such value-added services as could be provided by Bartleby and the others that inhabited his twilight realm. But equally important, in this southwestern desert the good Tinker was an unlikely epicurean, or in the modern parlance, a foodie, and as such could be relied upon in the matters that mattered most.

The beans Hensley liberated from the hermetically sealed jar were devoid of the glistening chocolate sheen that indicated over-roasting. South American by the aroma. He located the kettle and the French press and set to with a will born of fatigue.

As the grounds steeped, he peeled open a breakfast burrito—egg, bacon, serrano—and took an inaugural bite.

It had a kick that let you know it was playing for keeps. He didn't know if it came from El Chile Toreado, but it would do. In spades.

He took another bite and savored the endorphin-generating capsaicin glow.

As he sipped a second post-prandial cup of the silky-smooth medium roast a quarter hour later, the front door opened. A familiar rotund figure approached the bar, dropped on a stool, and hooked a boot heel over the rail.

"What's the strongest thing you got?" Tyler said.

The poor kid looked like he'd been kicked in the stomach. Hensley checked the clock. Eight a.m. He spun a cocktail napkin in front of his patron. "It's a bit early for the general populace."

"I ain't the general populace."

"No, sir, I knew that from the moment we first met." Hensley grabbed a coffee cup. "Could I recommend my drink of choice this morning?" He poured the last of the French press into the cup.

Tyler scowled. "I can get coffee anywhere."

"For the desperate, a variation is available."

Hensley selected a bottle of Powers, pride of Ireland, and splashed in a generous pour to top off the mug. He shoved it across the bar. "On me." He pulled a few bills from his wallet and stuffed them into the till. "Have you yet had occasion to break your fast?"

Tyler shook his head and took a wincing sip of the coffee. It wasn't the heat, so it must have been the whiskey. Tyler's act reeked of bravado.

Hensley snagged the second burrito from the bag and offered it to Tyler. "What are your thoughts on the serrano question?"

"Huh?"

"Can you take it hot?"

Tyler locked eyes with him. "Bring it."

"Consider it brung." Hensley placed the foil cylinder in Tyler's outstretched hand.

As Tyler peeled away the foil, Hensley took the opportunity to case the situation. Something was changed in the young man who sat before him tearing off substantial bites of turbo-charged taco.

"I must confess this is my first morning shift. Are you a regular at this hour?"

Tyler shook his head and gulped down the coffee.

"Then perhaps you could entertain me with the story of how this precipitate reunion has come to pass."

The last third of the taco disappeared down the Tyler gullet. He followed it with the rest of the coffee and presented the mug with the obvious expectation of a refill.

Hensley responded with a calculating gaze and took the mug. "Only the first one is free." He turned to the task of warming water, grinding beans, and the rest of the process. "But I offer discounts for interesting stories."

"Then I get the discount."

Hensley regarded him over the burr of the grinder. "I'll be the judge of that."

Tyler took a deep breath. "We're up in the Companas. Custom house. Spraying texture. As usual, it takes me half an hour to untangle a hundred-foot extension cord Brian rolled up around his elbow yesterday."

"Ah, the age-old cord-rolling controversy." Hensley dumped the grounds into the French press and poured the water. "The elbow roll is the province of mouth-breathers. Personally, I prefer the figure-eight flake over the coil-and-twist, as it is less prone to knuckles."

"Sure." Tyler shrugged. "Works for coiling braided lines on a sailboat. But for extension cords on a job site, it's the daisy chain."

"Of course." Hensley pressed the plunger down. "Easy to store. Easy to unroll."

"And if you start on the right end, you can undo as much or as little as you need."

Hensley poured them each a second cup of coffee. "I find your logic unassailable. Why has the Brian not adopted your technique?"

"Every time I try to daisy-chain a cord when we're packing up, he rips it out of my hands and rolls it around his elbow. Says it's beer-thirty and I'm wasting time. Or says we're working construction, not making arts and crafts for show-and-tell."

"And yet he doesn't mind losing thirty minutes on the front side of the day. I assume you pointed out this inconsistency."

Tyler sipped his coffee. "Yeah. All the time. But this morning I kinda lost it."

"Said some things you regret?"

"Nah. I don't regret a single word." Tyler took a swig of his coffee, then reached across the counter for the Powers and upped his ante.

"You're mounting up a tab," Hensley said.

"I got my severance." Tyler slapped a twenty on the bar.

"That'll go you for a bit." Hensley pushed his mug across the counter. "Now, let me ask you a question. You finished high school, I take it."

"Of course."

"And your best subjects?"

"Science. And math."

Hensley took a deep breath. So often these things just worked themselves out. "You can work construction if you want to, and there's no shame in that. Or you can do other things. Bigger things. But whatever you do, you do it for yourself, not for posers like Brian. Because whatever else you may be, you are three times the likes of him on an easy day and twice on Sunday."

The bravado faded away, and Tyler squinted at Hensley with an uncomprehending stare.

"My youthful friend, the best thing you have done in the past year was to cast aside the petty tyranny of this dubious Brian. You were meant for greater things."

Tyler regarded Hensley like a calf confounded by the sudden appearance of a new gate.

"You are just embarking on this crazy carnival-house ride I like to call life as we know it," Hensley said. "And you're thinking you need people like the odious Brian to get a leg up. But if you think back on your experience, you will see that Brian is nothing more than the guy who copied your work in high school."

Hensley paused to take a sip of the silky medium roast and to let this gem of wisdom soak into the consciousness of the acolyte across the bar.

"What does Brian have to offer you?" Hensley asked. "Technique. Mechanics. Valuable information, to be sure, but I suspect you've already gleaned all there is to be had in that regard."

Tyler considered this statement for a moment, then nodded to acknowledge the truth contained therein.

"For the likes of us, the challenge is not to compete with the likes of the Brians of the world. It's to protect ourselves from becoming the collateral damage of their mistakes. Like you did today."

Hensley emptied the French press as he refreshed both their coffees. He raised his mug toward Tyler.

Tyler responded with a raised mug and an expanded perspective. They clinked mugs and took their respective sips.

"I propose that from this day forth, your first order of business is to decide what business you intend to pursue. Then you look upon the Brians of this world not as mentors but as resources to acquire the knowledge you require to take the next step."

Hensley leaned forward on the bar. "Here is the thing. There are many of them, but there are only a few of us. And we, you and I, can choose to do whatever we want, while they are destined to do whatever they can."

Tyler seemed stunned into silence. His eyes glazed in an unfocused stare directed somewhere between their two mugs. Hensley knew better than to break the mood. He busied himself with clearing the wrappers from the counter and rinsing out the French press.

Eventually Tyler emerged from his trance and caught Hensley's eye. "But you're just a bartender."

"Of course I am. And you're just a drywall hanger." Hensley set the French press upside down on the edge of the bar to dry. "Or am I wrong about that?"

Tyler considered this for a moment. "Yeah. I mean, no. You're wrong." He finished off his Irish coffee and set the mug on top of the twenty. "Keep the change."

Then he slid off the stool and lumbered out.

Hensley watched him go. There was a kid who might do something. He wouldn't be surprised if, in five years, maybe ten, he'd see a write-up in some paper of what the boy had accomplished. Or not. Maybe Tyler would just do his thing and nobody beyond his own family would ever know about it.

But Hensley would know. Tyler would do something worthy of the challenge he had received today. And that was all Hensley needed to know, more than he took away on the average day. Even Julien of Galveston could go either way, but Hensley would stake his meager stake on Tyler. He would go the distance.

Hensley settled back on the stool and surveyed the empty bar, buoyed by the coffee. A couple of no-collar types, or maybe just blue collars who worked graveyards, wandered in, bought a couple of longnecks, and started up a game of eight ball.

He glanced at the pool players. They were either in group one or group two, the wolves or the sheep, and what could he do about it? It wasn't like they were looking for guidance. They would do what they wanted, or what they could, and he couldn't be held responsible for their decisions.

He checked the clock. Past ten. It was at least an hour to Albuquerque and an hour back. Add in all the medical stuff and it might be noon before Tink was back.

If he was going to track down Reggie, it might be helpful to know the current location of the major players, and that meant, reading in order from left to right, Sapphire, Percival, and D.B, and he had phone numbers for two of the three.

However, gaining intelligence of this nature required certain connections. He considered his options, not liking any of them. It was time to take his medicine like a man.

CHAPTER TWENTY-FOUR: LAUNCH

Hensley stepped into the office behind the bar, little more than a closet outfitted with a desk and mounds of folders filed on every available horizontal surface. He snatched up the phone and took it out to the bar so he could keep an eye on things.

The first call gained him the number of Davison's home phone in Austin. He answered on the third ring.

"Davison Fletcher."

"Many happy returns of the day, my good man," Hensley said. It had been a week since the meltdown in Galveston, and Hensley hoped that if the elapsed time failed to meet the requirement of healing all wounds, perhaps seven days would at least allow sufficient time for a scab to develop, saving him from outright hostility.

The long pause from the other end admitted of a multiplicity of interpretations. Hensley held his counsel and awaited further data before choosing an approach.

"If you're wanting bail money, you just wasted your only call."

Hensley breathed a sigh of relief. "Happily, I do not find myself in any such circumstance. But if you can grant me two-hundred and seventy seconds of your day, I have a story you might find of interest. Or at least diverting."

"The clock is running."

Surprised that Davison had not disconnected immediately, Hensley launched into an abbreviated brief of the tactical situation, emphasizing the need to extract Reggie from the clutches of desperadoes and to protect Sapphire from gaining a criminal record at her tender age, before laying out his immediate need of locating two cell phones.

"So you're not calling for money."

"It might have escaped your attention, little brother, but I survived the better part of four decades without calling you for money." Hensley took a few deep breaths. This was not the way forward. "My concern is for minors caught up in a crisis not of their making. If you can't provide the requisite services, I have other options. I just thought that you might have an interest in coming to the aid of the nephew neither of us knew you had until recently."

In the subsequent silence, Hensley used techniques acquired through multiple disciplines on multiple continents to bring his heart rate back to a rational level. There were larger things at stake here than his pride.

"Okay," Davison said. "Give me the numbers. But I'm retired. It might take me forty-eight hours to call in a favor off the record."

"I don't have forty-eight hours."

"And I don't have access."

"Fair enough." Hensley gave him the numbers. "I'll take whatever I can get."

"So I can reach you at this number in New Mexico?"

"No. It's a land line, and I'm following the best lead I have west."

"You have a cell number?"

Ah. Davison had put his finger on the operational flaw in Hensley's plan. "To date I have avoided such an electronic leash."

Davison made a noise that could be construed as a chuckle. "You might have to join the twenty-first century, old timer."

"I'll take it under advisement. Until such time, you can leave a message with Tink at this number."

"Okay."

A silence fell on the line, and the longer it grew, the more formidable it became. Hensley was not one to be intimidated by silence, but it was clear that something must be said.

"How's our favorite nurse?"

"Back in Detroit."

This was a surprising development. From what Hensley could see, Davison and Masie had become an item with potential. Masie gets the inheritance, Davison gets Masie, and Robert is your father's brother. And Hensley is the odd man out.

And then he realized that for the past three days, he had not given a single thought to the will. Not even when he dialed Davison's number.

"Putting her affairs in order?" Hensley asked.

"You'll have to ask her about that."

"And the will?"

"You'll have to ask her about that too."

Hensley chewed on this intelligence for a moment or two. "Perhaps I'll have that opportunity one day. Until then, I have certain matters to which I must attend. I'll be in touch."

"Do what you have to do. You always have."

Hensley sat with the phone to his ear, waiting for the next line. After a long pause, it followed.

"Listen," Davison said, but faltered.

Hensley waited.

"Look," Davison said. "Whatever has happened between us, it has nothing to do with these kids. If I can help you fix this, just say the word."

Hensley let out the breath he didn't realize he had been holding. "You can rely on me to do that very thing." He started to ring off but paused. "Oh, one more thing. Thank you, brother."

"I'm not doing it for you."

That stung, but it was no more than he deserved. "That's okay. I wasn't asking for me."

Hensley returned the phone to the office and took up his perch again. Thirty-seven years ago he had betrayed his brother, left him in the jungles of Angola with the doctor and his wife and faded into the world.

If he could go back, he might do things differently. Hell, who was he fooling? He would do things differently. There was not a day since that he didn't second-guess that decision. But every man did what he had to do at the time, didn't he?

No, he wouldn't resort to equivocating. He did what he did. He would own the consequences of that decision. But he didn't have to pass it down to the next generation. Right now all that mattered was Reggie.

And forty-eight hours was too long to wait to find the location of the principle players in this game. He would have to go to his second tier.

A few minutes before noon, Tink returned. Hensley dragged a towel over the bar. "How's your mother?"

Tink didn't meet his gaze. "They took some blood. We'll know in a few days."

Hensley considered digging deeper, but his experience told him that the world was full of seven billion stories and a man had to make his choices. He was inclined to focus on the path he had purposed in his heart, but there was a note in Tink's response that gave him pause. "About what?"

"How was the morning?" Tink answered gruffly.

"Probably much like many another morning," Hensley answered. He wished he could tell someone about the encounter with Tyler, but something told him this was not just another morning for Tink. He pushed the towel aside and turned to the gruff, gentle giant. "How's she doing?"

It was a bold move, pushing the envelope. Hensley wondered if he had gone too far, but sometimes you just had to go with your gut and conventions be damned.

"Poorly," Tink said. He looked about the space, searching for something to latch onto and coming up short.

Hensley stepped into the gap by pouring some beans into the grinder. "Coffee?"

Tink shrugged.

Hensley hit the button, and the noise gave them a respite from conversation for a blissful ten seconds or so. He dumped the grounds into the French press, poured in some boiling water, and wished he could do more, but it was the best he could offer. His instincts told him he was not built for moments such as this.

As he waited the five minutes for the grounds to steep, Hensley reached for the Laphroaig 10, set it on the counter, and then stuffed a twenty into the tip jar as a token of the momentousness of the moment.

He set two mugs on the counter to receive the silky South American brew, but the weight of the seconds proved too heavy. To cover the dead air, he found two tumblers and poured a few fingers of the frog. He pushed one to Tink, took the other, and held it aloft.

"She is a fine woman," he said.

Tink turned from the random activity he had chosen to distract himself, fixed Hensley with a virulent gaze, and snatched up the tumbler. "She is, and screw anyone who says different."

"A pox on their houses," Hensley said quietly.

They locked eyes, a fierce rage burning in Tink's gaze, a world-weary response in Hensley's expression. In silence they clinked glasses and downed the scotch.

She was a good woman who didn't deserve the ordeal to come, whatever it might be, but who did, Hensley wanted to know. All he knew was that it was Tink's cross to bear and if he could, Hensley would go to the mat to back him, but Hensley had his own cross to tackle, and Tink was on his own. As was Hensley, now that he thought about it.

To spare them both the ordeal of projecting the trauma to come, Hensley turned to the French press and did the needful, decanting it into their respective mugs.

They raised their mugs in silence, holding them aloft for a few seconds.

"May you be in heaven half an hour before the devil knows you are dead," Hensley said.

"I don't know whether to kick your ass or hug you," Tink said.

Hensley smiled. "I could name half a dozen who don't share your ambivalence on the subject."

They clinked mugs and drank deeply.

Hensley set his mug aside and hugged Tink. A few tears leaked out, but he wiped them on Tink's shoulder before anyone could notice. "I have to take care of a few things, but I'll come back," he whispered into Tink's ear.

Tink pushed him away. "Screw you and the horse you rode in on."

Hensley gained his balance and regarded Tink with a measured stare. "I couldn't have said it better myself. I have to see a man about a dog, but doubt not that before all is done, I will return and you will tell me your story."

"Since when did you care about my story?"

It was a question that delved into the depths of the Hensley, and he welcomed it not, but these were the elements of reality and he could not refuse it. "Since eight-thirty for those keeping score at home." He placed a hand on Tink's shoulder. "It will happen, but before that time, a lot of other things must happen."

He looked about the room. It was a few freckles past noon, and the crowd was rocking along on their own. He turned back to Tink. "In the meantime, I have to rescue the only creature on the planet who shares my DNA. Not counting my brother. You have a few C-notes to spare until I return?"

Tink regarded him with the craggy countenance that character-ized his dealings with the world, but as Hensley held his gaze, he saw the facade soften, and Tink disappeared into the back room.

Hensley cleared the bar and checked the room. The door behind him opened and Tink emerged.

He shoved an envelope into Hensley's hand. "I'll probably regret this."

Hensley pocketed the envelope without a glance at the contents. "Very possibly, my friend, but if I fail you it won't be from lack of trying."

He held out a hand. Tink took it, and they shared a single squeeze, Hensley holding his own against the giant opposite.

With his hand on the back door, Hensley turned. "One thing. If anyone asks after me, I'm headed to the Andes. I hear Machu Picchu is beautiful this time of year."

In the trailer, Hensley checked the envelope. Ten Franklins. He would go back and kiss the man right now, but he didn't have time to waste recovering from the pounding it would earn him. Instead, he distributed his holdings among several locations about his body, threw his meager collection of belongings into his bag, and stepped to the Patriot Pest Control van.

It was time to go see the man who wanted to horsewhip him in the town square.

Chapter Twenty-Five: Standoff

Despite the fact that it was in the nineties, Hensley took the precaution of parking the Patriot Pest Control van seven blocks from the Santacafe on the other side of the plaza. Not likely that Merle or Shotgun had reported the theft, but this was no time to be hobbled at the gate with a rookie mistake. Besides, it would never do for the judge to catch sight of him in that vehicle. He was likely as any man to connect the dots, and more than most.

Michelle caught his eye when he walked in and nodded to the courtyard. An unsmiling Judge Cox sat at a table with his back to the wall, commanding a full view of the entrance, a bottle of pale ale next to his left hand.

Hensley asked Michelle to bring a mineral water to the table, approached the judge, pulled out the chair, and sat down. "Thank you for agreeing to meet me on such short notice."

The judge's jaw muscles flexed in a surprisingly menacing fashion. "I'll give you five minutes."

Hensley accepted the mineral water from Michelle with a nod. "I left town as promised yesterday, but unforeseen circumstances compelled me to return." He picked up a menu. "Have you already ordered? The Reuben, perhaps?"

"You're not going to be here long enough to eat."

"Strange how we've talked twice in the last week, and both times you neglected to mention Reggie."

Cox pushed back his chair and stood. "Time's up."

Hensley watched him calmly for a moment before speaking. "Remember Percival Fisher? He has kidnapped Reggie to use as a bargaining chip to recover the stolen drugs."

Cox slapped both hands on the table and leaned forward. "What are you saying?"

Hensley dropped the menu. "I'm saying we dispense with the posturing and address the matter at hand. Forget what you think of me. Forget protocol. Forget the alphabet soup of federal agencies you chased me out of town with two days ago. Only one thing matters now."

If Hensley thought the flexing of jaw muscles intimidating, it was nothing compared to the cords of Cox's neck standing out like the pillars of Rhodes. He resisted the urge to check the vicinity for a bullwhip.

After a few moments, Cox dropped back down into his chair. "You have three minutes left."

Michelle arrived to take their order. "The Reuben, Judge?"

Hensley intervened. "Make that two. And a pale ale for me."

Michelle looked to the judge. He nodded, and she left.

Hensley finished off the mineral water and set the bottle aside. "You and I will never see eye to eye, but there are larger issues at stake—Sapphire and Reggie are caught up in the cogs of the machinery of the world at its worst. We can stand by and do nothing, or we can entrust them to the protocol of federal agencies with little capacity for nuance. Or we can find the tertium quid."

Cox stared at him without expression.

"The third way," Hensley said.

"I know my Latin."

Michelle arrived with the sandwiches and the beer and left.

"You were in 'Nam," Hensley said. "You know how the world works." He leaned forward and spoke in a voice subdued in volume but rich in passion. "You think you know me, but you are quite mistaken. I haven't seen battle, at least not in a war, and I thank whatever powers might be for that, but I have lived by my wits since I was sixteen, and I know the world. The best of it and the worst."

Hensley took a deep breath and backed off. He had to persuade Cox through logic, not intensity. "First, let us agree that the priority is to bring Reggie and Sapphire out of this thing alive and with a future. At whatever cost to ourselves."

In the silence Hensley left between them, Cox said, "Continue."

"Powell knows about Spud and Sapphire and the drugs thanks to my coming to you two of my own free will. I'm sure by now he's put together an interagency task force. But he doesn't know about Reggie. Or whoever else might have an interest in the drugs."

Cox nodded.

"Two worlds are converging on these two innocents." Hensley raised an eyebrow to indicate the latitude he afforded Sapphire in regard to the question of innocence. "One world that knows no rules. The other that lives by the rules. You have some experience in this regard."

Cox nodded again.

"Might I suggest that we can't afford to abandon Sapphire and Reggie to either side. This situation requires the oxymoron of a nuanced commando operation."

"And you're the one-man special forces contingent?"

"I am not without resources. If I can get a location on a few cell phones, I might be able to extract the parties in question before the showdown, and then we let the bad guys fight it out amongst themselves."

"You?"

"You might be surprised to learn that barely a week ago I went toe-to-toe against an international assassin on a lifeboat in the Caribbean and bested a few henchman before that. I can provide references from the Secret Service to that effect if required."

Hensley sampled the sandwich. Exceptional. He chased it with the beer and addressed Cox. "Or we can square off right now and settle it on the square. I'll handicap myself, of course, given the age difference."

Cox's nostrils flared. "I could break you in half without breaking a sweat."

"I have no doubt, if you could get ahold of me properly. But could you?"

Hensley set to on the Reuben. The hour was coming on two and he hadn't had anything since the breakfast burrito with Tyler.

After a few minutes, the judge followed suit. Between bites he said, "I'm going to tell you right off I don't like you. It was guys like you that burned their draft cards and ran off to Canada to save their butts and screamed 'baby killers' when we came back."

Hensley nodded. The judge had him all wrong, but he wasn't the issue at hand. Let the man have his say. He'd earned it. "If it's any consolation, I was a tadpole in the jungles of Angola at the time. But continue."

Cox tossed his sandwich down in disgust. "Tell me this. If you had possessed even an ounce of honor twelve years ago . . ." He took a deep breath and started over. "Okay, let's concede that you didn't know the future when you took your little bike ride. But if you had had the guts to come back and stick out it, do you think we would be having this conversation right now?"

Cox grabbed his napkin from his lap and threw it on the table. "Screw this." He stood up.

Hensley stood to face him. "Judge, I don't deny anything you said. In fact, I agree with every word. When this is over, I'll face you outside the courthouse barehanded. You bring your horsewhip, and I'll do my best to escape it. I've faced worse odds in my day."

They stood—Cox breathing heavily through his nose, Hensley feeling like he might deserve a bit of penance but thinking a literal horsewhipping might be pushing it.

Cox slowly ramped down and dropped into his chair, looking every bit of his seventy-odd years.

Hensley sat and waited. He was weary of outbursts when the situation called for more action and less outrage. It was the judge's move now. Hensley would do what he must, either with him or without him.

After a while, Cox looked him in the eye. "Truth is, I can't do much. By the time I could pull in favors for tactical measures, this thing will be over."

Hensley nodded. "But you agree that the best path forward, if we can manage it, is to extract our persons of interest before the authorities swoop in?"

Cox softened a millimeter. "When Chrystal came out here, I promised her father I would see to her, but a body's going to do what a body's going to do." He shook his head. "Forget all that. As things are, between the drug lords and the Feds, I don't see how Sapphire and Reggie have much of a chance. So if you have a plan, I won't stand in your way."

Hensley held up his bottle. Cox regarded him for a long moment, then picked up his bottle and clinked it against Hensley's. They both took a sip.

Something happened in that moment, a meeting of two worlds that could not be more opposed, but each focused on a common goal.

"I'm headed for the northwest," Hensley said. "But if I could get a bead on the location of the relevant parties, it would be in the interest of all concerned."

Cox turned to his sandwich as if nothing had occurred. When his plate was half empty, he cleared his palate with a slug of pale ale. "There's a guy. Down in south Texas. Utopia." He pulled a pen from his jacket, wrote a number on a napkin, and held it out to Hensley. "Just tell him 'Simon says' and he'll get what you need."

Hensley nodded and reached for the napkin, but Cox didn't let it go.

The judge caught his eye and held it with an intensity that would wilt a lesser man. "You only get one shot at a thing like this. If I was younger, I'd horsewhip your sorry butt and do it myself. And if you fail, I'll hunt you down and do it anyway."

Hensley relaxed his pull on the napkin. "If I fail, I shall welcome my penance at the hand of the one man on this planet most qualified to administer it."

They sat there for several seconds, the napkin suspended between their outstretched hands, each evaluating the other. Then Cox relented, and Hensley slipped the napkin with the number into his shirt pocket.

They finished their sandwiches in silence.

"Tell me one thing," Cox said. "Why didn't you come back?"

Hensley considered this for a longish time. There weren't many good answers to the question. In point of fact, zero by his reckoning. No man could undo what has been done. Or could he?

"Give me a few days and maybe it won't matter. As much."

Simon Cox snorted, stood, and walked away.

The jury of one was still out.

Hensley signaled Michelle for the check and inspected the number Cox had scrawled on the napkin. It was time to acquire the technology for this operation.

He walked the seven blocks to his van, as he had come to think of it, having traded in what would likely be a very expensive rental car before it was all over. He popped open the glove box and extracted the photo of Reggie, eternally poised with his foot on the ball, eyes squinting into the sun. He flipped it over and saw the date on the back. It was taken last year. He looked once more into the squinting eyes.

Would this boy, his son, welcome the return of the father that once was lost but now was found? Or would he send him away like everyone else was intent on doing?

Hensley returned the photo to the glove box and drove down Cerrillos Road for the next item on his agenda. As he passed the Santa Fe Railyard Park, he noticed a sign in the strip mall across the road. Premier Precious Metals. He turned at the next light, backtracked to the store, and bought two state quarters—Kentucky and Vermont.

Back in the saddle, Hensley proceeded to Walmart, where he bought his first pocket phone, a little flip-job that made him think of a Star Trek communicator. In the van, he flipped it open and dialed the number on the napkin. After half a dozen rings, a fluid voice of indeterminate age and gender answered.

"Identify yourself."

Hensley smiled. "Simon says you can locate a cell phone or two for me."

"Answer the question or you are dead to me, no matter what Simon says."

"Reginald Hensley Fletcher, most recently of Santa Fe, as of even date, requiring your services in what I hope is a simple matter of triangulation."

"Do you even know what you're talking about?" A heavy exhalation of breath. "Okay. Method of payment?"

That question caught Hensley off guard. "Credit card."

"Let's get one thing straight up front. I'll take your card, but if I don't receive payment, I can jack your life up in ways you can't even begin to comprehend."

While Hensley doubted that a life such as his, lived off the grid and off the radar, could be jacked up by a hacker, he appreciated the possibility that the guy on the other end of the line could render Chrystal's card inoperable within seconds and thus hamper his agenda. "If you have any qualms, rest assured that Simon will assist you in any efforts in that regard. You shall have your money, sir."

After a short pause, the voice responded. "Okay, give me the number."

"There are two phones I need to locate."

"No, I mean the credit card number."

"Ah. Before we go any further, may I have the pleasure of knowing with whom I am conversing? For the sake of convenience."

"You can call me Twink."

"Excellent. Mr. Twink, based on Simon's recommendation, I place the utmost confidence in you to provide the information required to return two children to the bosom of their family."

"TMI, Mr. Fletcher. Just give me the number, and I'll see what I can do."

"I do appreciate your competence in this matter, but if you will indulge me, one simple detail from you will aid in establishing the trust I require from my side to commit the funds for this transaction."

"What?"

"Could you share with me your drink of choice?"

"What?"

"A simple snippet of information that can in no way compromise your confidentiality, but which will set my mind at ease."

A longish pause followed. "Flor de Caña," Mr. Twink finally said.

"Neat?"

"Dubonnet Rouge, Benedictine, and Cointreau."

"Ah," Hensley said. "I see we can do business." He provided the information from memory. "I'd like a trail of as many coordinates as you can provide starting with Santa Fe."

"You'll hear from me within twenty-four hours at the number you called from. I'll place a hold on your card immediately for the service, but I won't place the charge if I don't find actionable information."

"Mr. Twink, you exceed all reasonable expectations of service. It seems that Simon's trust in you is not misplaced."

"Whatever."

The line went silent, and Hensley pocketed his phone. He reached for the key to start the van, but paused.

Perhaps he should call Ellis for information on the will. He pulled out his newly acquired pocket phone, but after a moment's consideration he reconsidered. As the executor of the estate, Ellis was duty bound to pursue the last known legal will, and from what Hensley had learned, that meant Ellis must take steps to award the Stone estate to Masie, irrespective of his personal preference.

If Hensley wanted to contest the will, he would have to engage his own lawyer, and who would that be? And what could he give them to go on, other than the medical report?

He shoved the phone back in his pocket and started the van. It was a long way to Portland, and the clock was ticking.

Chapter Twenty-Six: Sally

Hensley went back inside Walmart to stock up for the drive. It was over a thousand miles to Portland. He could do it in two days if properly provisioned. He took a page from *On the Road* and bought bread and sandwich meat, although he upgraded to whole grain and thick slices of roast beef and swiss from the deli. He passed on the chips and opted for carrots. The last thing he needed on a marathon was to succumb to a carb coma. He topped his cart off with grapes, a bag of almonds, and a case of bottled water. He scanned his change, found nothing of note, and pocketed it.

Next stop was the AAA office, where he scored a roadmap of the western states from the helpful Brenda. Back in the van, he spread the map out on the passenger seat. Santa Fe to Portland. The fastest route would avoid the mountains, and that meant I-25 down to Albuquerque and US-550 up to Farmington, then pick up I-15 in Provo to I-84.

Hensley shoved the key into the ignition but stopped short of firing up the engine. The question of the hour was not the fastest way from Santa Fe to Portland. It was WWSD. What would Spud do?

Hensley leaned back in the seat and attempted the impossible—entering the mind of a hormone-crazed teenager who thought that stealing half-a-million dollars in drugs from militia wing nuts was a viable exit strategy to a new life.

I'm at D.B.'s compound. I somehow get the drugs without being detected. Next stop Portland.

Or was it? Hensley opened his eyes and grabbed the steering wheel. Would Spud take the rocket to Portland or would he lie low and take his time? Either way, he didn't start from Santa Fe. He started from the compound.

Finding Pagosa Springs on the map, Hensley looked for the most direct route. From the compound, Spud could head west to Monticello and then north to I-70 and hop on I-15 in Provo.

Or he could take the unlikely route north to Salida and catch US-50 all the way up to Grand Junction to hook up with I-70. It added 150 miles to the trip, but when your destination is 1,500 miles away and you want to fly under the radar, do you care that it will turn into 1,650 miles?

Hensley was leaning toward the under-the-radar option when he realized that time had solved this little puzzle for him. Spud had a week's head start. Even if he had lain low for a few days in Salida, he was probably in Portland by now. So Hensley pointed the van south on Cerrillos toward I-25 and Albuquerque.

As he slowed to a stop for the light at Airport Road, the flashing lights of several SFPD cruisers on the opposite side of the road caught his attention. Hensley couldn't get a good view due to the traffic, but he got the impression several officers had their weapons drawn.

The light turned green, and the traffic began to move, albeit sluggishly due to the roadside show near the entrance to the mall. As Hensley approached, he caught sight of the focus of everyone's attention—the handcuffing-in-progress of a large man bent over the hood of a black Jeep Cherokee that seemed to be missing a windshield.

Inside, his hands clearly visible on the steering wheel, Archie glanced over at the Patriot Pest Control van and yelled. Hensley couldn't hear him over the air conditioner, but he was pretty sure it was on the order of "That's him right there!" Archie looked around at the cops to see if they were paying attention.

It turned out that they were indeed paying attention. The ones on his side of the car yelled back, using their weapons for emphasis, and Archie grabbed the wheel again, spewing what were doubtlessly curses of the most intense variety.

From his semi-prone position on the hood of the Jeep, Merle craned his neck up, revealing a bruised face, and locked eyes with

Hensley, who snapped a three-finger salute in his direction as he proceeded past the SFPD headquarters and down Cerrillos to I-25.

Those boys would think twice before they stole a highly recognizable car again.

Once he was up to speed on the interstate, Hensley pulled a water bottle from the case behind the seat, cracked it open, and took a long drink. He used a few deep breaths to calibrate his mind to the rhythm of a two-day drive.

He'd been operating at a frenetic pace, pulling the pieces together to marshal his resources and outguess a wild card. Now that he had established a plan, it was time to activate his mental governor before his brain whirled itself into self-destruction.

Hensley snatched a handful of almonds and chased it with grapes. It was time to return to the bigger picture. But which bigger picture?

There was the matter of Sapphire and Spud and the drugs. There was the matter of Reggie. There was the matter of Chrystal and his last chance at reconnecting with the closest thing he had ever experienced as a soul mate. And then there was the eminently practical matter of Uncle Rex's will and operational sustainability as a living and breathing organism on the planet.

As he took the exit from I-25 to US-550 toward Shiprock, the problem laid itself out as a tapestry, the threads crossing and intermingling in a complex pattern that defeated the finite mind. Logic collided with intuition, and Hensley backed off to take things one at a time, focusing on the most practical issue as a creature of his world must do to survive.

Life at its most basic level came down to sustaining the connection between body and soul. For the average individual that meant a day job, the nine-to-five struggle to keep the wolf at bay.

But Hensley wasn't the average individual. It wasn't a matter of pride. It was more a function of the Gaussian curve that explained so much of the natural world. The majority of society lived in the fat part of the curve, but Hensley had lived his life in the skinny part, and a body that lived by its wits was acutely tuned to the demands of basic needs—the base of Maslow's pyramid. One could aspire to the higher good but only as long as that one could satisfy the foundational requirements of existence.

Hensley believed every word that he had spoken to Judge Cox, but what did it profit a man to rescue the son he never knew he had if he couldn't provide for his own needs, much less those of his own flesh and blood?

So, even if he did somehow come to rescue Reggie, in the end it came down to what Hensley had to offer, and that meant it came down to the question of the will.

The van slowed into a coast as Hensley's foot relaxed with the realization that everything rested on Masie and what she did next. She could accept the estate and dispense favors like some medieval queen, or she could reject it, and then who knew what came next.

When a pickup that was half rust and half Bondo whipped around him, Hensley realized he was coasting at half the speed limit. He pressed the accelerator and pulled the newly acquired pocket phone from his pocket.

Davison answered on the third ring. "Davison Fletcher."

"Hensley Fletcher, at your service."

A longish pause ensued. "I said forty-eight hours, not four hours."

"I have a few leads that I am confident will lead me to Reggie."

A longer silence. "Let's forget the games. What do you need?"

"Masie's phone number."

Hensley could hear the squinting eyes through the ether.

"And how does that figure in?"

He should have known that he couldn't finesse his brother. "Let's say I extricate the munchkin from his current dilemma. What then?"

"You return him to his mother and you return to whatever it is you do."

"Or I provide for him the life he deserves."

"Ah. So you've found an angle."

"Think of me what you will, but this isn't about me," Hensley shot back before he thought.

"It's always about you."

Hensley corralled his emotions and held his tongue. He saw how it looked. His own self-interest tracked with the best interest of his son, and he would be hard pressed to differentiate the two. But Davison had his own weak spots. "Consider that I want for him the same advantages that I was denied and that you enjoyed. And I'm thinking Rex might side with me on this one, if that means anything to you."

The silence that followed caused Hensley to check the pocket phone to see if they had been disconnected. He was new to the ways of cellular communication, but he had heard others complain about the vagaries of coverage, and he was by many definitions of the term out in the middle of nowhere.

The indicators on the display showed several bars, so he returned the phone to his ear and waited it out. After all, the first to break an awkward silence put himself in the weakest position.

Evidently Davison was no stranger to this strategy, which meant Hensley had the opportunity to steer with his leg as he snagged a few more almonds and a splash of water.

Finally Davison relented. "If you're wanting to find out about the will, you'll have to ask her."

"I can appreciate that. Thus my request for her contact information."

"Good luck with that."

Hensley frowned "You expect me to believe that you don't have that information?"

"You can believe whatever you want."

"It is the way of all flesh to feel secure in their own beliefs, but I'd prefer a straight answer to the implied question."

"I don't know where she is or how to contact her."

This response gave Hensley pause. Based on the events of the final few days he had spent in their company, he had expected them to be sharing much more than phone numbers. Did this mean she was indeed the gold digger he had suspected all along? That once the payoff was assured, she had cut the bait loose? "If that is so, I must say I am sorry for this turn of events."

"And I must say I don't give a damn about what you are sorry for. If you need help in returning Reggie to his mother, let me know. Otherwise, lose this number."

A glance at the phone told Hensley that the ensuing silence was due to a disconnect. He tossed the phone into the passenger seat, then thought better of it and retrieved it. He dialed the next number from memory, got past the gatekeeper, and greeted the family lawyer with a warmth born of the coldness of an interaction with Davison.

"Ellis, my main man, what is the latest on the will?"

"May I take it I am speaking to Hensley Fletcher?"

"You may take that to the bank."

"I have submitted the extant will to the court for probate."

"And being translated into the vernacular . . ."

"It is in the hands of the court."

"And if I want to contest it?"

"You must engage counsel."

"Any recommendations?"

Ellis provided three names and numbers. Hensley thanked him, dialed the first number, filled him in on the situation, and referred him to Ellis for the particulars.

Having dispensed with existential matters, Hensley turned his attention to the higher orders of Maslow's hierarchy.

He had left Galveston in search of Chrystal, had kicked over one rock too many, and an heir had crawled out. Of course he had to snatch the pup from the fire, but then what?

Chrystal had made her point, had punctuated it with a pistol-shaped exclamation point. No help wanted. Hensleys need not apply.

If Hensley was to achieve the goal of a lifelong, mutually affirming relationship, he would have to resign himself to a non-optimum, non-Chrystal choice, as painful as that might be. And as the quintessential realist, he could see his way through that trial. After all, there were countless other options.

In all his years, he had never met another Chrystal, but it must be noted that he hadn't been seeking a Chrystal when he had stumbled upon her. Who was to say that fate or destiny or the randomness of the universe or even something more transcendent wouldn't lead him to that destination again? After all, lightning did strike twice, conventional wisdom notwithstanding. And maybe the odds were better now he realized he'd been searching for the wrong thing.

He reduced his speed as he drove through Cuba. Then, as he accelerated on the other side of town and took the long, sweeping curve to the west, it hit him, and he slapped the steering wheel.

Hensley didn't have to resume his pilgrimage through the world in search of the second lightning strike.

Reggie was the second strike.

Yes!

He slapped the steering wheel again. He'd allowed Davison and Masie to seduce him into the quest for a soul mate, matching every option against the image they had imprinted on him as if he were a baby duck.

It had never occurred to him that the purpose of the last few weeks had been to prepare him for the possibility of Reggie.

What if his soul mate was not a long-lost love but was instead his own son?

Leave the world a better place than you found it.

And what better way to do that than to use the family motto to break the family curse? To become the father to his son that his own father had never been to him?

Sure, from all appearances Chrystal would welcome this news about as much as she would a case of the hives enhanced with food poisoning, but perhaps eventually he could redeem that relationship as well.

All he knew was that this time he wouldn't make the same mistake of failing to recognize the miracle. He pressed down on the accelerator. The sooner he got to Portland, the better.

DAY 8: THURSDAY

Chapter Twenty-Seven: Portland

Hensley bedded down on the north side of Salt Lake City in an RV park. To stay off the radar, he paid with cash.

After five hours of sleep, he set out again at dawn on Thursday, the temperature a bracing fifty-something. He donned the Oxford shirt and his sports coat and drove three hours with the heater on.

There was little to divert him beyond the rugged landscape and spotty radio reception. Until he got some coordinates from Mr. Twink, he couldn't even make a plan. But he could guarantee that once he got the information he would be prepared to act.

Before his westward trek across the heartland of America back in the nineties, he had spent a few years in Portland. Assuming they were still around, and he had no reason to think otherwise, he could draw on a few off-the-radar resources to assist in his efforts.

Considering the mounting hosts of combatants in this scenario, once he located Reggie, he might require some muscle to effect the extraction, and Hensley had a few options to pick from. Tru Pak would be the first choice, assuming he'd managed to stay out of jail during the interim. There were other, less predictable options, but as he frequently said, one did not always have the luxury of examining the dental integrity of gratuitous equines. He would build a band of brothers from the available members of the Baker Street Irregulars and hope for the best.

The day gradually warmed up, and by the time he joined with the Oregon Trail in Bliss, Idaho, he was able to shed the coat. He paused for breakfast at the Oxbow Cafe.

He shivered his way across the mountains, but by one o'clock he was through the worst, and his wardrobe was adequate for the climate.

As he trekked along the Columbia River, the forests of Washington state stood proud on the other shore. He hit downtown Portland around four in the afternoon.

The city was much changed in the past decade and a half, and he scouted in vain for familiar landmarks. As he navigated the city center, he spied a Goodwill store at Tenth and Taylor. He whipped into the parking structure across the street and sequestered the Patriot Pest Control van on the ground floor.

With a groan, he unfolded himself from the driver's seat and straightened out his legs. Hensley considered himself as limber as any man of his age, but covering thirteen hundred miles in two days would take it out of a youth in his prime, and Hensley was far from that.

As he stretched, he considered his wardrobe. He had the white-linen, French-cuff shirt, the blue Oxford button-down, and a Tommy Bahama, but he figured some undershirts layered with plaid would not only suit the climate better, but would also provide him with a degree of anonymity by virtue of protective coloration.

From the moment he stepped into the Goodwill store, he realized his instincts had failed him. It looked more like a fashion boutique than a thrift store. Sleek vases with arrangements of budding branches, a shiny cocktail shaker surrounded by highball glasses, trendy lamps. He threaded through the gleaming aluminum racks featuring dresses and slacks and shirts on wooden hangers and eventually found the long-sleeved shirts, all brand name, brand new, and marked at $29.99. Given his limited resources, he limited himself to two.

After a change in the van, Hensley ventured back onto the street and wandered down to the Starbucks on Ninth. He snagged an Americano and took a seat at a sidewalk table for some decompression time after the forced march from the high desert over the mountains to the west coast. It had taken Lewis and Clark over a year to travel a similar distance, and Hensley felt every minute of it.

He had spent a few years here in the late nineties, taking things as they came as he always did. At that time, Portland was in flux, riding the rising tide of the dot com boom. Evidently the bust had come and gone in his absence as he had journeyed from Santa Fe to South America to Europe, North Africa, Turkey, India, Nepal, and then back to the States, summoned by Uncle Rex.

But it appeared that things were once again on the rise. The sidewalk traffic that passed by as he sipped his coffee consisted of professionals and hipsters and shoppers and tourists, all intent on some personal agenda. As was he, when it came down to it.

Hensley resisted the urge to measure his particular quest against the likely concerns of the passersby. A tempest in a teacup was still a tempest, and lacking the perspective to gauge its relative significance, at any given moment in any given life, the angst of an individual would expand to fill the available awareness of a soul.

In terms of urgency, his desire to rescue his son from peril was equal to the theoretical panic of the man walking past to score the requisite number of lobsters to accommodate the dinner party that could impress the right people to take his career to the next level.

And who was Hensley to judge? That man might be bent on the same thing as Hensley—securing the future of the next generation.

As Hensley sat thus engaged in reflection, he realized that despite recent urban development, this corner felt familiar. He inspected the surrounding buildings, but nothing presented itself. He finished off the Americano, closed his eyes, and cast his mind back to the late nineties.

During the intervening time, he'd probably traveled half the distance from the earth to the moon, but in the distance from birth to death, it felt like a mere blink of the eye.

Then it came to him. The Virginia Cafe, where he had spent many a pleasant hour, was a block over and up.

Hensley took the short jaunt, only to discover that the local landmark that had survived since the time of Prohibition had been replaced by a chain-link fence surrounding a concrete-lined hole that took up a quarter of the block.

As in uffish thought he stood, he noticed a dapper man in a three-piece suit and red power tie approaching in the crosswalk.

Hensley raised a questioning finger. "Excuse me, my good man. I find myself flummoxed by the apparent annihilation of that peerless institution that was the Virginia Cafe."

The man paused, gave Hensley a quick appraisal, and gestured west down Morrison Street. "It moved five years ago. Take a left on Tenth."

"Thank you." Hensley did as instructed and found himself two doors up from the very Goodwill where he had replenished his wardrobe.

At the new location of the Virginia Cafe, Hensley took a seat at the bar and ordered a glass of white wine from a thirty-something Rasputin, by the looks of him. When it arrived, he said, "Hensley Fletcher at your service, back in town after a decade of wandering."

The bartender held out his hand. "Wally."

Hensley grasped the outstretched hand. "I'm fresh off the trail from Santa Fe and feeling the need for a bit of sustenance. What do you recommend?"

Wally took a moment to size him up. "The club sandwich. Cajun spicy fries."

"Excellent." Hensley pushed the menu aside. "Make it so."

Wally conveyed the message to the kitchen gnomes and turned back to the bar. "So, where have you been for the last ten years?"

"In reverse order, Santa Fe, Philadelphia, DC, Galveston, Cancún, Nepal. For starters." He took a sip of wine. "I'm looking for a room for a week or so. Is the Rutherford Arms still in business?"

The bartender shook his head. "A lot has changed in the last ten years."

"It was ever thus. Any recommendations instead of the lamented Rutherford?"

"Try the Everett Street Guesthouse. A few blocks north of Burnside." Wally wrote the info on a napkin. "Terry's a classy lady."

"I shall most assuredly do so."

Hensley's club arrived, and he set to with a will born of two days on the road with Kerouac sandwiches. The task was complicated by the fact that the multiple layers rose up like the Rock of Gibraltar, but he regarded the problem in a manner similar to the USSR surveying eastern Europe and used much the same tactics in execution of his policy.

As he was thus engaged, an electronic twirping impinged on his enjoyment of the meal. He glanced around and caught Wally's eye. "What is that loathsome noise?"

"I think it's you."

Hensley frowned, and then realized it was indeed him. Or rather the pocket phone in his sports coat. Only one person knew this number. He pulled it out and flipped it open. "Hensley at your service."

"I have a bead on the numbers you gave me."

"Mr. Twink. I never doubted you for a second."

"Both numbers track from Colorado to Oregon."

"As have I since we last spoke. Can you narrow it down further?"

"The 7346 number is in east Portland around Eighty-Second Avenue and Flavel. I tracked 9263 east on US-26 to a place forty miles out called Rhododendron before it faded."

So D.B. was in town, and Sapphire was holed up somewhere in the woods. "Can you get me next to the second number?"

"No coverage to speak of in the Mt. Hood National Forest. And I'm guessing your target is not equipped with a sat phone."

"Highly doubtful."

"I could pin it down to within a few meters, but I'd have to be onsite and within two hundred meters of the phone."

"When we speak of the Mt. Hood National Forest, what are we talking about? Size-wise."

After a few seconds of clicking keys, Mr. Twink replied. "Over sixteen hundred square miles."

That put things in perspective. "Fret nyet, my little pet. I shall take it from here."

"Fine. Expect a charge on your card. If you need anything else, you know where to find me." The line went dead.

Hensley pocketed the phone, hoping the cash he left behind in Chrystal's house would cover it. What Mr. Twink lacked in social graces he made up in competence, but even he had his limits. The way forward called for someone closer to the locus of interest.

D.B. was over in Felony Flats, doubtless for good reasons. Perhaps he had family there, but either way, the important point was that he evidently had even less information as to Sapphire's whereabouts than Hensley did.

As to the location of Reggie, that depended on the location of Percy, and on that point, Hensley was as clueless as a vegan in a butcher shop. He had only one thing to go on—Percy was hunting Spud. So perhaps the best strategy was to find Spud before Percy did, and then lie in wait for him.

Hensley returned to his sandwich, but before he had downed the second bite, something began niggling in the back of his mind. Something Mr. Twink had said. Something about Sapphire's number. Rhododendron? No.

Mt. Hood National Forest. That was it. Back in Chrystal's kitchen in Santa Fe, Toni had mentioned a cabin on Mt. Hood. That the young Tatum had family in the area. Perhaps in Felony Flats.

That was the thread that would lead him to the center of the maze, and Hensley knew just the person to pull it. He signaled Wally.

"My good man, could I trouble you for a phone book?"

Wally frowned. "A what?"

"The yellow pages, to be more precise."

The confused bartender glanced around the area and turned back to Hensley. "Pages?"

"A directory of local phone numbers."

The gleam of intelligence kindled in Wally's eyes. "Who are you looking for? You can probably just google it."

"I lack the requisite infrastructure for such an operation. But surely a stroll through the listings will serve as well for my purposes."

"You were just on the phone a second ago."

Hensley presented the pocket phone for Wally's inspection. "This device is designed solely for telephonic communication."

"Where did you find that? In a museum?" Wally pulled out the rectangular item known as a smartphone among the bourgeoisie. "Who are you looking for?"

"McMillan Bail Bonds."

Wally pocketed his phone and produced the number from memory.

Hensley made the call. After he got past the gatekeeper, he heard the voice of Cecilia, or Cecil to her friends.

"Fletch, is it really you?" The familiar raspy voice brought back memories.

"As far as I can tell."

"What time zone are you in?"

"I'm partaking of the early bird special at the Virginia Cafe as we speak. I strongly recommend the Cajun fries."

"You're in town?"

"And seeking information only someone with your expertise can provide."

"Save me a seat. And order me a Tom Pollens."

"A Tom Collins?"

"Pollens. Just tell Chris. He knows what to do."

Hensley looked around the room. "What does he look like?"

"Like the love child of Zach Galifianakis and Rasputin."

Hensley eyed Wally. "Chris?"

Wally turned. "Yes?"

"Cecil has requested a Tom Pollens."

Wally nodded and turned to the bottles behind the bar.

Hensley kept an eye on him as he reached for a bottle of Hendricks. "What's your ETA?" he said into the phone.

"Five minutes, tops."

"I shall count the minutes."

Hensley hung up the phone and followed the movements of the bartender as he squeezed a lemon into the shaker, added honey simple syrup, and pulled an unlabeled bottle from under the bar.

"Pardon me, Wally, or is it Chris?"

Wally, a.k.a. Chris, paused with the bottle suspended above the shaker. "Yes?"

"Would you be willing to communicate the secret ingredient you are administering to this concoction?"

Wally held up the bottle. "This? Rhubarb bitters."

Hensley raised a hand of affirmation. "Of course. Nothing takes the taste of shame and humiliation out of your mouth quite like rhubarb."

"Bebopareebop, baby."

Hensley nodded. More Rasputin, less Zach. Definitely. A young Rasputin. "Your own invention?"

"I have a few tricks up my sleeve."

No doubt, Hensley thought. "I take it you are acquainted with Ms. McMillan. In what capacity?"

Wally added a dash of rhubarb bitters and thrashed the mixture about until the shaker was rimed with ice. "I think it would be fair to say that we have both been of service to each other."

"Professionally?"

"Yes," Wally said, but he drew it out to the degree that Hensley inferred an additional layer to the relationship.

"Say no more. We are men of honor and do not bandy a woman's name without regard to propriety." But he appraised Wally in a new light. Rasputin indeed. "Perhaps you could mix a second one for me."

Wally nodded.

Hensley finished off his supper and pushed the dishes aside as Wally set the two tumblers on the bar. The door opened, and Cecil walked in. Such was the force of her entrance that Hensley immediately stood up from the bar stool where he had been perched for the better part of an hour.

It was coming on fifteen years since he had last seen her, but other than her hairstyle, she looked unchanged. Five-ten and slender, blonde hair now cut in a page-boy that curled forward, and sporting a retro dress suit with padded shoulders, she gave off the air of the Andrews sisters in their prime but transported into the early sixties, even though she was approaching sixty herself if his memory served.

She held out her arms as he approached. He offered the cheek-to-cheek air kiss of which she was so fond in the nineties, but she pushed past that and drew him into a full hug. He reciprocated and breathed in the sandalwood scent she had always favored.

He began to disengage after a few seconds, but she clung to him, and he renewed his efforts until he felt her grip relax. He pulled back, holding her by the shoulders, and took her in.

"Cecil, dare I say you stand as a shining example of one of the verities in this uncertain world." He motioned her to the stool next to his. "I begin to suspect that you have an aging portrait sequestered in an attic somewhere."

Cecilia grasped the drink before her and extended it toward him. "Oh, Fletch, you have no idea."

Hensley reciprocated, they clinked glasses, and he took a sip. It was a bit sweeter than he normally took his drinks, but it was apparent from the first taste that Wally was no tyro. He tossed an appreciative nod to the artisan, and Wally acknowledged the compliment without a word as he attended to his back-bar duties.

Reaching for a menu, Hensley said, "Perhaps an appetizer would be in order."

"Chris, the usual," Cecilia said.

Wally nodded and stepped back to the kitchen.

Hensley pushed the menu aside. He had an agenda, but he pushed it aside as well. "Tell me all, Cecil." He saw that her glass was empty, so he slid his to her.

She finished it off and took a deep breath. "How much do you know about teenage girls?"

"Mercifully, almost nothing."

"Then thank your lucky stars."

Wally emerged from the kitchen door, and Cecilia placed her order by nodding to the empty tumblers on the bar. Then she turned to Hensley.

"There's something I have to tell you." She arrested Hensley's attention with an intense gaze.

Hensley looked into her brown eyes with a sinking sense of dread. "I await your pleasure."

"I have a daughter. Fourteen and impossible."

For the second time in forty-eight hours Hensley faced the news that another zygote had gone the distance and discovered America mere months after the confetti had been cleared up from his going-away party.

How many more revelations could he sustain before he wilted under the glare of the Ghost of Transgressions Past? Did he even have the strength to ask the question?

"I understand impossibility is a prevalent characteristic of the species," he said in as calm a tone as he could muster.

Wally intervened with two more Tom Pollens.

Cecilia snatched hers up immediately and drank half of it. "You have no idea."

Hensley took a sip and gave Wally points for consistency. "I must confess that up to this point, I have not had the opportunity to acquire the requisite experience to become conversant with the demands that doubtlessly weigh upon the soul of one encumbered with such a responsibility." Thankfully, he added to himself with a frisson of trepidation.

"And her father is no help at all."

"No doubt he means well."

"What if he did? That and a quarter will buy you a ticket on the road to hell. I'll take actions over intentions any day of the week." She took another slug of her drink.

Hensley dosed himself with a strong administration of Wally's concoction and prepared himself for the final blow. Might as well get it over with.

"And who is the lucky fellow?"

"Oh, you don't know him."

The relief that flooded Hensley's soul dawned on him like Dorothy Gale pulling open the black-and-white door to reveal the Technicolor realm of Oz pouring through.

But almost as quickly, he realized this response was unworthy of him. Here on the next stool was an old friend in distress and in need of consolation. He set aside his own concerns and laid a hand upon hers.

"How bad is it?"

Cecilia took in a ragged breath, glanced away, and shuddered for a fraction of a second. "You have no idea," she whispered.

A single tear escaped from the corner of her eye and began its descent down her cheek as Wally arrived with a plate.

"Spicy tater tots." He took in the situation, looking from Cecilia to Hensley and back. "On the house," he added.

Without moving a muscle, Hensley embraced Wally with a knowing look. "Good man," he breathed, and turned back to Cecilia. "Then tell me," he said.

The expression she turned on him would have melted the heart of the sphinx. And he was no sphinx. "Oh, Fletch." Her eyes overflowed and she reached for a bar napkin.

Hensley motioned to Wally to refill their drinks as Cecilia dabbed her tears.

"She thinks I'm a monster," she said. "And maybe I am." She tossed the napkin aside. "I'm just trying to save her from making the same mistakes I did."

"Of course you are." Hensley took her hands in his. "It's what we all want. And in time she will see that. Maybe sooner than you think."

Cecilia graced him with a look of gratitude that made him feel like an impostor. What did he know of being a parent? He had only just discovered he was a member of that fraternity, but without the time in the trenches she had endured for over a decade.

Of course he wanted the best for his son, but as Cecilia had said, actions counted for more than intentions, and Hensley wondered if he had the constitution to sustain the day-in day-out reality of turning those intentions into consistent actions.

He regarded Cecilia with a newfound respect for sticking it out alone for fourteen years. Changing diapers. Potty training. Parent-teacher meetings. Last minute science projects, although that at least evoked some level of interest.

But then came adolescence and the morphing of the tadpole into a froglike bundle of hormones and teen angst. Hensley had barely survived his own transmogrification from child to adult. He doubted that he could endure the trial of attending the process from the other side of the window, shared DNA or otherwise.

On the neighboring stool, Cecilia sloughed off her personal trials with a visible effort and another application of the napkin, reached for a tater tot, popped it into her mouth, and turned to Hensley. "Let's talk about something else. What brings you to town?"

Hensley could switch context with the best of them, but this taxed even his considerable talents. To give himself time, he snagged a spicy tater tot. It seemed to embody the perfect combination of deep-fried trans fats while delivering the kick that transcended the oeuvre of mere comfort food.

He turned to Wally, who in the tradition of the best bartenders had been busying himself with nothing in particular while remaining available to attend to the needs of his public. "Please convey my compliments to the chef."

Wally nodded but refrained from intruding upon the cocoon of intimacy that Hensley and Cecilia had established.

Hensley smiled to himself, thinking back to Julien at the rooftop bar of the Tremont, and suspecting that in due time he would attain this hallowed level of bartenderdom.

He turned back to Cecilia. "I find myself in a consonant, if not commensurate, situation. I seek to gain information that might lead me to my son."

Cecilia froze with a tater tot halfway to her mouth. "You have a son?"

"So I have recently discovered." In the next few minutes, he related an abbreviated account of his recent history, leaving out the less savory details. "I called you in the hope that you might have some history with the local Tatums."

"History? They're what we call a franchise in my business. Job security."

"Is there a chance they have a place in the Mt. Hood National Forest that Spud could disappear into while the heat fades?"

"They're clustered over in Felony Flats."

Hensley's reflexive twitch upset his glass, and a goodly portion of his drink splashed onto the bar. It couldn't be a coincidence that D.B. was infesting a neighborhood associated with Spud's antecedents. "Any Tatums haunting the area around Eighty-Second and Flavel?"

"They lie so thick on the ground you can't swing a dead cat without loosening the fillings of a half dozen or so."

Cecil drained her glass and looked down the bar. "Chris, darling, can you mix up another round?" She turned to Hensley.

Wally approached their position.

"And perhaps a carafe of water might not be amiss," Hensley added. Hydration was not to be neglected under such circumstances.

"The Tatums have generated enough cash flow over the years to score any number of hideouts outside the city," Cecilia said. "Mt. Hood. Depending on where they bought, they could be in Hood River County or Clackamas County. Either way, I can have someone do a search to see if any Tatums own land out there."

"I would be eternally in your debt."

Cecilia graced him with a weary smile. "Don't be ridiculous."

"Have I ever been otherwise?"

She considered the question as Wally delivered the goods. She sampled the Tom Pollens. "You have a place to stay?"

DAY 9: FRIDAY

Chapter Twenty-Eight: Dragon

Despite the implied offer from Cecil, Hensley got the studio cottage at the Everett Street Guesthouse for a reasonable rate, had a relaxing nightcap while assessing the state of his wardrobe, and then flicked off the light and slept the sleep of the just.

The next morning, he donned the second plaid shirt and ventured forth in search of comestibles. At this early hour, eight a.m. being early by Hensley's standards, the temperature was in the high fifties under a clear sky and a light breeze. He was glad of the jacket he had picked up in Santa Fe.

He found the City State Diner a few blocks east, took a seat at the bar, and on Ann Marie's recommendation, availed himself of the Freddie with seared grits. Thus engaged, he reviewed his thoughts of the night before.

The way Hensley saw it, he had to navigate three entities—the Spud-Sapphire alliance, the Percival-Reggie contingent, and the lone operator D.B. And where he found one, he was likely to encounter the others, either simultaneously or in short order.

While Hensley preferred the simplicity of working alone, the odds were not in his favor, especially against armed opponents, which was the most likely scenario.

It was time to summon the Mouseketeers. The premier mouse among that clan was Tru Pak, and that meant a drive down to Beaverton.

Hensley persuaded Ann Marie to look up the number to the Pacific Rim Martial Arts Academy, placed a call to the worthy establishment, and discovered that Tru was teaching a jujitsu class in an hour.

He finished off his breakfast, returned to the hotel, and arranged for his meager wardrobe to be laundered before mounting his trusty steed and heading southwest.

The half-hour drive to Beaverton gave him time to consider the quality of the reception he might experience after an absence of fourteen years. So far he'd been in the States barely three weeks, and the only person who had been glad to see him was Cecil.

If memory served, Tru approached life with a sober intensity that would make Judge Cox look like the class clown, and Hensley approached life like . . . well, like Hensley. If he had to put a label on it, he might call it a playful cognizance.

Even though Tru was ten to fifteen years his junior, Hensley had the impression that Tru had always regarded him with aloof amusement, as if he were watching the antics of a puppy. A less grounded man might have found it insulting.

They had met at the dojo. Hensley had signed up with the goal of maintaining the skills he had developed in China. As Hensley later discovered, Tru used the dojo to work off his lingering anger at being uprooted from his life in Seoul by interfering parents, a situation that resonated with Hensley from the get-go.

They were unlikely comrades—Tru in his early twenties and Hensley in his late thirties—but in addition to martial arts, they shared a love of classical music.

Hensley was partial to string quartets, particularly of the late nineteenth and early twentieth centuries. Tru was enamored of Bach fugues and inventions. He was the only person Hensley knew who owned both the 1955 and 1981 Glenn Gould recordings of the Goldberg variations. To keep things lively, Hensley frequently dismissed Gould as a showoff. After the first few times, Tru refused to rise to the bait.

But that was over a decade ago. Tru was approaching the age that Hensley had been when they first met. A lot could change in a decade, as Hensley had been forced to acknowledge several times in the last few weeks.

Hensley parked near the academy, checked at the front desk for the location of Tru's class, and proceeded down the hall. He slipped through the door and stood to one side. He recognized Tru immediately.

Tru glanced in his direction and then back to the two men sparring. The rest of the class watched in zazen position from the sidelines.

The taller sparring partner launched a punch, and the short one wrapped himself around the outstretched arm, using the momentum to roll his opponent to the mat, and then it was a writhing knot of limbs and torsos as each struggled for mastery.

Hensley looked back to Tru, who had evidently dismissed him and was studying the match. A little more meat on the bone, a little less hair on the dome, but still the same intensity, even while observing.

It occurred to Hensley that Tru was no longer an angry young man in his twenties. He might have acquired obligations, a life as some called it, that would predispose him to respond disfavorably to Hensley's proposition of a quest.

He seemed to remember that in the late nineties, Tru's father had swung him a position with Intel or Tektronix or some such going concern. Some kind of low-level number-crunching job that Hensley hadn't paid much attention to. By now he could be well and truly settled.

Eventually the match concluded in favor of the short guy, and after a post-mortem and other formalities, the class dispersed.

Hensley stepped forward, and Tru approached.

"You have returned."

Ever the stoic, that Tru. "Quite." Hensley held out his hand.

Tru took it. "For how long?"

"Is there a place around here we can get some coffee?" Hensley said. "I'd like to catch up."

A voice chimed in from behind Hensley. "There's Jet Set down in Tigard."

The winner of the sparring match stepped up, hand outstretched. Hensley shook it. "I'm—"

"Brother Hensley." He smiled.

"You have the advantage of me, sir." Hensley took a closer look, and the scales fell from his eyes. "The Jesuit!"

"In the flesh, as usual," the cleric said, his smile growing by the second.

"Brother Joseph, or is it Father Joseph now?"

"Brother. I did not pursue ordination."

"Doubtless for good reasons, of which I desire to know more. Brother Joseph, if you would be so kind as to lead the way to this Jet Set of which you speak, I will treat the party to the caffeinated beverage of choice and regale you with a story the likes of which you will not soon encounter."

Hensley waited in the lobby while Tru and Brother Joseph changed into mufti, and they caravanned a few miles south to a strip mall, the Jesuit leading the way in a 1995 Volvo 850 wagon held together by bailing wire and a decade of Hail Marys. Tru followed in a late model red Mitsubishi, and Hensley brought up the rear in the van.

Soon they were situated at a coffee table next to a mural of a space-age airline terminal. Hensley took the chair, leaving the couch opposite for Tru and Brother Joseph.

After a few pleasantries, Hensley began assessing the landscape. "Tru, other than classes at the dojo, how are you occupying yourself these days?"

"I have a consulting business."

"Ah." In Hensley's experience, more often than not the word "consultant" was a euphemism for "unemployed," and if that was the case, Tru might be open to a side venture with some excitement. "Of what nature?"

"I take care of the due diligence on investment opportunities for venture capitalists."

In other words, mind-numbing perusal of the books of aspiring startups. Even better.

Startup was a code word for "long on dreams and short on cash." Surely after years of ferreting out the minutia of the cash flow of delusional visionaries, Tru would welcome something more in keeping with the adrenaline-laced days of his youth in South Korea.

"And you find this fulfilling?" Hensley sipped his espresso.

"My girlfriend didn't complain about the BMW I gave her for her birthday."

As Hensley searched for a chink in Tru's armor, Brother Joseph spoke up.

"And the story you mentioned?"

Yes. That was the way in—appeal to Tru's romantic nature. Hensley blessed the Jesuit for this inspired interruption. "Precisely so."

Hensley pulled the photo of Reggie from his inside jacket pocket and placed it on the coffee table.

Brother Joseph picked it up. "Who is this?"

"Therein lies a tale." Hensley let the story flow, being careful not to muddy the waters with distracting details.

Two star-crossed lovers separated by a national disaster, the man without a country exiled by virtue of his stateless existence, the faithful lover not daring to hope that he had survived, raising their son through the intervening years with the assurance that the only thing that could keep his father from returning was his tragic demise in a distant and exotic land.

It was for a story such as this that Hensley was born, and he spared no heart-wrenching twist to the narrative. The Jesuit hung on every word, letting his cappuccino grow cold in his hands. When Hensley got to the part where Reggie was kidnapped by a drug-crazed militia extremist, Brother Joseph gasped.

Hensley arrested Tru with a piercing gaze and closed with a call to arms. "I appeal to you, my friend and former companion. Will you join me on this quest to rescue an innocent from the clutches of evil men?"

Tru stared back, as impassive as the Buddha. He took a sip of his coffee and set it aside. "You want me to walk into a snake pit of inbred right-wingers to kidnap your bastard son who doesn't even know you exist?"

This was not a response worthy of the tale Hensley had spun. But before he could answer, Tru leaned forward and spoke with a low, hoarse voice.

"You of all people should know better than to ask this of me." He stood.

The Jesuit reached to pull Tru back to the couch. "Brother Pak, consider the—"

"No!" Tru jerked his arm from Joseph's grasp. "He asks too much. Not even for you—" He bit off the rest of the sentence and walked away without looking back.

Hensley and Brother Joseph watched in silence as Tru pushed his way past a couple entering the shop and disappeared from sight.

Brother Joseph was the first to break the silence. "Don't take it personally."

Hensley stared at the door and shook his head, trying to figure where he had gone wrong in his pitch. From everything he knew of Tru's background—

"If you knew his story, you would understand that it's not about you."

Hensley turned to Brother Joseph. "How so?"

The Jesuit contemplated his response before answering. "I think we've earned a glass of wine. Are you up for an early lunch?"

"Lay on, Macduff."

Hensley followed Brother Joseph's Volvo a few miles down a boulevard, left past a church and into an upscale neighborhood, to a parking lot surrounded by trendy shops. They took a seat at the bar of a homey little place called The Olive and the Grape. Hensley befriended the waitress and ordered a cheese board and a couple of glasses of wine. Thus fortified, Brother Joseph began his tale.

"It is not easy to conquer a dragon. And once it is vanquished, it is no small thing to summon it."

Hensley loved a cryptic opening as much as anyone, perhaps more than most, but he was no match for the Jesuit. "Shall I write this down?"

Brother Joseph smiled. "What do you know of Brother Pak's history?"

"Back about twenty years ago, his parents moved from Seoul to the States because Tru was mixed up in some gangs."

"In 1990, the South Korean government cracked down on the local mafia, and the gangs moved into the resulting vacuum and built their own criminal empires. Turf wars ensued."

Brother Joseph paused for refreshment and then continued. "Brother Pak was an impressionable teenager fascinated with martial arts. His father thought he could profit from the discipline." He lowered his voice as if for fear of being overheard. "Truthfully, I fear the elder Pak focused most of his energy on his career instead of his son." The Jesuit took a deep breath and a deeper sip of wine. "It is one of the innermost needs of the human race. Acceptance. Belonging. Communion." He looked at Hensley. "Do you know what hell is?"

"Accordions and banjos playing Pat Boone's greatest hits?"

"Forget fire and torment. Hell is isolation. Separation from the divine."

Hensley nodded. "So the same thing, really."

Brother Joseph graced him with a slight smile. "In the gangs our friend found his tribe, a close-knit society that looked after their own. But a society of violence and rage. And he distinguished himself in battle. On many occasions.

"It was the very battle scars that he wore as a badge of honor that alerted his parents to his secret life. To save their son from the gangs, they emigrated to the US. But they couldn't save Brother Pak from himself."

An image from fifteen years ago arose in Hensley's mind. The time he and Tru left a performance of Schumann string quartets at the Alberta Rose Theater and stopped by a bar for a drink, Hensley opting for a fine single malt and Tru drinking his usual tonic water and lime.

As they left the bar, they happened on a half dozen punks harassing a high school couple. Before Hensley could raise his voice to reprimand the reprobates, Tru launched single-handedly into them, and Hensley had felt compelled to find a pay phone and summon an ambulance before they quitted the scene.

It was uncanny. Barely an hour earlier, they had been sitting in the theater enjoying a string quartet, and now several punks would likely need a serious course of physical therapy to walk normally again.

Hensley looked at Brother Joseph and nodded. He had seen the dragon unleashed. In fact, he was counting on that dragon to occupy Spud and Percival and D.B. while he spirited away Reggie. And Sapphire, if she would come.

But now it appeared the dragon had been banished, and Tru wasn't interested in offering it amnesty.

Hensley picked up his glass. "So much for putting the band back together." He finished off the last of the wine and signaled the waitress for another round.

Brother Joseph brushed crumbs from his shirt. "In the interest of a worthy cause, I will talk to him, but only once. It is a wise man who knows his limits."

"Tell him it's just a one-time thing."

"Would you offer a recovering alcoholic a drink as a one-time thing?"

"Not on purpose."

The waitress arrived with two glasses of wine.

Brother Joseph stood. "Just one for me."

She reached for his glass, but Hensley waived her off. "I'll take care of it, Sue. And can you bring me a menu?"

As the waitress left, Hensley turned to Brother Joseph. "So I'm on my own, then."

"Would you sacrifice a brother to save your son?"

It was a tough call. Hensley hoped it was a rhetorical question, because he had no intention of answering it.

Brother Joseph held out his hand. "You have my sword. Metaphorically. For what it's worth."

Hensley shook his hand. "How can I contact you?"

"My living arrangements are . . . flexible." He held out a card. "My cell phone number."

The Jesuit left, and the waitress returned with a menu. Hensley glanced at it and ordered the elk meatloaf sandwich. Then he addressed one of the glasses before him and commenced to engage in some serious cogitating.

In the minus column, he was down one dragon. In the plus column, he was up one Jesuit. All things being equal, it didn't come out equal.

He still had one card left in his hand. But it was a wild card and he wasn't sure he wanted to play it.

CHAPTER TWENTY-NINE: TATTOO

Hensley found Sea Tramp Tattoos right where he had left it fourteen years ago. He parked in the lot across the street. The door was open, and a guy with a white beard stood behind the bar, a wall of flash behind him.

As he crossed the expanse of red and white tile, Hensley nodded to the guy. "Don, my good man. You appear to be holding up admirably."

Don squinted his right eye through his wireframe glasses. "Do I know you?"

"I am long gone and much altered, so I am not surprised that you don't recognize me." Hensley held out his hand. "Hensley Fletcher."

Don shook his hand. "Nope. Doesn't ring any bells."

"No matter. I'm hunting for Whyte. Is he available for consultation?"

"Does he owe you money?"

"No, just an old friend in town for a few days and thought I'd catch up with him."

"He's freshening up some ink. Should be out in a bit."

"In that case, where can I find a good cup of coffee?"

"Try the Half Pint Cafe half a block down Ash."

Hensley tipped an imaginary hat and walked east on Ash Street. In the mid-afternoon sun the temperature approached the seventies. Hensley started to pull off his jacket but spotted the Half Pint across the street, checked for traffic, and darted across.

The microscopic cafe occupied the southwest corner of a four-story brick building and was housed in what used to be a freight elevator. The two tables out on the sidewalk were occupied. He popped in, got a cup of their Damn Fine Coffee from Marco, and strolled up Sixth while sipping.

He wasn't certain engaging Whyte qualified for the best idea of the month, but with Tru out of the picture, the pickings were of the slim variety. The problem was that while Whyte had a keen eye, a steady hand, an iron jaw, and a powerful punch, he was something in the nature of a bovine placed in unfortunate proximity with fragile dinnerware. Enthusiastic, but perhaps overly so. Unpredictable was the word. In spades was the qualifier.

He could stand by and look menacing, or he could launch into a flurry of appendages and pain, and irrespective of previous planning and guidance, no one knew which would happen at any given moment. Not even Whyte.

As he passed Ankeny Street, Hensley took note of a Thai place that bore further investigation and continued on.

The problem was that Hensley would definitely need someone to have his back if he was to brace the lion in its den. Especially since he didn't know how many lions would occupy said den at T time on D day at L location, also details that remained unknown.

In fact, the only thing he knew for sure at this moment was that Whyte was refreshing some ink, and even that was hearsay.

There was the Jesuit, but despite his willingness and the fact that he won the sparring match, Hensley questioned whether Brother Joseph had the sand for such an expedition.

In his wanderings, Hensley came upon Burnside Street and realized he was only a mile from his lodgings. He turned west toward Grand, passing in front of a Japanese restaurant that called to his inner depths, but he would have to check it out later.

His stroll down Grand didn't offer any tempting venues, and he entered Sea Tramp to see Whyte alone at the counter concentrating on a sketchbook.

From what Hensley could see, he hadn't changed much. Maybe a little heavier, but he had always been in need of a few pounds to fill out his six-three frame. He still had the skunk stripe in his thick black hair. Hensley had never been able to determine whether it was natural or an affectation that Whyte had adopted due to his name.

"Roberto," Hensley called out as he approached the bar. "I see that age does not wither nor custom stale your infinite variety."

Whyte looked up with an expression of expectation, frowned, and took a second look. Then the frown melted. "Henz. You got old."

"Nor does absence alter one whit your legendary wit. I see you are finished with your client."

"What client?"

"The refreshing of the ink?"

"Oh. That was for me." He held out his right arm to reveal the glistening new layer of red on a Woody Woodpecker tat.

"So you are free for a bit of conversation?"

"Absitively." He slammed the sketchbook shut. "How's Times Square?"

"I expect it is proceeding admirably under its own steam."

"Isn't that where you went off to?"

"Ah, yes, that was my intended destination, but I got sidetracked in Santa Fe and thus begins my tale. Shall we take a seat?" He gestured to the black and chrome chairs in front of the bar.

"Sure, but let's take it down to the Lovecraft."

"Is this some kind of romantic cruise?"

"H.P. Just down the street." Whyte glanced at his watch. "They don't open for another hour, but I know the bartender."

"I place myself at your mercy."

They walked two blocks south, Whyte texting the whole way. They arrived at a glass storefront plastered with macabre posters. Whyte pushed the door open, gestured Hensley into the dimly lit interior, and locked the door behind them.

The walls were plastered with Lovecraft-themed art. Whyte stepped up to the bar, and Hensley joined him.

"Hey, Ermen, you remember Hensley?"

Ermen had black lips, jet black hair with maroon streaks, a fair accumulation of metal bits, and a profusion of tats, doubtless courtesy of Whyte. She looked up from her back-bar preparations for a nanosecond. "Hi."

Hensley assessed her age to be thirty at the most, which meant she was in high school when he left the state. "Charmed, I'm sure." He grabbed a bar menu and skimmed the specialty drinks. The first on the list was called The Other Gods and featured absinthe. "What do you recommend?"

Whyte didn't bother to check the list. "The Defenestrated Zombie."

"I don't see it on the menu."

"It's Ermen's creation."

Hensley tossed the menu aside. "The Zombie it is then."

"Erm, two Zombies."

She replied without turning around. "Don't hold your breath."

Whyte smiled. "Don't pay her any mind. She likes to jerk my chain. So what's this story about Santa Fe?"

On the walk down, Hensley had revised his planned peroration, paring it to the minimum of detail in response to a fresh exposure to Whyte's basic nature.

"I have returned to the great northwest to extract an eleven-year-old boy from the clutches of his kidnapper. Singular. As in one kidnapper."

Whyte listened with the expression of a dog watching a man eat a steak.

"I don't know his exact location, but I have reason to believe that the kidnapper is tracking two teenagers who are likely hiding out in a cabin on Mt. Hood."

Ermen shoved two highball glasses garnished with lime wedges in front of them. "Two Defenestrated Zombies."

Hensley sniffed the drink. There was rum, some kind of anise liqueur, and an oddly medicinal aroma. He sipped it. It was simultaneously intriguing and disturbing. "My compliments. If I may ask, what is the secret ingredient?"

"Becherovka and two kinds of rum."

That covered the obvious. "And?"

"Gummidge's wort."

"She harvests it herself from the Tillamook State Forest," Whyte said.

"But there's something else." Hensley took another sip. "Almost industrial."

Ermen blushed and looked around before leaning forward and whispering, "Three drops of formaldehyde."

Hensley nodded appreciatively, pushed the glass aside, and turned back to Whyte, who was finishing off his drink. "My question for you is whether you would be interested in assisting me in this endeavor."

"Sure. I'm not doing anything this weekend." Whyte nodded at Hensley's glass. "You going to drink that?"

"I must confess to a congenital aversion to Gummidge's wort."

Whyte shrugged. "Your loss." He grabbed the glass and drank half of it in a single gulp.

"And perhaps yours as well," Hensley murmured. "My next step is to pin down the location of this cabin. Give me your number, and I'll call you when I have a plan."

"Roger that."

Whyte scrawled the information on a bar napkin and shoved it toward Hensley, who scanned it, verified a few questionable digits, and escaped to the afternoon sunlight.

He walked north, spotted a restaurant, crossed the street, and took the table by the door without consulting anyone. After a few impatient moments, he spied a waiter approaching.

Before the man could get a word out, Hensley said, "Can I get a glass of water immediately?"

The waiter regarded him quizzically for a few seconds, then departed and returned with a glass.

Hensley chugged it, set the empty glass on the table, and turned to the waiter. "Please forgive my importunity, but I was in serious need of hydration and dilution. I await enlightenment as to the fine fare I expect you offer."

The waiter's quizzical expression morphed to amusement. He handed Hensley a menu. "Something else to drink, perhaps?"

Hensley skimmed the offerings. "I'll try the Masaya Red."

With a nod, the waiter slipped off to the kitchen, and Hensley glanced at the front of the menu. Nicholas Restaurant. Lebanese. The luck of the Fletchers was making a comeback.

When the waiter returned with the wine, Hensley ordered the Arabian Breeze Mezza platter and set to a concerted bout of reevaluation.

As the memory of his Portland days reasserted themselves, he recalled that Whyte was less of a wild card and more of a loose cannon, but it couldn't be helped. This was not a one-man job, and due to psychological encumbrances, his best man wasn't available.

But the weak link in his plan, if it could rightly be called a plan, was the precise location of the one he had come to rescue.

He had hoped to find Sapphire and Spud through her cell phone, but the best Twink had been able to offer in that regard was "somewhere in the Mt. Hood National Forest."

It seemed that D.B. had followed a more direct route by focusing on those most likely to be able to provide a specific address.

As he sipped the wine, an excellent blend from the Bekka Valley, he considered following D.B.'s lead by infesting the environs of the southern end of Felony Flats, but just as quickly dismissed the idea. If D.B. were to spot the Patriot Pest Control van, things could go pear-shaped at the speed of pain.

Then the warmth of the wine brought him a sudden moment of clarity. He was wasting time trying to find Sapphire on the off-chance that it would allow him to lie in wait for Percival, who would have Reggie in tow.

All this time he should have focused his efforts toward cutting out the middle man. What he needed was Percival's number. Once he triangulated on Reggie's position and extracted him from the locus of felonious activity, he could address the secondary goal of saving Sapphire from herself. And from the Feds.

Hensley extracted his pocket phone, dialed 411, and asked for a listing for Percival Fisher in Santa Fe. Nothing. Pagosa Springs. More nothing. Albuquerque. An abundance of nothing.

He hung up and composed a mental list of those who might know, or be able to find, a mobile number for Percival.

Ronnie, queen of the compound, emerged as the most likely contact. But he had no way of contacting her.

D.B. would know, but that was a nonstarter.

Judge Cox? He might be able to get it.

As Hensley scrolled through his contacts, the waiter arrived and set the platter before him.

Fried cauliflower, falafel balls, and roasted garlic eggplant. And other stuff that would bear investigation.

"My good man, you have surpassed my greatest expectations."

"Do you need anything else?"

Hensley glanced at his wine glass. "I suspect that within the next ten minutes I shall feel the need to sample the cabernet."

"Of course."

After a nibble at a falafel ball, Hensley called the judge.

"You better be calling to tell me you have them and are headed back."

"Good evening, Judge."

"So you don't have them."

"Not yet, but I'm hoping you can procure information that will accelerate the process."

"You're forty-eight hours in and you got nothing?"

"Half of which was spent in transit. I have information on D.B.'s movements and have narrowed down Sapphire's location somewhat, but I lack the requisite information to pinpoint the subject of most interest, Percival."

"That is the least of your worries."

"Do you have the means to ferret out a mobile number for the person in question? If so, our mutual friend can do the rest."

"Powell arrived in Portland about the same time you did."

"Sheriff Powell?" Hensley could scarcely credit the statement, but Cox was not given to coarse jesting. "How did he—"

"Because he didn't attain the position of sheriff by being a complete incompetent. He's already liaised with the locals—city, county, state, federal. He knows as much as you do about the location of all concerned parties. Probably more than you do."

"But—"

"Powell called yesterday. After our conference in my office on Tuesday, he called Chrystal, and she told him everything. He knows about Percival and Reggie. The only thing he doesn't know is that you're there. That's just because Chrystal doesn't know, or he would know that too."

Hensley's mind raced, grasping at alternatives. "But he can't do anything. He's out of his jurisdiction. And since they've crossed state lines, the Feds are going to muscle their way into this thing and sideline the city and county and state guys into supporting roles. It could turn into a turf war between the FBI on the kidnapping and the DEA on the drugs. That should buy us some time. If I can just get Percival's number, I can find Reggie before—"

"Here's what you're going to do. You're going to forget about Reggie. The FBI will handle that better than you could ever think about doing. You're going to get Sapphire out of there before the DEA shows up and she ends up in a jail cell."

Forget about Reggie? He was the only reason Hensley was here at all. "But Reggie is my—"

"Yeah, yeah. Reggie is your son. The one you never wanted and didn't know about until two days ago. Let's get one thing straight. If you want to get your merit badge, forget about Reggie and focus on Sapphire. Because when it comes to her, Powell's hands are tied. He has to let the DEA take her. He can't spirit her away. Only you can do that."

Of course Powell was here. And it was Hensley's fault—confronting the sheriff on his own turf, practically handing him everything he needed to eliminate Hensley from the picture. If Hensley went after Reggie now, he could end up in the custody of the FBI himself.

But just back off and forget about Reggie? Abandon him?

The waiter showed up with a glass of cabernet, but his smile faded as he saw that the wine in front of Hensley was still half-full and the platter untouched.

Hensley held out his hand for the cabernet. The waiter shrugged and handed it to him. He drank half of it in one go. "Perhaps we could—"

"Mr. Fletcher, the only 'perhaps' in this equation is that perhaps I didn't make myself clear. The only standing you have here is to stand down. If I hadn't taken leave of my senses I would order just that. But against all evidence and reason, I still hold out a glimmer of hope that you can make one small contribution to the life of a young woman that you could have done better by if you had possessed the honor to sacrifice your whims for her needs. A small enough sacrifice in the larger scheme of things."

How could Cox ask him to turn his back on the one thing that might give his life meaning? Yes, Sapphire's situation demanded attention, but not at the expense of his own flesh and blood. Surely Cox could see that.

"I only wanted—"

"What you wanted is as irrelevant as what I wanted. What stands before us, what stands before you right now, is what is required. God knows I've demanded more of many a good man, many whose names are engraved in black granite in DC. So are you going to accept the task before you, or do I have to listen to what you wanted out of this?"

A longer silence followed, one that was interrupted only by the sound of scotch pouring into a glass and a bottle set down on a desk.

Hensley stared at the empty wine glass on the table, the half-empty glass beside it, the uneaten platter before him, the restaurant slowly filling up with customers, but without taking any of it in.

It was over. He'd come all this way—both in distance and understanding—to snatch his only son from mortal peril, and now even that was snatched away from him by an interfering Boy Scout. His only reason for being here had evaporated. The dream of reconciliation with his soul mate. The hope of breaking the family curse.

In the space of a single phone call, he was suddenly set adrift in the universe. For all practical purposes, his situation was no different than it was a year ago, before he had awakened to the possibility that with Chrystal, what he had always considered an illusion was perhaps possible for one such as he. Before he learned he had a son.

In truth, things were quite different now. There are some doors that, once opened, cannot be closed. And now fate had slammed that door shut.

Hensley flipped the pocket phone closed, dropped a couple of twenties on the table, and walked out the door onto Grand Avenue.

Chapter Thirty: Nadir

Some period of time later, Hensley found himself standing at the bar in the Lovecraft in the middle of Unhappy Hour, death metal filling the spaces between the people packed in front of him. He had no idea how he had come to be here or how long it had taken him to get here.

He was embedded in a throng of disaffected youths half his age. He surveyed the crowd, did a rough age-calculation, and revised his estimate downward.

Ermen of the black and maroon hair bustled about filling orders with an aloof competence that, under normal circumstances, would have elicited his approval, but all he could do was acknowledge it in an abstract validation of her skill.

Eventually the crush between him and Ermen thinned. He leaned forward and shouted "Defenestrated Zombie."

That got her attention, and she looked at him with a shock of recognition. "I thought you didn't like it."

Hensley shoved a twenty across the bar, and she turned to the task. Before he had time to process the rest of the scene, a highball glass sat before him. He flicked the mint sprig aside, slammed the drink, slid the glass toward her.

"Again."

She assessed him with a gaze that reminded him of his mother, an unsettling thought considering the age reversal, the clash in appearance, and the disparity of professions.

He pushed the thought away as she pushed the second Zombie across the bar. He drank it in the same fashion as the first and pushed the glass back to her. "Again."

Ermen shook her head. "Nobody gets a third Zombie. Not even you."

Hensley squinted at her. She stared back, uneasy but defiant. Ermen is squirming, he thought. "Okay, a gin and tonic." He slapped another twenty on the bar.

Before he got his billfold properly settled in his jacket, the drink appeared before him.

"That's it for you," Ermen said.

Hensley held the glass aloft. "Many felicitations of the day, Ermengarde."

He dismissed her shocked expression with a knowing wink. Did she think she was the only one in the room who had read Lovecraft?

Hensley slipped away from the bar in a fluid stagger, steadied by the crush of bodies. He wandered lonely as a cloud through the crowd, spied an empty chair against the wall near a youthful couple, and dropped into it in a pensive mood.

Hensley prided himself as a realist. A man of his indeterminate occupation didn't survive long in the world by harboring delusions of adequacy. Hensley saw the world as it was and bent it to his will more often than not. So take that, world!

He toasted the cruel world with a raised glass and took a generous sip of its contents. Then he glanced in the direction of the bar. Sweet Ermengarde, she had at least made his final drink with the good stuff. He struggled to his feet to go thank her for her generosity but thought better of it and sat back down.

It occurred to him that he was well and truly drunk, a state in which he rarely found himself, despite what some segments of the population might think.

And why not, he wanted to know. To everything there is a season. A time to be sober and a time to be drunk. Solomon might not have written those exact words, but God knew that he could very well have. Old Sol wasn't a man to shrink at any indulgence. And when a man has just been shoved out of the picture in the matter of his only son, well, there you have it.

Hensley leaned back against the wall and offered a studied toast to the ancient king and soul mate. Between the two of them they knew a thing or two about a thing or two.

But he had interrupted himself. He was thinking about something. About reality, self knowledge.

Yes, that was the thing or two of which he had thought. He took his reality straight, no chaser. But there was no need to overdo it. Reality had to be tempered with perspective. After all, as some noted philosopher had said, there was no evidence that life should be taken seriously.

But the judge had judged him and found him wanting.

"Take a number," Hensley shouted from his perch.

The girl at the next table glanced at him with alarm but turned away when he met her gaze.

Hensley had made a career of spurning such judgments, starting with his father back in Angola. He took a deep drink from his glass, draining it, and slammed it down on the table next to him. The flighty girl screamed and jumped up, jostling the table and spilling the drinks.

A tall boy with ear gauges and a sleeve tattoo loomed over him. "What's your problem, old man?"

Hensley regarded him without moving. "Settle down, mate. Nobody's yanking your chain."

"Well, I'm about to yank yours."

In an indifferent motion, Hensley planted his feet squarely on the floor and rippled his body from its slumped position. "Don't let your mouth write a check your body can't cash, junior."

"You wish." The kid lunged forward.

Hensley shot out his right foot between the kid's legs, hooked the left ankle, and swiped out to the right. As the kid teetered at an angle, Hensley sprang from his chair, grabbed the kid's shoulder, and spun him face down onto the floor. The next second, Hensley had his knee in the kid's back, ratcheting his arm up to his shoulder blade.

Then Hensley was being dragged to the door by a guy the size of Vermont. He knew better than to resist. The guy dumped him on his back on the sidewalk, raised a boot over his head to stomp him, thought better of it, and went back inside.

Hensley rolled to his hands and knees and struggled to his feet with the aid of a lamppost.

It was still light outside, although the shadows were long. Pedestrians gave him a wide berth.

"You should see the other guy," Hensley said to no one in particular.

He headed north to the Sea Tramp and the van, but when he got there, he paused for an assessment. It was only a mile to his rooms. Better to take a twenty-minute walk than to be sidelined with a DUI.

Hensley sauntered north to Burnside, turned right, and continued, but two blocks over he happened upon the B Side Tavern. He walked in, took a seat at the bar, and ordered a Fearless Porter from Laura.

As he waited, he cased the joint. It reminded him of a Texas roadhouse, complete with the aroma of cigarettes wafting in from the back patio. The light boxes above the bar featured medical x-rays of various body parts.

When the beer arrived, he took an inaugural sip, sighed with satisfaction, and thought about life and green things in general. The thing was, he had a son. Eleven years old. And he'd never seen him. And if the conversation with the judge was any indication, might never see him.

And that didn't set right with Hensley. Not even a little bit. He straightened into an erect posture on his stool and took a generous swig of the porter.

Forget Judge Cox. Hensley was here for his son. That was the only thing that mattered. All he had to do was find Percival, get Reggie, and get out of town. Oh, and snag Sapphire while he was at it. Couldn't let Powell and the DEA get their hands on her.

He pulled out his pocket phone and called Mr. Twink.

Mr. Twink answered immediately. "Now what?"

"I need a mobile number and current location for Percival Fisher."

"You need a reality check."

"I am a paying customer in good standing."

"Yes on the first. No on the second."

"Elaborate."

"I received a call from our mutual friend. I can help you on the 9263 number, but that's it."

"I can pay."

"I don't care."

"Cox isn't a part of this."

"Look here, *Robin Bumstead*. I don't want to hear about your personal problems. If I get a signal from 9263, I'll call you."

"Just one number. That's all I need."

Twink didn't respond.

"Hello?" Hensley checked the phone.

Disconnected.

Hensley took a long drink, wiped his mouth with his sleeve, and took a second to get his bearings. The judge had not only dressed him down but had effectively stripped him of options.

Not that Hensley was without his resources, but he couldn't summon them on a dime, and with Powell in town stirring up the natives, slow and steady would not win the race.

Hensley mentally reviewed his local contacts in Portland but found the cupboard bare. Then came the epiphany.

Davison! He hadn't exhausted all his resources. Sure, calling him was a long shot, an act of desperation, really, but he was desperate, so it made sense. Plus, a mere forty-eight hours ago, give or take, had Davison not said to call if he needed help with retrieving Reggie? Yes, he had.

He flipped the phone open and scrolled through his half-dozen contacts. As his finger hovered over the button, he paused. This would be a delicate call. Bar noise would not lend credibility to his cause. He dropped some cash on the bar and walked down to the corner.

He turned down Seventh and put a block between himself and the Burnside traffic before he pushed the button. As it rang, he checked the time. Eight p.m. in Texas on a Friday. Davison could be having a nice dinner with . . . no, evidently Masie was back up in Detroit and who else would he be dining with? Not the lovely Angela, surely. So he was probably at home—

"There's only one reason you should be calling this number."

"And a pleasant June evening to you, my brother. Have you hit a hundred yet down there?"

"Ninety-three. A cold front. What do you want?"

"I called for precisely the reason you suspect. Do you think you can avail yourself of whatever back-channel resources remain at your disposal to find a mobile number for Percival Fisher and perhaps a last known location? I have a strong reason to suspect that he's currently in Oregon in the confines of the greater Portland metropolis."

After a longish pause, Davison responded. "Don't you think this is a matter for the FBI?"

"We both know they won't listen to me. They'll start from scratch and take a week to learn from other sources what I already know. And they'll probably wreck a half-dozen lives in the process."

"What about the girl?"

"Sapphire? Somebody else is working that angle."

"Who?"

It was Hensley's turn for the long pause. "A friend of the family."

"Why can't he get Reggie while he's at it?"

"He's Sapphire's father, so naturally he's focused on her. And naturally I'm focused on Reggie for the same reason."

In the following silence, Hensley scanned his environment. A couple had parked on Ankeny and was strolling up to Burnside arm-in-arm, a beau courting his chosen belle. It was a rare sight in this modern age, and he allowed himself a small smile. In the midst of his troubles, it refreshed his spirit to see a flicker of goodness in the world. He considered going back to the B Side for another drink but thought better of it.

"What's your plan?" Davison finally said.

"Once I locate the rogue knight, I shall engage a few confederates." At this point, he was thinking he'd have to settle for Whyte and Brother Joseph and hope for the best. "I will insinuate myself into his lair, and between the three of us, we will subdue him, extract Reggie, and leave him to his own devices in the matter of recovering the drugs."

"You're going to let a kidnapper go free?"

"I could call 911. Anonymously."

"And tell them what? There's a kidnapper tied up at the following address, but when they get there they won't find a kid who's been napped or any evidence that will support an arrest, much less a conviction?"

"I must confess that I haven't given much thought to the matter of bringing Percival to justice. I've been focused on bringing Reggie to safety." Hensley took a deep breath. "And if I have to sacrifice the former to effect the latter, I won't lose sleep over it. Percival will get what's coming to him eventually, with or without my help."

"If ever there was a fool on a fool's errand . . ." Davison blew out a gust of breath. "There is so much that is so wrong about this, and almost nothing that is right. I know I'm going to regret this. No, strike that. I already regret it. But I'll see what I can do."

Hensley scarcely believed what he was hearing. The call was a Hail Mary at best, but it seemed Mary was coming through. "Given the timeframe, I need the information by tomorrow morning. I'll need time to reconnoiter and develop a plan before sunset."

"You realize this is Friday night, right?"

"And surely you of all people realize that tomorrow morning might be too late? I am in the position to offer inducements of a financial nature to expedite the request, if necessary."

"Whose credit card do you have now?"

That one cut a little close to the bone, but Hensley let it slide. When this was over, he'd pay off Chrystal's card. But Davison didn't have to know about that. "If you're still worried about those charges on your card, rest your mind. I'm good for it. Interest. Penalties. I'll cover it."

"I'm not holding my breath."

"Which is fortunate, since there is no need."

"I'll call you when I have something."

"Davison . . ." Hensley didn't trust himself to finish the sentence. "Well?"

"I am not incognizant of the sacrifice of your offer. It might be— no, it is the most important thing I have ever asked of you. Even more than granting me my freedom in 1980."

While everyone else in the compound in Angola is out in the clearing welcoming the supply plane, Hensley slinks behind the clinic, slips into the house, and pulls the backpack from under his bed. For months it has laid buried behind boxes and books and stuff, like a land mine. Inside, clothes, food, rope, matches, a knife, a compass, a little money, anything that would be useful on the road.

More times than he can count, he has used the distraction of the supply plane to grab the backpack with the intention of leaving once and for all. And each time he has stood, frozen like a sungazer lizard on a rock, until the noise of the locals hauling boxes to the clinic breaks the spell, and he buries the pack again and goes to help.

But not this time. He senses that if he slips the strap off his shoulder and slides it back under the bed, he'll never leave. He scans the room one more time and spots the red and green folders, faux-leather quad-fold albums with die-cut, coin-sized holes, one each for US pennies, nickels, dimes, and quarters. The folders Uncle Rex gave him back when they still lived in the States and anything seemed possible. Even going to the moon or getting his face on a coin.

He shrugs out of the straps, unzips the backpack, slides the four albums in, and hoists it on again.

Lurking in the undergrowth on the edge of the clearing, Hensley lures Davison from the flurry of activity around the plane and draws him into the shadows. Far enough that the moist, soft edges of the jungle kill every noise but its own and the sound of their feet on the trail.

Then Hensley drops to one knee, pulls the folders from his backpack, and holds them out to Davison.

"You're nine. The same age as when Uncle Rex gave these to me. Now it's your turn."

"But don't you want to—"

"I travel light." Hensley slings on the backpack, shrugging his shoulders to settle it, avoiding Davison's questioning squint.

"You're—"

Hensley whirls around and drops a hand on Davison's shoulder. "Shh."

Davison chokes his words back, tears springing to his eyes. Hensley forces himself to hold eye contact, frowning like Dad when he will brook no argument.

"I have to, Davison. But you can't tell anyone."

"But Dad—"

"No one," Hensley whispers fiercely, squeezing Davison's shoulder. "Now you take care of those coins, and one day I'll be back to check on you. But only if you keep this a secret. Otherwise, I'll never come back."

Davison's eyes teem. "Okay."

Hensley tousles Davison's hair and backs away, maintaining eye contact until he turns away with a jerk and runs through the jungle, heedless of branches and roots and rocks.

Hours later he pauses for water and then walks, scouting out a good place to make camp for the night. And he doesn't see Davison again for six years. Dad's funeral.

In the long silence on the line, Hensley glanced up Seventh toward Burnside, watching the traffic flow past. Hensley had offered his thanks to Davison based on his own perspective—that as important as that moment in the jungle had been for him, this moment dwarfed it.

But in the rush of emotion, he had failed to take into account Davison's experience. For his nine-year-old brother, that day in the jungle represented the ultimate betrayal. A day he had never forgotten and had never forgiven. And a day that Hensley had never given Davison a reason to forgive.

Sure, in the past month he had come to Davison's aid more than once, had liberated him from imprisonment at the hands of murderous thugs, had joined him in battle against an international assassin, had even spurred him into action when he faltered in the matter of Masie and his chance at embracing the blessed state that had eluded them both.

But for the most part, it was easy to trace the path of self-interest in everything Hensley had done, not only in 1980, but in the last few weeks, both in Cancún and since their return. In his defense, from the perspective of others, the self-interest theme in recent episodes was more of a projection of previous behavior than actual motivation. But not everyone would see it that way. And not one person in particular.

Hensley broke the silence. "Pardon my foray into less pleasant times. I merely meant to say—"

"I'll call you when I have something."

The line went dead. Hensley snapped the phone shut and shoved it into his pocket. He took a deep breath, walked back up to Burnside, and turned east.

He didn't blame Davison for his skepticism. For his resentment. But the landscape had changed, even if Davison couldn't see it. When a body discovered he was a father, it changed things.

A block later he came across The Wurst. On the other side of the plate glass, a crowd of weekend warriors engaged in pool and darts and skee-ball and other entertainments. An obsidian bar flanked with red-backed barstools beckoned.

Suddenly thirsty, Hensley pushed through the door and found an empty stool on the back side of the bar. He picked up a menu. After the phone call with the judge, he'd stormed out of the Lebanese restaurant without touching the platter he had ordered.

He evaluated his choices. Sausages of various types. A bartenderette spun a napkin in front of him. "What'll it be?"

"I'm torn between the Mo' Rockin' Lamb and the Trophy."

"They're both my favorites, but I lean toward the lamb."

"That settles it for me. And a Trumer Pils at your earliest convenience."

A few minutes later, he had a frosty pint glass in his hand. He turned to watch the crowd of twenty-somethings inaugurating the weekend. Young, energetic, invincible. Hopeful.

In ten years, Reggie would be of age, sharing the vista of a new generation with infinite potential, endless opportunity. Hensley pictured himself playing pool with his son, but the realization that by then he would be in his sixties crept up on him. And what twenty-one-year-old kid with the whole world before him would want to be shackled with an old man three times his age on a night like this in a place like this?

Hensley pulled the photo from his jacket and looked at the next-generation incarnation of his former self.

But I am not your typical off-the-shelf father, Hensley responded. Before the thought was fully formed, he saw it for what it was. Hubris. Self-importance.

It was the way of things for the old to give way to the new. Nothing personal. Just reality. Every season a generation of spent leaves spread out in a carpet, providing the nourishment for a fresh batch of foliage that would in the fullness of time dance its own spiraling descent to the forest floor.

Who was he fooling? He was nothing more than a leaf in denial, clinging to the branch that had no more use for him. So he had a son. So what?

What did he have to offer Reggie? Tips on how to game the system to his advantage? Pointers on how to survive until the next opportunity came along?

Up to now, Hensley had prided himself on his ability to live moment by moment like the lilies of the field, not giving a care for the morrow. Was this all he had to offer in the way of counsel? Take it as it comes, make the most of what stumbles into your path, give no thought to the future.

What kind of father would raise his son like that?

The clink of a plate on the bar jolted Hensley from his meditations.

"One Mo' Rockin' Lamb with sauerkraut, pickle, and chips," the bartenderette said.

Hensley spun back around on his stool and slapped Reggie's photo face-down on the bar. "May angels sing you to your rest," Hensley said, but it felt hollow even to him. He glanced at her left hand, saw the ring, called out on an impulse. "Excuse me."

She turned back in anticipation of a request for condiments or some such.

Beneath the makeup, Hensley detected dark circles due to late nights and early mornings. Too much partying? Or something else?

"I didn't catch your name."

She eyed him cautiously. "Jessica."

"Hensley." He gestured to her ring. "You're married?"

Jessica nodded.

"Children?"

Her face relaxed a bit. "A girl. Three next month."

"Then perhaps you can resolve an issue I've been contemplating." He took a deep breath and collected his thoughts. "A friend of mine has recently learned that he has an eleven-year-old son from a former relationship. The mother had kept this information from him. He discovered it through other channels."

She took no pains to hide the skepticism that flashed across her face as she glanced at the photo on the bar.

Hensley pressed on. "He is now in a quandary as to his next steps. The mother has remained unattached all these years, and my friend is concerned that his son is entering a phase in his life when a male role model is critical."

"And?"

"Should he disrupt the status quo to fill the void?"

"What about the mother?"

"In what sense? She's an admirable woman. Exceptional. Un-equalled."

"Does she want him back?"

"You raise an excellent question. Let us say that she is less than enthusiastic as to the prospect."

"So she's against it."

"Admirably and succinctly put, Jessica. You have captured the essence of her position."

"What about your friend?"

"He's a good sort. Independent. Resourceful. Charming in his own way."

Jessica peered at him. "Are you in advertising?"

"My interests are wide and varied."

"Independent? Resourceful?"

"Quite."

"Like your friend."

Hensley could see that Jessica was not a woman to be trifled with, but he would expect no less from a gal who dealt them off the arm in a rowdy establishment such as The Wurst.

However, for the sake of the story, he chose to maintain the ruse. "We have much in common. It is the basis for our long-standing friendship."

He paused to refresh his spirits with the Trumer. "It comes to this. Should he step in and assume the role fate and biology have thus ordained?"

A young man of the hipster persuasion bellied up to the bar with an empty pint glass. "Double Mountain Homestead."

Jessica performed the needful as Hensley addressed himself to replenishing the nutrients the human machine required for continued operation.

When the hipster departed, Jessica turned to Hensley. "I don't know enough about the situation to call it either way. And I don't want to know. But I can tell you this." She placed her hands on the bar and held Hensley's gaze. "There is nothing better than a good father. And there is nothing worse than a bad one."

Jessica spoke with the conviction of experience, and Hensley felt the weight of her pronouncement settle on him like a layer of ash after a volcanic eruption.

She picked up his empty pint glass. "Another?" Her voice indicated that she sensed he was in need of an additional dose.

"You're probably right."

As she pulled the pint, Hensley finished off the sausage. She placed the glass before him like a nurse on the battlefield administering morphine. "I hope your friend makes the right decision."

Hensley lifted the pint toward her. "I shall relay your wisdom to him."

As he drank deeply, Hensley realized that Jessica was right. And Chrystal was right. Judge Cox was right. Even Davison was right.

Hensley had nothing to offer Reggie that he couldn't glean from a boxed set of "Worst-Case Scenario" booklets and a copy of Ecclesiastes.

If he had any honor, he would call the FBI right now, tell them everything he knew, and fade into oblivion. He pulled out his pocket phone, flipped it open, and then realized it wasn't that simple.

First off, he needed a number. Not the number of the Portland field office, but the number of the special agent in charge. Second, he needed credibility. Otherwise the agent would blow him off, and it would be for nothing. Third, well, two was enough for him right now. He would work out the third thing later.

Instead, he called the lawyer working on the will. It had been two days since he'd put the man on the case. An update was in order.

He answered on the fourth ring. "Bornhouser."

"Hensley Fletcher calling. Do you have a minute to discuss the status of the Stone estate?"

"Do you realize that it's . . . two-fifteen? A.M.?"

"That had escaped my attention. On the other hand, it's Friday. The night is young."

"Yeah, but I'm not." The line went dead.

DAY 10: SATURDAY

Chapter Thirty-One: Materiel

Hensley came to life in the Everett Street Guest House feeling half dead. He blamed it on the formaldehyde. He checked the time. Ten a.m. He'd seen worse.

As he worked through the requisite post-binge steps, starting with a blistering hot shower, the major points of the previous day bubbled to the surface.

All his machinations in regard to extracting Reggie from his plight faded to irrelevance as he recalled his conversation with Jessica at The Wurst. Not only would the FBI have a better shot at bringing Reggie to safety and Percival to justice, but Reggie would probably have a better shot at life without the potentially devastating tectonic shift of the knowledge that he'd had a father all along. The wrong sort of father.

But there still remained the matter of Sapphire. Most likely the best thing he could do for Reggie, and Chrystal was to disentangle Sapphire from the web of complications into which she had fallen. In the case of a raid, as a duly sworn officer of the law Powell couldn't pull her aside and whisk her to safety. Only a civilian such as Hensley could effect that outcome.

And when it came down to it, if he could pull it off it might be the best thing he had done in his life. In which case, his efforts were not in vain. But he would still need a posse to effect the rescue. Which meant he needed to ascertain the exact location of the Spudster. And Cecil was his best bet on that score.

She answered on the fourth ring.

"MacMillan Bail Bonds."

"Cecil, how goes it with the battle of the generations?"

"Fletch?"

"At your service."

"Oh, I knew I forgot something. Now where is it?" The sounds of rustling paper ensued. "No, that's not it. Ha! Gotcha." The noise subsided. "In 2007, one Melvin Tatum purchased a cabin on a ten-acre lot in the southern foothills of Mt. Hood. Paid with cash."

Hensley jotted down the details. "Business must be good."

"They always pay me on time. Hey, I was thinking of doing happy hour at the Virginia later on. Want to meet me there?"

"Nothing would give me greater pleasure, but first I have to see a man about a dog. If I'm not there by five, start without me, and I'll catch you up at a future date."

"Don't let the grass grow under your feet, because I'm telling you right now the seat next to me at the bar won't stay empty for long."

"I have no doubt, my succulent one."

Hensley disconnected and immediately called Whyte, whose voice croaked across the ether.

"Yeah?"

"The game is afoot, my plucky companion. Meet me at the City State Cafe posthaste. Ann Marie will prepare a feast such as to spur us on to heroic deeds."

"What?"

"In the interest of efficiency, I shall restrict myself to words of one syllable. "Get up. Food now. City State Diner." Hensley shook his head. "Sorry about the last part, old chap, but the owners didn't see fit to employ a name consonant with our syllabic requirements."

"City State?"

"Across from the Coca-Cola plant. I'll meet you there."

Hensley completed his morning ablutions and packed. There was no way to tell how things would shake out today, and he had learned from long experience to be ready to evacuate at a moment's notice. Sometimes sooner.

He started the coffee brewing, gathered the various foodstuffs he had accumulated on the trip, and bundled them into the shopping bag from Goodwill. They were headed out to the trackless wastes of the Mt. Hood National Forest and wouldn't be able to dart over to a beanery whenever the mood struck them.

Verifying that he had left nothing behind, Hensley stowed his duffel bag in the Patriot Pest Control van, locked it up, and set off on the five-block trek.

Steam rose from his coffee in the mid-morning chill. They would have to take Whyte's car, whatever that might be. If Spud or Sapphire caught sight of the van, it could spook them, as they would naturally assume it was someone from the compound come to get them.

At the diner, Hensley greeted Ann Marie, ordered a few breakfast sandwiches and coffee for starters, and took a window seat.

He pulled the map from his bag of provisions and spread it out on the bar. Looked like it was about forty miles to Mt. Hood Village, which was on the western border of the park. Hensley glanced at his notes on the location of the cabin, but the map didn't give that level of detail. He'd need to get another map, which would probably require a drive into town to Powell's or some such establishment.

A black Jeep Wrangler pulled up across the street. Whyte emerged, squinting like a bear disturbed during high-REM hibernation.

As he crossed the street, he caught sight of Hensley and scowled. Hensley folded the map as Whyte dropped into a seat and took a gulp of the coffee awaiting him.

After downing the house sausage sandwich, Whyte turned to Hensley. "Why can't we snatch this kid at a reasonable hour like civilized people?"

"I'm afraid the target has changed and the timetable has accelerated." Hensley filled him in on the details. When he got to the part about needing a map of Mt. Hood National Park, Whyte pulled out a smartphone.

"You got the coordinates?"

Hensley placed the paper before him. In fifteen seconds Whyte turned the phone toward him. "You need to ditch that Star Trek communicator thing you have and get one of these."

The screen showed an aerial shot of a cabin embedded in an evergreen forest next to a creek. Hensley took it from Whyte's hand to look closer, but the image disappeared, replaced by a matrix of icons.

"I think I broke it." He held the phone out to Whyte.

"You have to hold it by the edges." Whyte restored the image and set the phone on the counter. "Pinch to zoom in. Other way to zoom out. Swipe to pan."

Hensley tried it. "Yes, I can see the appeal."

Whyte slipped off his stool. "You figure it out. I'm getting something that'll stick to the ribs."

Hensley zoomed out until he found Mt. Hood Village and panned to the right. A few miles east he saw Rhododendron. That rang a bell. A few seconds deliberation identified it as the place Mr. Twink lost Sapphire's signal. A few miles farther, a blacktop road veered off to the northeast and zigzagged up to Henry Creek, where the cabin stood a hundred yards past the end of the road.

Whyte set a plate teeming with carbs and protein on the counter. "What do they call this concoction?" Hensley said.

"Breakfast meatloaf deluxe." He set an omelette in front of Hensley. "It wasn't on the menu. I just told Ann Marie it was for you."

Hensley pushed the phone aside and sliced the omelette. It appeared to feature several types of cheese, spinach, and bacon. He turned on his stool, caught Ann Marie's eye, and blew her a kiss.

Whyte was already halfway through his mountain of food. Hensley turned the phone to him.

"To get to the cabin, we take off Highway 26 here, but there's no way to approach it by road without being seen."

Hensley panned farther east. "Instead, we stay on Highway 26, skip the next road, and take the third one. At the first bend, we take the Jeep off-road up to the Zigzag River, cross on foot, and hike the half mile up to the cabin."

He panned the map to follow the directions. "With this kind of cover, we can get a three-sixty view of the cabin, identify all the exits, try to discover who is inside, and formulate a plan."

Whyte nodded at Hensley's sports coat and cowboy boots. "You got to suit up."

"Plus gear and supplies." Hensley dug into the omelette. "Bottled water, binoculars, flashlights, rope, a good knife, zip ties, blankets. The usual."

"Andy and Bax," Whyte said as he scooped up the last of the grits and chased it with what was left of the coffee.

"Precisely." The military supply and outdoorsman emporium had been outfitting treks into the wilderness for decades. It was only a block from the Sea Tramp. In fact, Hensley had stumbled past it on his way to the van last night.

Hensley stood. "Since we don't know what we'll find up there, I'm going to call in reinforcements."

On the short drive, he called the number Brother Joseph had given him, but got voicemail. He left a message and devoted the next hour to provisioning for the trip. He replaced the cowboy boots with hiking boots, the sports coat with a camo jacket, and added a black touk. Then he remembered what Mr. Twink had said about losing the cell signal and bought three walkie-talkies.

It was in the high sixties a little past noon when they set out on the hour drive to Mt. Hood Village.

After a few minutes, the urban cityscape gave way to suburban strip malls and big-box stores, then that fell away to a rolling landscape with the occasional structure.

About halfway there, the density and hue of the foliage deepened until they were riding through a tunnel of evergreens. At Mt. Hood Village, vestiges of the tourism industry sprouted in the form of signs for cabin and cottage rentals.

It got a little more redneck as they approached Rhododendron, where the structures sacrificed aesthetics for utility.

Remembering what Mr. Twink said about losing the signal in Rhododendron, Hensley tried Brother Joseph again and left another message.

After they passed the Dairy Queen, the view improved, and a few miles later they spotted the blacktop road that led to the Tatum hideaway and turned left on the third road.

Whyte negotiated a path through the brush, and after a few minutes, they were overlooking Zigzag River, completely hidden from the road. Whyte turned the Jeep around for a quick exit, and they debarked and prepared for the hike.

Hensley took stock of the conditions. Clear blue sky and seven hours of daylight left, although under the canopy they would have an early and extended twilight.

They weren't quite at two-thousand feet elevation, but the temperature had fallen over ten degrees to the mid fifties. The exertion of the half-mile hike uphill would keep them plenty warm, but that would quickly fade during the ensuing hours of surveillance, which would involve long periods of stillness punctuated with careful movements. Hensley would need the jacket well before sunset.

Chapter Thirty-Two: Cabin Fever

Whyte locked up the Jeep, they crossed the Zigzag River, which was more of a creek, really, and started up the hill to the north.

The area was cluttered with cabins, and Hensley and Whyte did their best to remain covert. When they topped the next rise, the terrain dropped away in a gradual slope for about thirty feet to where a road cut across their path. A solid road carved into the granite of the mountain, barely the width of a single vehicle and quite rough. Anyone approaching by car would have to move slowly.

"Our destination lies beyond the next switchback to the east." He nodded to the hairpin curve to their right. Preferring to stay off the road, Hensley crossed it and pushed up the rise on the other side. It was steep going, and he paused at the top to catch his breath and allow Whyte to join him. They had left the cabins behind. Before them lay another stretch of rough road.

They crossed it and scaled the next rise with considerable effort. Hensley turned right at the ridge and led Whyte east. To their right lay the lower leg of the road, to their left the upper.

After a few minutes, the blacktop to their left played out into a gravel track leading into a clearing about fifty yards across. The corner of a weathered cabin appeared through vegetation.

The sun glinted off two square casement windows on the south side of the cabin with a chimney between. On the west side, facing them, an awning shaded a shallow porch that was three steps up from the ground. On either side of a closed door, Hensley spied two double-hung windows twice as tall as the others.

Hensley dropped down behind a flaming red rhododendron, and Whyte crouched beside him. The cabin appeared to be about twice as deep as it was wide. No vehicle parked out front.

"Looks like nobody's home," Whyte said.

"Their means of transport could be sequestered behind the cabin." Hensley squinted at the windows but couldn't see anything through the glare of the sun. "Or one of them has ventured out to the trading post for supplies and the other is waiting behind the door with a shotgun."

"That too."

"Assuming we are at the right place, we're looking at two, one, or zero people inside."

Whyte grunted.

"I propose that you proceed to the right, I'll go left, and we'll meet on the other side to compare combs."

Whyte repeated his grunt, slid down below the ridgeline to the south, and crept eastward.

Hensley watched him for a few seconds. The kid had skills. Just as long as he kept the crazy on a leash, he might work out okay. Hensley retraced his steps until the cabin was obscured by the forest and scrambled down the incline to the edge of the road.

He waited for a full minute, watching and listening for the approach of a vehicle or a pedestrian. The shadow of a hawk flashed across the blacktop, and he glanced up to see it disappear behind the tree line on the other side of the road. Taking this as an invitation, Hensley darted across the road and into the foliage on the other side.

Turning eastward, Hensley eased forward until he once again had the cabin in sight. On this side of the road, he was on the same level as the cabin or slightly lower as the grade dropped to the west. He settled in a zazen position, emptied his mind, and contemplated the vista before him, alert for any movement on the grounds or behind the windows.

After five minutes, Hensley decided to give it two more. He caught sight of a quivering branch up on the rise to his right. He froze, wondering if they had been made. After a minute or so, he concluded that Whyte must have lost his footing and grabbed a branch for support. Could happen to anyone.

Hensley pulled back into the brush and eased up the grade of the mountain until he had a full view of the north side of the cabin. It featured two double-hung windows with a small casement window between them. Without the glare from the direct sun, Hensley could see plaid curtains drawn in all the windows. He watched them for a while, surveyed the entire clearing for some revealing detail, then continued east, keeping well back from the splash of sunlight falling on the southern edge of the tree line.

When he cleared the back corner of the cabin, he saw a brown LTD at least a few decades old. The ozone killer Toni had described.

"So, two little piggies are at home," Hensley breathed to himself.

As he proceeded to the corner of the clearing, he noted the back of the house had a small attic window and, like the front of the house, two double-hung windows with a door between them. Unlike the front, there was only one step down from the door, as this side of the house was farther up the grade. Curtains obscured the northernmost window, but the other window was open. Everything inside was in shadow, but he caught the glint of chrome and suspected this was the kitchen.

A few yards outside the kitchen door, a counter-height deal table obviously served as a cleaning station for fish or birds or rabbits, whatever quarry was appropriate for the area. The small wooden out-building about twenty yards behind the cabin was either a shed or a pump house or both.

Hensley connected with Whyte up on the slope, thirty feet into the foliage directly behind the cabin. "In case you were dying of curiosity, that's Spud's car down there."

Whyte nodded. "So it's two against two."

"Unless they've picked up some friends. Anything of interest on the south side?"

"Two windows, chimney, electrical meter, possible root cellar." Whyte said. "How about you?"

"Two windows, most likely two bedrooms." Hensley nodded to the back of the cabin. "Projecting the interior from exterior clues, I'd say the front door opens into a large area that extends to the back of the cabin, living room in front, kitchen in back, the fireplace heating the area quite admirably. On the north, two bedrooms separated by a bathroom. Possible stairway or ladder to an attic or loft space, given the window in back."

"So, one of us takes the front while the other covers the back?"

Hensley thought for a moment. "Those bedroom windows are big enough to serve as an emergency exit. Before we brace them from the front and rear, I'd like to see if we can insert an operative into one or both of the bedrooms. With the windows covered, they're blind on that side unless someone deliberately pulls the curtains aside."

Whyte issued a doubtful grunt.

Hensley shrugged. "We should at least have a body covering the north side in case someone tries to slip out when we burst in."

Whyte conceded the point with a shrug of his own.

Hensley extracted his pocket phone. No signal. "I shall return to the Jeep and drive west in search of a signal to check on my third man to cover the windows. You should take up a position on the western front by the road, which will allow you to observe any comings and goings."

He stood, pocketed the phone, and held out his hand. Whyte considered for a few seconds, then relinquished the keys. They proceeded around the southern perimeter in a stealthy fashion and split ways at the southwest corner of the clearing—Whyte to his observation point and Hensley to the Jeep.

Hensley turned west onto Highway 26 and watched his pocket phone as he retraced their route. A mile down the road he came upon Rhododendron and caught a glimpse of a signal—one bar and then another. A buzz and a beep sounded from his phone like the one he heard in the hospital, but he was no wiser as to the cause.

He pulled into the Dairy Queen parking lot, backed up to the tree line to monitor the road, and dialed the Jesuit.

"Brother Joseph speaking."

"Are you still in?"

"Brother Hensley?"

"The same."

"I'm in."

Hensley gave him directions to the clandestine parking spot by the Zigzag. "Dress for maximum agility and minimum visibility. And bring a flashlight."

"It'll be at least an hour."

"That fits our timeline admirably." He hung up and checked the time. It was getting on toward four. At least four hours until sunset. He glanced at the Dairy Queen. A burger or two might not be amiss during the interim.

As he slid out of the front seat, a brown LTD with superannuated shocks careened off the highway and into the parking lot, rocking to a stop in a manner as to claim a portion of four parking slots. The driver's door sprang open with a metallic squawk and a wiry-haired kid of about six feet and one hundred fifty pounds unfolded from the front seat. He looked up and down the highway and hurried into the DQ.

Hensley dropped back into the Jeep, keeping one eye on the LTD and the other on the road on the off-chance that Spud's paranoia was justified. After ten minutes, Spud emerged with a white Dairy Queen bag, popped into the car, and swung back onto the highway in the direction from which he came.

Now was no time for relying on assumptions. Hensley cranked the Jeep and followed the LTD at a distance calculated to keep him just in sight on the broad curve of the highway. As he suspected, the LTD veered off onto the blacktop road to the cabin.

Hensley cruised past, turned around at the next turnoff, and returned to the DQ. He rushed inside, made a show of scanning the place as if expecting to meet someone, and then strode to the bored munchkin behind the counter.

"I was supposed to meet someone, but he's not here. Maybe you've seen him. About six feet. Skinny. Hair like an exploded bedspring."

The vague suggestion of a smile flickered across the munchkin's visage. "He just left."

"Curse the luck!" Hensley dashed toward the door but stopped halfway and glanced back. "Did he order something to go?"

The munchkin's gaze wandered up and to the left. "Six-piece chicken strip basket with country gravy, two half-pound flamethrower grill burgers."

"I knew he'd get it wrong." Hensley walked back to the counter and ordered half a dozen half-pound burgers and a wheelbarrow-load of fries and onion rings. Thus provisioned, he drove the mile to the third road and backed the Jeep into its former spot.

He considered trotting up the hill to deliver rations to Whyte, but the round trip would use the better part of an hour, and he didn't want to risk being absent when the Jesuit showed up. Instead he dined and contemplated the implications of Spud's order. Either Spud loved him some burgers or there was a third person in the cabin. The wisdom of summoning the Jesuit was now evident.

That raised the question of how to effect the rescue. Given the possibility of a third person, maybe a rogue member of the Tatum clan, perhaps they should have supplemented their supplies with a few flash-bang grenades. But as it now stood, Hensley's motley band was in no position to employ shock-and-awe tactics to overwhelm the occupants of the cabin.

Under the circumstances, Hensley felt that their greatest assets were the force of his personality and the ignorance of the fugitives. He had faced longer odds with less at his disposal and lived to tell the tale.

As the Jesuit's Volvo wagon idled into view between the trees, Hensley crumpled the paper from the second burger, dropped it into the bag, and stepped out to meet the cavalry. He thought he detected a passenger, but the afternoon sun dappled the windshield with an intermittent glare, and he couldn't be sure.

Brother Joseph backed into a space between two trees on the other side of the Jeep. The passenger door opened and Tru Pak got out.

"He called me," Brother Joseph said as he climbed out of the car. "I didn't think you'd mind."

Hensley eyed Tru. "And the dragon?"

Tru stared at him intently but didn't respond.

"We want everyone to walk away from this," Hensley said. "Without need of a cane or prosthetic limb. I wouldn't trust any of them alone in a room with a suitcase of money, but they're not the enemy. They just pose an inconvenience to our plan of saving Sapphire from the otherwise inevitable consequences of her ill-conceived actions."

"I'm not looking for a fight."

"I told Tru her story," Brother Joseph said. "Bad company. Impetuous decisions."

"I just want to make sure the girl gets a second chance," Tru said.

"Can you keep it on a leash?" Hensley said.

Tru nodded.

"It's this way." Hensley grabbed the burgers and started through the woods.

They made the half-hour hike in silence. When they hit the road, Hensley led them east to the observation post.

Whyte glanced over his shoulder as they approached, then took a second look. "What are we going to do? Pray them out?"

Hensley glanced at Brother Joseph, whose dog collar was clearly visible in the growing gloom against his black shirt and jacket. "He's a Jesuit."

"Zat so?" Whyte inspected the diminutive cleric, shrugged, and turned to Tru. "And who is this guy? The pope?"

Hensley opened the bag and passed out burgers and such. "We have about three hours until twilight proper."

Whyte took a huge bite and talked around it. "While you were gone, a beanpole kid left in the LTD and came back about fifteen minutes later."

"He ordered two burgers and a chicken basket from the DQ."

"Three meals?"

"He's a growing boy. But we have to plan for three. Whyte, you'll cover the back. We need eyes on the door and the windows. Get in close, maybe use the outbuilding for cover."

Hensley nodded at the south wall. "Nobody's going through those windows unless they throw a chair through them first, and still it'll be chancy.

"Tru, I want you to cover the north side. There are two windows just like the ones in front. Somebody could try to break through that direction. You can get in close when the shadows deepen. Maybe even check to see if you can slip inside without being noticed."

Tru nodded.

"Brother Joseph, I want you to stay here and keep an eye on the front in case we get company." Hensley reached in the bag, pulled out a walkie-talkie, and hung it on his belt. He handed a second one to the Jesuit and the third to Whyte. "Sorry, Tru, we have only three, and if we get activity, it will probably center around the doors, not the bedroom windows."

"What about you?" Whyte asked.

"I'm going to knock on the front door and see if Sapphire can come out and play."

Chapter Thirty-Three: Gambit

Hensley scrambled down the embankment to the road and walked up the gravel drive to the cabin. The clearing had been in shadow for close to half an hour and now the shadows were deepening into twilight. The temperature had fallen into the low fifties.

As he approached, he could see that the curtains were drawn, but a sliver of light peeked through the window on the right—the one that was likely the living area. He took the three steps to the shallow porch, pulled open the screen door, and knocked on the wooden door, careful to stand to one side.

After a good thirty seconds of silence, he knocked again, a little harder. The sliver of light went out.

Hensley smiled and shook his head. These goobers should thank him for bringing their spree to a premature end. With slick moves like that, they wouldn't last long against militia types. He cleared his throat.

"Sapphire, it's your Uncle Hensley. Remember me? Piggyback rides and snow cones?" He tested the door handle. Locked. "I was in your neck of the woods and thought I'd drop in for supper."

He thought he detected movement inside but wasn't sure. "By the way, I know what you're thinking. Uncle Hensley died in a mountain-bike accident in Peru. That's what everyone thought. But as you can see, I survived. Just took me a while to get back to the States."

The curtain to his right fluttered. "Your mother asked me to stop by and see how you're getting on. And Spud, I must make your acquaintance. Everyone has told me so much about you."

Hensley walked to the south edge of the porch as if looking for another door. He glanced west up the hill in the Jesuit's direction and returned to the door.

"Spud, I understand that you weren't particularly popular in high school. I must confess that neither was I. But in your case, that has all changed. Why, just off the top of my head I can think of half a dozen people who want to meet you in the worst way."

Hensley held up a finger. "Of course there's D.B. Always a dicey proposition, getting in good with the father-in-law. But he's keen. Very keen. He's been in town for a while, hanging around Felony Flats. Asking questions. I'm quite certain he'll find his way out here in a day or two. Just a matter of time, really. You know how he is when he gets his mind set on a thing."

Another finger popped up. "And Percival. He's even more anxious to see you. But I can see why you might prefer to avoid that little reunion, and that's why I'm here. To see if we can't sort this thing out before it goes pear-shaped on you."

A rustling came from the vicinity of the door handle, and the door swung open. Hensley waited for Spud or Sapphire to open the screen door, but nothing happened.

"Spud?"

"Come inside and close the door behind you."

Hensley glanced up at the Jesuit's post on the hill and slipped inside the cabin where the gloom deepened. To the right, the two squares up high on the south wall didn't let much light in, and the front and back windows were curtained. He could make out the darker shadows of furniture to the right—a couch against the south wall under a window, end tables and armchairs on either side, coffee table.

"Shall I turn on a light?"

"What you shall do is don't move or I shall light you up like a Christmas tree."

A table lamp flickered to life on the far side of the couch, casting the room into an amber glow that transported the scene to the 1970s.

Spud loomed above the lamp, his features casting weird shadows on his face like a kid telling ghost stories around a campfire. Sapphire stood behind him next to the fireplace, her arms crossed like she was cradling herself. In the decade-plus since Hensley had seen her, she had grown into a woman with features that hinted of Chrystal. But she sported a defiant, scared posture.

The most prominent feature of the tableau was a handgun the size of Haystack Rock in Spud's hand pointing directly at Hensley.

"I'd feel a lot better about things if you would put that cannon away."

"And I'd feel better if you would stick your head in a garbage disposal."

"While that is certainly an appealing alternative, I'm afraid we have a few things to talk about, and the presence of weapons of personal destruction are not conducive to civilized conversation."

"Sit down if you want, but we're staying right where we are."

Hensley glanced around the room. The living area was open to the rafters. Beyond the fireplace, a ceiling brought down the space over an L-shaped kitchen that occupied the south and east walls. Six chairs surrounded a kitchen table littered with the remains of a DQ meal. On the north wall, a door revealed the gleaming porcelain of a sink and toilet. On either side, one bedroom door was closed and the other was cracked open slightly.

He took the armchair facing the room, the one with its back to the front window. "It comes down to this. If you stay here, you'll end up in jail at best and dead at worst."

Spud scowled, but his youthful features detracted from any sense of menace he might have intended to project. "How do you figure that?"

"What I told you is true. Both Percival and D.B. are in town, both hunting you. I got here on Thursday, and it took me less than forty-eight hours to find your lair. They've been here three or four days. It's only a matter of time before they come knocking on your door. But that's not the bad part."

"What do you mean?"

"Percival snatched Reggie and is holding him hostage."

Sapphire gasped, a hand fluttering to her mouth. "Reggie?"

"I get the impression he's planning on trading him for the drugs."

She stepped forward and laid a hand on Spud's shoulder, but he brushed it away. She came up beside him, closer to the light. "But Spud, they have Reggie. We have to—"

"Shut up. He's probably making all this up to get us rattled."

The aim of the gun wavered as Spud lectured Sapphire, but they were too far away for Hensley to disarm him.

"You want proof, call Chrystal. Or Fagan. Or call Melvin Tatum."

"We can't get a signal out here," Sapphire said.

"I get the feeling D.B. or Percival or both have talked to Melvin by now. I tracked Percival's cell phone to Felony Flats three days ago."

Spud's brusque confidence melted as the possibility sank in. "Uncle Melvin would never . . ." He glanced around the room with desperation. His eyes settled on something in the dark corner between the back door and the bedroom wall.

Hensley squinted at it and gradually made out the shape of ladder rungs built into the wall leading up to a trap door in the ceiling. Three guesses as to what was up there.

"But that's not the worst part," Hensley said.

Spud snapped back toward Hensley. "What do you mean?"

"I've had a phone call from Sapphire's great-godfather, the federal judge. As of yesterday, the DEA and the FBI have been informed that you are in the area and of what you brought with you, and they're working overtime to track you down." Hensley stood. "So as I said earlier, you can't stay here."

"Spud, we have to drive into Rhododendron and call Percy."

"What we have to do is find a new place. If this bozo found us, the rest will too."

"But poor Reggie. He's probably in hysterics by now."

"The way your mom spoils him, he could use a little toughening up."

"Sapphire is right," Hensley said. "You have to give the drugs back."

"Like hell."

"You want Reggie's life on your conscience?"

"He'll be alright. Percy's too much of a wimp to hurt anyone. Even a kid."

"I suggest that we split up to reduce the risk of getting caught. Sapphire can come with me and you can meet us at—"

"You ain't going nowhere," Spud said. He raised the gun and trained it on Hensley. "Ever again."

Sapphire grabbed at his arm. "Spud, what are you doing?"

At that moment, the walkie-talkie crackled to life with a single whispered word that Hensley couldn't make out.

"What was that?" Spud demanded.

"Just my ringtone. A text."

"You can't get a signal out here."

"Sure I can. Look." Hensley reached in his pocket.

Spud raised his other hand to the gun to steady it. "Hands where I can see them."

Hensley raised both hands slowly.

As he did, the Jesuit's whisper came from the walkie-talkie again. "Incoming."

"That sounded like a radio," Spud said. "What's going on?"

Incoming? Who was it? The Feds? D.B.? Percival?

"I think we're about to have company." Hensley stepped around the coffee table and held out his hand to Sapphire. "Quick. We'll go out the back."

"Get back," Spud demanded.

Hensley walked around the other armchair to Sapphire. "Think of Reggie. Think of your mother."

Sapphire looked from Hensley to Spud and back. "But . . ."

Hensley took her arm and led her a few steps toward the back door.

"I'm warning you," Spud said.

"No," Hensley said. He stopped and turned toward Spud. "I'm warning you. You've made several bad choices in the past few days. But we can still fix it if you put that gun away and come with us."

Sapphire looked back. "Spud, they got Reggie."

"But Saff, this is our only—"

He never got the chance to finish the sentence. The front door slammed open and a shotgun appeared in the doorway, followed by D.B.

Spud whirled around, raising his gun.

Hensley pushed Sapphire away and launched a kick at Spud's forearm. It connected. The gun clattered across the floor and slid under the couch.

Spud scrambled for it, but D.B. lunged forward and slammed the butt of the shotgun against the side of Spud's head. Spud collapsed on the coffee table.

D.B. stepped back from Spud and turned the shotgun on Hensley. "Who are you?"

"Hensley Fletcher, at your service." He held out a hand and stepped forward. "Doing my best to extract your daughter from this regrettable predicament."

"Stay where you are." He glanced over Hensley's shoulder. "Saffie? You okay?"

Sapphire stepped out of the semidarkness of the kitchen into the weak light of the table lamp. "Daddy, they took Reggie."

"We'll find him." A gleam of recognition dawned in D.B.'s eyes, and he lowered the shotgun as he looked back to Hensley. "Weren't you dead?"

"Happily, no."

"You cut your hair."

"I see you retain the lightning powers of observations for which you are justly famous."

"How did you—? Never mind." D.B. gestured to Sapphire. "Come on, punkin. Let's go."

Sapphire took a few steps, then glanced at the inert form sprawled over the coffee table. "What about Spud?"

"If he's any kind of man, he'll chop his own cotton, but either way, he's no concern of ours."

Her lower lip trembled. "He's a concern of mine."

D.B. stepped to Sapphire and wrapped his free arm around her shoulders. "Punkin, if he really loved you, he never would have got you into this mess. Now let's find Reggie and go home."

Hensley walked past them. "That is a course of action I can thoroughly endorse." Just as he reached the front door, he heard the rush of boots on the steps.

Chapter Thirty-Four: Quietus

A foot thudded into the trapezoid of yellow light streaming out the door, and a bull-necked man in black shoved the muzzle of a tactical shotgun against Hensley's chest and pushed him back into the cabin.

Hensley stumbled back to his right. The man dragged a kid into the room with his other hand.

Reggie.

As Percival, for the man in black could be none other, leveled the gun at D.B. and Sapphire, Hensley lost his battle to regain his balance and tumbled to the floor. He rolled to his knees and turned to face Reggie. Even if he hadn't seen the pictures at Chrystal's house, he would have seen his own face in this face.

The crazy scene unfolding around them faded as Hensley stared at his son for the first time. Reggie glanced wildly around the room, but when his eyes fell on Hensley, they didn't move away.

Maybe it was because he recognized something in Hensley. Or maybe it was just because Hensley was the only person in the room looking at him instead of the crazy man with the assault weapon. There was a bruise under Reggie's left eye that had faded to a dim yellow, and his expression said, "Help me."

Hensley crawled to his feet and stepped toward Reggie. The barrel of the shotgun swung his way, and suddenly the voice that had been yelling came into focus.

"Take one more step and you're a dead man."

Hensley looked up from Reggie to Percival and arrested his forward progress, coming to rest lightly on his feet. It was no small thing to stare into the black hole of the abyss, but it was also the third time in recent memory that someone had shoved a gun in Hensley's face, and he was beginning to feel a bit resentful at the prospect. "Now that you've found what you were looking for, perhaps we can remove the child from the equation."

Percival squinted at him. "Mister, I don't know who you are, and I didn't come here to kill you, but I will if you make me. You got one chance to learn to listen, or you'll never get a chance to learn anything else."

Hensley winked at Reggie and took a short step back. "Or you could put that gun down, and we could see who teaches a lesson to whom."

For half a beat Percival eyed Hensley like maybe he had missed something. It was clear that from Percival's perspective, he had the drop on everyone and was holding all the cards, or at least holding the baddest gun in the room, which amounted to the same thing. And even if he went mano a mano with the old man, he had the advantage of six inches, fifty pounds, and martial arts training.

And the thing was, Percival was right. Most likely he could wipe the floor with Hensley. But the way Hensley saw it, at least it would give Reggie a chance to dart out the door, and they could sort it all out after, with or without Hensley, depending on the outcome.

"Listen up, old man. You don't have a dog in this hunt, so if you want to get any older, the best thing you can do for your health is to shut up every chance you get."

Hensley shrugged.

Percival reached back with a foot and kicked the door shut. Then he slung Reggie around to his right and planted him in the armchair that backed to the front window. "You move and you know what'll happen."

Reggie gave Percival a single nod and looked to Hensley. Hensley rolled his eyes, looked back at Reggie, and shook his head dismissively, trying to look as much as possible like a teenager enduring a lecture. Reggie frowned his confusion. Evidently this was not how grownups were supposed to respond in this situation.

For the first time since Percival arrived, Hensley took notice of the rest of the room.

D.B. stood to Hensley's left next to the armchair by the kitchen, shielding Sapphire with his body. Between them and Percival, Spud remained sprawled over the coffee table, his head hanging between it and the couch. His handgun still peeked from under the edge of the couch. D.B.'s shotgun lay on the floor next to the coffee table, evidently as a result of negotiations that had taken place while Hensley's attention had been occupied elsewhere.

"Just take the drugs and get out," D.B. said.

"Oh, I aim to take the drugs."

"And if you value your sorry hide, don't bother going back to Colorado. We don't need your kind."

"We? Who is we? And what kind is that? The kind that sees what needs doing and does it?"

"You want to join forces with the agents of anarchy, you go right ahead. But that's where we part ways."

Percival bared his teeth in what might have passed for a grin in his world. "The enemy of my enemy is my friend."

"See? There it is right there." D.B. shook his head. "How do you think this country got into the mess it's in? That's the whole Middle East right there. Trying to fight devils by joining forces with other devils. You follow some kind of twisted logic down a rabbit hole and the next thing you know, meth heads are your friends."

Hensley nodded with appreciation. D.B. might have unconventional methods, but his reasoning was sound. You stare into the abyss long enough, and you better start counting the silver.

"How many times have I . . ." D.B. threw up his hands. "Forget it. Go ahead. Take the drugs and get the hell out of here. Just don't come back to my place, or I'll introduce your belt buckle to your spine with one round."

The smile that slithered across Percival's face wasn't a pleasant thing to gaze upon. In fact, Hensley was fairly certain that the ambient temperature of the blood in his veins dropped a good five degrees just from watching it.

A ripple of muscles coursed through Percival's shoulders. "There's another thing. It's always 'my place' this and 'my place' that, when me and Merle and Arch have put as much work as you into building it. More."

"You got paid. Good wages too."

"I never figured myself for a wage slave. That place is my stake as much as it is yours."

"I didn't see you put up any money to buy the land or the materials. And you sure didn't turn down the paycheck."

"There's such a thing as sweat equity."

Hensley stole a glance at Reggie, who seemed to be holding up. "And there's such a thing as attending to the matter at hand. Perhaps we can effect an exchange—the drugs for the tadpole—and you two can continue this discussion over a cup of joe. I can highly recommend Jet Set Coffee in Tigard."

Percival shot a glare at Hensley that approximated the force of a round from his outsized weapon. "I don't remember pulling your string, old man. So put a cork in it."

A rustling from the southern quadrant of the room drew the attention of the collective to the groaning form of Spud rolling off the coffee table onto the floor next to D.B.'s shotgun. He rubbed his head gingerly and peered up at D.B. "What'd you do that for, man?"

Percival stepped forward and kicked Spud in the gut, then shoved him against the coffee table, which flipped over against the couch, legs poking out toward the middle of the room.

Sapphire gasped and lurched toward Spud, but D.B. pulled her back.

Spud curled up into a ball, protecting his ribs. "What the hell, man?" he gasped.

"This is the part where you return what you stole and beg for your miserable life," Percival said.

Hensley stepped forward. "If I may intrude, I have found that civil discourse is more effective than—"

Percival swung the muzzle of the gun around. "Keep that up and I'll intrude a slug right between your eyes."

Hensley held up his hands. "Of course there are many views on the subject, and while I can't fully endorse it, doubtless from some perspectives yours has merit."

He took stock of the situation. Percival was now a few feet in front of Hensley, D.B. and Sapphire to Hensley's left. As he figured his chances of removing the rogue knight from the equation, it was one or none and Percival held a gun that could cut a man in half. Not a set of odds Hensley would have backed in his old life, but the stakes had changed.

Percival aimed another kick at Spud. "You know what you did, you idiot?" He tossed a glance at D.B. "Because your future father-in-law has no idea how to fund a movement, I had to short the dealer."

"You . . . what?" Hensley blurted it out before he could contain himself. If he understood this miserable trailer-park trash excuse for a visionary correctly, the weasel had somehow contrived to acquire an as-yet-undisclosed quantity of crystal meth by deceiving the dealer as to the payment he had delivered. And of course meth dealers were notorious for a forgiving view in such situations. Everyone knew that.

Suddenly the thought of the Feds descending upon them was a welcome alternative. Hensley looked around the room to see if anyone else had grasped the gravity of the situation.

The way Hensley saw it, at this point, when the dealer arrived with his posse, anyone in the vicinity of the drugs in question would be holding the short straw. He checked on Reggie. His son seemed to be watching the proceedings as one would watch a movie. In 3D. In spades. With knobs on.

Hensley's attention was distracted by another kick at the fetal Spud.

"Until you came along, it wasn't a problem," Percival said. "Quick turnaround, I pay the difference after I sell the package, and everybody's happy. Until you get a bright idea."

He delivered another kick, then turned to D.B. "All this nonsense wouldn't be necessary if you had the balls to step up to the plate. But no. With you it's all dig in and hunker in the bunker. It's time for a regime change."

Percival pulled up the shotgun. Hensley feinted away from D.B. toward the door. As Percival swung the gun wide, Hensley launched to the left and delivered a kick that slammed the barrel of the shotgun upward. A deafening round discharged into the rafters.

Spud tried to scramble away, and Hensley tripped over him, falling in front of Reggie. From the corner of his eye, he saw D.B. dive toward his shotgun by the coffee table.

As Hensley struggled to his feet, the door exploded open, and a biker the size of Detroit barreled in, throwing rounds about the room like May flowers.

Hensley snatched Reggie from the armchair, turning away from the gunfire and sheltering him with his body. Reggie grasped at Hensley's camo jacket.

Then Hensley felt a searing pain blaze through his right shoulder and gasped. He stumbled forward, kicking the end table aside, and grunted as he pushed Reggie into the southwest corner of the room.

"Stay down," he growled, and threw his body in front of Reggie, facing outward to take on whoever made the mistake of coming within his reach.

He felt the movements of Reggie cowering into a ball in the corner and wondered for the first time if this was all his fault. All of it. Sapphire going off the rails. Reggie getting sucked into it. Him being here now. Meth-cooking bikers and conspiracy-theory militia wing nuts converging in a conflagration of gunfire.

A round hit Percival in the leg, and he let loose a wild volley of shots that raked across the ceiling as he went down. D.B. was on the floor in the middle of the room, but he pulled up to one knee with his shotgun and aimed at the biker when a dark form swung down from the rafters and took the biker out with a kick to the throat.

Two more bikers shoved through the door to take his place, but Tru, who was the dark fighter, threw his weight onto his right foot, launched into a horizontal spin, and connected his left foot with the first biker's head. The biker stumbled into his buddy, and before either could recover, Tru stepped in and delivered two rapid throat punches. Both bikers dropped their weapons as they staggered back out of the door, Tru following.

Next to the coffee table, D.B. swung his shotgun this way and that, searching for a target.

Hensley caught a movement in his peripheral vision and glanced over to see Spud push the coffee table aside and scramble for the handgun lying under the couch. Hensley tried to snatch it away, but it was more of a wish than a movement, and in response to the searing pain in his shoulder, he fell back against Reggie to guard him.

Then the back door burst open and a fourth biker rushed through with a shotgun, scanned the scene, and centered on D.B., the only person in the room holding a weapon.

As the biker swung his shotgun around, Whyte charged through the back door and launched through the air, planting a well-aimed boot at the biker's kidney. The biker arched back, the shotgun lighting up the room as it blew out the front window.

From his recumbent position, Spud swung the handgun he had managed to retrieve toward the noise, but Whyte rolled to his feet and kicked it across the room, where it thudded to a rest against the front door.

A figure in black appeared in the doorway, kicked the gun aside, and stepped into the room. D.B. whirled toward the door, and seeing a priest in a dog collar, paused in confusion.

"I'm one of the good guys," Brother Joseph gasped between ragged breaths from his sprint down the hill to the cabin. "But the other good guys are coming up the road in force, so you might want to drop the firearm."

"You still with me?" Hensley rasped over his shoulder.

"Yeah," Reggie whispered.

D.B. studied the Jesuit for a moment, then set the shotgun down.

"If I may," Hensley said from his corner. He attempted to struggle to his feet, but gave it up after a few seconds and instead turned so he could see Reggie, who was crouched in a ball in the corner.

Hensley propped himself up on his good elbow and addressed the room. "I'd prefer to present to the authorities only those in need of adjudication."

He turned to D.B. "Get your shotgun and get Sapphire back to her mother."

Tru stepped through the front door. "In future, if you're going to kick a gun up to discharge in the rafters, please notify me in advance."

Hensley nodded and jerked his chin at Tru, Whyte, and Brother Joseph. "Make sure they make it. And go with them." He pulled the walkie-talkie from his belt. "And take this."

"What about him?" Whyte nodded at Reggie.

"He stays with me."

"Okay, then what about you?"

"We'll catch a ride with the sheriff."

"What about me?" Spud croaked.

Whyte ignored him and turned back to Hensley. "You've been hit."

"I'm guessing they have a first aid kit." His mind raced to cover all bases. "But do me a favor. Get my keys from my right pocket and get my bag from the white van parked at the Everett Street Guest House. Wherever they're taking me, I'm going to want it."

As his posse left out the back door, Hensley craned his neck to see over the coffee table. "Here's the story, Spud. The drugs were your idea." A spike of pain shot from his shoulder through his body. Hensley gritted his teeth and took several short breaths to get it back under control. "Sapphire didn't know anything about them until this afternoon. When you told her, she didn't want to have anything to do with it and left before everyone else showed up. And D.B. and my crew were never here."

"You want me to lie to the police?"

Hensley had no doubt that Spud's first words were a lie to the police. "Do you love Sapphire?"

"Well, duh."

"Enough to take the blame for your own mistakes and save her from jail time?"

Hensley let him think it over and glanced back at Reggie, who was now sitting with his back against the corner, at eye-level with Hensley. "Is this your first rodeo?"

Reggie nodded tentatively.

"If I have anything to do with it, it will be your last." Hensley smiled and thought about reaching out to him, but he was lying on his good side and couldn't move his other arm.

He'd been shot before, but one didn't get used to an angry chunk of metal ripping away flesh and bone. When it came to excruciating pain, every time was the first time.

Now that the adrenaline was fading, his first instinct was to roar and curse and demand an explanation for why he should be singled out for this torture, but he choked it back for the sake of his son. Instead he closed his eyes, drew in breaths through his nose, and forced them out through gritted teeth. After a few moments, he got a handle on the pain.

He locked eyes with Reggie, who stared at him, tears brimming.

"Are you going to die again?" Reggie said.

"I'm not an easy man to kill."

Reggie scooted over and leaned against Hensley's chest. "I always knew you would come back."

Hensley's first thought was wonder at the faith of a child. His second was that the kid wouldn't last long in this world if he indulged such fantasies. His third was that the second was unworthy of him. He repented.

Then the Feds crashed through the door.

The first phalanx were cannon fodder with Kevlar vests and automatic weapons. Two figures lurched to either side of the door and raked the room with their eyes and weapons.

Hensley scanned the room to assess their targets. Two unconscious bikers lay on the floor, and Spud and Percival lay groaning by the coffee table. And of course an unarmed man in the corner shielding a kid. Nothing to shoot at.

The next three or four agents rushed through and cleared the bathroom and bedrooms. Then they directed their attention to the main room, performing liveness tests, which the bikers passed, and securing Spud and Percival. One agent called in medical support for Percival while another turned toward Hensley.

"We're good," Hensley breathed. "Although I could stand a little stitching up and an opiate or two."

As the agent set his weapon aside and inspected Hensley's wound, the next wave entered, consisting of the special agents connected with the FBI and DEA, and then the paramedics, who focused on Percival before turning their attention to Hensley.

As they pulled off Hensley's jacket and cut away his shirt, Sheriff Powell strode through the door.

Powell focused an unforgiving glare on Hensley. "What the hell are you doing here?"

Hensley pushed Reggie forward. "Make sure this one gets to his mother."

Powell nodded and held out a hand to Reggie.

Reggie hesitated and looked to Hensley.

Hensley nodded.

Reggie reluctantly allowed Powell to escort him out the front door.

Hensley waited until his son disappeared across the threshold. Then he took a deep breath and allowed himself the luxury of passing out.

DAY 11: SUNDAY

Chapter Thirty-Five: Admission

Hensley awoke in a hospital bed with tubes and wires attached. It was a first for him. He'd spent more hours than he cared to count in a clinic in Angola washing bandages and stocking shelves and such, but for all the multifarious experiences of his checkered career, he'd never been incarcerated in a Western hospital.

He couldn't say that he was buoyed by the prospect of being surrounded by the wonders of modern medical technology. But one did what one must to connect one moment to the next and keep body and spirit in one piece.

Memories of doors blasting open and bikers charging in and flashes of automatic rounds flooded his consciousness for a few moments, and he breathed deeply to calm himself.

As far as he could remember, Reggie survived the ordeal and was escorted to safety. He regulated his respiration and took inventory. All seemed well with the exception of a persistent, dull, pervasive ache in the right side of his body. To be precise, it seemed to be localized to the upper torso.

Overlaying all was an overwhelming sense of fatigue. He wanted to ripple his muscles from top to bottom, take inventory of the corporeal self, but he lacked the energy to execute the movement.

The more he thought about it, the more he wanted to just resign himself to the oblivion of sleep. Then he caught the sound of someone doing the very thing that he was contemplating.

Hensley turned his head to the right and caught sight of Chrystal in a chair under a thin hospital blanket, writhing for a more comfortable position.

Half asleep. Fully desirable.

How long had she been there? How long had he been here? How long was long?

Darkness embraced him and the next thing he knew, a nurse was holding his wrist and looking at her watch. He peered at her through half-lidded eyes.

"I never trust these machines," she said.

Hensley nodded. Or at least he thought he did. Sound woman. He said so. Or least thought he did. But she just looked at him strangely.

The next time he awoke, Chrystal stood next to the bed looking toward the door, her hand on his arm. It was warm and damp, and he had never felt anything so wonderful. It reminded him of Georgia peaches and fresh-grilled waffles and the close humidity of a jungle night and . . .

He was jolted back to consciousness by a male voice.

"The prognosis is excellent. No infection. No important nerves impacted. It's just a matter of convalescence at this point."

Hensley forced his eyes open in time to catch the back of a lab coat exiting the room. He rolled his head to the right and there was Chrystal looking back at him.

"Hello," she said.

"Exactly."

"How are you feeling?"

"Like I've been shot."

"They said you took out four armed bikers by yourself. Was that before or after you were shot?"

"I couldn't really say. It's all a blur."

Chrystal smiled, but her expression was tempered with something. What, exactly, he couldn't say. He felt that his powers of observation and deduction were diminished. Perhaps by something in the drip. Or maybe it was due to being shot.

"What day is it?"

"Sunday night. You've been here twenty-four hours."

"Where am I, exactly?"

"Legacy Mt. Hood Medical Center."

"How's Reggie?"

"He's with Sapphire at the hotel. Probably staying up too late watching TV and eating too many potato chips."

"It is the way of his people."

"Which people?"

"The Fletchers are not known for moderation."

"Take a number." Chrystal stroked the back of his hand along the tendons to the fingers.

Hensley closed his eyes and savored the moment. Maybe it was the drugs, assuming there were some drugs in the drip, or maybe it was reality. At this point, he didn't care which, and who was to say there was a difference?

Life was what it was, experienced moment by moment, and he would take this moment, because who knew how many more like this he would be granted.

"He recognized you."

Hensley opened his eyes and looked into hers. Brown, flecked with gold.

"He knows who you are."

Hensley nodded.

"If you break his heart, I'll kill you."

He didn't doubt it. And he didn't blame her. He had set out on this quest in search of something real. The thing Davison had found. The thing his father had found, as much as it galled him to admit it. But Hensley had found something else. A something that confounded all his expectations. A son.

For the past four decades, Hensley had taken life as it came, maximizing the experience, relishing the ephemeral as one savored the fragrance of a flower that would wilt on the morrow. Nothing lasted forever.

But now he had a son. And one day his son might have a son. Or a daughter. Some things did go on.

Perhaps he could repair what he had broken with Chrystal, but no matter how transcendent that experience might be, it would die with him.

But Reggie. This was the horse of a different color.

One could live life to its fullest, or one could nurture another life. Like Chrystal had done. But could one do both?

Hensley had a thousand questions roiling in his head, but beneath each one lay a potential land mine, so he took the path less traveled and kept his mouth shut.

"Bobby said you were guarding Reggie with your body when they came in."

Hensley nodded.

She was silent for a long moment. "Thank you."

"I know you didn't want me to—"

"I'm glad you did."

She was looking away when she said it. Hensley took a baby step.

"Reggie said he knew I would come back."

Chrystal jerked her hand away and pierced him with a steely glare. "How could he think you would come back? You were dead. That's been the story since before he was born. Nobody knew different. Not even me."

"Why didn't you ever hook up with the sheriff?"

"What?"

"Seems like a good man. Probably good with kids."

"What kind of meds do they have you on?"

"You had already consigned me to the grave. And he seems keen. Very keen indeed." Hensley shrugged, and his shoulder reminded him that such movements were not welcome. Through gritted teeth, he said, "He is undoubtedly the type that would dote on you. You would live like a queen."

"You see me as the kind that needs doting on?"

"Actually, I was thinking more of Reggie."

"If I wanted to raise Reggie to be a cog in the machine, I would have married Bobby a long time ago."

"He seems to have been looking for a father for a long time."

Chrystal blew her bangs up. "Well, what did you expect? If I have to choose between someone who would break his spirit or someone who would break his heart, I think he's better off like he is."

Hensley wondered how women came by their wisdom. Instinct or experience? Or maybe word of mouth. Whatever the source, most of them seemed to instantly know things that would never occur to a man in a million years.

"So you're saying fatherhood is not a case in which something is better than nothing?"

Chrystal turned away, her hand rising to her eyes. "Damn you, Henz, why couldn't you have left well enough alone and stayed dead?"

This was not the direction he had hoped the conversation would take. As she wiped her tears with the heel of her hand, he gazed at her profile. He was sailing uncharted waters, and it seemed to him that in these climes, there be dragons.

Hensley had never been party to a conversation of this sort because he was always gone long before it would have become necessary. As he had just discovered, a seemingly benign comment could scuttle the ship. He cast about for a wind to pull him clear.

"Chrystal, I don't deny that I'm a cad. Or at least I have been . . . No, that's not it. Two months ago I got a telegram from Uncle Rex and . . . No, that's too much . . . There's something I have to tell you, something that happened last week on a cruise ship . . . Let's skip over that for now. Night before last I experienced an epiphany due to a waitress named Jessica—"

"That's enough." Chrystal held out a hand, palm thrust toward him, head turned away. "It's too much. You hung around for two years. You disappeared for twelve years. So which one is real? Which one can Reggie count on?"

"Last night as I lay bleeding on the floor of that cabin and guarding Reggie with my life, I realized—"

Chrystal wheeled around, her hair flaring out. "You can't just breeze in here and play the hero and expect to cancel out everything. How can I know what you will do two years from now? Or even two months from now?"

She jerked her purse from the chair where she had been sleeping and strode out. She stopped at the door. "I won't gamble Reggie's future on the chance that you're suddenly reformed."

And then she was gone. Hensley couldn't blame her. She'd had twelve years to get used to the idea of a new child and a dead Hensley. Here he was shocked with the discovery of an unexpected son, and there she was shocked with the return of a live Hensley. It was hard to say which was more brutal to the psyche.

What was more, she might be right. Reggie needed a father, but who was to say Hensley was the father he needed? The father to prepare him for life as he would know it?

Of course Hensley had something to give. Ask Julien at the rooftop bar in Galveston. Ask Tyler at The Tinker's Dam. Ask any of the hundreds of souls adrift in the world that Hensley had steered toward trade winds in the past several decades.

Hensley's speciality was triage for desperate men, rudderless and casting about for a bearing. By contrast, Reggie had a home, a family, a safe port. Such advice as Hensley had to offer might cause him to founder instead of bring wind to his sails.

It had been years since Hensley had found himself lost at sea, and it wasn't a pleasant sensation.

He was distracted from his ruminations by an irritating noise. It took him a moment to fix on a closet in the corner as the source of the twirping. It took him a few more moments to identify it as the ring of his pocket phone, doubtlessly still in the pocket of his pants.

A few seconds of stirring about was all that was required to convince him that even if his shoulder would allow it, freeing himself from the wires and tubes was ill-advised. He glanced about and discovered a wired remote with a confusing set of buttons. On a hunch, he pushed the red button at the bottom.

Half a minute later, a nurse with the physique of the Lusitania in her finest moments entered the room. "So we're awake, are we?"

"Yes, we are." Hensley set the remote aside. "Could we be so kind as to retrieve the phone from our pants?"

"We discourage use of cell phones in the rooms."

"Wise counsel, but we just heard it ringing and we suspect our family on the East Coast is concerned for our welfare. The kindest course of action is to assure them that we are in the best of care and convalescing at record speed."

The nurse paused for a few seconds, then relented. She delved into the closet and presented him with the phone. "Try to keep it short. You need your rest."

"I assure you, my good woman, no one is more cognizant of that fact than I."

As he took the phone with his left hand, it made a sound he'd not heard before. A buzzing with a ding. He turned his attention back to the nurse. "And if the commissary is open, I'd like to order a nice Speyside single malt. Old enough to drive if possible."

She glanced through his chart and shrugged. "I don't think the doctor would mind. Chocolate, vanilla, or strawberry?"

Hensley sighed. "Chocolate would serve nicely."

The nurse nodded and left.

He flipped the phone open. One missed call from Davison. He hit the button to call back.

Davison answered without greeting or preamble. "I don't have a location on that number. Retirement has its drawbacks. And an OPR investigation tends to put a damper on extra-departmental cooperation."

"I appreciate your effort, but I was able to extract Reggie from the nexus of danger, free of harm, and return him to the bosom of his family."

The exhalation of breath was audible a half-continent away. "Good."

"Perhaps one day you will have occasion to meet your one and only nephew. I commend the experience to you."

"We shall see," Davison said. "I have a question for you."

"Shoot."

"What did you tell Masie at that rooftop bar in Galveston?"

Hensley raised an eyebrow. The left one. The one farthest from his wound. "We spoke of many things. Would have spoken of more had you not so precipitously intervened."

"Did you ask her for anything? A part of the estate?"

"I did nothing of the kind. As I recall, up until you arrived, our conversation revolved around the life philosophy of the bartender and his prospects."

"Of course it did."

"You can confirm with her if you doubt my recollection."

"I did. So where did you find Reggie?"

"Strangely enough, I didn't find him. He came to me in a cabin in the foothills of Mt. Hood. A peaceful setting. Idyllic, you might say. Surrounded by blooming rhododendron."

"So what's next?"

"That, my brother, is very much in play. I have prospects, but nothing is set in stone as of even date."

"You're back in Santa Fe? Or still in Portland?"

"On the coast for the nonce. This time of year the climate is much more forgiving than the high desert. You should come out. Bring Masie."

"Maybe I will."

Hensley raised the left eyebrow again. This cryptic comment didn't fit the mental template Hensley had established for this brother. "Shall I reserve a room for you at the Everett Street Guest House?"

"No need. Too much is in play at the moment."

"Ah, well, then . . ." Hensley suddenly found himself at a loss for words. Must have been the medication in the drip.

"Later," Davison said, and the line went dead.

Hensley looked at the phone for a moment, puzzled by the absence of hostility. Perhaps Davison was just relieved that Reggie had been rescued without incident.

He set the phone aside just as Lusitania entered the room with a large paper cup on a tray. She set it in front of him, unsheathed a straw, and stabbed it into the cruciform slit on the lid.

"One chocolate malt. Don't tell the doctor." She winked at him, a most disconcerting wink.

"You render me speechless," Hensley blurted.

"It's our little secret." She winked again and steamed out of the room.

Hensley sipped distractedly, wondering how much of this was real. He needed to get out of here before they measured him for a white jacket with inconveniently long sleeves.

He made use of the proximity of the phone to make a second call.

After five rings, an answer. "Bornhouser."

"Once again, Hensley Fletcher here. Have you discovered anything about the Stone estate issue?"

A long pause followed. "Uh, yes, Mr. Fletcher, I have discovered something very important to the case."

"Excellent. Do tell." Hensley took a sip of the milkshake.

"I have discovered that you will need to engage someone else to settle the estate. Don't call me again."

The line went dead. Hensley checked the time. It was barely midnight on the east coast. In the case of lawyers, evidently diligence was required to engage one with the proper sense of urgency.

As he set the phone on the cabinet to his left, a slight figure carrying a duffel bag slinked through the door. Tru Pak.

Hensley jerked his chin toward the closet and checked the doorway, but it remained unviolated. "Where's Whyte?"

"Standing lookout."

"For bikers or officers?"

Tru shrugged.

"I trust you ushered D.B. and his daughter to safety."

Tru nodded.

More than most, Hensley appreciated a man who avoided superfluous conversation, but it could be taken to extremes. But then, Tru was a man of extremes. Or had been, at any rate.

"Good work out there on the mountain," Hensley said. "You've learned a few tricks since the nineties."

Silence followed his words like a stream filling the empty space left by an oar. Hensley let it settle, relaxing in the remembered rhythm of hanging with Tru.

The Korean stood halfway between the closet and the bed, relaxed but alert. Breathing. Looking at nothing and everything.

Hensley smiled. Another man would have rushed in with words to fill the void, not understanding that silence was not an emptiness to be filled. It was the space that gave speech significance.

After a period of time that had no measure, Tru spoke. "Next month my son will be born."

Hensley nodded. "Congratulations to you, my friend."

"That is why I called Brother Joseph." Tru locked eyes with Hensley. "I was wrong to refuse aid for your son."

"A man learns the shape of his shadow by stepping into the light."

"When a man turns toward the light, he leaves his shadow behind."

"Then may we both learn to face the light, my friend."

Tru nodded and left.

DAY 12: MONDAY

CHAPTER THIRTY-SEVEN: DISCHARGE

The next day Hensley was awakened by a six-foot-five nurse taking his vitals. "You have visitors," he said.

"I am not at home for visitors." Hensley looked around for a clock. "What time is it anyway?"

The nurse checked his watch. "Eight-oh-six."

"Tell them to come back at a civilized hour." Hensley closed his eyes. "Two-thirty or three. Or later."

"You can tell them yourself."

Hensley opened his eyes. The nurse was halfway to the door. Sheriff Powell stepped aside to let him pass and then came in, followed by a drone in a suit and a third in jeans, t-shirt, and flight jacket.

This was a most regrettable turn of events. Hensley preferred to take such interviews on his own terms, which was to say never, but here he was confined to a bed attached to tubes and wires and such and the agents of the law blocking his only escape. He let out a long breath. "Please tell me you brought coffee."

Powell glanced at the third man, who backed out of the door and called to someone out of Hensley's sightline.

"South American medium roast, black," Hensley called out.

"This is Special Agent Cheatham of the FBI." Powell nodded to the second man. "And Special Agent Wall of the DEA." Powell indicated the third man stepping back into the room.

"I hate to trouble you at such short notice, Agent Wall, but it suddenly occurs to me that I require an Irish coffee for this occasion," Hensley said.

Agent Wall frowned at Hensley and glanced at Powell, who shook his head and stepped to the side of the bed, his back to the other agents.

The whole scenario puzzled Hensley. Why would a county sheriff be running this interview with federal agents following his lead? He took a few breaths to clear his head.

"Gentlemen, I am moved by your concern for my welfare. Most unexpected, if not to say unwelcome. However, I have experienced a trying few days and my doctor insists on silence and bed rest for at least seventy-two hours."

"Your doctor cleared this interview," Powell said.

"I insist on a second opinion."

"We have a few questions about the events of Saturday night."

"Don't we all?" Hensley closed his eyes and took a deep breath. Many issues presented themselves, all of them more pressing than this tedious debrief.

He regarded the assembled representatives of the law with a less than charitable view. "I assume that we have all the relevant players in all the appropriate slots in the local hoosegow. I trust you are adequate to the task of sorting them out and consigning them to their respective fates."

"Not all," Powell said. "We have testimony and physical evidence of actors not presently in custody." He consulted a notebook. "A ninja that attacked three gang members. A second man who assaulted a fourth gangbanger."

Hensley tilted his head. "A ninja, did you say?"

Powell rolled his eyes toward the agents behind him. "Special Agent Wall took the statements."

Wall stepped forward. "Three gang members corroborated the presence of a person dressed in black who dropped from the rafters and attacked them."

"The first gangbanger shot me. I don't have a clear memory from that point forward, but I can say with confidence that I didn't observe any ninjas on the premises, neither before nor after commencement of the festivities."

Special Agent Cheatham stepped forward. "Maybe you can tell us how you happened to be at the cabin Saturday night."

"I was there to pick up Reggie."

"And how did you get to the cabin?"

"Spud gave me a ride." Hensley looked at Powell. "Didn't he tell you?"

"Spud lawyered up."

"Well, there it is. Percival dropped off Reggie. He was leaving when a motorcycle gang showed up, and I don't mind telling you the wheels came off at that point. Lucky for us, the cavalry showed up. Although I'm still not clear on that detail."

Hensley caught Powell's gaze. "Good thing you did, though. A lot of people would be in a world of hurt if you hadn't."

Special Agent Wall stepped up to the side of the bed. "You mean to tell me that—"

"I think we'll get better information when Mr. Fletcher has a chance to recover," Powell said.

"But—"

"We have plenty of other leads to pursue," Powell said. He turned to Hensley. "We'll be back tomorrow. Get some rest and be ready to answer some questions."

Hensley nodded gravely. "I shall do my best, gentlemen."

Despite what he thought of the eternal Boy Scout at his bedside, Hensley had to admire the man. Faithful to a fault. Disdain emanated from Powell in waves, but he would do nothing to jeopardize Chrystal or Sapphire. It was the only thing in the world that the two of them had in common, but it was enough. If he had been capable, and if Powell would have allowed it, Hensley would have embraced him at this moment.

Powell fixed Hensley with a parting glare. "Tomorrow." He turned and walked out the door. The two Feds reluctantly followed.

As they disappeared from view, Hensley let out a cleansing breath and sank into his pillow.

Then Davison rounded the corner and walked up to his bedside. "You're keeping strange company these days."

Hensley didn't have to look at the monitor to know that his heart rate spiked. It hadn't been twelve hours since they had spoken. How did he get here so quickly? And why? "So what are you? The closer?"

A strange frown crept across Davison's face. Not the usual disapproving expression Hensley had come to expect. Something else.

"Maybe." Davison inspected the equipment connected to Hensley. "I hear you took a bullet."

"That's what they tell me."

"On purpose."

"Believe me, I neither invited nor welcomed such an outcome." Davison nodded.

A silence fell upon the room, interrupted by the occasional chirp of the monitor. The six-foot-five nurse glanced in. Hensley acknowledged him with a jerk of his chin and the nurse faded away. Good man.

Davison pulled up a chair and dropped into it.

As Hensley waited for Davison to make the first move, he found himself thinking about his son. As Davison said, he'd taken a bullet for Reggie. Instinctively. Without thinking.

Hensley couldn't recall the last time he'd done something without thinking. He reviewed the past two weeks—searching for Chrystal, searching for Sapphire, searching for Reggie. All premeditated.

He cast his mind back to the two preceding weeks. Lying in wait for Davison at his home in Austin. Following him down to Cancún. And before that, making the trek to the States in response to the telegram from Uncle Rex.

Come at once. Say nothing to Davison.

Every move calculated. He extended his search to the preceding decades.

It came over him in a cool wave like the sensation of stepping out of the African sun into the shadow of the jungle canopy. Hunting. Synchronizing his perception to the rhythm of the world.

No. His unthinking reaction to protect Reggie seemed more elemental than primal. Beyond instinct to the insensate reaction of a molecule guided by unseen forces.

If he needed any proof, this was it. For the first time in his life, when the moment came, he gave no thought to his own welfare.

Even as Hensley pondered this possibility, his conscious mind asserted itself, the constant companion that had saved him and plagued him through the years. Sure, in the face of an existential threat, adrenaline and reflex kicked in, but that was no way to live.

Davison cleared his throat.

Had it been one minute or ten? Suddenly a question pressed itself to the forefront of Hensley's mind. Why was Davison here? When was the last time Davison had willingly spent time with him?

It was decades ago, before the moment Hensley handed Davison his coin collection and faded into the wide world.

"You remember when you broke Mom's record?" Davison said.

"As I remember it, you broke it. *Camelot*."

"You pushed me."

"Doubtless I had good reason."

"I've been listening to it these last few days."

Hensley tried to imagine Davison clearing up the breakfast dishes in his comfortable Austin home, singing along with Julie Andrews on "If Ever I Would Leave You." The ghost of a smile teased his lips.

Davison didn't seem to notice. "Can you imagine her leaving him? Or him her?"

Hensley regarded Davison as he would a stranger. "I sense you are going somewhere with this."

Davison took a deep breath and let it out slowly. "I'm done."

"Done?"

"Done with whatever happened in the jungle when you left."

Hensley sank back against the pillow with the weight of three decades of regret. "I meant to come back. But I couldn't—"

"I'm letting it go." Davison caught Hensley's gaze and held it. "What you meant. What you didn't mean. It doesn't matter."

"But . . ." Hensley ground to a halt. What could he say, except, "Why?"

"Because I want what they had."

Hensley glanced away for a moment, attempting to connect the dots. "What does the one have to do with the other?"

Davison's gaze didn't waver. "A good woman told me . . . well, several good women, but this time I finally decided to listen."

Hensley waited for the payoff, but Davison's resolve appeared to waver. While his eyes were still on Hensley, he seemed to be seeing something else, something a long way off. Then he took a deep, shuddering breath, clenched his jaw, and looked back at Hensley.

"If you want to embrace the future, you have to let go of the past."

Hensley fought back the surge of anger that coursed through him at these words. His kid brother, of all people, should know what it was like for him. For both of them. It took a few deep breaths before Hensley trusted his voice. "He was—"

"It doesn't matter. What he did. What you did. There's only this—what do you want, and what are you willing to do to get it?"

Echoes of a long-forgotten conversation reverberated in Hensley's brain. What had the sensei said back in Guangxi?

Everything is empty except the open hand.

Hensley had thought he understood it at the time, but now Davison was here in this hospital room in Oregon to teach him what it really meant. How can you walk away from something if you never let it go?

He'd been running from the clinic in Angola for more than thirty years, only to discover that he'd never left it behind. He'd been dragging it behind him for a lifetime.

Was that what it took? Could he do it? Suddenly the room felt like it was back in the jungle. Stifling.

"What you do with it is up to you, but I've made my choice." Davison pushed up out of the chair.

Hensley struggled for words. It seemed that Davison had found a way to let go. That was why he was here, not to lecture to Hensley but to release him. And evidently to release himself as well.

However, it was one thing for Davison to walk away from resentment, and it was another thing entirely for Hensley to free himself from regret. But that wasn't Davison's problem. "Thank you."

The faintest of smiles relaxed Davison's face. "I didn't do it for you, but you might think about doing it for yourself."

Could he? Would he? Although Hensley and Davison were poles apart, they had this thing in common—retreat disguised as a life. Until now. But if Davison could . . .

"What they had," Hensley said. "Do you think it's possible for the likes of us?"

"With the right woman, yes. If you want it bad enough." Davison turned to leave, but stopped at the door. "I almost forgot. Masie decided to accept the terms of the will. Tomorrow I'll award the estate to her. The way Uncle Rex wanted it."

Hensley took a deep breath. Two hundred million dollars had vaporized in a few sentences, but for some reason he couldn't bring himself to care. "I can't think of anyone more deserving."

"But she was insistent on one detail. She wants to give you the house on the Main Line."

"Why?"

"Plus a stipend to cover operating expenses. I talked her down from a yearly amount to a lump sum."

Hensley felt the tectonic shift. This could change everything where Reggie was concerned. "Very wise of you."

"It will maintain the property for twenty years based on the average expenses of the last five years and indexed for future value. After that, you're on your own."

Few things could render Hensley speechless. In fact, as he looked back on his mercurial career, he could count the occasions on one hand and have fingers left to scratch the odd itch.

The path forward to reunite with Chrystal was far from smooth, but surely the future of their son meant as much to her as it did to him. This was the one thing he could bring to the table.

Once installed in the mansion, Hensley had no doubt that, freed from the existential imperative to keep the place running, he could take the time and effort to ingratiate himself with the local power structure and assure a career path for Reggie that would eclipse that of his siblings.

"This is most generous and most unexpected."

"You have to sign a statement relinquishing all other claims to the estate."

"I'm sure Ellis is equal to the task of drawing up such a document to the satisfaction of all concerned parties."

A long silence followed.

"Is she the one?" Davison finally said.

"You have the question backward."

"You think you can stay put in one place for twenty years?" Davison said.

"I have an eleven-year-old son. He'll fly the coop in half that time, and then we shall see."

"Ten years in one place? She must be some woman if she can rein you in."

Hensley retreated into the familiar. "She is what we call in the trade the horse of a different color with the shoe on the other foot."

"I've heard of those."

Hensley closed his eyes for a bit. He was feeling the weight of his wound and of the events of the past few days. But, more than that, he was feeling the sensation of a non-confrontational Davison.

Davison broke the silence. "So what is Chrystal like?"

"She is like Masie in that she cannot be compared to any other woman."

"How did you meet her?"

"It was fate or chance or destiny or whatever you like to call these things. I was just passing through, but it took me two years to leave."

"And why did you?"

Hensley thought long and hard, but no matter how he searched, he returned to the only possible explanation. "I was an idiot."

Davison nodded. "At last, something we can agree on."

The Brobdingnagian nurse stuck his head in the door. "Shift change. Need anything before I go?"

"One thing," Hensley said. "What's in the drip?"

The nurse responded without looking at his chart. "Saline with a one gram antibiotic dose twice a day."

Hensley nodded. So much for the painkiller theory. The nurse left, and Hensley turned to Davison. "This is my chance."

"For what?"

"To get out of here. Get my clothes from the closet."

Davison shook his head, but he did as requested. Hensley was dressed in mufti in a few minutes. He directed Davison to grab the duffel bag, and they shuffled down the hall to the elevator, Hensley leaning on Davison.

"Hit the button." Hensley leaned against the wall to catch his breath.

Davison hit the button. "Where are you going?"

"To the next thing."

The elevator dinged, and the Lusitania nurse exited, but Hensley turned away with a faked cough and slipped through the doors before they closed. Davison followed.

Hensley leaned into the corner. "Don't worry. I'll take it from here."

Davison pulled some papers from his jacket and handed them to Hensley. "The details of the deal. Call Ellis if you need help."

"I'll manage."

The doors opened. Hensley found a seat in the lobby and settled down.

Davison dropped the duffel into the adjoining chair and gazed at Hensley for a longish moment. "It's not too late. For either of us."

Hensley grimaced, worn out from the effort. "That remains to be seen. But I'll give it the good old college try."

"You know where to find me."

"You might live to regret that little detail."

Davison nodded and headed to the exit. He paused at the door and turned back. "I don't think so. Thanks to Masie." He graced Hensley with a two-finger salute and disappeared out the door.

For the first time in decades, Hensley found himself entirely without precedent. He wanted to attribute the lightness of being to the meds, but salt and antibiotics weren't mood-altering drugs.

He spent a few minutes gathering his breath and his thoughts. Chrystal was obviously conflicted, particularly regarding the view that, where Reggie was concerned, a little bit of Hensley was worse than no Hensley at all. And he had to admit that, judging by form as she was forced to do, it was a defensible position.

When it came to relationships, the Hensley on record was a spotty fixture—good out of the gate but questionable in the stretch. And his most recent accomplishments, while admirable in their own right, did nothing to contradict that view. They didn't trade in the currency of Chrystal's concerns. When evaluated dispassionately, they demonstrated initiative but failed to convince in the matter of staying power.

Maybe the Hensley that stepped off the cruise ship in Galveston was not the Hensley that now sat in the lobby of the Legacy Mt. Hood Medical Center. Contrary to everything he thought he knew about himself two weeks ago, Hensley was prepared to place his hand on a Bible and swear to the fact that he was indeed a changed man.

And if it would help the cause, he would do it in a heartbeat, if not sooner. But recent events had revealed that what had been Hensley's greatest strength was now his greatest handicap.

In his long and varied experience, Hensley had found few obstacles that would not yield to the finesse of a patter finely crafted to the psychology of the individual. Outside of Davison, few were immune to its seduction.

But when Hensley found himself in Fagan's townhouse looking down the barrel of a gun, he had discovered that such methods failed to persuade the one person who mattered most.

What was called for in a situation where words were worthless was the wordless statement that spoke for him. And Masie, bless her heart, had handed him exactly that.

After all, if a mansion on the Main Line funded for the next twenty years didn't scream "in it for the long term," Hensley would like to know what did.

Not that Chrystal could be bought with the promise of a life of luxury. He had recognized that while sipping scotch in Uncle Rex's study, now soon to be Hensley's study. What mattered was the opportunity this change of fortunes would afford their son.

That was something worth sticking around for, and when Hensley explained it, Chrystal would see that he was laying a foundation for the future. Their future. Together.

Hensley pulled out his pocket phone and scrolled to Chrystal's number.

"Hello?"

"Chrystal, how are you on this fine day?"

"Hensley? Where are you?"

He realized the Santa Fe area code of his pocket phone had confused her. "At the hospital. I was hoping we could get together today for a chat about what comes next."

"Oh." There was a short pause. "We're headed out to Haystack Rock."

"An excellent plan. Why don't you stop by and pick me up on your way?"

A longer pause. "Are you up to it? Will they let you out?"

"Surprising as it may seem, they have tired of my company, and I am free to occupy myself as I see fit. And nothing would give me greater pleasure than to join you and the assorted crew on your excursion. If you will have me."

"Uh. Okay."

"I shall count the moments until your arrival. You can pick me up in the lobby."

Her hesitation spoke volumes, but Hensley suspected she would see things differently before the sun went down.

Chapter Thirty-Eight: Haystack

Even if Hensley had possessed the energy to launch into the thick of it with all four feet, such a conversation wasn't possible with Reggie and Sapphire in the back seat, so he leaned against the passenger door and napped for most of the ninety-minute drive to the coast.

He woke up when Chrystal parked the car, and they hiked down to the beach. Sapphire struck out ahead of the group, defiant in her captive independence.

As they reached the sand and Haystack Rock hove into view, Reggie abandoned all pretense of protocol and took off running toward the primeval giant. Since the tide was out, he was able to get right up to the base and climb among the rocks, peering into the surging water as gulls circled above.

Hensley and Chrystal approached the landmark in a more cautious manner, silent and braced against the wind. He was glad of the jacket he had scored at Andy and Bax, even if it did have a blood-stained hole in the right shoulder. The ambient temperature was in the low sixties if he was any judge, significantly attenuated by virtue of a stiff salt breeze.

As the water surged in the tidal pools, Hensley spied starfish and sea urchins and all manner of marine life. There was something reassuring about this monstrous rock providing a haven for the vulnerable. It looked the same as he had seen it fifteen years ago, and probably the same as fifteen hundred years ago when Beowulf braved the depths of a different sea to slay a monster.

"What is the longest time you stayed in one place?" Chrystal asked.

Hensley gave it some thought. "Once I left Angola? Three years."

"Where was that?"

"A Buddhist monastery in the mountains of Guangxi. But the second longest was in Santa Fe. With you."

"And you left both, eventually."

Hensley had to find a way into this conversation, and this was not it. He opted for the non sequitur. "Would you say Reggie is bright?"

"He figured out who you were in about ten seconds."

Point taken. "And his prospects?"

"Good. Until you showed up. Now . . ." She turned away and scanned the beach for Sapphire, who had found a relatively dry boulder to perch on and was gazing out to sea. She glanced back to the rock where Reggie was popping bubbles in a strand of seaweed.

"Surely you know that when I left to bike the Andes, I had every intention of returning."

Chrystal didn't take her eyes from Reggie. "Until the next thing came along."

"I had no choice. There were extenuating—"

"No choice?" She turned to him with a fierceness that made Hensley take a step back. "I missed the part where you were hand-cuffed and forced into slave labor in a vineyard in Argentina."

Obviously Chrystal didn't appreciate the nuances required when engaging a functionary at a border crossing, particularly at a time of national crisis. Hensley had no doubt that lack of imagination was a basic qualification on their résumé.

"There were considerations—"

"There are some things worth fighting for," Chrystal said with a quiet intensity barely audible above the surf and wind.

"Yes, but then I didn't . . ." Hensley stopped himself before he went a word too far. *Then I didn't know about Reggie.*

He was unable to hold her fiery gaze. He glanced at their son. What if Hensley had known about the potential Reggie? Would he have braved heaven and hell and the Feds to claw his way back to the child he had never envisioned nor desired? To the eventuality he had gone to great pains to avoid? Maybe not then, but things had changed. He had changed.

But that couldn't be Chrystal's question, because she knew he was unaware of Reggie's existence at the time. No, she was asking an altogether different question.

Wasn't she worth fighting for? Worth demanding that the insensate universe yield to the overwhelming passion of two star-crossed lovers?

Hensley took a deep breath and looked past Chrystal to the coastline fading into the haze.

"If I have a besetting sin, and I have no doubt you could extemporize at great length and in blistering detail on the topic, it is that I seem to recognize the value of what I have only in retrospect. In a less sanguine person, that flaw might lead to a life of regret, but happily I have escaped that melancholy fate."

Chrystal's snort was audible over the wind and surf.

Of course she was cynical. He turned his gaze to her. "Until now."

She met his gaze, waiting.

"The biggest mistake in a lifetime of mistakes was the day I let a troublesome passport stand between me and the only soul mate I have ever found in decades of circling the globe."

Moisture rose to her gold-flecked eyes, but judging by her expression she remained unmoved.

He chanced placing his good hand on her shoulder. "And my greatest fear is that I have come to this realization too late."

Chrystal brushed Hensley's hand aside and wiped her eyes. "That was a nice speech, but if you came out here to give me your class ring and ask me to go steady, you wasted a trip."

Hensley frowned. If nothing else, surely the hint of tears meant that his words had hit home.

"If I wanted a boyfriend, I'd already have one. This isn't about us. It's about Reggie."

Obviously Hensley had got hold of the wrong end of the bull. Setting aside the question of how he would fight for a son he didn't know existed, Hensley hastened to deliver the goods.

"Last night you asked me which was the real Hensley. I hope this will allay those concerns." He reached into an inside jacket pocket, pulled out a few sheets of paper, and handed them to her.

Chrystal skimmed the text on the first page and looked up at him. "What is this?"

"This is our house. You and me and the kids."

"How is this our house?"

"You remember Uncle Rex." Hensley pulled the last page from the bottom, the one with the photo of the mansion. "This document gives me ownership of the Stone family home along with a stipend covering operating expenses for the next twenty years."

Chrystal shoved the papers back at him with a confused frown. "Good for you?"

"If this doesn't demonstrate my intention to settle down, what would?"

"You got a house in . . ." She snatched the papers from his hand and scanned through them. "A house in Philadelphia?" She waved the pages in his face. "You want me to rip my kids out of their lives and away from the only home they've ever known and move two thousand miles on the off chance that somehow you'll decide to stay in one place like a civilized human being?"

Hensley gestured toward their son. "Just think of the opportunities a move like this could open up for Reggie. And Sapphire, of course. And you could quit your job."

"I happen to like my job, thank you very much." She stuffed the pages into his jacket pocket. "In fact, as hard as it may be for you to believe, I happen to like my life just the way it is."

Clearly, as much as Hensley had learned in the last few weeks, he had a lot more learning to do. Who knew offering to settle down in a mansion with the mother of your child would precipitate World War III?

Chrystal ground a boot heel into the sand as she turned and strode away, but after a few yards she came back, shaking a finger in his face.

"And I don't need you riding in here like some kind of white knight trying to fix everything. God only knows how we survived for the past twelve years without you."

She wheeled around and set off again, veering in the direction of Sapphire's rock, but she stopped when she saw it was empty.

Hensley scanned the area and saw Sapphire crouched on a ledge at the base of the rock next to Reggie, who was poking at something in the water with a bit of seaweed.

Chrystal corrected her course in the direction of the kids, and as Hensley watched her stomp on the edge of a receding wave, he wondered if maybe he should have bought a ring and gone that route.

He set off to follow when she spun around and stomped back to him, her hands on her hips.

"The only thing on the table is whether you have the guts to stay around and be a part of your son's life."

Hensley couldn't have been more confused if he'd been a cat in a clothes dryer. He took a moment to compose himself. Evidently protecting his son with his very life wasn't sufficient proof of commitment, and neither was stepping up with the goods to assure an enviable future with unprecedented opportunity.

After a deep breath, he set out to lay a trail of breadcrumbs to the pot at the end of the rainbow. "That is an excellent question, one that I have been asking myself for the past week. As you have so eloquently and accurately pointed out, past performance doesn't elicit optimism regarding future results."

Chrystal nodded.

"It took me a while to accustom myself to the concept. But twenty-four hours on the road offers ample time for reflection, and somewhere around Cuba I realized Reggie was the one thing that could irrevocably alter my peripatetic existence."

Hensley's gaze turned inward as the thought of that moment and the second, more telling moment. "Even so, I continued to question myself until last night I realized that when I saw Reggie in danger, I rushed in to protect him without thinking."

He focused back on Chrystal and was puzzled by her unchanged skepticism.

Chrystal shook her head slowly. "For you, it's like a Hallmark commercial and a superhero movie all rolled into one, isn't it?" She leaned forward. "Tell me, what will you do when you're asked to work the concession stand every Saturday afternoon for an entire season to fund new uniforms?"

Given the papers in his jacket pocket, Hensley could just buy the soccer uniforms, or hire a gnome to work the stand, but he sensed that such practical solutions were not desired at this moment.

"Or you get the fifth call from the school telling you he's not doing his homework? Or you find out at nine p.m. that his science project is due the next morning and he hasn't even started it?"

These situations required more finesse, but given the fiery responses to his previous attempts to answer her questions, Hensley preferred to treat this set as rhetorical.

"Or he comes down with fever and vomiting and diarrhea and has to be fed by hand for three days between changing the sheets and constantly doing laundry?"

It occurred to Hensley that all these hypothetical scenarios were alarmingly specific and likely not hypothetical at all. His expression evidently reflected this thought.

"Because, yeah, it's nice when a white knight charges in and takes a bullet for his son, but guess what? That doesn't happen that often. In fact, never, for most kids."

His own father had never taken that kind of interest in Hensley. Or Davison, for that matter. In the early days it was med school and internship and residency and crazy hours. Then it was the clinic, where you would think he could have scaled it back, but no, he never wavered from the same punishing schedule, right up until the day he died. With his boots on and in the saddle.

But that was the point, wasn't it? Do the opposite of the old man. Then Davison's voice intruded into his thoughts.

I want what they had.

A vision of bacon-wrapped dove breasts on a spit over a fire flooded in. Dad pulling Mom into a casual embrace. The kiss.

That was the flaw in Hensley's master plan. What about the things Dad got right? Because, as Davison had come to realize, the old man got at least one thing right.

Hensley's chin dropped to his chest. The joke was on him. By rejecting everything about his father, he had unwittingly relinquished control of his choices to the very man he despised. He had sown the wind and reaped the whirlwind.

He squeezed his eyes shut. How badly did he want this? Enough to admit that the old man did at least one thing worth emulating? Enough to let it go? All of it?

Hensley took a deep breath and opened his eyes. But Chrystal wasn't finished.

"And how is a guy who flits around the world like some kind of attention-starved butterfly going to teach his son about how to treat women? Or were you planning on the 'do as I say, not as I do' approach?"

He considered reaching out a consoling hand but desisted. Besides, his shoulder cried out for a painkiller. "You have every reason for concern. The fact that you're still talking to me at all, even if it is to dismantle me one brick at a time, is a testimony to your generosity of spirit."

"Damn straight."

"Before I proceed further, may I entreat you to allow me the luxury of seeking comfort?" With his left arm he gestured to the rock Sapphire had abandoned.

Chrystal softened slightly and nodded. Hensley shuffled across the sand, settled in, and prepared for the final attempt.

"While I am cognizant of the futility of words in such a circumstance as we find ourselves, I can think of no other avenue for bridging the divide between us."

"How about you just tell it to me straight?"

"An admirable suggestion. You may be surprised to learn that I agree with your assessment. I am what might be called a high-risk alternative. Or at least I was until quite recently."

"Is this what you call straight talk?"

"Ah. Let me try another approach. These past few days, I have come to realize that I have made serious miscalculations in my approach to life."

Hensley paused, but when Chrystal responded with knitted brows, he pressed forward.

"I mean to say . . . given my nature and the unique circumstances of my early life . . ." There was no way to finesse this inconvenient truth. "Not to put too fine a point on it, I have been an utter fool. In every sense of the word."

Based on Chrystal's puzzled expression, he had got through the first level of defense.

"I can explain, at great length if required, the context that led me to act as I have done for the past three decades and counting, but the details are not germane to the matter at hand. As alarming as I find it, for the bulk of my life I have evidently been clueless regarding something as essential and basic as love. How to give it. How to receive it."

Chrystal tilted her head to one side. "But—"

"Exactly. But something happened in Cancún that started me on the path back to you. And when I discovered Reggie, that changed everything."

Hensley struggled to his feet. "I stand before you, a willing student, ready to learn how to be human." He spread his hands.

"The facts are these, put as succinctly as possible. First, I am prepared to abandon all schemes and stratagems to assure that I am present for any and all circumstances in which Reggie will require my presence. Second, I retain the hope, foolish though it may be, that I shall be granted the honor to do so at your side, undeserving though I might be."

Chrystal drew in a deep breath as if to launch a response, held it, and then let it out. The frown she focused on him was not one of disapproval but of consideration.

Hensley pressed his advantage. "To speak plainly, nothing would give me greater pleasure than to correct the greatest error of my life by spending my final years in the company of my son and the one woman in my life whom I regretted leaving."

"What about the mansion in Philadelphia?"

Hensley pulled the papers from his pocket, tore them in half, and tossed them into the wind. "My home is with the ones I should have never left."

Chrystal watched the papers blow away.

Hensley pulled his passport from his back pocket and offered it to her. She squinted at him as if trying to figure his angle.

Hensley flipped the passport open, ripped it in half, and tossed it aside. "Since I was sixteen, I have been a man without a country."

This was no time for half measures. He dropped to one knee in front of Chrystal. "But if you are willing, I will no longer be a man without a home." The moisture brimming in Chrystal's eyes echoed his own and gave him hope.

She shook her head. "I won't leave Santa Fe."

"Then neither will I."

Chrystal looked down on him, a tear trickling down one cheek, and turned away. She walked a few steps toward the surf and looked out toward the ocean. After a moment, she wiped her eyes and turned back to him.

"It's too much too soon."

Hensley struggled to his feet, his left hand on the rock. "We can take it slowly."

"You can't move in."

He nodded. "I have a place in Santa Fe. And a job."

"On probation. One day at a time."

"I'm familiar with the concept."

Chrystal stared at him for a measureless moment. "I must be crazy." She shook her head.

"I suspect the sheriff and the judge will have strong views on the subject."

She shrugged. "Nothing I can do about that." She checked on the kids and turned back to Hensley. "You have a place in Santa Fe?"

"Just outside of town. You remember Tink?"

"Scooter Bell?"

"The very one. My landlord and my employer."

"Is the bar still a dive?"

"With a capital V, my dear. But I have some thoughts about expanding the revenue by bringing in food trucks, which I shall lay before Tink upon our return." He looked southward toward civilization. "Speaking of which, I am feeling in need of sustenance. If I'm not mistaken, Mo's is about a half mile down the beach. A peerless establishment where one can acquire a quite serviceable bowl of chowder on a blustery day."

"I'm ready for something warm." She took a few steps toward the rocks. "Reggie! Sapphire! Lunch." Chrystal angled toward the restaurant.

Hensley pulled up alongside her. "There is one small matter I must apprise you of. To execute the master plan and deliver the tadpoles from their dilemma, I required access to a rental car. And as you know, one cannot hire a car without a credit card. I left enough money at your house to pay the full balance and more, costing you no interest and leaving your credit score better than I found it."

Chrystal stopped. "You stole my credit card?"

"I merely utilized it as a tool to overcome an obstacle."

"You stole my card."

"It is in your house this very minute, next to the computer. I used it for the single purpose of hiring the transportation required to effect this happy outcome. For everything else, I paid cash."

Chrystal froze him with a hard stare. "Okay. I get it, but you just added a year to your probation period. And Reggie can't know anything about it."

"About what?" Reggie skidded to a stop next to them.

"Nothing."

"About this." Hensley reached into his left pocket and pulled out three coins. "I noticed you had some gaps in your collection."

Reggie took the coins and inspected them. "Wow! Oklahoma. Those are hard to find."

"But worth the wait when you finally get it."

Reggie looked up at Hensley with a smile. "Thanks!" A look of uncertainty flashed across his face before he added, "Thanks, Dad."

A wave of emotion washed through Hensley, something he'd never felt before. He wasn't sure what to call it. It was like satisfaction and longing were fighting a cage match in his soul. He grunted as he knelt on one knee in front of Reggie.

"You're welcome. I'm just sorry it took me so long to bring them to you."

He reached out and took Reggie in his arms, hugging him. "But I'm here now, son." Reggie hugged him back.

The sun rode high in the sky over Reggie's left shoulder, ten degrees or so beyond zenith.

Hensley closed his eyes and raised his face to its faint warmth.

BRAD WHITTINGTON

ENDLESS VACATION

{ A NOVEL }

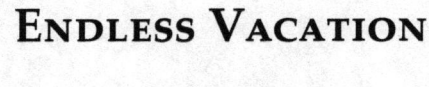

ENDLESS VACATION

CHAPTER ONE

In three days, life as Dave Fletcher knew it would end, and his biggest regret was that he had failed to equip the chair across from his desk with an ejection seat.

He would miss many things about life as a special agent for the Secret Service. Vanek was not one of those things.

Vanek sat in that chair, that lamentably underpowered chair, regarding Dave with the stare of a hyena standing just out of reach of a wounded lion, waiting for the moment it staggered to its knees. Waiting for the moment he could snatch the corner office from Dave, and the title of lead agent of the Austin regional headquarters.

A smile that was more like the baring of teeth flickered across Vanek's doughy face. "I envy you."

Dave stared back, declining to comment.

Vanek was barely fifty but looked well past the mandatory retirement age of fifty-seven. He worked hard, partied harder, and smoked like a beater with a broken head gasket.

"This time next week, you'll be chilling on your deck with a Mexican martini. I'll be stuck here, chasing leads like a rabid pit bull in a day-care center."

Dave almost smiled. The only way Vanek would chase anything was if it had a kolache tied to it. "Speaking of which, how about you just cut to the chase?" He glanced around the room. "Come to measure for curtains, maybe?"

Vanek's pained smile fractured into a grimace. "About the Rivera investigation." He rolled his chair closer to the desk. "Looks like we maybe caught a break."

Dave was annoyed to hear that Vanek had been working the one case he had held onto, but he remained impassive, refusing to give the satisfaction of a reaction. "How so?"

"Word has it Rivera's got a guy on the inside."

The suggestion was too absurd to deserve a response. Dave had scrubbed the case down to the bare metal. There was no agent in regular communication with Rivera—not Secret Service, not DEA, not FBI. In fact, the only agent to come in contact with Rivera was Dave himself, back when he bought the Jenny from him. Back before the counterfeit money surfaced.

"Every time we get close, the mole tips him off, and Rivera fades."

"A convenient theory." Especially convenient for one who preferred speculation to investigation. "Any evidence to back it up?"

"We have a bead on a guy with a past connection. Pretty solid."

Despite himself, Dave leaned forward, his elbows on the desk. "Who?"

Vanek leaned back in his chair, suddenly casual. "No need to worry. It'll take a few days to round him up. You'll be gone by then."

Dave leaned back in his own chair, echoing Vanek's posture. Best not to give the hyena even a hint of interest. Despite his incompetence as an agent, Vanek excelled at politics. Every conversation with him had to be treated with the care of a biological weapon.

The grin returned to Vanek's face. "But you might be surprised."

Me, Dave thought. He's saying I'm the inside guy. He suppressed the urge to punch Vanek out of daylight saving time and clear into the next time zone. Instead he leaned across the desk and planted his hands with a sudden intensity that threatened to topple the smug scavenger out of his chair.

"What?" Vanek barked in an unnaturally high octave.

"Careful. Don't do anything you'll regret."

Vanek returned Dave's glare with a calm stare. "Just giving you an update."

"It had better be a joke."

"Who's joking?"

Dave suddenly realized he no longer had to play this game. "Whatever it is you're doing, keep me out of it." He left Vanek sitting in the corner office he had lusted after for more than a decade.

"Hey, where you going?"

All Dave gave him was a wave of his hand over his shoulder as he strode past the cubicles and through the front door to the hallway.

The closing of the door mercifully cut off Vanek's reply. Too impatient to wait for the elevator, Dave took the stairs eight floors down in a controlled fall. In the parking garage, he put the top down on his Z-51 Corvette and escaped downtown as fast as traffic would allow.

Not content with finally taking the corner office, Vanek had evidently concocted some harebrained scheme to implicate Dave in a corruption charge. That wouldn't last long. Anybody with a brain would see through it.

Now that he had escaped Vanek's nauseating company, Dave looked for a destination and settled on an hour of aerial therapy in his restored WWI biplane, the Jenny.

As he wove through the pre-rush-hour traffic, his mind wandered to Stephanie. He wondered what she would say about his pending retirement. Probably something like, "It's not Friday, yet. We'll see."

If he'd left the service fifteen years ago, he wouldn't have lost her, wouldn't have taken the promotion to lead agent in the Austin field office to escape her memory. Unsuccessfully, as he would have known if he'd been thinking instead of reacting. He was still thinking about her fifteen years later.

He turned west onto Southwest Parkway and changed the subject—the security company he planned to open. As usual, the main hurdle was financial. Borrowing against his retirement account and pulling the equity from his house would get him, at most, three to six months of operating capital, not the three years Uncle Rex had suggested he accumulate before retiring.

Dave pushed that thought aside as well. He was taking the Jenny out to decompress, not to increase his stress. He'd resume worrying when he was back on the ground.

The last vestiges of Austin fell behind him and the road split a hill. As he topped the rise and the road curved left, the limestone walls dropped away, and Dave got a glimpse of the Hill Country. It was his favorite spot on the drive.

Layers of ridges coated with scrubby juniper and a few live oaks drew him toward the horizon, Spanish oak lining the watercourses in the ravines. Condos poked up between the trees like prairie dog mounds.

He caught a red light, and the stagnant air settled around him like a cocoon. A cloud drifted across the sun, cutting him a break of a few degrees. It was a mild day for the end of May, barely in the nineties.

At Lakeway Airpark, he drove past the Ercoupe perched on a pole by the entrance, idled up to the last T-hangar in the row, and saw something that spiked his pulse higher than a visit from Vanek. A candy-apple blue Lamborghini.

He had the car door open before the engine stopped. He strode to the access door, threw it open, and scanned the dim interior for Rivera, but something else commanded his attention. A Glock 26 pointed at his forehead.

CHAPTER TWO

Dave stared down the barrel of the gun at Rivera.

"Oh, it's you." Rivera squinted at him and lowered the gun to his side.

"Who were you expecting?" Dave tended to resent it when someone pointed a gun at him. He set his foot on a toolbox, bent forward, and came up with his own Glock pointed at Rivera. "Now, how about you set that gun down on the floor and back away?"

Rivera's eyes narrowed and his body tensed, but his voice was as casual as a pair of flip-flops. "Dave, my friend, you wound me."

Dave nodded at Rivera's gun, keeping his aim steady. He wasn't in the mood for banter.

Rivera bent over, not easy given his size, and placed the gun on the concrete.

"Good. Now kick it here."

Rivera gave it a nudge.

"Back away."

Rivera took three steps back.

Dave stepped forward and kicked the gun into the corner by the door. "Now, let's talk about why you're here."

Rivera's gaze drifted from the gun in the corner to the gun in Dave's hand to the expression on Dave's face. "You have not been returning my calls. It is not polite."

"No point. We both know it's not going to happen."

Rivera glanced at the Jenny. "Sell it back to me. Name your price." He stroked the fabric on the upper wing.

"It's not for sale."

"Of all people, my friend, you know that everything is for sale. It's just the finding of the right price. Fifty thousand."

Dave shook his head.

"A hundred. I can fix it so it's tax-free."

One hundred thousand dollars. Plenty to set up that office downtown. He shook his head again. Even if he wanted to sell, he couldn't do business with a suspect. "Go home, Rivera."

"Two hundred." When he didn't get an answer, Rivera's gaze wandered around the hangar. "I always felt free in the Jenny."

Dave watched him, ready for a sudden move, but Rivera seemed focused on nothing, or maybe something only he could see.

"Sometimes a man just needs to go." Rivera grabbed a polished wooden wing strut. "To turn his face forward and not look to what is behind." He turned a resentful gaze on Dave. "Selling the Jenny to you, that I regret the most."

Dave's phone vibrated. Without taking his eyes off Rivera, he dug it out of his pocket and held it so he could see both Rivera and the caller ID. The name surprised him. "Uncle Rex. Can I call you back? I'm in a meeting."

"How about joining me for dinner?"

"Give Mr. Stone my regards," Rivera said.

Dave took a step forward, gesturing with the gun for Rivera to move back. "Sure. How's next week sound?"

"I'm thinking seven o'clock."

Dave frowned, both at the phone and at Rivera, who hadn't moved. "I can't get to Philly by seven."

"Probably not, but you can make it to Bee Cave."

"You're in town?"

"The Emerald, seven o'clock."

The call disconnected before Dave could respond. Uncle Rex was not an impulsive man. If he made the trip down from Philadelphia, it had to be for something that couldn't be done on the phone. Most likely bad news.

Dave pocketed the phone and returned his attention to Rivera, his pale face easily visible in the gloom of the hangar. Here was another man whose sudden presence was disturbing and whose reason for coming was equally unclear. Not likely it had anything to do with the Jenny. After all, Dave himself didn't know he was coming here until thirty minutes ago.

"Why are you here? How did you get in?"

"Even trade, the Lamb for the Jenny. You can keep the Z-51. And the cash."

Did it have something to do with Vanek's absurd claims? "Why were you waiting here for me? With a gun?"

"I just wanted to see the Jenny again, make sure it was in good condition."

Dave shook his head. "That's not it. Try again."

"I want to fly it, once more. I will pay for the fuel." Rivera reached for his billfold.

Dave jerked his gun, gesturing Rivera's hand away from his pocket. "Are you wired? Is that it?"

Rivera responded with a scowl.

"Your shirt. Take it off."

Rivera studied Dave for a minute, then shook his head and unbuttoned his shirt.

"Set it on the wing and step away." Dave waited until Rivera was ten feet from the wing and then inspected the shirt. Nothing. "Drop your pants."

"My friend," Rivera said, shaking his head. "You go too far."

"Just do it."

Rivera reluctantly complied until he was standing in his boxers and cowboy boots.

"Kick them here."

Dave checked the pants for a bug of some kind, especially the oversized belt buckle, but found nothing. He stepped back toward the door and gestured with the gun for Rivera to get dressed.

He debated what to do with the pathetic figure. Arrest him for breaking and entering? That would waste everyone's time, and he'd miss his dinner date with Uncle Rex.

Instead, Dave cleared the path to the door. "Get out of here."

Rivera buttoned his shirt as he left, but stopped at the doorway. "Maybe one short flight, my friend?"

Dave raised the gun. "I'm not your friend. I'm just the guy who made the mistake of buying a plane from you."

Rivera shrugged and bent toward his gun.

"Leave it."

Bent halfway over, Rivera frowned at Dave. "I have a CHL."

"You can pick it up at the office tomorrow." When Rivera hesitated, Dave said, "It's a lot cheaper than bail for burglary and assault with a deadly weapon."

Based on the glare Rivera focused on Dave as he straightened up, Dave doubted he would get a Christmas card from the man this year. As he watched Rivera's bulk fill the doorframe on the way out, he reflected that instead of *Güero*, Rivera's nickname should have been *Gordo*. Or maybe *Oso*.

Dave kept his gun trained on the doorway until he heard the Lamborghini drive away. Then he checked his watch and turned to the fully restored 1917 Curtiss JN-4D biplane.

He'd flown a lot of planes, but nothing gave him the open-cockpit experience of the Jenny. Even the cargo plane in Angola that had infected him with the flying bug as a kid couldn't compare. Buzzing low and slow to feel the rush of the terrain as it whipped past. Teasing the bottom of the clouds as you hit the inversion layer with a ride like a bucking bronco in the sky. Hovering above the earth close to stall speed, barely moving, like a hawk searching for dinner. Falling through the air and pulling out into powered flight, nothing between you and the sky but your clothes and a dose of adrenaline. Try that in a Learjet.

Dave still had enough time for a short flight before dinner, but the conversation with Vanek and the visit from Rivera seemed too much for coincidence. He scanned the hangar to see if anything was missing or disturbed, but all seemed as it should be.

Rivera didn't take anything away. Did he leave something behind? Perhaps Dave had been right about being bugged, but the room, not the body. He made a more thorough search with equally unsatisfying results. When he checked his watch again, he realized he was going to be late for dinner.

Figuring out the mystery of Vanek and Rivera would have to wait until tomorrow. Right now he had to figure out the mystery of Uncle Rex.

Chapter Three

Dave pulled off Highway 71 into the gravel parking lot of The Emerald, a small outpost of Irish culture established by the Kinsella family in 1984. In the intervening decades, civilization in the form of country clubs, subdivisions, and upscale shopping malls had gradually encroached on the little cottage nestled among the oaks, but it had stood its ground.

Near the door, Dave spotted the Mercedes that Rex kept at his Tarrytown house. He parked next to an SUV big enough to have its own ZIP code. As he entered through the vestibule of the rock cottage, a young woman with long, dark hair approached.

"Rex Stone," Dave said.

She directed him to the back room, where he found Uncle Rex, martini in hand. Rex set the glass down and stood, his arms outstretched.

Dave grabbed a hand to shake it, but Uncle Rex pulled it free and embraced him in a hug, one with plenty of bone and muscle behind it. Dave hesitated, then hugged him back.

Something was definitely up. He couldn't recall a single hug from Uncle Rex, not even the day Rex came to the boarding school to tell Dave his father was dead. The East Coast side of the family went for the polite handshake or the air kiss to the cheek. Mom had been the only exception, but Dave assumed she had picked it up from the Texas relatives, Dad's side.

Before Dave was fully seated, the woman placed a matching martini on the table and disappeared. Dave held his martini aloft. "You're not over the hill until the hill is over you."

Uncle Rex lifted his glass. "To life without regret."

Regret? Uncle Rex?

"Dave, good of you to meet me for dinner."

"Nonsense." Dave wouldn't miss a dinner with Uncle Rex if he had to break out of jail to attend. "But what brings you here in May?"

The Kinsella woman returned with flambéed onion soup.

Rex sampled it. "Bridget would have loved this."

Dave nodded. "Mom knew how to enjoy the finer things, even on a nurse's salary."

"You remember this?" Rex pulled a slender silver chain from the breast pocket of his jacket, a familiar pendant hanging from it.

Dave reached for it. A chip from the Rock of Gibraltar, fashioned from the mountain itself, the limestone edges smooth after four decades of service. He flipped it and read the inscription.

I SHALL NOT BE MOVED

The Stone family motto, a weapon that Bridget Stone had turned against the family itself.

Rex returned his attention to the soup. "We could all take a lesson from your mother in living without regret."

Twice was two times too many to ignore. "What's all this about regret? Think of all you've accomplished."

"Exactly! I've done quite well." Rex leaned over his bowl. "For myself."

"And others."

"But think of what I could have done."

The familiar intensity of Rex's gaze was mixed with a new element, something Dave couldn't quite place. Something that wasn't Uncle Rex.

"If it weren't for you, I would be living in a shack in Angola and giving inoculations to squirming babies." The life Dad and Mom had planned for Dave, the life he had escaped when they sent him to the States for his schooling.

Rex took the necklace from Dave's hand and rubbed the worn ridges with his thumb. Dave waited for an explanation. Rex resumed in a more relaxed tone.

"When Bridget turned twenty-five, took control of her trust fund, and ran off to Africa with Reggie, the family was outraged.

Married to a nobody? Yes, he was a doctor, but no connections, no money, and worst of all, an idealist. Oh, the shame!"

Dave never tired of this story, but Rex didn't finish it. Instead, he returned the necklace to his pocket and finished his soup.

"I won't deny that your father had his faults—perhaps overzealous at times, completely inept at managing investments, prone to rash decisions and extremes. Especially at the end. But he recognized what was really important. And Bridget believed in him. Few people achieved that honor." His voice dropped to a whisper. "I sometimes wonder if she didn't make the better choice."

All this second guessing didn't sit well with Dave. As his early retirement approached, he'd done enough of it for both of them. "Uncle Rex, it's not like your life is over. And even if it were, you have nothing to regret. Or apologize for."

With his own disappointing financial situation, Dave felt like he had more reason to complain of wasted time than Uncle Rex, who had a long list of accomplishments.

The next course arrived before Rex responded. Dave sampled the Dublin Lawyer Special: lobster tail in a flaky puff pastry, simmered in heavy cream and Irish whiskey. Dave wondered why anyone ever prepared lobster another way.

Rex savored a bite with his eyes closed, and then went for another. "When was the last time you saw Hensley?" he asked without looking up.

"Same time you did. Mom's funeral."

"Do you know where he is?"

"I know as much about Hensley's whereabouts as he cares to tell me. Which, as you know, is nothing."

"Track him down."

"He knows how to find me."

Rex started to reply, but stopped himself.

Dave speared a bit of lobster and considered this new line of conversation. Did this mystery have something to do with Hensley?

They were nearly through with dinner, and Dave still had no more idea of why Rex was here than he did of why Rivera was in his hangar or why Vanek was playing games.

They were silent as the dishes were cleared away and the dessert delivered: fresh oranges and orange marmalade in a chocolate-covered pastry puff accompanied by Irish coffee.

Uncle Rex took a slow, appreciative sip. "Angola wasn't easy on Hensley."

Dave snorted. "I made it through okay."

Rex studied him. "After a fashion." He took a bite of the dessert. "It's not a one-size-fits-all world, Davison. Some of us are more broken than others."

"Hensley's world is every man for himself and the devil take the hindmost."

As much as Rex had done for Dave, for the family, he wasn't there when Hensley handed Dave his coin collection like a consolation prize and disappeared forever. When he made a token appearance at Dad's funeral and disappeared immediately after. And the same at Mom's funeral.

The dance had gone on long enough. Since Rex had already breached the line of reticence behind which the two of them typically kept personal matters, Dave decided on a little plain speaking. "Uncle Rex, pardon me for saying, but you don't seem to be yourself. What's going on?"

Rex cleared his throat. Dave watched him, but Rex focused on his coffee cup.

"Davison, I did my best as I saw it at the time, but . . . I thought Reggie was misguided. Sincere, but naïve. I . . ." He finally met Dave's stare, eyes misting. "I hope you know how much I treasure the years we've had, but I didn't do right by you. I'm sorry."

Dave's confusion prevented him from speaking. This was the reason for the evening? An apology for doing the right thing? He studied Rex, really saw him for the first time tonight. Rex was changed from the dynamo of industry Dave had always known. He seemed frail, diminished, defeated. Dave wanted to avert his eyes from the unwonted apologies. The making of excuses for Hensley, who had betrayed the family.

"You did more for me than my own parents did, or could do." Dave struggled to keep his voice steady, not sure that he had succeeded.

Rex held his gaze, his eyes moist. He seemed on the verge of speaking, but instead retreated behind his coffee.

Dave waited, both desiring and dreading an explanation. There had to be something else, but if it was more comments in the vein of apologies and suggestions that he hunt down his prodigal brother, Dave wasn't sure he wanted to hear it.

But Rex seemed to be done. He stirred his coffee and stared at the Irish crème swirling around the vortex.

What had happened to the Uncle Rex who had built a commercial empire with business interests on practically every continent? Where was the man who preferred results to excuses, who didn't take no for an answer, who had eliminated the word "failure" from his vocabulary?

Neither side of Dave's family, the Stones or the Fletchers, talked much about feelings. But in the past five minutes, Uncle Rex had exposed more emotion than in the past thirty-six years combined. It left Dave unsure of how to respond. He felt like he should offer something to restore Rex to some kind of balance. The words were out before he realized he had said them.

"Maybe I'll hunt down Hensley."

Rex's expression as he glanced up from his coffee was an improbable mixture of doubt and hope.

THE DEFENESTRATED ZOMBIE

The Defenestrated Zombie came into being through the auspices of one Jeremy Grigg, the Groover of Perth, who divined the perfect ingredients.

Of course, any zombie must contain light and dark rum. Due to the Defenestration of Prague (independent research advised), we required a Czech liqueur, and Becherovka came to our aid.

However, the drink as conceived by The Griggster and described by Ermen on page 219 is impossible to make, due to the largely imaginary nature of Gummidge's Wort (although the etymology of "wort" is interesting in this context, as is a perusal of the story of Worzel Gummidge) and the inadvisabililty of ingesting formaldehyde. (For the record, one would have to drink 200 Defenestrated Zombies to get a lethal dose of formaldehyde, whereas the alcohol would get you after 20 drinks or so.)

Consequently, I engaged the services of Chris Wall (aka Wally), gnome-at-large at Cafe Malta in South Austin. (Attendance required at your earliest convenience.) I told him the story and charged him with the task of creating a drink that could be legally assembled and consumed. He discharged his duties admirably.

The complicating factor in this drink is the blood orange syrup. If you can't find any, you can make your own by reducing blood orange soda.

The Defenestrated Zombie

1 1/4 oz light rum
1/2 oz orange juice
1/2 oz cranberry juice
1/4 oz lime juice
1/4 oz Bechorovka

Mix in shaker and decant into glass. Drizzle blood orange syrup into a layer on the bottom. Float dark rum on top.

Acknowledgements

Thanks to Brenda Hughes for helping bring Chrystal to life.

Thanks to Chris Wall for creating the recipe for the Defenestrated Zombie.

Thanks to Mark Flegal for Portland location scouting and Sueann Flegal for joining the location scouting expedition.

Thanks to Tosh McIntosh for firearm advice.

Thanks to John Cokendolpher for construction site controversy input.

Thanks to Patrick Barry for martial arts assistance.

Thanks to Mark Spyrison, Jeremy Grigg, Gordon Atkinson, and The Woman for early draft feedback.

Thanks to Christopher Campbell for medical input.

Thanks to U2 for inspiring the structure of the novel with "Moment of Surrender" from No Line on the Horizon.

Thanks to Chad Wall for Santa Fe location scouting.

Thanks to critique groups NIP and El Gee for feedback.

Thanks to the newsletter subscribers for providing feedback on draft four.

Thanks to Rebecca Leach and Charlene Good for making the inside better, and Brian Wootan for making the outside look good.

— BRAD WHITTINGTON —

Sign up for the newsletter to get other sneak peeks and freebies.

BradWhittington.com

ABOUT THE AUTHOR

Brad Whittington was born in Fort Worth, Texas, on James Taylor's eighth birthday and Jack Kerouac's thirty-fourth birthday and is old enough to know better. He lives in Austin, Texas with The Woman. Previously he has been known to inhabit Hawaii, Ohio, South Carolina, Arizona, and Colorado, annoying people as a janitor, math teacher, field hand, computer programmer, brickyard worker, editor, resident Gentile in a Conservative synagogue, IT director, weedcutter, and in a number of influential positions in other less notable professions. He is greatly loved and admired by all right-thinking citizens and enjoys a complete absence of cats and dogs at home.

BradWhittington.com